The Circle Game

By

Tanya Nichols

2

Alternative Book Press
2 Timber Lane Suite 301 Marlboro, NJ 07746
www.alternativebookpress.com

The Circle Game
This book is a work of fiction. Names, characters, places and incidents are the product of the author's imagination or are used fictitiously. Any resemblance to actual events, locales, or persons, living or dead, is coincidental.

Publication Data
Tanya Nichols [2018]
The Circle Game/ by Tanya Nichols—2nd ed.
Ask Publisher for Further Publication Information

ISBN 978-1-940122-38-0
Printed in the United States of America
10 9 8 7 6 5 4 3 2 1

4

"Tanya Nichols' *The Circle Game* sets two memorable characters on a collision course: Bernadette, an idealistic attorney overwhelmed by courtroom challenges and more personal questions of identity and purpose; and Julie, her anonymous birth mother, whose story unfolds decades earlier in a dingy trailer parked behind a biker bar. Nichols' prose consistently grabs the reader with its lyrical clarity, and implicates us in the lives of complex and engaging characters. The novel moves us deeply in all the best ways..."
--John Hales, author of *Shooting Polaris: A Personal Survey in the American West*

"California's great Central Valley long has been fertile ground for novelists eager to write about immigrants, busted dreams and the moral questions facing real people in their everyday lives. With *The Circle Game*, where the ghosts of the past lurk in the corners of every chapter, Tanya Nichols zeroes in on good intentions that lead to fatal consequences. It's a tale of families, motorcycle outlaws, lovers, and redemption. You won't soon forget it."

--Bill McEwen, *GV Wire*

"*The Circle Game* has the power to show us that, even after years of great tragedy and loneliness, only forgiveness can open the circle of family and let in those we need most."

-- Kristin FitzPatrick, author of *My Pulse is and Earthquake*

There is no cry of pain without, at its end, an echo of joy.

--Ramón de Campoamor

For Darby Jay

One

2005

An angry heat burned from deep inside, flushing Bernie's neck and cheeks to crimson, blotching her pale skin like a sudden attack of poison oak. She didn't need a mirror to know what she looked like. She knew what happened when her rosacea kicked in. Normally, her pale skin would simply flush to a warm pink across her cheeks and nose, but too much heat, too much stress, or too much alcohol ignited the rosy pink to a flaming red. It was a weakness, a gambler's tell.

In through the nose, out through the mouth, in through the nose, out through the mouth. One of her therapists suggested controlled breathing to manage stressful situations. But even a thick layer of concealer and pressed powder failed to dim the harshest flush, the type she could feel breaking through as the elevator groaned its way downward. Gripping her briefcase tighter, Bernie focused on slow, steady breathing as she studied the profile of Stuart Reilly, opposing counsel and well-known courtroom bully.

One by one the illuminated numbers above the scratched and dingy chrome doors ticked off their steady descent, five . . . four . . . three, gears grinding and creaking at an endless job. Bernie watched the flashing lights, praying there would be no stops along the way. The sooner she could get out of the cranky elevator, the better. Reilly's curled lip made it clear what the next few months would involve. Trial would be vicious, not only for her, but for Carlos. And it was Carlos she had to worry about, not her blotchy skin.

Finally, as the number two light flashed on and off, a quick exit just a floor away, Bernie responded to an earlier jab in court. "I'm perfectly aware of the mediation process, Mr. Reilly. I was simply suggesting you prepare your clients to bring some serious cash to the table."

The doors parted and she stepped out quickly, rushing ahead of any snappy comeback. Timing is everything, and a courtroom elevator was not the place to battle; it was simply a place to flex a little of her own muscle.

The corners of Bernie's mouth slipped into an uncontrollable grin as she pushed through the double glass doors and out into the mid-morning sunlight. This really was the best case she ever had. Stuart Reilly might have a dozen associates to jump at his bark, a big, fancy office stuffed with eager law clerks and secretaries, and the bench stacked with his former partners, but they were no match for a cute little six-year-old boy when it came to winning over a jury. Carlos's parents were dead and Reilly's rich client was to blame—simple stuff for any jury to understand. And she, better than perhaps anyone, knew the hell Carlos was going through. She couldn't give him back his mom and dad, but she would make sure he was well compensated, that he would have a chance at a future.

A whisper of clouds stretched across a fading lavender sky and a light breeze offered a bit of hope from a relentless summer that had stretched into October. Fresno was famous for summers that burned like hell itself and dreary winters of dense fog that shrouded the valley in a blind mist. This was one of those rare in-between days, the type of day that must have lured those first settlers to stop and begin planting crops and building homes.

Courthouse Park was a scattered patchwork of cool shade and deep shadows where grey squirrels darted across the grass and up the mottled branches of the meandering magnolias, Chinese elms, and tall pines. A constant parade of deputies in and around the courthouse made it a safe playground for the kids whose parents fought inside, battling over couches and televisions, weekend visitation and child support. Bernie quickly strolled through the park, ignoring the napping winos stretched out on the grass, past benches filled with bored civil servants and frightened jurors munching on bagels and muffins from the coffee cart that stood in the breezeway, all under a perfect sky above.

As soon as she rounded the corner of the courthouse annex, Bernie stopped to peel off her suit jacket. Temperatures might escape the century mark for a change, but it was still too hot for the professional outfits court demanded. She preferred loose pants and blouses that flowed about her like watercolors. After discovering a small import boutique in Berkeley, Bernie had filled her closet with exotic-sounding colors: coral sea, lavender mist, and iced geranium, all in soft cottons, fine silk, and washed linen. But she did not dare wear those flowing ensembles to court. Not anymore. Not if she wanted to be taken seriously.

Once upon a time, Bernie had appeared in court in her favorite celery linen suit, thoroughly wrinkled after a five-minute car ride, and the judge asked her if she had been up all night working or if she had merely slept in her clothes. And when she wore a flowing teal blue and purple floral suit, the same crusty judge asked her if there was a luau going on in the breeze-way that he didn't know about. Everyone laughed, even her, but she never wore anything that wrinkled instantly or flowed softly into court again. All public appearances featured her in only the most conventional and professional attire of tailored suits, serious navy blue or black with the occasional basic beige or charcoal for variety. Some of the newer young female attorneys came traipsing into court in short skirts with bare legs and strappy sandals, but she knew it wouldn't last.

Juries and judges in this conservative town look at more than evidence; they consider everything from a prosecutor's shoes to the defense attorney's watch. To be safe, a complete ensemble hung in her office closet for emergency calls to court. Appearance might not be everything, but it certainly counted for something, and there was no need to make her job any more difficult than it already was, especially on the back of her clients. So even when temperatures soared above one hundred degrees, she suited up, pantyhose included, and prayed she wouldn't melt in the process.

The soft day lured her into walking the four blocks back to the office. She took her time for a change, taking in the city streets in a way that wasn't possible through a car window. Most of the larger law firms had deserted downtown and set up shop in new modern office complexes out north, a good twenty-minute drive from court, opting for climate control and energy-efficient sterility. But Bernie liked being close to the action, and she liked the graceful old houses of downtown. In an odd way, she felt somehow connected to the depressed atmosphere of old Fresno. White-collar flight had quickly changed a thriving downtown to a dusty stretch of classic urban blight. The Fulton Mall, a six-block walking mall, was an outdoor museum of art and flowing fountains. For years it brought cars and busloads of folks to town for shopping, lunch at Woolworth's, and a matinee at the Crest Theater, but the flight of businesses and newer shops out north had turned it into a string of empty storefronts or sandwich shops, the beautiful sculptures and fountains left to collect dust and graffiti. The rumor was that it would be ripped out and cars would once again roll down the avenue. She'd been drawn to this area since she was a kid; she had fond memories of shopping with her grandmother for school clothes at JC Penney and chocolate malts at the Newberry's lunch counter. Ripping up the mall would be like ripping up those wistful days, but those days were gone.

A cool breeze elicited a broad smile for the old Mexican man selling the ginger candies he kept tied in plastic bags to the handlebars of his bicycle. His brown skin, thick and leathery from a lifetime of working in the sun, made his white shirt radiant. He stopped, gestured to the candies and nodded his head at her, grinning sweetly.

"Señora," he said, pointing to the candy, his smile broadening.

"No, gracias, Señor," she said softly, wishing she had tucked a few dollars in her pocket, but she only had her ID and a credit card in her bag. Bernie dragged her rolling briefcase behind her, letting it drop off the curb with a thud, yanking it up at the next block, the sound of the turning wheels an even rhythm as she trudged along.

The thought of Stuart Reilly's smug face in court was maddening. He was still strutting from their last battle together, one where she was on the losing end. Not so long ago, she had believed in Arnold Kramer's case just as she believed in all of her cases, invested thousands of her own dollars in experts, worked tirelessly, spent countless hours building a top-notch case. By the time depositions rolled around, she was convinced the case would be worth at least three quarters of a million, maybe more if she got lucky with a good jury. Arnold Kramer's days of driving big rig trucks were over; his injured back unable to stand the long hours behind the wheel without pain medication, and it was impossible to take drugs as a driver.

The whole case crumbled at Kramer's deposition when Reilly brought in a video for all to see. There was Arnold carrying bags of concrete, shoveling dirt, swinging a hammer, and, just in case there was any doubt about his abilities, he could be seen diligently operating a jackhammer to hack away at an old concrete slab. He was just helping his sister in an emergency, he'd explained, his eyes pleading and searching for understanding. That one day of physical labor sent him to bed for a week, he cried. He really was hurt, hurt bad, he had pleaded.

Before the day was over the six-figure case that Bernie was counting on settled for a measly fifty grand. Bernie didn't make a cent after paying all the costs, and doctors and rehab experts and even shelled out five-grand to Arnie to get him to agree to the settlement. All that work and not one dime to show for it. A sole practitioner can't handle many of those hits and expect to stay in business.

Bernie stopped for a moment to inspect the new beds of flowers at Lisle's Funeral Home, a gorgeous white colonial mansion surrounded by beautifully landscaped grounds. The gardener replaced the flowers every few days, before any blooms had a chance to fade. The only ones that were constant were the purple agapanthus that bordered the sidewalk and circle driveway. She loved the way their blossoms seemed to explode like violet fireworks from long arching green necks. It was a sin, she thought, that most people who visited the place probably never even noticed the old guy's hard work.

Like the old funeral home, Bernie's office was located in an old clapboard Victorian home. A hundred years ago, Fresno's finest social set jostled along the tree-lined street in buggies or on horseback. After World War II, the homes slowly turned into rundown monoliths, many chopped up into cheap apartments. Eventually, some real estate tycoon had the bright idea to renovate some of the grand old homes into professional offices that offered the charm of antiquity with a costly visit to your lawyer or accountant. Only one or two downtown houses were still actually home to the stubborn old folks who refused to run away, choosing to install iron bars on the windows or wrought iron fences around their yards instead of moving to some fancy retirement center in the suburbs.

Bernie loved her office, the Gordon Home, with its polished hardwood floors, grassy front yard, and casement windows that opened to the outdoors. She loved the long, covered porch and filled every corner with pots of lacey ferns and succulent jade. A basement, naturally cooled by the deep earth that held it tight, was perfect for her library. But her favorite feature was a large stained-glass window at the top of the stairs that sent a shaft of red and yellow light over the reception area, an illusion of a good aura floating in the air. On the south side of the house, a Modesto Ash spread its branches wide just outside her office window, offering its protective shade from a vicious sun. She had an ever-changing view, fluttering greenery in the spring, a shower of orange and gold leaves dropping to the ground in fall, and, finally, naked branches of winter floating in a haze of fog. An old hitching post stood on the side of the house where she occasionally imagined a chestnut gelding waited to carry old Dr. Gordon off to some medical emergency.

The landlord had done a nice job of restoring the old house, choosing a subtle green-grey color for the walls, a sharp burgundy and creamy vanilla for the layers of trim around the windows and door frames. The front porch gable featured a curlicue accent that reminded her of the cursive line she used to scribble beneath her name when she was twelve, when signing her name was still a work of art, practiced again and again with care. If an office would be her second home, she wanted it to be a real home.

By the time she reached the bottom of the four steps that led to the front door, a thin band of sweat darkened the back of her pale silk blouse and her cheeks were flushed, this time from heat, not anger. The day was gorgeous, but still too warm for walking in pantyhose and silk. She climbed the broad steps and crossed the painted porch to the front door. Through the large oval of leaded glass, she could see into the old living room, now reception area, and back to the old dining area where Crystal sat working at her desk. Before she could even get her keys out of her pocket, Crystal pushed the button hidden beneath her desk; the buzzer sounding as the lock released with a loud, clanging snap.

"Mediation," Bernie announced from the doorway, pausing just long enough to slip out of her shoes and kick them through the door to her private office, tossing her jacket onto a guest chair. "Can you believe it? Mediation already? We haven't even answered interrogatories for Christ's sake."

After twisting a handful of limp, rust-colored hair into a knot on top of her head, Bernie grabbed a pencil from the cup holder and jabbed it through the makeshift bun to hold it in place and off her damp neck. Bernie didn't let many people see her hair pulled up, but Crystal already knew that her boss had big Dumbo ears that turned the color of strawberry Jell-O; she'd seen them light up more than a few times. A fantail of wild hair stuck up in the air while several loose straggles hung limply down Bernie's back, but it worked in a sort of fashionable messy way that she would never strive for.

"I'm not surprised." Crystal yanked the headset from her ears, swung around in her chair and followed Bernie into the small kitchen area near the back door. "Why did you walk? I wanted to get out and pick you up, my morning reprieve, you know."

"I'm sorry, it was just so nice out and I felt like I needed a breath of fresh air, a little think time." It was easy to forget how dreadful it must be for Crystal, tied to her desk and telephone all day, every day. "Anyway, the judge gave us ninety days to get it done, so set it out as far as you can."

Bernie grabbed her cup from the dish drainer, a rose-patterned, bone china teacup she had bought for a quarter at a yard sale the first month she opened practice. The cup had survived an uncertain past and sat alone on an old card table, fragile and beautiful, unchipped, unbroken. A quarter seemed too low a price for such a treasure.

"What's the rush?" Crystal asked, pouring the last of the pot into Bernie's cup. She placed the empty pot in the sink and let the water spill in and over the rim while she spooned fresh grounds into the gold cone filter.

"Judge Baldry. He doesn't care that my clients live out of the country or that discovery isn't even halfway done." She rested her back against the counter, peered into the brackish liquid, took a sip, scowled at the bitter taste, and set the cup down. "Think I'll wait for fresh."

"Why don't you have some ice water? You have that," she pointed to Bernie's face and circled her index finger around, "that look."

Bernie recognized Crystal's polite attempt to point out what she already knew—her face was the color of a maraschino cherry.

"What look?" she asked, sarcastically wide-eyed and innocent, her left eyebrow raised, the only one she could control, offering a wry smile. "Don't worry, kid, it's just the heat. I just walked six blocks in pantyhose and heels. Besides, my dad always said hot coffee was the best thing to drink on a hot day."

"It's only four blocks," Crystal said, sliding the coffee filter into place.

Bernie ignored the correction, lifted the overflowing pot from the sink. She dumped out the tap water and filled the carafe from the water cooler, a slower process, but she swore she could taste chemicals in the city water. As fresh coffee began to sputter out, the two women moved on to Bernie's office, Crystal stopping to grab a stack of pink phone messages, notepad, and pen.

"Who's Joan Bennett SS?" Bernie asked, quickly shuffling through the pink squares of paper, skimming the names of the morning callers.

"She's with Social Security—that's the SS. Said it was personal." Crystal picked up her boss's jacket from the chair and hung it on a wooden hanger behind the door, carefully smoothed the wrinkles with her hands, then gave it a gentle pat as if it was some kind of pet hanging there.

"Must be about Noni." She set the stack of messages down next to the phone on the credenza behind her as a visual reminder that she had calls to make, then swung around, unzipped her briefcase and pulled out the manila file folders she had taken with her to court that morning.

"Also, Reilly's secretary called to schedule Carlos and Rosa's depositions, wants to know if you'll bring them here."

"Of course, he does. And if he wasn't such an ass, I'd agree." She studied the files briefly before handing them over to Crystal, removing her legal pad covered in scribbled notes to keep with her at her desk.

"So, what? You're going to go all the way to Mexico for deps because you don't like the guy?"

"Sure, why not?" Bernie shot one quick glance across her desk, just a flicker of eye contact, before shuffling through a mass of papers and pens, searching for her casebook, a thin notebook of detailed case information. She might remember every word in there, but she was lost without it at her fingertips. It was like a touchstone, all her projects condensed to one black binder. She knew she had an uncanny recall for detail, but she also knew she had gaps, things she couldn't remember at all. The casebook and meticulous files let her sleep at night, knowing all the names, dates, and numbers were safe if her memory failed.

Crystal tossed the file folders onto the red velvet sofa behind her and considered her thoughts. "Well," she said, "a trip to Mexico is expensive for one thing. And couldn't that sort of backfire on you?" She leaned forward, her steno pad resting on the edge of Bernie's desk, pen in hand, ready to record the long list of instructions her boss would fire off in a torrential pace once she got settled in to work and really going.

"The costs will be covered when we settle, so that's no big deal, but tell me, why do you think it can backfire?" Even though Bernie always questioned her secretary's opinions, she liked hearing Crystal's take on things, the occasional quirky feedback that might surprise or even anger her with inadvertent racism and misogyny, but almost always proving helpful somewhere down the line. It helped her predict the swing of a jury pool.

"Well, their life is pretty meager down there. It's not like here."

"I've been to Mexico. I know what it's like," Bernie said.

even have indoor plumbing. It wouldn't take a whole lot of money to change their life. I mean fifty-grand in Mexico is probably like a million here. Doesn't that kind of lower the bar? You know, a jury will think 'Why give them all that money when it takes so little to live there?'" She tapped her pen on her notepad for emphasis. "Aren't you, I don't know, kind of shooting your own case in the foot? You know, feeding that idea to Reilly."

"No, no, no, I don't think so," Bernie said, flipping through the pages of her casebook, pausing to give full attention to her answer. "First of all, plenty of people are just as poor in Fresno County and plenty of people in Mexico live quite well. But, that aside, you're forgetting that Carlos Luna is a U.S. citizen. He was born here. He lived right here until his grandmother took him back with her after his parents died. His mom and dad worked for the same guy for eight years with no indication they would ever return to Mexico. Carlos is entitled to the same amount of compensation as any white American boy. His life and his parents' lives were just as precious and just as valuable as any little blonde family in Clovis."

"And," Bernie said, continuing her argument, "Carlos would be living here now if Mr. Simpson hadn't plowed his truck into the Lunas. That little boy lost his mom and dad and the only life he knew. Just because he's living in Mexico with his grandmother doesn't make the loss of his parents worth any less."

Crystal twisted the corner of her mouth, scooted back in her chair, and looked down at the notepad in her lap. "Okay. I'm sure you're right," she said, her voice barely above a whisper. She nervously flipped a couple of pages as if she was looking for some note, scribbled "Bitch" then quickly crossed it out so that a small blue inky square was all that remained of her blasphemy.

Bernie turned to her left and hit the power button on her computer, avoiding her secretary's wounded gaze. Crystal was the best assistant she'd ever had, and Bernie needed her, so she turned to her and smiled, vowing to compliment her at least five or six times before lunch. "Yes, well, you're right too. That's my biggest worry, actually, that a juror will think like that. There's plenty of racism to go around, so I have to make sure they see it my way. Besides, I'm still hoping we can settle this thing at mediation. So," she swiveled back around to look directly into Crystal's unblinking eyes, and said as sincerely as possible, "we have our work cut out for us. I can't do it without you; you know that. We're a team."

Crystal nodded and flashed a brief smile; her frosty mask cracking, her jaw softening. "So, you really want to go to Mexico for deps?"

"Absolutely."

Crystal began to write as Bernie turned to the computer and logged on, quickly typing in her username and password, Birdie, her Dad's pet name for her when she was a kid. No one called her that anymore.

"Call Lance Parker and see if he can help us out with numbers. We'll need a structured settlement plan." She spoke without looking at Crystal, her eyes focused on the monitor, her mind racing.

"Parker's not taking any new cases for a while. I talked to his secretary yesterday and she said his wife's sick, so he has his nephew working with him now. Want to give him a try?"

"Sure. Give him the basic facts: five-year-old child, mom and dad were farm workers—but stable, working for the same man—you know what to say. And he'll need details like the specific ages of the parents, what they earned, so make sure you look all that up before you call. Ask him if he can give me some preliminary numbers on damages and structured settlement figures. I'd like to know that before we take the deps." With the click of the mouse a long list of e-mails ap-peared. "Actually, see if he can come in. I want to meet him, go over this one in person."

"Okay, I'll call him this morning."

"You know, another thing, Reilly won't want to travel to Mexico himself—I'm sure he's afraid to drink the water. That guy might act all tough, but he's really a pussy about some things. He'll send some lackey in his place, which is a really good thing. Reilly would probably scare poor Carlos and his grandmother to death; he's so intimidating." She gave a shudder at the thought of his constant neck popping, bulging biceps, shoulder rolls, and jutting chin. "When you call his office, tell them we can't bring the Lunas here before ninety days—immigration issues, border problems, and oh, I don't know, they've been through enough this year; it would be too much on an old woman and small boy to travel out of the country—something genuine. But be very nice about it, like we're unhappy about having to make the trip, too."

Bernie popped open an e-mail, read the content and hit delete as if she was squashing a bug. "I hate when people send me this crap."

Without taking her eyes from the screen, she talked to Crystal while reading, eager to lighten the mood, or at least change it, with the latest story of their resident ghost. "Hey, did I tell you Mrs. Gordon paid us a little visit last night? She found a file for me."

"What file?"

"Jenkins. I looked everywhere for it, and I mean everywhere. I wanted to take it home, but I couldn't find it. When I came in this morning, there it was on the floor, just inside my door, lying on the floor. How weird is that?" Smiling big, she wiggled her fingers in the air and lightly moaned, "hooooooo."

Crystal didn't laugh, but she did give a hint of a grin. "You must have dropped it on your way out, had it all along or something. I really don't think ghosts are much into litigation these days."

"Nope. I swear I didn't." Bernie cast a mischievous glance to her secretary, knowing how much the poor girl hated Mrs. Gordon ghost stories. "It has to be Mrs. Gordon. She's nosey, or bored, likes to read our files when we're not here. It's kind of like gossip for her. Actually, I think she wants us to start handling some juicy divorces."

"Stop it. You know that stuff creeps me out." Crystal shuddered as if she were freezing, but her smile had returned. "I'm afraid of ghosts and I'm the one who has to stay here by myself all day when you go to court."

Bernie ignored Crystal's pleas, further humoring her to lighten the mood. "You know, Crystal, she was a rich doctor's wife. And they certainly didn't have computers when she was around, so she probably won't erase important documents, but she might look over your shoulder to see what you're doing, or pace around upstairs, make a little noise, just enough to make us all nervous. Maybe we should have a séance and see if we can contact her. I could bring in my Ouija board and some black candles. You've got to do it by candlelight."

"No thank you," Crystal said, shaking her head, smiling again. "Leave the Ouija board and candles home. Can we just get on with work now?"

"Yes, you're right. Lunas. Let's talk about that." Bernie felt better knowing she had melted the earlier tension. Stressful work was one thing, and she could handle plenty of that, but personal stress and relationships left her drained and empty.

"You know, I doubt there's a decent hotel in the village where Mrs. Luna lives. Tell them we'll bring Mrs. Luna to Mexico City if they pay for her and Carlos to spend the night there. Make sure we get a nice hotel with a conference room and a swimming pool. Oh, and let's take our own court reporter. We'll need an interpreter, but you can find one there."

Crystal tapped the end of her pencil on the steno pad. "Got it. What else?"

"We need to subpoena Simpson's cell phone records. I need to prove he was talking on the phone when it happened."

"I already did; I ordered his driving record too. They should be in any day now," Crystal said, clearly pleased with her initiative.

"You're so good; I told you, I could never do this

without you," Bernie said. Another compliment, she noted, certain it took at least five times as many compliments to offset any single hostile remark. Six was even better for building up a nice reserve to quash any future ruffled feathers a difficult day might deliver. Bernie placed the palms of her hands down on the pile of folders in front of her. "Okay, I'm going to tackle this stack here. You let me know about dates and when the numbers guy can come in."

Crystal stopped in the doorway on her way out, opened her mouth to speak, then shook her head and turned away. She grabbed the doorknob and was just ready to pull the door closed when she finally spoke. "You know, at the risk of sounding unusually cruel, and please don't take this the wrong way, but it would almost be better for Carlos if he didn't have a grandmother."

Bernie couldn't help but flinch involuntarily at the comment. "Why would you say that? So that he'd have no family at all and be completely alone in the world? Wow, Crystal, I thought you were the nice one."

"Well, if the grandmother hadn't taken him to Mexico, he'd still be living here." Her shoulders lifted and lowered as she spoke, as if it was a foregone conclusion. "You know, in the States, where he's used to living, where he would get a good education."

"That doesn't mean he'd have a better life—living with strangers. He'd probably be in some foster home. The fact is, Crystal, he has a grandmother and she loves him, so it's up to us to make sure he's taken care of, and educated, even in Mexico, where, by the way, they love their children and grandchildren just as much as we do."

"Don't you think it's weird, though, you getting this case? I mean, how many lawyers out there lost their own parents in a car accident?" Her eyebrows lifted as she pressed her lips tight, her face forming the question mark. "You're the only one I know of, and you end up with a case where the parents both die in a car accident." She took a deep breath, opened her eyes wider than usual, and whispered, "Kind of freaky. Stranger than any lost file if you ask me."

"It's not as unusual as you think. People die all the time, even young parents."

"Not like that."

"No, sometimes even worse. Really shitty things happen all the time, even to nice folks like you. And me. And Carlos. Just read the paper."

Bernie narrowed her eyes and turned back to the computer screen, avoiding the discriminating gaze of the woman who had come to know her well, but not nearly as well as she believed. There were things that Bernie didn't share with anyone. Except Noni.

With her back turned to the door and Crystal, ending any further discussion, she picked up the first phone message and started pushing buttons. At the soft click of her door closing, she set the phone down. With the tips of her fingers, she gently massaged her forehead and breathed in and out, slowly counting, and waited for the flush to fade from the tops of her glowing ears and across her burning chest. *This case is going to cost me a lot of compliments*, she thought.

By the time Bernie finished going through the morning mail and ventured out of her office in search of a coffee refill, Crystal had arranged for the new economist to come in for a meeting. "He'll be here tomorrow at three," she announced.

Bernie was barefoot, the pantyhose she'd worn to court that morning tossed in the garbage can under her desk. "Who?" she asked.

"Parker's nephew, Don Fielding."

"Oh, good. That was quick work; thank you."

Bernie poured her coffee and sipped it thoughtfully as she sauntered back to her office, tugging her blouse free from her waistband, slowly unraveling to get as comfortable as possible for the rest of the day. Crystal, busy flipping through the calendar, the phone tucked between her shoulder and right ear, flagged her down, handing her another phone message, multitasking with her usual calm. She might be irritating at times, Bernie thought, but in the end, she made it all happen.

Crystal was in charge of running the office: worrying about things like deadlines, scheduling, transcription, and even how much money was spent on each case. Five years ago, when she came to work for Bernie, Bernie didn't trust anyone else to handle her calendar, let alone her company checkbook. During her first week, Crystal showed Bernie a picture of her husband, Denny, a baseball player for the local farm team, and said she could hardly stand to look at it he was so cute. Bernie was convinced she'd never last a month at the job. But she was wrong. Crystal was smart, extremely organized, and kept the practice running smoothly, even though Bernie still cringed inside when she saw the girl occasionally reach out and gently touch Denny's picture, knowing he was out on the road somewhere playing ball, still hoping for the big time, drunk on dreams.

The two women worked well together, though their views of the world were not only through different lenses, but through different lenses facing in completely opposite directions.

Crystal believed in lifetime soulmates, recreational shopping, glossy fashion magazines and regular manicures. She never missed Sunday morning services at People's Church where the parking lot was filled with BMWs and big shiny SUVs—all things Bernie scoffed at openly and frequently, but Crystal simply smiled at her jaded comments. If they bothered her, it didn't show.

Bernie was more interested in trying to do something to fix those situations where destiny screwed up and real lives were damaged, even if the only repair came in the form of a dollar sign. She put her trust in things she could control and manipulate on command, like hard work, recycling, and responsible voting—not monolith churches run by guys with expensive suits and bad hair, singing pop song hymns and passing the gold offering plate.

It's not that she didn't believe in God; she just didn't think any one group of people had a special claim to their idea of God. What made Catholics or Baptists think they knew more than Presbyterians or Jews or Muslims, for Christ's sake? They all seemed to think they had a fix on this elusive spirit, God. She preferred to think of God as this force that lives way out there, quietly peering through a small crack in the sky, quietly watching the daily struggle on this lonely planet and probably a few others, too. Sometimes he laughs at man's folly and blows a kiss on a soft breeze; other times man's cruel recklessness makes him angry and sad, so instead of a whisper of love, he sends a deadly hurricane or tidal wave as punishment. And then there are the times he simply turns away, leaving the crack open for private wishes, prayers, and dreams to drift through to the other side where they float around unnoticed. Of course, that tiny gap between worlds also allowed unseen spirits, angels and minions alike, to slip through for some earthly fun. But, even when it seems the small fracture line is abandoned and still, the two worlds existing as distant strangers, a timbre of light shines through. Bernie was certain that the light was the most important part.

It wasn't that she didn't believe in love or lifelong relationships; it just hadn't happened for her, not in any real way. Most people longed for the passion that fuels stars, but Bernie knew where such passion could lead. She knew how the end of that passion could rip your heart from your chest and everyone in its path. Distance, emotional distance, allowed partings to simply slough away. There might be a little sting, but no permanent damage.

The very idea of only one soul mate was preposterous, like only one flavor of ice cream or religion for everyone. There were, she was certain, many possible mates for people. Her one semi-long-term relationship had ended painlessly three years earlier when her boyfriend got a job with a firm in San Francisco. Weekend visits became further and further apart, and slowly they learned to live without the other, sometimes forgetting to call, forgetting to answer messages. Their final break-up took place on the phone, both of them agreeing that whatever they'd had was no more. They remained friends, still exchanged occasional phone calls and funny e-mails, but a casual friendship was all that remained, like a fading suntan at the end of summer.

What Bernie had come to realize and appreciate was that Crystal's romantic and often prudish nature was often the same view of local juries, people who were shaped by the nightly news, Sunday sermons, and popular sitcoms. Even though her secretary could make her dizzy with questions and mind-boggling philosophies, Bernie had come to rely on her for more than her clerical skills. After one year, Bernie gave Crystal a ten-percent raise. The second year, she got another ten percent and a fancy title, Firm Administrator. The third year, Bernie started a profit-sharing program and invested $7,000 in a mutual fund for her secretary.

When Bernie suggested one day that Crystal go to law school, even offered to help pay for it, Crystal laughed out loud as if the very idea was ludicrous. "No thanks, I want a life," she said.

Later that night, as she worked at home, crafting an opposition to a motion for summary judgment, Bernie stopped and thought about Crystal's comment. What was wrong with her life? She had a life, damn it, and a good one too. She just wasn't married with two kids and a dog. She knew better than anybody that being married didn't necessarily mean a happy life. Marriage could be tragic.

Two

1968

The air was sticky with plums, their sweet scent intoxicating and heady. Fat Betty's, a road-stop tavern, was surrounded by an orchard of Santa Rosa plums, a niche carved out among rows of overgrown fruit trees hungry for picking. Neglected branches were propped up on wooden stakes like crutches; the abandoned fruit was soft and rotting on the ground, rank with sweetness. Occasionally, a stray breeze would deliver the musty odor of the Tule River that flowed nearby to mask the fermenting spoil, but the men lingering outside the old dive bar, drinking beer and smoking cigarettes, didn't care about things like soft breezes, picking plums, or a forgotten harvest.

A row of menacing choppers lined the edge of the dusty parking lot that stretched out to the empty road. The bikes were mostly customized from modified stock, some with ape hangers, others with extended forks, machined metal tubes screwed onto the forks. Their overheated engines were finally quiet and cool after a long day of endless streaming down the 99 corridor and winding mountain roads. Loud and fast, their riders were fierce, and their bond was tighter than blood. The Vipers owned the road as they weaved fearlessly in and out of traffic, passing on curves, daring cars to get in their way. They rode until the sun disappeared behind the Sequoia skyline, ending the day at the small bar surrounded by plum trees.

Fat Betty's was a favorite stop for the night. No one ever hassled them out there next to nowhere. They would swap road stories, drink buckets of beer, brag and tell lies, smoke a little dope, and, if this night was like most Saturday nights, there would be plenty of girls hanging around. But this night was different. On this night, one particular girl was being offered up for their pleasure. And it wasn't just some young thing picked up along the road. This one was someone they knew, one of their own. It was Juicy, Freddie's old lady, off limits to the other guys until now. She had been accused of taking club money and that was unforgivable. She had to pay.

"She's all yours," Freddie had yelled to the bar. "She owes us, brothers, so get your money's worth."

It didn't take long for the steady trek out back to begin. Some would simply linger outside, never setting foot inside the trailer, but plenty would take advantage of the opportunity to do Freddie's girl then make their way back to the bar for more beer, bragging about their time with Juicy. And then there were the three men who ventured in together, looking for something rougher than just a turn with a pretty girl. All the men ever saw in the small trailer was Juicy, all yellow and spooked, naked in the single bed. None of them noticed her baby who slept peacefully under the small drop-down kitchen table.

The baby was as far away from her mother as possible, buried beneath a pink and yellow cotton quilt Juicy had stitched together by hand during the months when her belly grew too large for sitting on the back of Freddie's Harley.

The edge of a faded, red vinyl tablecloth hung low, nearly hiding the sleeping child from view. Only her frightened mother would look across the small space to see the bottom of the basket, making sure it remained untouched. Hopefully, the little bit of Jack she'd mixed in Ginny's milk bottle would knock her out for the whole night. She had guessed that two or three tablespoons would do the trick, reasoning that booze was really just like cough syrup. She hoped she was right. The last thing she needed now was a crying baby. *Just stay asleep*, she silently prayed. *Sleep.*

During those brief moments when she was able to move around, Juicy would quickly peak under the table cloth, stroke her baby's cheek softly, then return to the bed and resume her living nightmare. Even with the roughest of them, she never refused any command. She knew better, so she tried not to think about the sweating pig on top of her or the dirty hands holding her down, wrenching her wrists. To survive, she slipped right out of her skin and while one man after another grabbed her; she focused on her jail cell, the small trailer with grimy walls and cheap furniture, imagining it at an earlier time. Imagining it as a happy place. *Before, before,* became her mantra of hope. *Think of before.*

The dingy aluminum hut was brand new once, she told herself, someone's little home. Surely, she fantasized, some man and woman had eaten supper right there at that little table, maybe pot roast surrounded by tender carrots picked from their garden or maybe it was a tuna casserole, even though the woman hated fish. Right at the edge of an orchard of plums, two people might have feasted on ears of corn and the sweet air and soft breeze of a summer evening, happy to be there with each other in this room. They probably made love on this bed, sweet and gentle, then slept peacefully in each other's arms.

The happy couple fantasy never lasted long. The stench of sweat, stale beer, and sour breath would drag her out of her sweet dream and wrench her back to reality, to the pressure and weight of yet another man on top of her, his dirty fingers wrapped in her tangled hair. Eventually, they all left, the last one laughing at her painful groans as he let the cheap screen door bounce and slap behind him.

36

Three

2005

When the doorbell rang, Bernie was busy returning three days' worth of phone calls, her bare feet propped on her desk, a strand of hair twisted in her mouth. While she punched telephone buttons and talked on the handset, she watched the still leaves just outside the window, willing them to flicker or drift with any hint of a breeze; anything would do. The heat had returned for a final performance and no amount of air conditioning or shade could cool the old house to a comfortable level. She dropped her feet to the floor when she heard the door open and watched him walk across the reception area to Crystal's desk. That can't be him, she thought, and turned to the next message. He must be some kind of salesman or something, not her economist.

"Hi, I'm Don Fielding." His voice drifted across the reception area, light, yet filled with confidence. "I have an appointment with Ms. Sheridan."

Bernie listened in disbelief. *No way, she thought. He's Don Fielding? He looks like a college kid, too young to be an expert witness.* Most economists were older, more experienced, like Lance Parker. *And,* she noticed, *he's Asian.* That intrigued her more than his youth; Lance Parker was white.

"Oh, hi, I'm Crystal. I spoke with you on the phone. Ms. Sheridan will be right out." Bernie could see Crystal stand and offer her perfectly manicured hand in a professional and yet personal welcome. "Why don't you have a seat in the conference room?" She pointed him to the large mahogany table across from her desk where she already had the Luna files laid out neatly, along with a fresh legal pad, blue gel pen, mechanical pencil, and various-sized post-it notes. All of Bernie's potential needs were, as always, ready for her in advance. Crystal hurried to Bernie's office door, her heels clicking and scuffing on the oak floor. She tapped lightly on the wall just inside the door and pointed toward the conference room to make sure she saw him come in. "He's here," she said softly.

Bernie motioned for her to come in and close the door while she finished leaving a telephone message. "This is Bernadette Sheridan again. I guess we're playing phone tag. I'm going into a meeting right now, but you can call me after four. Thank you." She hung up the phone. "He's the economist? Lance's nephew?" she whispered, her index finger pointing to the other room.

"Yeah, why?"

"He doesn't look like Lance, for one thing, and he's awfully young, isn't he?"

"I don't know how old he is." Crystal shrugged her shoulders, pursed her lips, not thinking like her boss, already worried how a jury might feel about an expert who looks like he's twelve. "Maybe they're related by marriage."

"I just hope he's good," Bernie said, searching her desk, shuffling the same papers and red file jackets that had been there for three days. "Where's the file?" she asked. No matter how many times Crystal prepared the conference room for her, she would still ask where the file was, almost as if it was a ritual.

"It's all in there, ready to go."

"Oh, thanks." She slipped her bare feet into a pair of well-worn Birkenstocks, combed her hair as best she could with only her fingers, letting the side strands fall loose around her face to camouflage her cursed ears, then hurried to meet the man that waited for her in the conference room.

"Mr. Fielding," she said as she passed through the double doorway, chin lifted, shoulders back, her right hand extended before her, ready to give a good strong handshake. "Hi. I'm Bernadette Sheridan. Nice to meet you."

He stood as soon as she entered the room and readily met her outstretched hand with a single grip and a quick release, no repetitive shaking; it was as if the hands gave a simple hug and retreated. "Nice to meet you," he said, grinning and nodding his head eagerly with each word. "Please, call me Don." He waited for her to sit before returning to his seat.

"Okay, Don." She looked at him closely, noticed he looked directly into her eyes, no quick look up and down or over the shoulder. She liked that. It was one of the first things she looked for in a person, certain she could detect liars and phonies in an instant, though she'd been proven wrong many times. But she instantly liked his smile. It wasn't just a movement of the mouth or nod of the head; when Don Fielding smiled, his whole face smiled, and his dark eyes seemed to twinkle. A jury would like that. "Can I get you a coffee, tea, glass of water?"

"Water would be nice."

"I'll get it," Crystal said. "Would you like some, too?" she asked Bernie.

"Yes, thank you, Crystal. And could you put some ice in it?" The two women exchanged brief, knowing smiles at Bernie's request for ice water, finally taking Crystal's unwanted advice for her flushed face.

Bernie sat directly across the table from Don, at the place where the files and supplies had been laid out for her. "So, tell me about yourself," she began, "where do you come from? Crystal says you recently moved to Fresno." What she really needed to know was if he had the experience to stand against the attacks of Stuart Riley. That guy loved nothing more than pummeling an expert witness.

"Well, I recently moved here from Seattle. I brought a copy of my CV," he said and reached down and grabbed his leather satchel, a soft-sided case with a fold-over top and tarnished brass closure. The leather looked soft and worn, like an old catcher's mitt. His initials were burned along the edge, DAF. He pulled the snap open as he set the bag on the table in front of him, reached in, pulled out a forest green folder, and handed it to her. "That has everything, CV, business card, letters of reference, and fee schedule."

"Very nice," she said, examining the professional portfolio, admiring the embossed logo, his name in block letters, square and strong. "Why on earth would you leave Seattle for Fresno where we're still running the air conditioner in October?"

The sliding pocket doors rumbled open and Crystal slipped in with two tall glasses of ice water, carried on a black, lacquered tray. "Thank you, Crystal."

Crystal simply nodded in response, leaving the tray and the room without saying a word, closing the doors behind her.

"I actually grew up around here, so when Lance called and asked if I'd like to come and help him out, it seemed like a good thing to do. Most of my family still lives here, and," he paused to grin, his eyes nearly closing in happiness at the thought, "to tell you the truth, last summer, when I was on vacation with my family at their cabin, I bought a little cabin of my own."

"Nice," Bernie interrupted. She had always dreamed of having a cabin, a place to escape from work, phones, life, everything.

"Yes," he continued. "Up near Huntington, in Camp Sierra. I've been working on it every chance I get, and I really love it, so I decided to move closer so I could actually spend more than a couple of weeks a year there. I'm sort of going back and forth right now, still tying up some loose ends in Seattle. I have a couple of cases still going on there that I need to finish up."

"Huntington Lake. It's gorgeous, but gee, I haven't been up there in a couple of years, I guess. I'm not sure I even know where Camp Sierra is."

"Well, you'll have to drive up and visit, see what I've done. Maybe spend an afternoon on the water. I have a little boat."

"Sailboat?"

"Of course." He dipped his head a bit, as if it were the end of his sentence, a physical period. A lock of his dark hair fell over his face and he gently lifted his thin fingers to comb it back into place. "It's just a little daysailer."

"Sounds fun."

"Do you fish?"

"No, not since I was a kid." Bernie flashed back to a forgotten day on the Kings River, sitting in tall grass with her dad, their poles held loose in their hands. How old was she? Seven? Eight?

His dark eyes scanned the conference room walls, the molded ceiling and cool green walls. "This is a great office," he said. "I love these old houses."

"Thank you. I do too." She looked around at the familiar room, still gratified that her choice to open her own practice downtown was the right thing to do, no matter the risk.

Bernie opened the folder and studied the long list of qualifications and accomplishments. "I see you went to UCLA."

"Yes, for grad school. I actually did my undergraduate work here at Fresno State. As you can see, I have an MS and PhD in Economics. My bachelor's is in Psychology, a little bit of a shift from Econ, but helpful in forensics work."

"Impressive . . . Dr. Fielding." She nodded approvingly as she continued to scan the long list of professional papers he had authored, and the longer list of legal cases where he served as an expert witness. "You don't seem old enough to have done so much. You've been busy."

"Yes, and thank you." He paused for a moment before going on with his history, allowing Bernie more time to peruse his information. "Why don't I give you the brief version? For the past ten years I've been working in Seattle, consulting in legal matters and teaching part time at the university." He paused again to grin, amused at his own life, at least the part he was about to reveal. "And, in my free time, I was playing bass guitar in a local band there, well—it's a club band. We play mostly originals, but a few covers."

She laid the folder down, intrigued, and leaned a bit closer to make sure she caught every word he shared, truly interested. "Let's see, you're a sailor, forensic economist, professor, and a musician? That's quite a mixed bag of skills there. How do you have time for all of that?"

"I don't know. I guess you just make time for things you want to do." His palms rolled slowly upward, as if there could be no other way imaginable for him to live. "And, just give up the rest." For the first time since he'd walked in the door, and for just a moment, he wasn't smiling. "Don't ask me what's on television because I don't know."

Bernie measured her words carefully, knowing her next question could come off as offensive or too personal, but she was curious, and asking sensitive questions was what she did. She knew that if she had a question, probably someone else did, too, so it was better if she knew the answer up front. "At the risk of seeming politically incorrect, actually, *knowing* it is politically incorrect, you don't look like Lance."

"No, I don't." He shook his head slightly, but never shifted his gaze from her face.

Bernie offered a warm smile. "I'm just curious," she said, "and I decided a long time ago to just ask my witnesses and clients about anything. It's better to be direct than leave a meeting with any questions in my head."

"Actually, I don't look like any of the Parkers or the Fieldings. Most people hear my name and expect to see a fat, bald guy in a cheap suit smoking a Cuban cigar, not a skinny Asian guy, though they are never surprised that I'm pretty good at math." His face lit up when Bernie smiled freely and genuinely at his humorous jab at racial stereotypes and himself.

"Oh dear," she said, grimacing.

"I'm not sure if it's much a story, but my name was given to me when I was adopted. I am, by birth, Vietnamese. I was one of those children taken out of Vietnam at the end of the war and brought to America for adoption."

"Really? You were adopted?" This captured her interest even more than his CV, musical skills, or mountain cabin. The minute she'd seen him, she'd wondered if he was adopted. "How old were you when you came here?"

He blinked slowly, smiled slightly, and seemed pleased to share his life story with her, even though they had just met. "I was just five when I came to America. I don't really remember much about Vietnam, bits and pieces of faces, smells, and a small house, but most of it is just a blur. I remember flies for some reason, a lot of flies, but I'm not sure if that was Vietnam or Fresno; my folks live out in the country and there are still a lot of flies, so I don't know where the flies come in. I wish I remembered the language, but I don't, not a word. I do remember sitting in school, struggling to understand English, never quite sure what the teacher was saying, but I had a good tutor so I caught up."

"What about your parents, your real ones; don't you remember them? I remember things from when I was five. And your name? You must have had a different name." Her questions ran into each other, leaving no time for him to answer. That was not her style, at least not the one she used in depositions, but this was not a deposition. This was different.

"You really are direct. I'm not sure what any of this has to do with your case, but I'm used to these types of questions. Most people just aren't as, as you say, direct." He paused for a sip of water then continued. "Believe it or not, my name was Danh, almost Don, just more nasal. I don't have any real sense of hearing it that way, it's been so long, and I don't really remember my *birth* mother and father, just flashes of faces, teeth, smells, snippets of sounds, if that makes sense."

"So, you were in an orphanage, right? I'm assuming your mother and father must have been killed in the war." She closed Don's business file and lightly pressed her palms down on it, as if she held it in place. There was nothing on his resume nearly as interesting as what he shared of his own life.

"I'm not sure about that." He leaned back and looked at the ceiling as if it were a window to his past. "If I was in an orphanage, I don't think it was for very long, because I don't remember anything like that. I mean I remember being on the plane with a bunch of other kids and being in a big room with cots or something for a very short time, but I was lucky, I guess; I was adopted by a family as soon as I got here. I was part of what the government called Operation Baby Lift; are you familiar with that?"

"No. I know the U.S. brings in a lot of Hmong refugees and Fresno's one of their relocation places. Is it part of all that?"

"No, this was long before they started bringing in the

Hmong people. I've been here since 1975, the year the war ended. The Americans took thousands of children out of Vietnam and brought them to the States for adoption; it was a big baby market. Some were orphans, but not all. From what I've read and been told, a lot of parents gave their children up so they could live in the States and have a better life. They didn't want their children to suffer like they did. I like to think that I was one of those kids. I even have this vague memory, or maybe it's a dream, of my mother crying and someone taking me out of her arms, but I could have made that up." He shifted in his seat as though he might be uneasy, revealing more than intended in this first interview with a potential client. "You know, I was a bit of a crybaby when I was small, so it might have just been me crying when I had to go to school or something. Don't worry; I don't cry much anymore."

"Well that's good to know."

Don may have been uncomfortable revealing so much history, but Bernie found his candor intriguing and appealing. Such unfettered honesty and glib humor eased any tension that may have been hiding in the corners of the old room, transforming the meeting into a pleasant exchange. Two people sat around the long table getting to know each other, just like a couple of folks meeting over drinks, instead of two plotting professionals gathered in a law office surrounded by files full of legal documents, death certificates, police reports, and photographs of a dead man slumped over a bloody steering wheel, his wife face down in the dirt in the early morning dawn.

Bernie once again opened Don's file and quietly scanned the rest of his CV, the long list of clients and cases.

"So, Don," she paused and nudged the folder away from her, "this case is, in some respects, a slam dunk. I represent a five-year-old boy with two dead parents and the paternal grandmother who lost her son and daughter-in-law. The maternal grandparents are deceased. So, the good thing is there's only two plaintiffs. Sometimes these cases can have ten or fifteen claimants, but this is an unusual situation all around. In fact, it might just be too unusual."

"How's that?"

"Well, you are an orphan, a child who lost his parents at the age of five, which is exactly what our plaintiff is—a child who lost his parents at the age of five. And," she paused, clearing her throat before continuing, "and, this is not something I usually share, but it only seems fair to let you know that I am also an orphan, though I was much older. My mother and father were killed in an accident when I was thirteen."

"Huh." He sat silent for a moment. "What a coincidence. But, like I said, I'm not sure I was an orphan. I prefer to think my mother gave me up; I think she wanted me to have more than she could ever give. You've had to have heard the jargon, not giving up, giving more, all that. I think I would remember if she were killed. And I don't."

The air conditioner hummed softly. Bernie didn't want to talk about his birth mother's sacrifices and Madonna virtues, but still, the whole idea of some selfless woman sending her child to America was endearing, even noble. It was the kind of rags-to-riches immigrant success story that a Fresno jury would eat up. She could try to work that in on the witness stand, innocently slip it in with his background during qualification. She much preferred the orphan concept to some mother just parceling him out to some unknown situation, but this was his story, his life, not some fairytale.

"Yes, I've heard about the ultimate sacrifice of a mother not giving up, but giving more; well, that's often a rather romanticized version of giving away an unwanted child, but I suppose in your case it probably was the best thing that could have happened, I mean . . ." Bernie swallowed her words, realizing her faux pas by the scrunched eyebrows and tight lips across the table. She felt his gaze hard upon her and blushed. "What I mean is that it was a true sacrifice in light of the war and all. I can't imagine . . ."

Nothing she could say was going to sound right, at least not now. She was trespassing on sensitive territory and rattled by Don's face as he struggled to grasp what she said, looking like he was suddenly nauseous or holding back a lifetime of disgust all sitting across a table from him.

"Let's just say this is an unusual situation with respect to the similar losses shared by you, me, and Carlos Luna, regardless of the cause," Bernie said softly, hoping to smooth the ruffled feathers.

Don's jaw loosened, and he nodded, a sign of understanding, agreement.

Bernie took a deep breath and let it out slowly. "I'd like to think our personal commitment to this case will be somewhat enhanced by that shared experience and, ultimately, we will present stronger testimony . . . for Carlos's sake."

hand. Bernie picked up the thick file jacket and pulled out a single manila folder. "Do you know the basic facts of the Luna case?" she asked.

"A bit. Crystal gave me some very basic information over the phone. She told me your clients are from Mexico." His congenial getting-to-know-you manner seamlessly shifted to discussing the Luna case, his voice lowered to a more earnest tone of compassion and intelligence. He was one of those rare people whose entire demeanor committed to the moment at hand. He sat taller in his chair, and his chin edged up higher.

"Not exactly. Right now, they both live in a little village in Michoacán, in southern Mexico, but Carlos, the little boy, was born here in Fresno. He actually lived out in Madera until six months ago when he went to live with his grandmother. She wanted him with her, and she couldn't come here, so . . ." She didn't finish the sentence in words, just motioned the obvious with the wave of a hand.

"Hmmm. That complicates things a bit."

"Yes, quite a bit, actually. Grandma, pardon me, Mrs. Luna, I should say, was accustomed to her son, Carlos's father, sending her money just to take care of herself." She watched him slowly nod in agreement as he began to recognize the problems that festered hundreds of miles to the south during a time when borders were difficult to cross. But Crystal was right; he was nice. He needed a haircut, but other than that, he seemed like a good choice for this case. "She no longer has that income and now she is raising a small child in difficult circumstances."

"Wouldn't she be entitled to benefits? Social Security? Insurance? Something to maintain her?"

"We're working on getting some advance money from the driver's insurance company, but nothing has come through yet. I've advanced a small amount myself to cover initial expenses, but it won't last long. We need to settle at mediation, if possible. I don't want to put them through a trial if I don't have to." She didn't mention that she, too, would rest easier with some cash flow increase. "In fact," she added, "I don't know if Crystal mentioned it to you, but we're going to mediate this case within ninety days."

"Yes, yes, she informed me of that, so I worked up some preliminary numbers," he said, "very preliminary, based on what I had, but they're pretty loose. I'll need documents and details to come up with anything solid." From his satchel he retrieved a red file folder which held several pages of columns of figures. He slid the page across to Bernie with the tips of his fingers. Again, Bernie noted the graceful manner of his hands, the long, slender fingers of a guitar player.

As she examined the itemized list of categories and potential values, she pressed her lips together and dipped her head from one side to the other, just like her mother used to do when she studied a report card of evenly mixed As, Bs, and Cs. It wasn't great, but it wasn't terrible, either. She was impressed; she had to admit. The guy had done his homework before showing up for her party.

"What I've done is project the estimated income for the parents through their life expectancy. I've also figured in the cost of housekeeping and maintenance that they would have provided until the child turned eighteen."

"Good, and of course this is all in addition to the

emotional damages, which will be significant." She was talking to herself more than the expert, but he assumed the comment was for him.

"Right, well that's for you to establish. That's always a mystery to me—figuring out what someone's life was worth—emotionally. How do you truly measure that with any certainty?"

Bernie studied the individual across from her for a moment, considering how to paint the picture of emotional damages for him as she did for juries, the perfect sales pitch to match a specific buyer. What would he respond to? What would work for this particular man?

Her voice was low and gentle when she spoke, compelling trust and confidence. "You're a musician, so I know you understand an attachment to something like an instrument. So, think about this: What's more painful? Losing Willie Nelson's beat-up old flat top that's covered with a lifetime of signatures, all those autographs, the history there, the wood worn through over the years, or losing the brand-spanking-new Martin you just paid ten grand for? I'm talking about emotional pain. Do you care more about the guitar you have held and played for years, that others have added a piece of their life to by signing their name, one you played until you've worn the wood away, an instrument that is irreplaceable, or do you care more about the new guitar, the one that's shiny and expensive, but you've never even changed the strings. Hands down, you'd be devastated at the loss of the personal, uniquely carved possession, a one-of-kind. Right?"

A slow smile formed, and he nodded his head up

and down.

"Now, imagine, and this is something I know you can do, just like I can, imagine losing your mom and dad, far more unique and precious than any hollow wooden box and six strings, no matter who played it or signed it. What's that pain like? What's that pain worth?"

His eyes shone when he spoke. "You're good. You know your audience and you know your guitars."

"I have to be. Rogelio and Lucero Luna might have been poor farm workers to the rest of the world, but they were everything to Carlos. And Rosa too. They can't be replaced, and we can't bring them back. They were one of a kind. But their loved ones, their child, Carlos, and their mother, Rosa, can be compensated financially. We can do that."

Don leaned back in his chair and listened to her, the tips of his fingers pressing against one another. He didn't say anything, just simply nodded in agreement.

"Unfortunately, most people associate value with wealth. They want to give bigger sums to good-looking white people with professional jobs, and that makes sense; the more earnings, the more lost, I know that. So, I need you to maximize the solid damages, the ones you can count and put into a nice little chart for the jury to see, give these folks some solid worth." She stressed her words: "We need to try to make the Lunas appear as valuable on paper as they were to their son, or as much as possible, that is. Those solid damages, the special damages, depend in large part on you. I'll take care of the rest."

"I understand."

"What else?" Her favorite question. She leaned

forward, and, now relaxed and at ease with her guest, unconsciously tucked her loose hair back behind her oversized ears.

"For the grandmother, Rosa, I need a little more information than what I have right now," Don said. "She was apparently dependent on her son for income, but I don't really know how much. It's unlikely that she had a bank account where he deposited the money directly, but you never know, we should find out. Her son probably wired her money, or gave her cash on an annual visit, if they did that sort of thing. I need something to verify how much money he actually contributed to her living and how he did that."

"I doubt she kept receipts, but I'll ask. I'm going to be talking to her sometime this week. Crystal's setting up depositions in Mexico, so I'll make sure she puts me on the line when she contacts Mrs. Luna. She's arranging for an interpreter to make sure there's no miscommunication. The other thing we can do is go through the parents' things they left behind. Some of it went to Mexico with Carlos and Rosa, but a lot of it is still here, in their old house. The Lunas lived with another family in Madera. I asked the woman to keep any papers and documents they might come across as they cleaned up their rooms, so I guess I need to drive out there and pick up whatever they might have found."

"Yeah, any receipts from Western Union, checking account deposit receipts or anything like, that would really help."

"I'll get out there this weekend."

In just over an hour, Bernie had signed the retainer agreement with Don Fielding and handed over copies of the

Luna's earnings statements and death certificates. While they waited on Crystal to make the copies, she filled Don in on some of the other details of the accident. The defendant, Mark Simpson, was driving his father's company truck while talking on his cell phone, missing a stop sign and crashing into the Lunas, t-boning their old Mercury sedan. She explained that there was a company five-million-dollar umbrella policy out there in addition to the personal policy with a five-hundred-thousand-dollar limit. If it had been a white professional couple named Smith or Johnson, she had no doubt the policy would be paid without question. But the death of two field workers would mean she'd have to fight for every nickel.

"So, you can see," she said, concluding the debriefing session, "this case is important. Really important."

"I understand."

"Good."

She was walking him to the door when the phone rang.

"Bernie," Crystal interrupted, "Joan Bennett is calling again. Do you want to take it, or should I take a message?"

"Oh, I'd better take it." She gripped his hand firmly and gave it a powerful shake. "Thank you for coming in, Don. I'll call you in a day or two after I go to Madera."

"I'm looking forward to it," he said. "It was a pleasure. I'm going to like working on this one."

She closed the door behind him and shuffled into her office, kicking her shoes off as she slid into her high-backed chair. "This is Bernadette Sheridan." Her voice was crisp and professional for the unfamiliar caller.

"Ms. Sheridan. Finally, we connect. My name is Joan

Bennett. I'm with Social Services, Department of Children and Families."

"Did you say Social Services? Children and Families? I thought you were with Social Security."

"No, I'm calling from Social Services."

"Is this about my grandmother, Isabelle Fierro?" Butterflies appeared and fluttered in her nervous stomach at the words *Children and Families*. They would not be contacting her unless there was a problem.

"No. This call concerns you, Ms. Sheridan. I have some information regarding your birth mother," the woman said.

And there it was.

When she was younger, she imagined getting a call like this. Every time she read about children finding birth mothers or birth mothers finding children they'd given up, she wondered if it might happen to her one day.

Bernie sat up straight and rested an elbow on her desk, her fingers slowly rising to touch her face, just next to her lips. She could feel an ache in her chest and heat rising up the back of her neck. "Go on," she finally said, "I'm here."

"We were contacted by your birth mother some time back. She asked for our help in locating you."

Bernie nodded her head, though the woman on the line could not see her. "I see. My parents told me I was adopted when I was very small, just a baby. So, after all these years, why now?"

"It's been nearly two years since we started the process." There was a pause as if she expected some congratulations on her diligence, or a question or comment from Bernie, but there was only silence across the telephone line as Bernie nodded her understanding to an empty room, speechless. "And now, she would like to know if you would be interested in talking with her, or possibly even meeting her."

A familiar weakness soared through her body, beginning at her head and dropping to her toes, an irrational anger buried long ago resurfacing and simmering with each second. Did she really want to meet the woman who gave her away? She'd thought about this for most of her life, convinced she knew what had happened. Undoubtedly, her birth mother was a kid herself who got knocked up in high school. And she couldn't be bothered with a baby. Caring for a baby at a young age would only hurt them both. And the baby would be better off with a mom and a dad, so she simply gave her child away. A familiar story, the guilt of an older woman who suddenly regrets her teenage choices.

Still, Bernie reasoned, the woman who gave birth to her was alive and out there and she should know; she should know what she'd done when she'd sent her baby off to her new perfect family. She should know what happened.

The phone trembled slightly in her hand. Bernie gazed out to the leaves of the familiar Ash tree for something, but what that was she didn't know. There was a time when she'd actually prayed for this call, silently willing her birth mother to find out that her baby's childhood had crumbled, but that was years ago, or days ago. Now, she wasn't sure. Why would someone want to show up thirty-eight years too late to say she wanted to be a mother? Or she was sorry? Or, hi, want to be friends now that you're a grown woman? She inhaled through her nose, exhaled out her mouth, slowly, counting to five as she inhaled, again as she exhaled. Yoga breathing. When she spoke, all that came out of her mouth was "Oh," the word cracking and breaking on the way.

"I realize this is sudden and probably a little shocking, but there's no way to ease into the subject." Again, the comment was met with nothing but silence on the other end of the line, so the woman continued. "Why don't you let this bit of news sink in, think about it, and we'll talk in a day or so. It's better if you let things process a little before moving on too quickly."

The woman's voice was soft and soothing. She probably made these types of calls often, and had experienced every kind of reaction imaginable. She was the one with all the information in front of her. She knew things about Bernie, her past, where she came from, things Bernie had only guessed at over the years. A stranger on the phone knew more than Bernie did about her own life, her history.

"Process, yes." She switched the phone from her right hand to her left and rested her forehead in the palm of her right hand. "You see, I'm really busy right now. I'm an attorney, but uh . . ."

"Yes, your mother was actually quite proud to learn that."

"She knows I'm a lawyer?" It puzzled her that the woman who gave her up also knew more than Bernie. She at least knew how Bernie spent her days.

"Yes, but she does not know your name or any details about you. Without your permission, we can only give non-identifying information. She doesn't even know the city where you live."

"That seems odd. She knows what I am, but not who I am." Bernie felt her heart pounding in her throat, not her chest, forcing a rush of heat up her face and down to her trembling fingers. "What if I were a cocktail waitress? Or, say, a welfare mom? Would you still be making this call?"

"Ms. Sheridan," she cleared her throat, spoke slowly and evenly. "Your mother was extremely anxious about your welfare, so during my last conversation with her, I let her know you were a professional woman with your own business, an attorney. That is all. She had no idea what your life was like when she began the investigation. Regardless of how you feel, she liked hearing that you had done well. If she never learns more, she was reassured with the knowledge that you are successful in your own right. That you seemed to have had a," she paused a bit before finishing, "a good life, the life you deserved."

"Good for her." Contempt hummed across telephone lines to a woman simply doing her job, the only one available to receive the jab and sting of Bernie's bite.

"Ms. Sheridan, this is never easy. Trust me, take a day or two, and think it over. We don't immediately bring the parties together. We usually start with letters. Perhaps you'd like to start by writing a letter. That is often easier than dealing with a face-to-face meeting right away. And, if it is agreeable, I can have your mother send you a letter, too. It would go through me, of course."

"I do need to think about this," she agreed, slightly regretting her hints at rudeness. "I'll get back to you."

"Thank you. We'll talk soon after some of this news settles."

Bernie hung up the phone and moved to the comfort of the red velvet sofa salvaged from her childhood, sagging, but comfortable. She pulled her feet up and wrapped her arms around her bent legs, hugging them close to her chest to form a tight ball with her body like she did when she was thirteen, huddled up and silent on that very same couch. Noni would urge her to do homework, go outside and play, set the table, anything to get her up and moving. But she would stay there in her silent cocoon until her feet tingled with a burning numbness. When Crystal walked in to say said good-night, Bernie was still clutching her knees to her chest, ignoring the pins and needles that pierced her calves and toes.

"You okay?" she asked.

"Yeah, just taking a minute." She leaned back, released her legs and stretched out long, throwing her arms back over her head. "Long week. I'm glad it's the weekend."

"Yeah, I'm taking off. Why don't you leave your briefcase here? Just relax for a change this weekend. If you want to do something, give me a call. I'll be around all weekend. Denny's going to Phoenix."

"Thanks, Crystal. Maybe I'll do that. You have a good weekend." Bernie knew she would never call Crystal to go out and have a good time. They only socialized for special occasions, celebrations, holidays. And that was at lunch, during the week.

"You too." She turned away and called up the stairs, "Good night Mrs. Gordon," her words lifting to a hollow echo as she bid a farewell to the phantom ghost of a woman that had lived where they now worked, the poor soul who was blamed for every lost file, each settling groan and creak the old house muttered in aging protest. The spiritual whipping post that never complained. "Leave the files alone," Crystal demanded as she walked out the door.

Bernie smiled at her, realizing that was Crystal's only goal.

"Mrs. Gordon," Bernie whispered to the now empty room, "what would you do? Would you want to meet the woman who didn't want you? Would you write her a letter?" She sat quietly and waited for a creak or groan in reply, but the house was silent.

When Bernie finally pulled herself up off the couch and out the door, Don Fielding was still out there, talking to a guy in coveralls splattered and stained with splotches and flecks of grey and brown paint. *Like a Pollock painting*, she thought, *a living and breathing canvas*.

Her landlord had recently added the Victorian next door to his portfolio with plans to turn the entire block into his own personal avenue of office buildings. Crews of carpenters, plumbers, painters, and landscapers paraded in and out of the tired, old house, slowly transforming it to a work of art. She had watched the workmen come and go for months, their hissing saws and pounding hammers forcing her to close all the windows and run the air conditioner on rare summer days when a cross breeze carried the scent of jasmine.

"Still here?" she asked.

He said something to the painter, who nodded, then walked over to where she stood by her car. "Yeah. I noticed they were working on this house and got them to let me in to take a look inside to see what they're doing. It's a great place.

Have you been in there?"

"No. Not yet. Are you looking for office space?" She opened the passenger door of her small Subaru and laid her packed briefcase onto the empty seat. Her head was still spinning with the news of Joan Bennett's phone call, a part of her talking and moving, her social skills on autopilot while she inwardly writhed in a slow simmer of anxiety and confusion.

"No. I work out of my house, well, apartment, for now. But, I'd like to buy a little house in town and fix it up myself. You know, have something to work on here when I'm not working on the cabin, so I was just looking for ideas." He pointed at the two houses side by side, her office and the vacant one. "I really like these colors. Nice."

"Yeah, they're nice." She followed his gaze to the roofline, then moved around to open the driver's side door, but waited to get in, the conversation not over.

"Well, I'm headed up the hill." Don glanced to the east for a long moment, then turned back toward her as if he wanted to say something more, but thought better of it. He bowed slightly and made a gesture with his hand in farewell.

"Have fun," she said. Bernie watched him slide into his small truck, his thin body moving like a dancer, fluid and weightless. He drove away slowly, his eyes already focused on what was ahead.

Bernie took the long way home, choosing the shady side streets, the ones she learned to drive on more than twenty years ago, avoiding the crowded freeway and Friday evening traffic. She rolled down the windows while she cruised along old Van Ness Avenue, moving away from downtown. She slowed her car at the sight of children splashing through a wading pool in their front yard and studied their tired mother sitting on the porch smoking a cigarette, her eyes resting on the boy and girl playing in the pool. Bernie recalled how her mother, the only mother she knew, anyway, used to watch her swim. They had a Doughboy pool in the backyard. Bernie had wanted a kidney shaped built-in pool, like Pam Wilson's, so her father built steps and a small redwood deck all around the pool. It was, he claimed, even better than a built-in because you were up higher. Her mother would sit in a lawn chair on the patio, smoking Virginia Slims and reading paperback novels, while Bernie jumped from the deck into the cool water again and again, cannonballs and dives, one right after the other. Her mother only looked up when the splashing stopped, afraid of the silence. When Bernie finally turned into her narrow driveway, she was still thinking of her mother, sitting and reading, struggling to recall even one time that her mother jumped in and splashed with her. She was sure she had, but she couldn't envision it. That memory was locked away somewhere. The only image she could conjure up at the moment was her mother looking up, startled and afraid.

She unlocked the door and entered the cool darkness. The small Tudor home was where she had lived as a teenager, then again as an adult after she moved Noni to the Nazareth House, accepting the gift of a home from her grandmother for the second time in her life. Of course, in exchange, she paid the monthly rent at Nazareth, which was far more than any mortgage on the old house would be. Bernie could hardly wait to tell Noni about the call from Joan Bennett, about her birth mother trying to find her. She was sure the old woman would spit on the ground, then mutter or curse under her breath in Italian. Noni knew everything.

Four

1968

She was sitting up, trying to clear her head, when Freddie stomped up the rough plank steps, each boot pounding and heavy-footed. Like most of his friends, the only shirt he wore on such a muggy night was a black leather vest, "Vipers" emblazoned in bold, white letters across the back, a red, hissing snake coiled up around the tail of the letter "p."

"Don't get excited—you're not done yet." He paused to rub the heel of his hand over his bloodshot-red eyes. "Two more, then you can go." He leaned his head to one side, lifted the edge of the red cover, glanced down at the sleeping baby then over at her mother before dropping the cloth from his fingertips. "Shit, that kid can sleep through anything. Must take after me," he added with a laugh, sinister and low. "Here," he said, picking a cigarette from his pocket, tossing it onto the bed where it landed between her legs. "Don't say I never gave you anything." He laughed again then tossed her the nearly empty pint of Jack Daniels that sat on the table. "You look like you could use a drink."

"How could you do this?" Juicy picked up the cigarette and tried to steady her hand as she put it in her mouth, then gently touched her face and winced in pain. He leaned over and lit the trembling tip with the Zippo she had given him on his last birthday, his twenty-fourth. The flame lit up her dirty face with streaks of smeared mascara and a purple shadow along the left side. Red blotches the size of fingers circled her upper arms. She inhaled deep and blew the smoke out in gasps. "I hate you. I really truly hate you, Freddie." She grabbed the bottle and took two big gulps before the burn of straight whiskey on a split lip brought tears to her eyes and caused her to choke and cough.

"Yeah, you'll get over it." Three perfectly round smoke rings popped from Freddie's mouth, then a final stream of smoke. He took another drag before talking, bathing his words in smoke. "Two guys just rolled in from Oakland. They're just having a beer first." He looked her over, his eyes moving from her face, down her naked body to her feet, and then spit on the floor. "And clean yourself up, for Christ's sake; you're a mess." He pushed the door open with a kick and a blast of the plum-scented air filled the trailer.

Through twisted metal blinds she could see Freddie standing outside smoking with his friends, their dark silhouettes blacker than the shadows of plum trees. She numbly watched one of them tilt his head back as he chugged a beer. Their voices drifted through the open window and dirty screen. She recognized him from the times when she'd been on the road with them, riding behind Freddie, her arms around his waist. "Fuck, man, you really got Juicy in there?" he asked.

"Took the scratch I was holding for our Bass Lake run next week. She's just paying it back in trade." They laughed again, and someone coughed and spit.

"That's cold, man."

There was the sound of breaking glass and then the

revving of engines. All night, there was the sound of engines, sometimes a lone humming and churning, other times a deafening roar as clusters came and went. When she was pregnant, she used to listen for the roar of a single engine, waiting for Freddie to come home from some weekend run or all-night party. She really believed that once the baby came, he might change. She had changed, and he could, too. Their lives would be better, she told him, if he would get a better job, one where he hung around with a different crowd. He should stay home with her and Little Ginny more too, she'd told him, especially at night. He ignored her when she suggested they get married and be a real family, but he didn't say no, and for a while, she was sure he was trying to be different, to be a good dad. He even fed the baby a few times, smiled when she grasped the bottle and grunted in hungry enthusiasm. "Yeah," he had said, smiling down into a perfect tiny face, "this kid likes to eat, just like her old man. Just wait till you taste an ice-cold Bud, you'll forget about this nasty stuff." Some folks might think it was a bad thing to talk to a baby about drinking beer, but Juicy knew he was just joking around; he was doing the best he could. But it didn't last. And their money didn't, either.

Even when her belly grew round like a basketball and her ankles swelled into tree stumps, Juicy managed to bring home enough money to at least keep them going whenever Freddie was out of work. Construction work always slowed down in the rainy season, and they never saved a dime, so when Freddie's paychecks stopped, Juicy picked up the slack. Every time. Six days a week, she would tie a stained, white apron around her waist, fix her hair and makeup, and head down to Nolan's Diner on the interstate. She served bacon and eggs all morning, filling coffee cups again and again, then shifted to the burger-and-coke lunch crowd, saying thank you for the quarter tip, smiling all the while she thought her lower back might break in two.

It was only fair, she thought, that after the baby was born Freddie would cover their rent for a few weeks, at least until she found a reliable babysitter. She could have gone back sooner, but she didn't feel comfortable leaving a newborn with Freddie all day. No doubt he'd be out in the garage, working on his bike, and forget all about his daughter inside—or he'd get high and pass out on the sofa, oblivious to the baby's cries to be held and loved, to have a clean diaper, a fresh bottle. She should have known something was up when he handed her the wad of bills and warned her, "You'd better hope we find a way to pay this back, or there'll be some serious shit to pay." She'd just wanted a little break, a chance to be with her baby, his baby, so she took the money he gave her and never asked where it came from.

With a convulsive shudder, as if she could possibly be freezing in the hot and stuffy trailer, she hugged her body tight, rocking and smoking, until finally she pulled hard on the last drag of her cigarette and crushed it out against the paneled wall, the ash and sparks spilling to the floor like a faltering fireworks display. Never did she imagine that those few dollars would turn her into one of those girls the guys trash talked after a wild night of partying with the "pass arounds," the ones willing to do anything to be a biker babe. Not her. She was Freddie's old lady, even better than a Mama. She was Juicy. Everyone knew her. Everyone liked her. She was like a sister to those guys, gave them free coffee and sodas when they showed up at the diner. She was one of them, or at least she thought she was.

In the dingy bathroom, she splashed cold water on her face, then pressed a cold washcloth between her legs and tried to ease the burning pain where she was tender and bruised. She scrubbed at a patch of dried blood on her inner thigh and along her knee. It burned to pee, but she had to go. She held her breath and closed her eyes to the pain and nausea that swept through her. There was nothing left for her to vomit, her stomach long ago emptied into the rust-corroded toilet.

The face in the mirror was only vaguely familiar to the one she had studied that morning, carefully lining the eyes, brushing on mascara, wanting to look good when they went out for a drive in Freddie's truck. The day had held such promise, the bike back in the garage while the three of them rode through the countryside together, a little family. Her carefully teased hair was now flat and matted; her skin a yellowish green, and she was sure that somehow the color of her eyes had changed, that any hint or trace of blue had leaked away. They were grey now, not grey-blue or blue-grey, just grey. Anyone who looked into those empty eyes would know what she had become in one night, what she had done, just to pay the rent. She wanted to kill him, kill all of them. She took one more drink from the bottle and returned to the filthy bed as the door opened. Two more.

Nasty Dan came in first, grinning like a fool, his stringy hair hanging in his face. Lizard was close behind, already unzipping his pants, his mouth wet with drool.

"Juicy, Juicy," Dan said. "Lizard here wants to watch a little first."

"Don't worry," Lizard said, laughing and wiping his chin. "I'm going to get in there, too."

Juicy cringed and struggled to find that place deep inside herself once again to hide her disgust. She squeezed her eyes shut as Dan unbuckled his belt, telling herself it was almost over, telling herself to survive the night, imagining this room at a happier time. It didn't matter what happened to her anymore, but Ginny needed her. Dan's dirty fingers squeezed her breasts hard, making Lizard groan in approval while Juicy groaned in pain. *Before this . . . After this . . . Before this . . .After this.* The stench of the men, Dan on top of her and Lizard nearly smothering her with his filthy fingers on her face, made her want to wretch.

Just when Juicy thought she might gag, from beneath the table came the sound of a small snore, heavy breathing, and then a loud cry.

"What the fuck is that?" Nasty Dan jerked back and nearly fell over. Wearing only his cut, his jeans bunched up around his ankles, Dan pushed away from the girl, letting go of her hips, freeing her from his grasp.

"It's the baby. My baby, Ginny." Juicy's words were slurred and thick, her mouth so dry her lips felt stuck to her teeth. She struggled to roll herself over onto her side, away from the arms of Lizard, stretched out across the head of the bed like a human pillow where he'd watched his friend. "I have the baby here."

"You brought a kid in here? What the fuck's wrong with you?"

"What else was I gonna do? Leave her on the bar? It's not like I asked to be here."

Nasty Dan was pissed off, but she wasn't entirely sure why. Her having a baby didn't have anything to do with him. He didn't have to worry about anyone but himself. He'd had his fun.

"Where you going?" Lizard moaned.

"She's hungry," Juicy said, sitting up, scooting to the edge of the bed. "It must be four. She's always hungry at four."

"Man, this is fucked up."

"Just let me . . ." Her words faltered as she winced in pain. "Just let me give her a bottle; she'll go right back to sleep." Everything hurt. Juicy struggled to the table and pulled the basket out from under the tablecloth. The hungry cries grew louder as she lifted the baby up from the floor and carried her back to the rumpled bed.

Dan pulled his crusty jeans up from around his dirty, black boots and stormed out the door as Freddie was coming up the steps. "You know she has a kid in there, man?"

"What the hell does that matter?" Freddie stood by the door, looking over at the skinny guy stretched out on his back across the bed, one arm draped over his face as if the dim light blinded him. "You done, Lizard?"

"I guess I am now." Lizard rolled off the bed and slowly made his way outside, zipping his jeans as he headed for the back door of the bar, still open for this crowd long after closing time. It wouldn't close until they wanted it to, and the owner wouldn't complain. As long as his pockets filled up with cash, the beer kept flowing. It wouldn't be the first time he stayed open all night, and it wouldn't be the last.

Five
2005

Noni liked living at Nazareth House. When her hips and knees failed to carry her weight for more than a few yards, she invested in an electric chair, but that was only good for weekly trips to Safeway or cruising around the block to have a cup of coffee with Maria Mello, the only neighbor left from the old days. Inside her overstuffed house of polished furniture, ceramic Madonnas, and colorful woolen rugs, the chair was a hazard. The old woman would limp and groan from room to room, occasionally finding herself on the floor, cursing her rickety joints.

After finding Noni stretched out in the hallway one afternoon, Bernie hired someone to come in during the day to clean house and cook meals, but the nights were a worry. For three months straight, Bernie spent every night with her grandmother, worried the old woman would fall in the night with no one there to help her up. Finally, Bernie simply moved back into the house where she had lived for many years. It didn't take long for the shrewd old woman to decide she'd had enough. "Put me in Nazareth," she said. "And you take the house. I won't need it anymore."

Since then, the eighty-six-year-old widow had lived in a small room at the Catholic home for senior citizens, surrounded by other frail and grey-haired folks trapped in wheelchairs or hobbling about with walkers and canes, while Bernie rattled about the little white house on Brown Street, surrounded by the things of her childhood, rooms of fragile memories.

Noni's days were busy caring for her jungle of potted plants that grew on the small patio off her room, reading every word of the Fresno Bee, attending morning mass, and sharing her meals in the dining hall where she frequently mentioned that her granddaughter, the lawyer, was coming to see her on Saturday. Sometimes, when she was lonely, she would call Bernie and tell her how many days or sometimes even hours it had been since she'd seen her, knowing that would ensure her company. On each visit, whether it was for a long afternoon or just an hour in the evening, Noni paraded her granddaughter up and down the wide hallways, introducing her to the same white-haired friends she had met before, all of them eager to talk to her, to touch her dark-red hair and smooth skin, reminders of what had faded and dimmed with the passing years of their lives.

"Hi-ya, gorgeous," Bernie said, leaning into the open doorway, tapping lightly on the doorframe.

"Bernadette," she said, "what on earth are you doing here now? It's Friday night. You don't usually come on Friday nights." She began to fold the newspaper she had spread out before her, carefully returning it to its original form, her fingers in a constant slight tremor. "I was just finishing the paper."

"Anything in there I should know about?" She bent down and kissed her grandmother's cheek, gently hugging her frail shoulders.

"Oh," she scoffed, "you know enough, I think." She pushed a small lever on the arm of the chair and the motor hummed as she swiveled around to the faded chair where

Bernie would sit.

"I brought candy." Bernie pulled a small, white bag from her purse and gave it a tantalizing shake. A pound of mixed Brach's candies, butterscotch, peppermints, caramels, and toffees wrapped in glossy pink, blue, yellow, and red foil rumbled like a cup of dice. Noni had always preferred the grocery store bulk candy to French truffles or Belgian chocolates. Brach's was her favorite.

"Just in time. That damned crazy Lolly was in here yesterday, stealing all my caramels and toffees." She shook her head in mock disgust then peeked in the bag, pulling out a golden butterscotch for herself before holding the open bag out for Bernie to take her pick, just as she used to do in the aisle of Safeway. Stolen sweetness.

"Guess I better get myself a maple toffee before Lolly swipes them all." Bernie plucked a red-foiled candy from the bag and relaxed back in her favorite chair, its worn rose pattern wrapping around her like an old glove. She slowly untwisted the shiny wrapper and took one small bite from the small candy, savoring its goodness, making it last.

"So, why are you here?" Noni asked. A press of a switch and the chair hummed across the floor to a maple bureau where she emptied the bag of candies into a shallow, oblong bowl of cut glass, her good crystal still nestled on their shelves in the built-in hutch on Brown Street.

"I got a phone call today from someone at Social Services."

"About me?" Her bushy eyebrows fluttered as she blinked twice slowly, a sign she was preparing to hear bad news. "What'd I do now?"

"No. About me, actually."

"What could they want with you? You're too young for Social Security, aren't you?"

"Social Services, Noni, not Social Security. You know children and families, social workers?" She paused, and a slow smile formed as it dawned on her that Noni herself had been a social worker before she made Bernie her life's work. "Like you," she said grinning at her grandmother's rare mistake. "Come on, you know all about that stuff. You were a social worker in your heyday. That's your department."

"Oh, you remember that, of course. You remember too much." The old woman nodded and looked pleased that someone could recall her life as the busy working woman before she was trapped in her aging body. "That was a long time ago, and a short career. I only worked after Joe died, after your mom was grown. Then . . ."

Noni's liquid eyes seemed to glaze slightly as her mind roamed back to another time, then with a blink she was gazing intently on her granddaughter, her lips trembling as she forced a smile, her thin hands fidgeting nervously, fluttering from her knees to the arms of the chair, then back to her knees. "What on earth could a social worker want with you?" Her smile faded as quickly as it had appeared; the customary worried expression she had worn for the past thirty years returning to her face.

"Well, Noni." Bernie paused and measured her words carefully, finally deciding it was best to just tell it like it was, matter-of-fact, no sentiment involved. No sugar coating was necessary or desired when it came to Noni. "You're not going to believe this, but it seems my birth mother is looking for me. Apparently, she'd like to meet me now that I'm all grown up and don't really need a mother."

"What?" Noni asked, gliding back to her spot near the old chair, her aged senses finally keen to the feel and pulse of her motorized carriage. No more crashing into walls and corners, scratching furniture, bruising her paper-thin skin that hung in loose folds from fragile arms and puffy legs marred with purple maps of varicose veins. Their eyes met and locked, each staring at the other. Noni's chin frequently trembled as if she were almost chewing, her jaw moving up and down rapidly. Finally, she spoke, responding to the news. "Well, I always wondered if she would."

"You did? Really? I used to think she might, but then I, I don't know, let it go or something. I don't think I want to meet her, in case you're wondering."

"Then don't. What good can come from it now?"

"That's my point, but don't you think it's weird?" She leaned her elbows on her knees to bring her face closer to the freckled scowl she once had feared, closer to the filmy brown eyes that had always watched out for her. "Come on, Noni— why now? I'm thirty-seven years old for Christ's sake. It's a little late for anyone to want to be my mother. Where was she twenty-five years ago when I actually needed a mom? It all fell on you."

With a flick of her wrist and shake of her head, Noni dismissed the idea that Bernie was some sort of burden that fell on her. "How do you know what she wants? She might just be curious; she's old now, too, I guess."

"She can't be that old. I'm thirty-seven; heck, she might only be in her early or mid-fifties. She was probably a teenager when I was born, don't you think?"

Noni gazed off to a corner of the room, avoiding the eyes of her granddaughter, the only family she had left in the world. "How should I know?"

"Come on, Noni, you know in the sixties all those young girls who got pregnant were sent to some home for unwed mothers and gave their babies up for adoption, usually to some stern-looking nun. I always figured that I was one of those babies—some unfortunate accident or nightmare to the prom queen or head cheer leader, something like that."

"Hmmmm . . . maybe . . . I don't know. Does it matter now? You're a grown woman; you don't need a mother. You had a mother, remember. And she was the best mother. Maybe this woman wants money, knows how rich you are." Noni was getting agitated; her trembling was more pronounced, and she seemed more annoyed than interested with Bernie and her news and her questions.

"Noni, I'm not rich."

"Compared to most people, you're rich. And everyone wants money, so hang on to your wallet."

They had this conversation at least once a month. Noni refused to understand how precarious being a plaintiff's lawyer could be, sometimes working for months only to have it cost her money for all her efforts in the end. Bernie knew she had to keep a healthy nest egg to keep her from going under and to keep Noni at Nazareth, and sometimes that nest egg nearly emptied. Like now. But that was something she could never share with her grandmother, and that would change as soon as she settled the Luna case.

"Hooh," her grandmother rolled her eyes, mocking her.

"Noni," she pressed, "that's not the issue here. I'm just saying it's curious that someone who abandoned me thirty-seven, heck almost thirty-eight years ago should suddenly decide she wants to know me." She aimed and tossed the crumpled candy wrapper into the small wicker wastepaper basket across the room, an easy shot after years of practice. "This isn't Oprah, and you know why I feel like this."

"How was anyone supposed to know what would happen?" Again, her brows twitched, and she smacked her lips nervously. "How could anyone know something like that . . .? We survived." She lowered her chin to her chest and closed her eyes, shutting out the cruel memories, just as she always did when she thought of her dead daughter, Bernie's mother. Bernie was never sure if she was praying for her mother's soul or simply blocking out all thoughts of that terrible time.

"But it wouldn't have happened if she wasn't selfish?"

"Who? Who was selfish? Your mom?"

"Not Mom. My birth mother. Giving me up was selfish if it made her life easier. If you think about it, it's really all her fault." Her weight fell back into the chair, her hands limply hanging at her sides as though all energy seeped away with the words that left her mouth.

"How do you figure that? What does that woman have to do with what your father did?"

Always, Noni blamed Bernie's father, never knowing how that blame tormented her granddaughter, never knowing how much she missed him still. "Well, I wouldn't have lost my parents. It wouldn't have happened to me, I guess. My birth mother is still alive, so I would have had a real mother." Careless words, she realized. "I'm sorry," she whispered. "I shouldn't have said that. Mom was my real mother."

Noni fidgeted with her cotton housedress, picking at

the pattern of blue pansies with trembling fingers, then smoothing the fabric flat against her leg, her head nodding slowly with understanding and fear, the dark circles and wrinkles under her eyes heavier than usual. Bernie had noticed a renewed sense of grief in her grandmother lately, somehow more pronounced now than all those years ago when the pain was fresh and raw. She attributed it to idle days surrounded by people so old and close to death themselves. This conversation only seemed to make it worse. Her birth mother might never know the hell of Bernie's childhood, but Noni lived it with her. Adoption didn't have anything to do with the fate of Ron and Patty Sheridan.

"No, you're right. It wouldn't have happened to you." She reached out to Bernie and took her hand. "But, if you weren't Patty's daughter, who would I have now?"

* * * *

They were fighting again. For three days they didn't speak a single word to each other, only passing messages through Bernie, their daughter. *Tell your father his dinner is in the oven. Tell your mother I took a check from her checkbook.* It wasn't the first time they'd behaved like spoiled children. At the time, she didn't give it any real thought beyond annoyance at serving as the messenger. In fact, sometimes when they quarreled, she rather liked it. They were so busy festering and stewing about the latest insult or angry glare they wouldn't notice it was bedtime or whether or not Bernie had done her Spanish homework or cleaned her room or whatever they usually nagged about. She became invisible and free to do whatever she pleased while her parents battled it out. She just figured that's how all parents behaved when they were fighting, but she learned all too soon that her parents were different. Memories of small arguments faded, but twenty-five years later, Bernie's memories of one particular night swirled and tumbled about, often surfacing in dreams, or at the odd moment spent at a stop light, or waiting in line at the supermarket. It happened a couple of days before that terrible night, their final fight.

They were all in the car, her dad's 1978 T-Bird, driving down a dark two-lane highway, going home from their weekly Sunday dinner at Noni's house. Bernie was stretched out in the backseat, but when she felt the car suddenly jerk to one side, she sat up, grabbing hold of the seat where her mother sat. They were going fast. Really fast. She saw her mother look back at her, then over to her husband, her face pinched and dark. "Ron," she said, her voice raw with fear, placing a hand on his upper arm. "Please slow down, Ron. Please. Bernie's in the car."

He glared at his wife, then slowly eased up on the accelerator. "Your mother needs to mind her own business," he growled at his wife. "She should have just let you leave instead of prolonging this, using a baby to keep you here. It's unconscion . . ."

"Ron, please," she begged, again touching his arm. "Bernie."

"Well, it's true, isn't it?"

When they finally slid into their driveway, her dad stormed into the house ahead of Bernie and her mom, charging up the stairs to their bedroom then slamming the door hard.

"Mom," Bernie said, "what's Dad so mad about?"

"It's nothing important. Don't worry; everything will be fine soon. Just go to bed."

Bernie's mother locked the front door behind them, a habitual effort to keep them safe from whatever danger might lurk in the darkness. "Go to bed," she said again, then kissed her daughter on the top of her head.

Two days later, when Monsignor Desmond came to Bernie's class and quietly asked her to go outside with him, she knew something was seriously wrong. It had to be serious if the monsignor came and pulled her out of religion class. Not a student helper from the office. Not Sister Catherine. Not even Father Harris. It was the monsignor himself.

The pudgy little man with fluffy white hair gently placed his hand on her thin shoulder as they walked side by side to the chapel. The day was dreary and damp, one of those days when the valley fog sits heavy and thick, reducing the world to a small, misty haze. Bernie liked foggy days. She liked the way everything just slowly vanished into white, the way she could disappear and hide in an open field just yards from the watchful eyes of the old nuns at Saint Helen's School.

"Did I do something wrong?" she asked Monsignor, her voice the pious and respectful tone she used in confession. An innocent asking forgiveness for some unknown sin.

"No, Bernie, you've done nothing wrong. Absolutely nothing wrong." His words were soothing and gentle as he gave her shoulder a light squeeze followed by a gentle rub that frightened her more with each step.

Bernie stopped inside the door of the church for a splash of holy water, careful to follow all the rules of Catechism and also fearful of whatever news was coming her way. She solemnly touched her forehead and chest with nervous fingers, searching her brain for any bad deed that would put her in this much trouble, quickly shifting from guilt to concern for Noni, the only person she really knew that might be old enough to die. She remembered the time Monsignor came for David Negrete when his grandpa died. She hesitated a moment before moving on and quickly prayed that Noni was okay. Her grandfather had died before she was born, so it couldn't be him. Her other grandparents died when she was small; she barely remembered them. It had to be Noni. There wasn't anyone else she knew that was old enough to die.

Monsignor stopped at the first row of seats he came to, the back row, and guided Bernie in ahead of him. She genuflected before sitting down, anxiously following all the rules in the presence of the holiest man she knew. The old pew creaked as she scooted down to allow room beside her.

For a moment, Monsignor simply stared at the altar. "I've never sat in this row before," he said quietly.

Bernie didn't know how to answer. She'd sat there plenty of times, usually with some pen and paper doodling or writing notes, anything to help pass the time. She pulled the hymnal from the back of the pew in front of her and held it in her lap thumbing the pages nervously, never looking at the printed pages, just fumbling with the book. The church seemed strangely dark. The fog softened the fractures of light that passed through the colorful stained-glass windows of the sanctuary. No bright stabs of red or blue sliced through the air as they often did on sun-drenched mornings. Bernie was afraid, already wanting to cry, though she didn't know why. She just knew she was going to, the lump in her throat already tightening. The monsignor was struggling, his face pained and flushed as he gazed up at the life-sized crucifix as if he silently pleaded for help from the wooden sculpture, the lifeless body of Jesus nailed to a cross.

He finally turned toward her, took the small, blue book from her hands and returned it to its proper place. He placed both of her hands in his, gently patting the back of her right hand. "Bernadette," he said, "I have tragic news to tell you. Tragic." His voice seemed thin and small, so different from the one that resonated from the altar announcing the body of Christ, the blood of Christ. "And there's just no easy way." Again, he glanced toward the front of the church while he tightened his hold on her thin hands, leaning closer.

"What is it? Did something happen to my grandmother?" Her nervous eyes narrowed with concern, fear of the tragic news that was coming her way. "Is Noni dead?"

"No, your grandmother is fine. In fact, she should be here soon. I've sent someone for her. Father Harris will bring her to you. It's your parents, Bernadette. Something has . . ." He swallowed, gripped her hands tighter still, focused his watery blue eyes directly on her face. "Something terrible has happened to your mother. And your father, too, I'm afraid." He paused again, the thin collar around his neck the only thing moving as his Adam's apple slid up and down, up and down.

Every muscle in Bernie's body stiffened and her spine became rigid as though a steel rod suddenly linked her neck to her tailbone. Her heart pounded furiously from her chest up into her throat and down into her gut. "What happened? Did my dad crash the car? Did he? Are they hurt?" Her body began to rock; she tried to pull away, but the old man held her hands and wrists tightly, keeping her in the seat beside him.

His voice turned somber and controlled, sounding as he did during communion offering. *The body of Christ, the blood of Christ,* was all Bernie could hear, but that was not what he said. She strained to hear, to understand, but the sounds of the Eucharist echoed in her ears and she searched the church for somewhere to hide, instinctively knowing she did not want to hear what the priest had to tell her. There should be incense, an organ, more people, a lot more people. The pews should be filled. She didn't want to be here alone with this holy man. She didn't want to hear whatever he had to say. *No no no no no no no no.*

"Bernadette, you must listen to me. Please. Please. There was no car accident. Something happened at home."

The body of Christ, the blood of Christ.

"Your neighbor, Mrs. Quentin, called first. She knew you were here and didn't want you to go home to . . . to . . . I'm afraid . . ."

The body of Christ, the blood of Christ.

"No," she finally said loudly, shaking her head from side to side, pulling away from his strong hands, her eyes filling with horror, her stomach turning and raising in her throat. "No," she said, even louder still. The church walls closed in, suffocating her with years of lingering stale incense and dead saints. Jesus in his crown of thorns, lifeless stained-glass stations of the cross, a marble statue of the Virgin Mary, all spiraling and whirling about her as the world seemed to slip out from beneath her pew.

"I'm so sorry, but your mother and father apparently had a . . . a . . . a violent altercation, and they have both passed . . ."

"No," she said again, almost screaming this time, her voice echoing in the empty sanctuary. "No, you're wrong."

The body of Christ, the blood of Christ. The words of the Eucharist haunted her, pain, death, redemption. "No, no, no," she repeated again and again.

"Bernadette, please hear me. I need to tell you what happened."

"No." Her head jerked violently from left to right, refusing to acknowledge him, refusing to accept his words, revising them in her head, changing them to the Last Supper, take this cup. Her eyes roamed the room, searching for an exit, a way out.

The body of Christ, the blood of Christ.

"I wish I could spare you this. I wish I could find a way." He wrapped his arm around her shoulders and pulled her close as the tears came and patiently waited for her sobs to pass into weak submission. When she was at last still, the struggle ended, he delivered the painful news as though the message were a grave secret, his voice a hoarse whisper.

"Mrs. Quentin said she heard shots, two of them. She rushed over to see what happened and found your mother. Your father, he apparently shot . . ." He paused, took a deep breath, and finished it, quickly. "Bernadette. Bernie. Your parents are both dead. I'm so sorry, so sorry."

She jerked away from him, covered her ears with her hands, and continued to shake her head from side to side, refusing to accept his lies, unable to imagine what had happened in her home while she had sat in the cafeteria and peeled the perfect orange her mother had put in her lunchbox that morning.

The body of Christ, the blood of Christ. The body of Christ, the blood of Christ.

She should have been there. It wouldn't have happened. She screamed and cried, "I want to go home. I want to go home now. I want to see my mom. Take me home now. Please."

The priest's painful words smoldered and burned deep inside her, erupting into a fear and terror she had never known, and in the end, all she really heard was a call to the Last Supper.

The body of Christ, the blood of Christ.

She wanted it to be like any other Sunday. She would walk behind her mother, in front of her father, a perfectly reverent family, and they would eat the bread and drink from the cup. They would keep their heads bowed and shuffle back to their seats where they would kneel, side by side, hands clasped in front of them, just as they had done hundreds of times, hundreds of times. This was what you did in church. The priest was supposed to talk about everlasting life, give you hope and the body of Jesus, not take everything away. He was wrong.

"Bernadette, I'm truly sorry."

"I don't believe you," she said, weeping, leaning her head on the pew in front of her, her face now wet and hot with angry tears. "He wouldn't do that. My dad wouldn't do that." She stood up, wanting to run and get away, wanting to go home and prove them wrong. Her mother would be there, doing laundry or cooking or watching *All My Children* on television. Her dad would be at work still, but he'd be home by six, just like every day, home by six. Dinner would be at six thirty. They were wrong. But the priest stood and caught her as she rose to her feet, grabbing her by the shoulders and pulling her tightly to him.

"Cry, Bernadette. It's time for tears." He held her close to him while her body shook with unleashed sobs. He then slowly guided her back down into the pew beside him.

"I don't understand. How could . . ."

"I don't understand it either. We can't begin to understand."

They sat side by side and waited there until her grandmother, confused and bewildered with bitter grief, arrived at the church with Father Harris. She would take her orphaned granddaughter home with her where they would weep in each other's arms all night.

Bernie would never remember leaving the church.

The days that followed would always be a jumbled mess in her memory. Her world had descended into the densest of fogs, everything disappearing into a silent mist, a black hole of grief and confusion. In years to come, bits and pieces would flash through her mind or appear in wild dreams, especially after drinking too much Tanqueray, but it was mostly a haze of images, nothing clear. Noni falling to her knees at the sight of the dark red stain at the bottom of the stairs where her mother had apparently fallen, a single bullet in her back. The pool of a darker stain on the landing at the top of the stairs where her father had ended it all for everyone. So much blood. How could there have been so much blood? The thick smoke and stench of incense that filled her nostrils for days after the funeral. Two dark wooden caskets side by side in a church filled with everyone Bernie had ever known. Pies and cookies, ham and lasagna, plates of cheese and crackers. Food everywhere. As if eating would fill the painful emptiness that tried to swallow her whole.

* * * *

Bernie looked at her grandmother now, old and sad, her weak eyes nearly lost in the drooping lids and dark circles. "I'm sorry, Noni. I shouldn't have brought it up." Noni was all she had, her grounding through everything, and it pained her to think she had upset her. Since that day, Noni was the only person on earth that Bernie loved and trusted. She was ultimately the person she had lived for all these years, constantly striving to make her grandmother happy, to make her proud. Such devotion was, at times, exhausting.

"No. You're right. You wouldn't have had the life you had. You wouldn't have lost your mom and dad, none of that, but you wouldn't be my granddaughter either, so . . ." She waved a hand in the air. "I don't know." Her voice trailed off, and her head seemed to tremble more than usual. "I don't know why things happen, but they happen for a reason."

"Noni," Bernie took her grandmother's brown-spotted hands into her own and kissed them one at a time, "please don't be sad." She sat silently, just holding Noni's trembling fingers, knowing the memories that haunted her grandmother. "You're right. This woman probably just wants something from me, like money, or I don't know, a kidney or something." Bernie tried to shed a different light on the whole thing, lighten the dark mood and sadness she had managed to stir up in a matter of minutes.

Noni pulled away and offered a slight lift of the right side of her mouth, almost a smile. "Then don't give it to her. You might need it when you're old like me."

"Yeah—and what if she's a nut? You know, maybe

she's been in a mental hospital all this time and now she wants a daughter to take care of her, or something. And how can I do that? I have crazy Noni to worry about." Again, she tried to get a full smile from the old woman. She should not have dragged these troubles into the room with a bag of candy as her only offering. But Noni was the only one who knew how she felt, who knew what she'd been through. There was no one else to talk to about this.

"You're the one who's," she raised her right hand and circled her fingers to help explain, "mezza mezza."

"What the heck is mezza mezza?"

"I guess I'm old. That's not the right word. That means so-so, I mean you're the one who is kooky. Thirty-seven years old, no husband, still hanging out with an old woman on a Friday night." She finally broke into a quivering smile and a low growl of laughter, then leaned forward, raising her old-age-spotted hands to grab the younger pair. The four linked hands formed a gentle knot of flesh and bone, embracing fingers and lives as one. "Bernadette, you know I love you more than anything. You're like my own daughter, but maybe there are things you should know. I don't know. I'm too old now to help you. Maybe I should have told you more." Her chin trembled, and the worried look returned again. "Maybe you should meet her." Noni pulled her hands away, but Bernie only grabbed onto them again.

"I don't know. I'm torn. Part of me is just curious, and another figures no good can come from bringing all the past back. Still, maybe . . . the woman from Social Services said to give it a couple of days." She raised the old woman's hands to her lips once more and kissed them again before resting back into the faded roses.

"Are you still cutting out newspaper articles? That might make you feel better." The chair hummed as she glided the short distance to the table where the neatly folded paper waited. "Here. You can have my paper."

"No. I finally quit doing that. Every once in a while I see something and save it, but not often."

For years, Bernie scoured the newspaper each night, searching the headlines for stories of suffering and loss, especially murder-suicides, domestic disputes that turned deadly, something to make her feel normal, less freakish. Knowing that she wasn't the only one this type of thing happened to was comforting. It was a part of her life she never shared, a secret. As far as anyone else knew, her parents died in *an accident*, and her grandmother took her in after that. She knew some of her grandmother's friends knew, but no one dared mention it. Ever.

"Well, take the paper. Maybe there's something really bad in there to make you feel better."

"Okay." She knew her grandmother needed to do something for her and giving her the morning newspaper was about the best she could do from a motorized chair in an old folks' home.

Noni was the only constant person in Bernie's life. Everyone else from her childhood eventually disappeared, sooner or later, but not Noni. She was always there. When Bernie moved in with her grandmother, she quit her job to be there for Bernie one hundred percent. She took her granddaughter to three different therapists, searching for the one that would say the right thing, anything to get the girl to sleep without nightmares, to go out with friends instead of staring at the television for hours on end. She lit hundreds of candles at Saint Theresa's, praying for her dead daughter's soul and the sad and angry child she left behind.

Slowly, Bernie fell into the very rhythm of Noni, a gradual healing from the constant aroma of garlic and onion in the kitchen, fresh air in the crisp sheets on her bed, the sound of her grandmother's voice calling her to breakfast, offering to drive her to school, and the certainty that on Friday night the ironing board would be up and Noni would iron a week's worth of shirts and dresses while she watched J.R. and the rest of the Ewings on *Dallas*. Like slow lapping waves that tirelessly caress the shore, retreating and returning, never ending, Noni was there. Now, it was her turn to be there for Noni. She owed her that.

"You're a smart girl, Bernadette, you will figure it out. So now I want to take you to see Mrs. Gianetta. She has a question about her will, and I told her you would help."

No matter how many times Bernie had asked her grandmother not to offer free legal services to the other residents, it did no good. It was just another way for Noni to brag and show her off, and Bernie could hardly deny her that small pleasure. Actually, she couldn't deny her anything, and Noni knew it. Noni knew everything.

Six

1968

The baby began to cry, a whimper that ruptured into an ear-piercing howl. She was hungry.

Freddie leaned against the doorframe of the small trailer, looking down at Juicy, then out into the darkness, but never stepping foot inside, where his baby wailed. "Get your shit together. We're going," he said, lighting another cigarette.

"Can I feed her first? She's hungry." Juicy laid the baby down on the bed and stood in front of him, naked and sticky with sweat. A slight breeze blew through the open door, fresh and sweet, cooling her down, reviving her a bit.

"No, I need to get my bike. The guys are leaving soon, heading north, and I plan on going with them. You're either staying here for good or going now."

It wouldn't do any good to argue with him, to ask for any favors. Things had changed during the last few hours; everything was all upside down and wrong. Juicy yanked a t-shirt over her head and fumbled around for her underwear, then remembered how the first bunch had ripped them off of her, or maybe cut them, she couldn't recall now. It seemed so long ago. When she heard Freddie draw a long angry breath, she gave up the search and just pulled her jeans on, wincing in pain as the rough denim rubbed her thighs and pressed on her tender private parts. She pulled a clean diaper from a pink and white striped bag in the corner and dropped it on the bed next to the baby. "It's okay," she said, her voice raspy and hoarse, thirsty for a drink of water, anything. "Shhhh. Don't cry, little girl. Don't cry," she urged, her own eyes filling with tears.

"I said let's go."

"Her diaper. I need to change it; she's soaked through."

"Now." Freddie turned away and stomped off in the darkness, keys jingling in one hand, the other balled up in a tight fist, ready to fight.

Juicy picked up her baby, still holding the clean diaper in one hand, grabbed her boots and the diaper bag, and started out the door. She heard the truck starting and ran after him, the baby screaming and bouncing, the bag slung over her shoulder, weighing her down, boots smacking her in the hips, rocks and stickers jabbing into her bare feet. "Wait," she cried. "Freddie, wait; God damn it."

He didn't look at her as she climbed into the old Ford. He pressed hard on the gas before the door closed, and the sudden force knocked her sideways, smashing her upper arm into the dash as she protected the baby's head. She gave him a hard look, "Are you happy now?"

"Shut that kid up."

"She's hungry and wet. You didn't give me a chance to feed her." She held the baby close and tried to stifle the screams with her aching breasts, rocking in the seat while she dug her right hand in the diaper bag, searching desperately for a bottle. Her fingers wrapped around the half empty one she had fed her a few hours ago as they drove fast down Highway 165. They had gone out for a ride, just trying out his new clutch, she thought. She picked up the bottle and shook it. It was warm, and probably old and sour, but she gave it to the baby anyway, rubbing the edge of the nipple along the bottom lip that quivered and shook with raspy cries, forgetting the bottle was laced with Jack Daniels. Juicy had no choice but to make her sleep through her mama's nightmare, and Jack was all she had. The little mouth grabbed the nipple and instantly sucked hard on the rubber tip, the cries quickly shifting to grunts of pleasure as her empty belly was satisfied.

"There you go," her mother whispered. "See, it's okay." She held her daughter close to her breast and patted her wet bottom, her diaper soaked through and leaking out the rubber pants to the legs of her soft cotton sleeper, patterned with little lambs grinning and leaping puffs of white across a field of blue and yellow daisies. "Oh, you're all wet," she moaned to herself, "poor thing, poor wet baby girl. Gin Gin Ginny Girl, gorgeous little Ginny Girl," she sang, her own lullaby.

While the baby sucked on the bottle, her mother began to unsnap the sleeper, slipping one arm out, then the other, pulling it down and off. The truck jerked and rattled and Juicy struggled to change and feed the baby simultaneously, but she knew better than to complain. Not now.

They rode in silence, Freddie smoking and driving fast down dark roads, streaming past orchards and vineyards, rolling through stop signs without stopping, sometimes without even slowing down. She didn't know what time it was, but knew it would be light soon. The earth had the shimmer and glow of predawn, the light beginning from the ground up, pushing the darkness out into the atmosphere. Just hours earlier, when Freddie had lured her out to the trailer behind Fat Betty's, it had been twilight, the first stars shining in a violet sky, a humming of night noises rising from the orchard where crickets, mice, and opossum scurried about, searching for food. By the time the roar of engines drowned out the buzz of hungry bugs and rodents, it was pitch black.

The voices, bodies, odors, and tastes of the night flashed through her mind, turning her stomach over and over, sickening her. As they drove the unfamiliar roads, somewhere near Porterville, she thought, or maybe Visalia, she began to wonder how she got there, how her life had turned to this. When she left her parents' home, a little more than a year before, she was so sure of where she was going, what she wanted. But she didn't know anything anymore, where to go, what to do. Finally, she spoke. "You'll never see me again. I mean it."

"Good." Freddie pressed harder on the gas.

"You're an evil bastard."

"You know what you are? You're a whore. You're nothing."

"Fuck you. I'm the mother of your baby—I'm . . ."

In one swift motion, Freddie slammed on the brakes and threw the back of his hand up and into Juicy's face, knocking her head to the side window. The bottle was yanked from the baby's mouth and flew across the cab as the truck slid sideways on the road. The baby screamed while her father grabbed a handful of her mother's hair and pulled her head back, leaning his face close to hers, his breath the familiar sour smell she knew too well. "You're lucky you didn't find yourself at the bottom of the fucking lake instead of just flat on your back." He gave her head a small shake. "You're a fuckin' thief." He shoved her head away, then smacked the side of her face with the back of his hand.

"I paid the rent, asshole, with the money you gave me. Your rent," she sobbed, moving as far away from him as she could, holding the baby close to her chest, trying to smother the screams with her body. "You're the one who stole it, or did you forget that part? What would Nasty Dan and the guys think of that?"

"All you had to do was get laid, Juicy, the only thing you know how to do," he screamed. "And shut her up, God damn it." He threw the truck into gear and, with a squeal of tires and spray of dirt, he sped down the two-lane road, furious.

Ginny's screaming was relentless and loud. No matter how her mother rocked and patted her, crying her own tears, the baby wouldn't stop crying. Freddie ranted and raged, his stream of curses filling the cab of the truck until he finally pulled over hard to the side of the road. He reached across her and opened the passenger door. "Get out."

"Just take me home and then I'll leave."

"Get the fuck out now." He threw the truck in park, leaned back against his door, and pulled his right leg up and around. She was falling from the truck before she even realized that he had kicked her, the baby falling with her, under her, screaming, the bag flying.

"Freddie. Don't," she screamed, scrambling to her knees, but all Juicy heard was the rev of his engine as he raced off down the highway, leaving her and a crying baby alone in the dark.

Ginny's cries were louder, she noticed, a sound she had never heard before, piercing through the night. Face down in the dirt, wearing only a dirty diaper and one half of a sleeper, the infant's arm was bent behind her. Wrong, all wrong, her mother thought. On hands and knees, she picked her up. The baby screamed in pain, intense pain.

"I'm so sorry," she said, weeping and moaning. "I'm so sorry." She strained to see, blinded by darkness, dirt and tears. She searched for the bottle, the bag, clawing at the ground until her fingers felt the canvas strap, then the round plastic bottle of formula. She struggled to her feet and lifted the screaming baby, covered in dirt and urine and held her tight to her chest, careful not to grab the arm that seemed deformed. She hung the bag around her neck and started running down the highway, her own body aching and throbbing with every awkward, painful step. "Help," she coughed, her voice hoarse and choked with sobs. "Help me. My baby's hurt."

The porch light was on, the house still dark. She pounded on the door until it opened, a man and his wife standing together, worried at the commotion on their doorstep waking them from their last seconds of sleep. They pulled the girl and her baby inside.

"What happened? Where did you come from? Who are you?" They wrapped the baby in a towel, helped the woman into the backseat of their Rambler station wagon. In less than five minutes, they were driving, the man behind the wheel, his wife beside him, and behind them sat the beaten woman, dirty, her face marred with smeared blood, holding the baby with the raspy cry, her little voice nearly gone from strain.

The sun was beginning to creep over the horizon as they reached the hospital. Juicy saw the ambulance in the parking lot, the glass double doors, then inside everything was blue and green and the baby was gone, behind a curtain, down a hallway, through two big swinging doors. Suddenly, everything was quiet.

Seven
2005

Like most Saturdays, it was nearly noon and Bernie still sat in her backyard with a mug of hot coffee and the morning paper, struggling with an eight-letter word for broth that fit with the boxes of letters she'd already completed in ink. A pound of red seedless grapes was nearly gone as she picked and nibbled away, doing anything to keep her mind off of Joan Bennett and who or what her birth mother might be and why she would finally decide to look for her after all this time.

It was easy for a day to slip away in the backyard retreat her grandmother had created over the years. Noni had turned the yard into an artist's paradise. Star Jasmine covered the fences and filled the air with a rummy sweetness. The rhythm of a three-tiered fountain flowing constantly offered an illusion of a mountain brook hiding in the beds of day lilies and petunias in their final stages of bloom. Reds, pinks, purples, yellows, white, and every shade of green filled the yard, but it wouldn't be long before everything would turn to amber with the falling leaves of the sycamores and mulberry trees. Bernie loved to sit on the deck and breathe in all the fragrances, letting the stress of Noni's health, lawyers, clients, expenses, and now birth mothers dissipate with each breath. It wouldn't be long before the cold weather would arrive and days of lingering in the backyard would end until spring brought a new wealth of sunshine.

Despite what Bernie told her grandmother the night before, she had already clipped one article from the front page of *The Bee*. The story that caught her eye that morning was about a big fire in the Sequoias, no murder, no suicide. The woman who started the fire was about to be sentenced and wrote a letter to the judge, a last-ditch appeal for some sympathy, an explanation as to why she would do such a horrible thing for apparently no reason at all. She wrote, "You could worry yourself sick trying to be a better person, spend a thousand sleepless nights figuring out how to live a clean, decent, honest life. You could make a plan and bolt it in place, kneel by your bed every night and swear to God you'd stick to it. And then out of nowhere, some catastrophe comes into your life and turns everything upside down and inside out forever." *That's it,* she thought. *This woman gets it. She's sitting in jail, probably will be sitting there for a long time, and now she's learned that in one day, with one act, your whole world can cave in around you and everything changes forever.*

Bernie had clipped the piece and hurried off to her bedroom. From under the bed, she pulled out the clear plastic storage box and popped open the lid. It was nearly filled with old newspaper clippings and magazine articles, some more than twenty years old, the paper faded to a tawny yellow. She gently laid the new story on top, then pressed down on the mound of newspaper print, smashing together years of death and sadness into one firm pile, snapped the lid shut, and shoved it back under the bed where it would stay until another headline would send her in search of scissors.

The crossword puzzle was more of a challenge than Bernie wanted, so she left it unsolved and moved on to the easier word Jumble. The words were too easy: biscuit, jargon, drudge, and private. As she solved the final puzzle with the word "driver," she decided to get up and make the drive out to Madera to see if there was any paperwork left by the Lunas. She needed to put this case together quickly. Not only was mediation less than ninety days away, she needed to do something for the little boy across the border. Sixty minutes later, she was driving slowly down Orange Avenue, searching for number 6245.

The street was lined with shabby, wood-framed houses: nearly identical boxes of chipped and peeling paint surrounded by patches of withered grass, tired and dying from weeks without rain. An occasional magnolia tree grew near the road, and at some time one or two of the homeowners had apparently attempted to do some landscaping; an occasional scraggly rose bush or overgrown hydrangea hugging the sides of those houses, but most of the yards were ignored and neglected plots of dry ground. She drove, hoping someone would be home. Hoping she would find what she was looking for.

A small boy, his hair buzzed off for the summer, played alone in front of the small house. He kicked a soccer ball back and forth between his bare feet, dribbling the ball across the yard, two skinny legs jutting out of a pair of navy blue shorts that hung to his knees, occasionally kicking the ball into a camellia growing next to the front door, scoring a goal, brown petals fluttering to the ground. Bernie parked across the street, away from any stray kicks that might find their way to the side of her car.

"Hey there," she said, trying to sound cheerful. "Do you live here?"

He kicked and jogged, casting a sly look up to her, but not stopping until he plowed the ball hard into the straggling bushes and raised his arms in a sign of victory. *Score one for the little kid against the dying bush,* she thought. "Hola," she said, trying Spanish on her second attempt. "Este su casa?" She pointed to the house, smiled big, and nodded vigorously. Her Spanish wasn't very good, and she suddenly realized she should have brought an interpreter along. "Este su madre at, uhh, el casa?"

He stopped and picked up his ball and gave her a toothless grin. "She's home."

"Oh good. You speak English. My Spanish is . . ." She exaggerated a big grin, pulling her lips back tight, and gave a shake of her head instead of finishing her sentence. When he laughed at her funny face, she reached her hand out to him. "My name's Bernie. What's yours?"

"I'm Moochie." He squinted into the sun and rubbed his palm back and forth across the top of his head, like he wasn't sure his hair was really gone yet, then stuck his hand out to greet her.

"Well, nice to meet you, Moochie." She gave his small hand one firm shake and let it drop. "How old are you, Moochie?"

"I'm six now," he said proudly. "I used to be five, but now I'm six."

"Wow, you must have just had a birthday then."

"Yeah. Last week." He hopped up and down and side to side, a flurry of constant motion.

"Did you have a party?"

"Yeah, my mom took us to the McDonalds and we could sit on the grass and see the fair. There was a big ride way up in the air."

"Did you go on it?"

"No, we just sat on the grass at McDonalds and looked at it. It was cool. People were screaming; they was so scared." His smile broadened at the memory and he laughed, his head tilted back, shaking side to side while looking up at the sky. "We didn't get to go in the fair. It costs a lot of money, but we got to see it."

"So, your mom's here?" She tried to keep up with his movement, constantly shuffling to keep his hopping body in view.

"Uh huh. I'll get her." He leaped up three steps, bent forward and peered through the dark screen door, cupping his hands around his eyes. "Mama, a lady is here."

From inside, a lively thrill of happy accordions, trumpets, and guitars bounced out to the porch where they ricocheted into soft harmonies before fading into quiet. A woman's voice yelled something in Spanish, a smaller voice shouting back, but Bernie couldn't understand any of it. They spoke too fast for her to understand. Finally, Angelica appeared, her dark hair pulled into a high ponytail, so tight her eyes seem to slant upward, exotic and painful. She wore cut off denim shorts, the button and zipper undone to make room for a growing belly, a new baby inside waiting to be born. A bright orange tank top stretched tight across her middle and the shorts showed off her fit legs, legs that didn't seem to go with the top half of her. "Oh, hello," she said, her broad face breaking into a wide grin. "You're the lady lawyer. I remember you. I go to your place that time, remember?"

"Yes. I was hoping you would remember me." She had only met Luis and Angelica Corona once before, when they came to her office with Carlos, just before he was sent to his grandmother in Mexico. The Coronas were the ones that called her after the accident. They got her name from Pedro Garcia, a former client happy with the quick settlement she'd gotten for him from a fall at the grocery store. The manager on duty had helped him out the door and to his car, not bothering to make a report of the fall, not bothering to call an ambulance, not bothering to offer him anything, ignoring the man's painful limp as he stumbled out the door on a fractured ankle, suggesting he see a doctor when he got back to Mexico. No one wanted to take that bout of egregious racism to court, so it was settled quickly. Pedro told them to call Miss Sheridan, a white lady lawyer. She would know what to do.

Just days after the tragic accident, they walked into her office, Carlos still speechless and hardly breathing or moving with the fear and pain that swallowed him with the news that his mommy and daddy were gone forever, a paralysis that Bernie recognized. Of course, she would take this case, she told them. She would do anything for the dark-haired child who clung to Angelica Corona's skirt, never letting go. He seemed fragile and helpless, sitting at the conference table like a lifeless mannequin, his eyes dark and open wide, watching for the next punch his short life could expect. Bernie wouldn't hesitate to represent Carlos, if his guardian agreed. Carlos's pain was palpable.

"Is Carlos back yet?" Angie asked, her voice sliding up a scale, the last word an octave higher than the first, her English sounding musical as if she learned it from the pop songs on the radio.

"No. I'm not sure when he's actually coming back, but I think he's doing pretty well with his grandmother. I'll know more soon. I'll be going down there to see them."

"Oh yeah?" she sang. "I don't go back, but I hear they coming here soon."

"Who told you that?" Bernie knew information flowed across the border with family members and friends brave enough to make the trip home to their family left behind in Mexico, only to return in a few weeks' time for the new picking season.

"My friend's cousin went down there. He said he saw Carlos and Señora Luna, and they say they coming here pretty soon."

"I don't know anything about that, but like I said, I'm planning a trip there to see them. Perhaps the message got confused." Bernie pointed to Angelica's stomach. "When's your baby due?"

"In December. I'm hoping December 12. In Mexico, down there, it is special to have a baby born on that day and you name her Guadalupe. It's the Day of Guadalupe."

"What if it's a boy?"

"Same. Guadalupe is boy or girl." She lightly rubbed the palm of her hand around her protruding belly, already petting her unborn child.

"Well, you're going to have your hands full. Three kids." Bernie spread her own empty hands outward, palms to the sky.

"My mother will be here, I think. And my husband, he will be back. We'll be fine. It will be good."

At least this mother will take care of her baby, Bernie thought, not hand her off for someone else to raise. Bernie's pleasantries and patience were quickly fading; suddenly all she wanted was to get moving, to get what she came for and head home. "Well, the reason I came by was I was wondering if you maybe found any paperwork that Mr. and Mrs. Luna might have left behind. Receipts, really. Do you remember I asked you to keep anything you found?"

"Everything I find I put in a box. Not clothes or things like that. I didn't think you'd want those. Just papers, some letters and some pictures."

"Photographs?"

"Uh-huh. I got photos."

"Great. Can I get it all from you today?" Her spirits lifted with the thought of what she'd find.

"Yes, yes. Come in. I'll get it."

She led the way into the small, dark living room, the one window covered with a faded blue sheet to shield them from the glare of the afternoon sun. The whole place smelled of Pine Sol and something else, something delicious like homemade soup with lots of onions and some kind of meat. What furniture there was had seen better days, probably donated to some Good Will or Salvation Army where it was salvaged to furnish the Coronas' living room.

The olive green and brown plaid sofa sagged in three spots where the cushions had gone flat in the middle from years of holding exhausted bodies, dirty and dust-covered after long hours of scrubbing floors, pounding nails, or picking grapes and tomatoes. Patches of frayed upholstery gave way for bits of padding to escape from the arms of the tired couch. An old RCA television sat on a royal blue metal trunk, its sides full of dents and rust marks. Two child-sized plastic chairs, one red and one yellow, sat side by side in front of the screen where Scooby Doo lapped at a puddle of water outside a scary castle. Scooby couldn't be heard over the pounding brass band that blared from a radio in the kitchen. Dark linoleum, industrial strength, covered the floors instead of the rustic hardwood Bernie imagined from the view from the street. She always pictured older homes with oak floors, sometimes hidden under stained carpet, but there hiding, a kind of saving grace or surprise for anyone brave enough to rip away the dirty rug. It was clearly a grace that didn't find the house on Orange Avenue.

A little girl lay on her back under the kitchen table, her legs in the air, feet pushing up on the bottom of the table.

"Maribel, get up from there, Mija."

The little girl dropped her feet and rolled onto her side. Her mother prattled off another stretch in Spanish that Bernie didn't understand, but knew by the pointing finger and stern look that it was some sort of marching orders for the kid. She scooted out from under the table and stomped over to the television, her thumb in her mouth, punched a button, and the screen went dark. Angelica disappeared, and a moment later the trumpets and singing in the kitchen were quiet, too.

Bernie stood in the middle of the room and watched Moochie and his sister crawl back under the table while their mother was out of the room. "This is all I got," Angelica said. She carried an old produce box, its sides weak and stretched from the burden of a load of onions or cantaloupe. A loose pile of papers and a few odds and ends were piled inside, but not much. She set the box down at Bernie's feet, stooped over, and picked up a couple of photographs. "See, that's them."

A small, dark woman, Lucero, her face round and flat, stood behind Carlos, her hands on his shoulders, almost smiling, but not quite. She cast a shy and hopeful look to the snapping lens. Beside her, his two hands loose at his sides, was Rogelio, Carlos's father. He was square and solid, his short, black hair parted neatly on the side and combed across his forehead, his white western shirt tucked into his blue jeans, revealing a large silver belt buckle. Carlos was standing pigeon-toed and grinning so hard his eyes looked closed, as if he didn't want to see what was out there in front of him.

"Who took this?" Bernie asked. "They look so nice." It was better than she'd hoped. This was a photograph of a family, a once living, breathing family.

"Oh, at church one day," her voice slid up a note, "the preacher's lady, I mean his wife," another high pitch, "she took pictures and gave them to us." She pulled one from the back and held it out. "Here's one of Carlos and Moochie."

Bernie smiled at the picture of the two boys, Moochie taller, both of them making silly faces, Moochie sticking his hand up behind Carlos's head to give him ears. Boy stuff. She remembered that from when she was a kid. Silly pictures with her friends, when life was consumed with sleepovers and Barbie dolls. She wondered if Carlos would remember the days of acting silly with his friend Moochie before he had to cling to someone's skirt to keep from sliding off the earth.

"Let me see." Moochie hopped up from his place under the table where he sat and watched the women talking to stand close to Bernie, who held the picture out for him. "Oh man, I remember that day. That's cool. Can I have it?"

"Not just yet. Tell you what, I'll get a copy made and send it to you. How's that?"

"Coooooool." He ran, threw both hands down on the couch and kicked his legs out behind him, spun around and fell backward on the couch.

"Do you miss Carlos?"

"Yeah, he's my best friend in the whole world." In one swift motion he quickly flipped his body over and buried his face in the sofa cushion, hiding from the lady who talked about his best friend.

Angelica fumbled through the papers, eager to please, proud of what she had collected. "Here's some more. I think they took these at the fair last year. The one in Madera." She handed Bernie three strips of black-and-white photos, one strip of Rogelio, one strip of Lucero, and one strip of Carlos. Lucero and Rogelio had four identical non-smiling headshots, the types of photos you see on a passport or driver's license. Carlos had one serious photo, just his little face looking into the light. The other three were silly, one with his tongue sticking out, one with his fingers pulling his mouth to the sides, and one with his nose pushed up flat like a pig.

Bernie couldn't help but chuckle a little when she got to Carlos's group of photos. "What a goofy kid," she said. "He's a cutie, that's for sure."

"He's going to get a lot of money, huh?" Angelica asked.

"What?"

"Carlos. He'll get a lot of money from the court, right?"

The question was jarring. Noni was right again—everyone wants money. "Well," she said, careful to protect her client's privacy but still keep Angelica happy, "I'm certainly going to do my best to make sure he's well taken care of. The money is important, but what we need to remember is that he lost his parents, his mom and dad. And Mrs. Luna, Carlos's grandmother, relied on her son, too. Money doesn't make up for what they lost, but it can help take care of them."

"How much will she get?" Angelica asked.

Bernie felt her spine stiffen, aware that Angelica was ignorant of any expected sense of decorum or finesse, but also aware of the lure of friends with money. She had learned long ago that there was no shortage of greedy people who want to help their friends and family win in court, hoping to be there when the check cleared. "I'm afraid I can't really talk about that with you. I realize you were close and lived together, but you're not a party to the case."

It occurred to Bernie that Crystal was right, how it must seem to people who have so little, the idea of even ten thousand dollars must be mind-boggling, a hundred thousand seeming like millions. This small house and its small rooms and covered windows had been home for two families. Where had they all slept? Unable to leave with any unanswered questions, no matter how trivial, she asked. "How many bedrooms do you have here?"

"Two."

"How did all of you manage to live together in such a small space?"

"We had a room and they had a room. We share the kitchen and living room. And the bathroom." Angelica seemed unbothered by the questions or the living arrangement they had shared.

"So, you and your husband and two kids slept in one room, and the Lunas slept in one room." Bernie tried to guess the size of the house, maybe seven hundred square feet, *maybe*. No wonder there wasn't much in the way of furniture. There wouldn't have been room for all the bodies. She tried to imagine seven people sitting around the small table, or gathered in front of the small television.

"Uh-huh." She grinned and nodded, eager to please, proud of her home. "After the accident, we were gonna have somebody else move in, but then my husband went to Washington for a while." She paused and pointed out the window with her finger, as if it was just outside. "Washington State. My mother and sister came and stayed and helped me, but now they went to Arizona to live with my brother. He has a good job there. So, we have lots of room now. My mom, she's gonna come back though and help me again."

Bernie continued with her questions. "Have you lived here long?"

"Oh yes, yes, I think five years maybe. I work for Mr. Tomassian, the owner. I clean his house and get cheaper rent. I clean lots of houses, not just his. You need help, you call me. I do very good work." She looked nervous and scratched at her tight scalp. "Can I ask you something?"

"Sure."

"Could Carlos come live with us? I mean, him and Señora Luna. They could share the extra room."

"I can't answer that, either. Mrs. Luna may want to stay where she is, raise Carlos there. In Mexico."

The question intrigued her, the mother's friend asking to care for the boy, take in his grandmother, too. She wondered, had anyone other than her Noni wanted to raise her? A friend of her mom, maybe? Was it just money that Angelica wanted, or did she care about Carlos, her son's best friend? Maybe her birth mother would have popped into her life earlier if she'd known there was life insurance money, or about the sale of the big home where she had lived until she was thirteen. That money paid for Bernie's therapy, college, law school, helped her start her own practice.

"But she's too old to raise a little boy."

"Pardon me?" The singsong voice interrupted her racing mind, snapping her back to the moment at hand.

"Señora Luna, she is old to raise a boy good. And Mexico is not so good—it's better here." Angelica knew how to plead a case, relentlessly jabbing away with her falsetto voice. "I have a green card. I live here eighteen years already. I speak English. I taught Carlos and his mother how to talk English. I don't think the grandmother speaks English very good. Carlos should come here. Better here."

"But she's his grandmother. She's his family. That's what matters now, family."

Bernie ended the conversation with a quick nod of her head and slight dismissive flick of the wrist, the same move she used on rambling witnesses. It was a good move, and most people picked right up on its intended meaning, but Angelica just smiled and nodded, still as happy as when Bernie walked through the front door.

Bernie shifted her gaze to the road, away from the poor woman who happily scrubbed her landlord's toilets and floors to live in his cracker-box house with its scorched yard and ugly floors. "I'll let you know if I can think of anything else," Bernie said as she reached for the carton, her manner softened. "Thank you for packing this stuff up. I'm sure it will be helpful."

Bernie picked up the box and carried it under one arm out to her car. There wasn't a whole lot in there, but she was sure that was all there would ever be. Angelica had probably gone through everything in their room by then, using what she could of their simple clothes, dishes, hats, tools, or pots and pans, giving away the rest. As promised, she saved all papers and receipts, even useless papers, in the cardboard box for the lady lawyer.

The highway was a quicker route, but Bernie chose to drive country roads back to town. There was hardly anyone else traveling on Avenue Fourteen; the empty landscape allowed her the space and time to reflect on her morning and develop a strategy for the days to come. She smiled at the memory of the pictures of Carlos and Moochie, and Carlos with his parents, but her frustration grew as she recalled Angelica's mention of money. Was she trying to get some of that money? Or, did she really want to have Carlos with her, a part of their family, because she cared about him?

Bernie knew the crippling grief of losing your mom and dad. Would she have clung to anyone but Noni during that first six months, when she was afraid to sleep alone for even one night? Her grandmother was safe and comfortable. Her grandmother was everything solid, not shifting under her feet. Carlos was, she decided, where he should be—with his grandmother, no matter where that was.

Noni had made sure they both went to therapy, to get professional help with their grieving. That's where they learned about clipping stories from newspapers. Would anyone other than Noni have helped her clip out those articles, reminding her again and again that bad things happen all the time to people everywhere? *Bad things happen all the time . . . to people everywhere.* She would make sure Carlos and his grandmother got therapy too.

Noni's words haunted her. Bad things happen all the time. Why, she wondered, did she never consider that horrific things might have happened to her real mother? Perhaps the one who gave her away was like one of those tragic victims whose stories were stashed away in a plastic box under her bed? Maybe there was a reason, maybe there was more.

***

Two hours later, Bernie sat at her dining room table with a cold Corona Extra and the mangled box of unopened mail and folded scraps of papers in front of her. Bits of earth sifted in the bottom of the box, remnants of the field where some immigrant pickers stooped and sweated for long hours in hellish heat so they could afford for their whole family to sleep in one room. Most of the papers were smudged and crumpled as if they had been headed for the trash bin at some time, but saved by Angelica.

Money. That's the end game of a lawsuit, but it doesn't resolve everything at stake, especially in wrongful death. Most folks don't realize that reality when they go to trial, seeking justice in the form of a dollar sign. And, to be fair, money buys a lot of peace and compensates for those solid damages, the dollars and cents of a human life. Money pays medical bills, puts food on the table and sends kids to college. Money matters, especially when you've lost your providers. Money would pay for therapy. She would make sure Carlos and Mrs. Luna would receive therapy.

Money. Noni had said everyone wants money. Bernie had to be suspicious or at least consider that her birth mother simply wanted someone to take care of her financially. It was daunting, and exhausting, always examining motives, especially when it came to money. And Bernie was always examining motives. Always. She hated that part of her life and had no idea how to turn it off.

Bernie tilted her head back and downed three big swallows of beer and kept shuffling, opening, reading, making piles of paper and envelopes, careful to keep everything. Some of the mail was unopened, delivered after the Lunas were dead; most of that was just junk mail. Piece by piece, she carefully examined the written fragments of a young immigrant couple. She had never met them, but the pictures and the words, even the ones in Spanish that she couldn't read, made Rogelio and Lucero come to life before her. When she unfolded three pale-yellow Western Union receipts, she couldn't help but smile and nod her head yes, yes, yes. Western Union receipts and photos of the happy family made her job much easier. What had Reilly said in court that day? *Her expectations are unduly inflated and simply not reasonable.* Jerk.

Sitting there, staring at the faded receipts and photographs, she experienced one of those rare moments when she wished there was someone else around so she could belt out a *whoohoo* or *hot damn!* Someone would come running to see what she was yelling about, and then maybe shout along with her or even pick her up and spin her around like they do in the movies, celebrating the little slips of paper that she held in her hand. A whoop or holler in an empty house just made her feel foolish when it echoed and bounced around unnoticed. She picked up the receipts and carefully slid them into a clear plastic sheet protector with the photo of the Luna Family on top, a reminder of the magnitude of the matter at hand, a lost family. They were more than receipts and structured annuities. She went to the kitchen for another beer.

Bernie sat drinking and considered the pile of junk mail, no intimate notes or personal messages gathered or sent. Joan Bennett had suggested that she write a letter. She supposed she could just write one and never actually slip it into the outgoing mail. That was another one of the tricks she learned from her therapist years earlier. "Write it all down, Bernie. Deal with it in some physical way." Maybe, she thought, she should write an honest letter, tell the woman about the hell she had walked through, then toss it into the fireplace and watch it burn. Her words would ignite into a fierce flame, then smolder and eventually crumble into ash. Maybe then she could make sense of the anger that seemed to linger deep inside her. That is what no one ever understood, her anger at the past. Sadness, folks understood, but not the anger. And now it was easy to focus that unresolved anger on the stranger who had given her up so long ago.

Writing letters was what she did every day, but the pen would not move. She held it poised a fraction of an inch above the yellow legal pad, but no words would come. She should write on something else, she decided, anything but a yellow legal pad. On her desk in the spare bedroom was a ream of blank white copy paper. That's what it should be, a blank white page, no guided lines, no color or design.

Back at the table, fueled by one more swallow of beer, Bernie picked up the pen and scribbled onto the blank white page, "Dear," and then realized she didn't know what to call her. She could not call her mother, and Joan Bennett had not mentioned even a first name. She wondered then if the social worker told her birth mother what Bernie's first name was. She stared at the single word, *Dear*. Why was the woman dear? Finally, she crumpled the wasted paper and tossed it on the floor.

She started again, a new blank page, and simply wrote "Hello." She looked around the room, searching for the right words. She couldn't simply say I only want to meet you to let you know what a fucked up childhood I had. She thought of Noni, and how it had hurt her when she implied she wished she'd never been adopted in the first place. Still, she kept writing, reminding herself that it would land in the fireplace, or maybe in the box under the bed, an exercise in expression. Noni didn't need to know about her private therapy. She wrote quickly, letting the words flow.

> *Hello.*
>
> *This is a difficult letter for me to write. I don't even know your name and I don't believe you know mine. Ms. Bennett informed me that you were looking for me. I don't know what you hope to gain by meeting me now after all these years, and I'm not yet sure that is something that should happen, but I will write this letter to let you know I'm considering the matter. I'm simply curious, that's all.*
> *Sincerely,*
> *B.S.*

For once, Bernie was pleased with her initials. B.S. She read back over what she had written, intrigued by the unexpected diplomacy of her own words, then crumpled that up, too, adding it to the other wads of paper scattered on the floor. Across the table the image of the young Luna family smiling at the camera caught her eye. She had not looked at photos of her family in a long while. She went to the closet and pulled the worn black photo binder from the top shelf. Noni had meticulously labeled each photo with dates and occasions, keeping her life story in proper order, the past leading into the present through transparent window coverings.

She flipped the pages, touching the faces of her mother and father, wishing she knew what had happened that day. What had made her father so angry that he would actually kill his wife, her mother, and then himself? Bernie knew he loved her very much. They both loved her, and she had loved them. She often imagined her mother being caught in some love affair; she was certainly pretty enough to turn other men's heads. But she was always home—when would she have had the time? What else would drive a man to such a horrific act? Other times, she considered the possibility that her parents lived some secret life using drugs that made him psychotic and delusional. Maybe he was hallucinating. A lot of normal-seeming folks are into things like drugs or kinky sex, why not them? But there was never an answer, just fragments of clues. Her life was full of endless questions that no one ever seemed to have an answer to, or at least answers they were willing to share. It was a stranger mystery than any situation that came across her desk. Not knowing was what pissed her off and drove her anger. She would never know what happened on the most significant day of her life. Of course, she was angry.

Bernie slowly closed the photo album and pressed down on the book with the palm of her right hand, willing her energy to the lifeless pages. Maybe it was time for at least one answer to one question. She picked up her pen and a clean sheet of paper. She wrote again, slower, each pen stroke deliberate and strong.

Hello.

My name is Bernadette Sheridan. I am the daughter you gave birth to on May 25, 1968 and abandoned or gave away, I'm not sure which, sometime later that year. I was adopted by Ron and Patty Sheridan of Modesto, California. Ms. Joan Bennett tells me you have been looking for me. I was not sure I wanted to meet you at first, but I have questions, and perhaps you have some answers for me. I will send this letter to Ms. Bennett and wait for her to arrange a meeting or provide additional information about you to facilitate further communication. For example, I don't know your name. Odd, isn't it? I look forward to hearing from you, or at least about you.
Regards,
Bernadette Sheridan

After reading it over three times, Bernie folded it carefully and slipped it into an envelope. She still wasn't sure she would actually mail it, but she would call that Bennett woman back and get the address on Monday. Sending this letter would set something in motion. She sensed there would come a time when she would ultimately meet her mother, talk to her, look at her. And there was no denying it—she was curious, overwhelmingly so. The process might drag on, she knew, anything involving a government agency took months. She would have to be patient, but she'd waited thirty-seven years; what was a month or two more? She could get things going, then change her mind. No one said she had to actually meet the woman; she could just ask a few questions, get a little family history. But one thing she was certain of—Noni must not find out.

Bernie smiled at the thought of Noni and her dish of candies, guarding them like bits of gold. She was the one who had sacrificed everything when she took Bernie in to raise. If Bernie did actually meet her other mother, she simply would not mention it. She'd spent years trying not to upset Noni, a small repayment for all she'd done for her granddaughter. This would be no different.

120

Eight

1968

A nurse stood at the foot of the bed, studying her patient's chart, occasionally looking over to the sleeping woman as if she needed to remind herself what the person she read about looked like. What kind of girl ends up running through the streets at night, beaten up and filthy, carrying a six-month-old baby in her arms—a baby with a broken arm and abrasions on her face and chest? How does anyone end up in such a horrible situation? She didn't believe they were really kidnapped. The pieces just didn't fit. All of the nurses were talking about her, trying to figure out what really happened. Some said she was probably a prostitute, while others thought her husband or boyfriend did it. One or two believed the kidnapping story, unwilling to believe anyone would lie about such a gruesome event. One thing was unquestionable—she and the baby were in some kind of trouble, and they both needed help.

The girl flinched in her sleep then slowly opened her eyes and winced in pain. She seemed confused, gazing around the room then down at her own body, the IV needle stuck in her hand. "Where's my baby?" she asked, slowly realizing where she was, remembering what brought her there, the night before flashing through her mind like a bad horror film.

The nurse slid the chart back into a metal rack at the

foot of the bed. "Don't worry, dear. Your baby's fine. She's in the pediatrics section, just one floor down." She moved closer to the head of the bed and lifted the woman's thin wrist into the palm of her hand and lightly pressed her second and third fingers on the groove just below the thumb and felt for the pulsation of the radial artery. Her pulse quickened as she grew more alert and aware of her situation.

"How's her arm? I think it was broke." Juicy's face screwed up and she pulled her wrist away and covered her eyes with the tips of her fingers, pushing them in as hard as she could, blacking out the world for just a moment, trying to dam the spill of tears rolling down her cheeks.

"You're right." The nurse spoke gently, hoping her calm manner would flow over to her troubled patient. "Her left arm was fractured, and she's got some pretty good scrapes and bruises on her chest, legs, and face, but we're taking good care of her." The nurse smiled down at her, touched her lightly. "Do you feel like talking about what happened? The police were back here earlier. I told them I'd give them a call when you were awake, and ready to talk."

The very thought of talking to the cops again made her want to jump out of the bed and run away, but her legs felt so heavy and she was so tired. So tired. She had managed to get through the first round of questions, the pictures they took of her, the awful exam she'd endured, painful and embarrassing. She rolled her head to the side and her eyes fell closed once again. Try as she might, she couldn't seem to clear her head. She felt weaker than she'd ever felt before, and all she wanted was a little sleep. If she could sleep for a couple of hours, she was sure she'd be fine.

"What's in there?" She pointed up toward the clear

bag of fluid that was flowing into her veins. *Fluids*, was what she thought they had said. "I feel kind of woozy like."

"The doctor gave you Diazepam to calm you down a bit and some Demerol for the pain. You're banged up pretty good too; you have a couple of broken ribs, some bruises and abrasions, not to mention the emotional trauma. He wanted you to rest; you were a little agitated."

"Agitated." She opened her eyes and looked down at her body. Purple bruises covered her forearms where she had been grabbed by she didn't know how many dirty fists and held down against her will. "Yeah, I guess I was." She nodded and repeated the word. "Agitated." She would never tell anyone what really happened, how she'd allowed it, really. She hadn't tried to run away from them. If she did, she wouldn't have gotten far, and she'd probably have more than a couple of broken ribs to deal with.

The nurse picked the chart up and scribbled a few notes while she listened to Juicy repeat the story she had concocted while riding in the back seat of a speeding car taking her and her baby girl to the hospital, the same one she'd told the doctor when he examined her earlier, the same one she'd told the police when they filled out their report. Her car broke down in the middle of nowhere and a stranger had given her a ride, raped her, beat her, and then tossed her and Ginny out on the road. It was serious. A rapist out on the loose —they would be looking for him now, but she didn't give them much to go on. No real description of the car. Nothing much on him other than she claimed he was tall with a beard. She couldn't even remember where she had left her car, where she'd been. The detectives were suspicious about her lack of details, and hoped to come back after she'd slept and have her fill in the gaps. They didn't want a mad rapist on the loose.

Juicy had given careful thought to her story, methodically running through the possible scenarios as the car raced down the highway. A car crash would be good, but there was no car. It was obvious she'd been raped; she had bruises everywhere, especially her inner thighs, upper arms and breasts. Her genital area was inflamed and battered. Her rectum was raw and painful. She knew to tell them that much of the truth—they'd examine her—but the whole truth would be a death sentence. Look what happened when she'd simply paid rent with their stupid trip money, money that Freddie handed to her. He would have killed her if she'd told the guys about that, and they would have probably killed him for stealing from his brothers. What would happen to the baby then? It was better for both of them, for her and Ginny, that she bear the blame and the punishment. She could only imagine what the club would do to her now if she cried to the cops. She didn't even want to think about that. If Freddie hadn't hurt Ginny too, she would never have stepped foot in a hospital. He really fucked things up this time.

"Where did you leave your car?" the nurse asked.

"What?" She blinked twice in painful confusion.

"Where did this guy pick you up? Where's your car? The sheriffs want to know."

"Oh, I don't know. I can't remember. It was out in the country somewhere. I was just driving, trying to get the baby to sleep—she likes the car—and it stopped." She winced in pain and closed her eyes to shut the prying woman out. "I'm really tired," she moaned.

"If you could remember, it might help them catch the guy. There might be fingerprints or something. What kind of car was he driving?"

"I told you I don't remember anything about it. It was big, I guess. It was dark, so I don't know. I don't want to talk about it right now." She covered her eyes with her right hand, blocking out the world.

The nurse stood quietly for a moment before speaking. "It must have been terrible for you and the baby. Especially the baby. She can't understand what's going on. She just knows it hurts."

The nurse checked the IV, running her clean fingers down the narrow tube, scribbled a few more notes on the chart, and turned to go. With one hand on the door and the other shoved in the pocket of her white uniform, she stopped. "You know," she said, her words halting, as if she wanted to say more, but hesitated, "the police . . . . Never mind. Get some sleep."

"What about the cops?"

"I'll tell them it would be better if they can come back tomorrow after you've had some rest, but I can't guarantee they'll do that. Just rest."

Only minutes later, as Juicy was drifting off to a dreamless sleep, a woman's voice was urging her awake. "Mrs. Jones, I'd like to talk to you for a moment. Mrs. Jones, can you hear me?"

Juicy struggled through the drugs and exhaustion to focus on the woman who sat beside her bed. She thought the nurse said she'd keep the cops away for a while. All she needed was a little sleep, just a couple of hours, and she'd be ready to go. She needed to get out of this place before she had to answer any more stupid questions. Thank God, she was at least smart enough to give a fake name and story when they admitted her. There was no reason to doubt her—yet. They would never track her down once she was gone, but this was too soon, too soon. She hadn't even had a chance to see Ginny, let alone find a way to sneak her out of the nursery. "What do you want? I'm not feeling well right now, if you don't mind."

"I need to get some information for the billing office; seems you didn't have any identification when you came in; also, I want to talk to you about what happened to you . . . last night . . . about where you go from here, really. And I want to talk to you about your baby."

"I already told the cops and the doctors and that nurse, too, everything that happened. I was attacked by some monster who threw me and Ginny out of the car and I fell on top . . . . He broke her arm."

"Yes, I know what you told them. And Ms. Dixon, your nurse, is actually a good friend of mine, and we've had a chance to talk—she's the one who called me in. Like I said, we need to get some details about your personal information for billing purposes, and also try to make sure you're taken care of." She paused for a moment, carefully choosing her words, but wasting no time trying to wiggle her way into the weakened woman's confidence. "You've been through a terrible ordeal. What I'd like to know is what you perhaps didn't tell your doctors or the police."

The woman scooted the chair closer to the bed. "No one should have to experience what you have, especially a young mother and an innocent child who can't defend herself. In the end, though, it is up to you, as her mother, to do whatever is necessary to keep your child safe. That's your job. It's my job to investigate the situation when a child is injured .

. . suspiciously. I need to make sure that your little girl is safe, Mrs. Jones. That's all. Ginny's just a baby and can't tell me how she feels, so I have to ask you, her mother." She reached her hand over and gently brushed some loose strands of hair back off Juicy's forehead, careful not to touch the purple knot above her left eyebrow.

Juicy's lips pressed tightly together and two hot tears ran down the sides of her face and disappeared into her matted hair. "I know it's my job . . . I'm her mother for Christ's sake. I love my baby and I take good care of her."

"Oh, of course you love her. No one doubts that. In fact, that's precisely why I want to talk to you." She pulled a tissue from the box on the counter and dabbed at Juicy's damp face, then handed her the tissue. "Sometimes," and now she took the girl's trembling hand into her own, mindful of the IV needle, "sometimes we get to be mothers before we're actually ready for such a big job. You seem quite young. Maybe this is all too much for you right now."

"What do you mean? I didn't do this to her." She pulled her hand free from the older woman's grasp to wipe her own eyes. "Who are you, anyway?"

"I'm Isabelle Fierro, a social worker here at the hospital. I'm here to help patients with their needs, financial and otherwise, to make sure you have proper care and services available when you leave here. I won't hurt you. You can trust me."

Juicy struggled to push herself up higher in the bed, but she was weak, and her body felt so heavy. Isabelle stood to help, lifted her gently at the shoulders and pulled the young woman forward to adjust the pillow. "There. Is that better?"

"Yes, thank you."

"Linda, may I call you Linda?"

Juicy nodded, remembering the name she'd given to admitting. Linda Jones, her best friend in sixth grade.

"Is there someone I can call to come and be with you? I'm sure your family is terribly worried."

"No, my husband is . . . he's in Vietnam." She wasn't sure where that lie came from, but it seemed like a good one. She thought of the skinny kid that had come to her restaurant with his girlfriend before he headed off to fight in a jungle. He was in a uniform, and his girlfriend looked terrified and heartbroken. Juicy liked the way the two sweethearts held hands and just looked at each other for the longest time, letting their eggs and coffee turn cold. In her mind, she would be that girl. He would be her husband. She tried to lock that image in her mind, told herself that she was that young girl and her name was Linda.

"So you have Champus?"

"What?"

"Medical insurance for military families, you know, when you can't get to the base? Don't you know about Champus?"

"Oh, sure, I just, I'm not myself right now. These drugs, you know." She had to watch every word; there was so much to remember, and she was so tired. If she could just close her eyes and sleep for a bit, just a bit.

"What about your parents? Are they nearby?"

"No, no, they live back east. I don't want to worry them right now. I'll call them later. Look, I'm really . . ."

"I can call them for you, if you like. Just give me their name and number."

"No, no. It's better if I call. My mom is the nervous type, and she's been sick. I'll call later. Right now, I . . ."

"How about a friend? Someone who can come and be with you?"

"No, really, I, we, uh, just moved here. I don't really know anyone. I'm fine, really. But, thank you." Finally, there was a pause; Juicy relaxed and closed her eyes. The woman smelled good. White Shoulders perfume, the same one her mother wore whenever Dad and she went out.

"Vietnam, huh? How long has he been there?" Her voice pierced the sleepy haze.

"What?"

"Your husband. You said he was in Vietnam; how long has he been gone?"

"Uh, six months, I think." Her mom would spray the air with her perfume then walk through it. Juicy wondered where she'd learned that trick. Who taught her to just spray the air and walk through the mist of flowery scent?

"So, has he even seen his daughter? Or was he already gone when she was born? She was born, in May, wasn't it? That's just five months ago—a bit longer than the time he's been gone."

Damn it, Juicy thought, again pulling herself back to the sterile hospital room and the nightmare she was living. She should have said two months or three months, anything but six months. *Stupid, stupid, stupid.* Now there would just be more to explain. "Oh, yeah, he saw her, he left right after she was born, so maybe he's been gone five months. That's right, you see, I'm not thinking right, I'm so tired. It's the medicine they gave me. Can't we do this tomorrow? I'm supposed to rest." She closed her eyes and prayed the woman would just leave, but she didn't.

"Is he in the Army? Navy? Marines?"

"Uh huh, Marines." She kept her eyes closed, wishing she could fall asleep and avoid these pestering questions. She wasn't in any condition to be making up answers. She wanted to sleep and dream of White Shoulders and the days before Freddie, when the biggest lie she told was that her homework was done so she could go to the drive-in with her friends.

"Well, I'm sure it's not easy for you—being a single parent while he's away."

Juicy didn't answer.

"You don't have anyone to help you?"

"No, it's just me."

"You said you lived in Bakersfield. Do you mind me asking why you would live there if you don't know anybody there? Was your husband stationed somewhere near there?"

"Yes, he's stationed there."

"Hmmm. That's interesting."

Juicy felt trapped, pinned down by an IV line and suffocated by the nosy social worker. "Do you mind if we do this tomorrow? Please, I need to sleep."

"Linda, I'll be honest. I'm not so sure that it was a stranger that did this to you. I don't mean to harass you; I'm just trying to make sure that baby downstairs with the broken arm and scraped up face will be taken care of properly. Like I said, it's my job to look out for her best interests. The doctors and nurses will take care of you, and the police will find whoever did this to you. It's just, there are many things that don't make sense to me. Why isn't there anyone you want us to contact about your condition? Are you protecting someone? And why can't you remember where you left your car, or what road you were driving on, or what kind of car your kidnapper was driving—and, I may be wrong, but I don't know of a marine base in Bakersfield. And this is probably the most troubling thing for me; why did both you and Ginny smell of alcohol? The blood results aren't back, and you may have a good answer, but these are all causes for worry. Maybe I'm overly suspicious, but I'm wondering if there isn't more to the story than what you're telling."

"Why do you care? I didn't do this to myself, and I certainly didn't hurt my baby." Juicy was scared. This was not going as she had planned.

"I care because if it is someone you know, like maybe a husband or boyfriend, it might, and probably will, happen again. Next time it might be more than a broken arm that your baby suffers."

She shook her head slowly and wiped her eyes. "There won't be a next time."

"How do you know that?" Isabelle again let her fingers grace the injured girl's forehead, extending her touch, offering a gentle hand.

"I just do."

"Look, if you want to tell me about it, it will just be between us. I won't tell anyone else. I promise."

There was a kindness in her voice, something Juicy hadn't felt in a very long time, and she smelled like White Shoulders. Such a sweet smell, pretty and light. When she was small, her mother would stroke her hair like that.

"I just want to help you. You can trust me."

"But you can't," was all Juicy could mutter, her words fading into the sterile air.

"Linda, trust me," Isabelle repeated. "I really can

help you." She played with the loose strands of Juicy's hair, slowly, patiently. "Let me help you, dear."

"I don't need your help. I just need to get out of here. I just want to go home." She pulled her head to the side, trying to pull away from the woman's soothing touch.

"We all need help now and then. There's no shame in that. It's my job to help people in trouble, and I'm pretty certain you're in trouble. Maybe I could arrange for housing, transportation, medical care for the baby. She'll need medical care after leaving here." Isabelle shifted her focus to the girl's slim fingers, gently stroking the back of the fingers, back and forth, softly.

"She has a doctor."

"Who is that? Maybe I can get in touch with him. It would help to get her records and we need to send him the records of her care here. He'll need to know about her injuries, document his file."

"He's in Bakersfield. Can you please come back later? I'm too tired to talk." Juicy was too nervous and emotional to keep up with all the lies she was telling to answer any more of the prying woman's questions.

"Sure, I can come back later, but..." she held the tips of Juicy's fingers in her hand, a gentle, but firm, grasp, like a mother with her small child. "I'm afraid that until I get some better answers, I'm going to have to take some precautions with Ginny." Her tone grew sterner, changing her to an annoyed mother chastising a rebellious teen. "You see, Linda, I think you're keeping secrets and I can't let that baby go while I have these suspicions about her welfare. It would be better if you would just talk to me, tell me the truth. I can help you and Ginny, but only if you let me."

The woman reached up again to lightly brush strands of hair from Juicy's forehead, her fingertips barely touching the tender skin. She stroked the girl's hair and whispered gently, "You're safe now. I won't let anyone hurt you. Let me help you."

"I can't."

"Oh, but you can. You need to think of that little girl, what's best for her. You can't just think of yourself now. You're not in any trouble with the law—you're just in a mess. We all find ourselves in messes now and then. I'm very good at getting people out of messes; trust me."

"I told you everything."

"Linda," she leaned in closely and whispered in her ear. "I know you're in trouble. I'm not the police. Let me help you; let me help your baby. All you have to do is talk to me."

The Demerol flowed through Juicy's veins while a crippling helplessness plagued her. Her resolve was weakened, her ability to lie and deceive was crumbling fast. For the first time in weeks, someone was being nice to her, really nice to her, like a mother. She smelled good. Juicy wished her mother had been like this, willing to help, not just condemn. She needed a mother more than ever. She needed someone to care about her. To care about Ginny. As if a truth serum had been injected into the translucent IV line, Juicy began to talk, to place her trust in the hope of White Shoulders and soft hands.

She cried as she told the woman how she had met Freddie at his sister's birthday party a couple of years ago, how he'd given her a ride home on his motorcycle, how much she loved him. She told her how things changed once she got pregnant, that he was going to marry her, but now he never would, how he would hardly look at her as she grew bigger with the baby, how angry he would get at the slightest thing. When he got drunk he called her terrible names, like bitch and cunt and whore, but still, he loved her and always made it up to her. And finally, she confessed that Freddie had taken some money from an old paper sack he had hidden in the garage, money that didn't belong to them. He'd given it to her to pay overdue rent, warned her that it would be bad if he couldn't replace it before the next ride. She knew whose money it was, and she knew he'd never replace it, but she took the roll of bills and stayed with him, hoping he'd find work, hoping the bad day would never come.

In the end, Freddie had tricked her into going for a ride, telling her it would do her good to get out for a day, let the baby get fresh air. They ended up at the bar where he gave her over to his dirty friends as payment, lying to them, telling them she'd stolen their money. She should have known better than to go with him that day. He didn't care if Ginny got out for fresh air; he didn't love her. She closed her eyes when she told Isabelle Fierro how the men had taken turns with her, and how she hid the baby under the table the whole time. She did what she could. She had protected her baby. She wouldn't ever let anyone hurt Ginny. She kept her safe. She kept her safe.

For a moment, there was silence in the room as if the words needed some time to settle down and soak in. Finally, the older woman spoke. "But Ginny did get hurt, didn't she?"

"I couldn't help that," Juicy whispered, her voice hoarse and weak. "I'd do anything for her. I love her more than anything."

"Good. I'm glad to hear that." The social worker rose

to her feet and paced around the room for a moment, as if she were searching for something. "Linda, I want to offer you a chance to give that baby more than you possibly can at this point, and in the meantime, you can give yourself a second chance, too."

"What do you mean?"

"I'll be blunt, because I know even now you're planning to get the hell out of here and I don't want to have to do something that can be avoided. I think you should consider letting a good family adopt your baby and give her all those good things you want for her. It's about Ginny, what's best for Ginny. You're still just a girl yourself."

"I can't give up my baby. I love her too much. There's no way. You said . . ." Juicy's breathing grew labored and her heart pounded in her throat as a crippling fear seized her.

"Oh, I know how much you love her. That's why I think you should consider it. It takes the greatest kind of love to sacrifice your role as mother to give your child a better life than you can at this point."

Shaking her head from side to side, fueled by fear and rage, Juicy refused the older woman's proposition. "No, I could never do that. Never."

Isabelle continued her case, ignoring Juicy's agony, ignoring her pain. She prattled on, her words a dissonant chant. "I know a lovely couple who would be happy to give your child a home, the kind of home that child deserves. The husband is a professional man. He makes very good money. His wife works, too. She's a secretary, but she would be happier with a reason to quit her job and stay home, to give her undivided attention to caring for a baby, to a family. They have a lovely home, two stories, and a nice yard just waiting for a swing set or playhouse. They just don't have any children, and apparently aren't able. A child is just the thing they need. You'd be making a family, a real family. You'd be giving the greatest gift possible, not only to the couple who wants children, but to Ginny. You'd be giving her a life and future that, sadly, is one you are not equipped to provide."

"But, she's my baby. Mine." Frustrated, angry, and frightened yet again by a situation out of her control, Juicy grasped the bed rails and silently prayed for the pushy woman to go away. "I'm her family. *I'm* her mother. She stays with me."

"I know that, dear, and I also know you want what's best for her. It takes great sacrifice to make a true family. We all have to sacrifice sometimes."

Juicy shook her head and rolled over onto her side, turning her back on the woman's unrelenting efforts to take her baby away, to give her to strangers. The heat of the woman's hand rested upon her shoulder, a stinging reminder of her lingering presence. With a violent shudder, Juicy jerked her arm away.

"Wouldn't you love for Ginny to grow up in a house with a mom and a dad? In a nice home in a nice neighborhood?" The mature woman's voice stayed calm, oozing with irritating sincerity and compassion. "Can't you imagine her riding her bike on sunny afternoons, opening piles of presents on Christmas, sleeping safe in her bed in a room of her own, a room with toys and books and a closet full of clothes. Can you give her all that?"

"Who's to say I can't?"

"Oh, I'm sure you'd like to. I just know how hard it is to be a single mother, working all day, up with a baby at night, never enough money, as you know. That is how you ended up here, a lack of funds, right? I also know how often women end up back with the very man who hurt them."

"Don't worry, I'm not going back there." She rolled back to face the social worker and met her piercing gaze.

"Where will you go, then?"

"I don't know. Home maybe. To my folks' home."

"Oh, I didn't realize your parents were willing to help you out. Yet you haven't even called them to come for you? Are they here?"

"No."

"They live back east, you said. Do you want me to call them for you? It might take them a while to get here." The woman's needling and prodding was relentless.

"No. I'll do it. I just don't want them to worry."

"I'm sure they'd want to know what happened to you."

"No." Again, she avoided the gaze of the woman on her right and focused only on the watercolor that hung on the wall. A river scene with drippy trees and a yellow sky, just how she felt. "I haven't actually seen them for a while. They don't know about Ginny, but they will love her. I know it."

"Oh, I see."

"They just hated Freddie."

"Uh huh, I think I can see why."

Juicy was tired of the questions, eager to be alone so that she could figure out what to do. "Look, I really need to rest now. You need to leave."

"Of course, you do. I'll be back later this evening, after you've spoken to the detectives. I won't tell them what you and I talked about just yet, but I'm sure they'll have the same questions I had. Probably more."

"What if I don't want to talk to the cops? Do I have to?" If this woman told the cops what happened and they went after Freddie and the guys, she was as good as dead and then what would happen to Ginny?

"Oh, I don't think you have much choice in that." The woman stood and took the girl's hand in her own one more time. "But if you change your mind, I can probably take care of that for you, too. I'm on pretty good terms with the authorities."

"No doubt," she muttered angrily.

"Get some rest, Linda." Juicy flinched as the woman gripped her hand tighter as she leaned in closer, adding, "That's not your real name, is it?"

Juicy didn't answer. She closed her eyes and waited for the smell of White Shoulders to be gone and silently prayed that the freight train pounding through her veins would halt, but the roar of pain and violence rumbled on like a falling echo, spinning and bouncing, refusing to be silenced.

Nine

2005

On Monday, before answering emails and phone calls, Bernie telephoned Joan Bennett to say she'd taken the advice to write a letter to her birth mother. All morning Bernie had weighed her decision, arguing with herself as she showered, reassuring herself as she applied mascara. Simply mailing the letter would not do any harm, she reasoned. There was no commitment by mailing a simple letter. She wasn't necessarily going to meet her other mother face to face. It was just a short note, the door cracked open, but not enough to get a clear view of what was inside. She could always change her mind later, let it end with that one piece of mail. By the time she backed her car out of the driveway, the letter was as good as sent.

After carefully addressing the plain white envelope to Joan Bennett, she would wait another hour before actually putting a stamp on the letter, and then another before dropping it into the outgoing mail basket on Crystal's desk.

Just before noon, Wayne, the chatty mailman, picked up the pile of white envelopes, most of them generated by Crystal, and offered his usual greeting as he passed her office door. "Morning, Counselor."

"Morning, Wayne." It was done.

Once the letter was on its way to somewhere unknown, Bernie forced herself to put the whole business of her curious past out of her head, to focus on the stack of unanswered interrogatories and files spilling over from her desk to stacks on the floor. If she'd learned anything in her years as a lawyer, she knew the snail's pace of red tape and government procedures. It would take weeks for her letter to go through all the proper bureaucratic channels: probably first reviewed by some secretary, then Joan Bennett, then photocopied before it would finally be mailed off to the unknown mother with an official cover letter explaining the content. Meanwhile, in Fresno, California, she had several cases and people that needed her attention, including Carlos Luna.

In some odd way, the mailing of the letter was a catalyst for manic-like activity. As if a director had called *action* and the slap of the clapboard marked time, Bernie propelled herself forward. With unleashed energy, a pounding soundtrack played in a loop, pushing her onward to the next scene. Running on overdrive, with all synapses firing automatically, not a breath of hesitation, Bernie grew lightheaded and dizzy with a strange sense of urgency not typical of her.

When she paused long enough to sit and enjoy the view of a hummingbird buzzing outside her office window, Bernie was overcome with wistful nostalgia. She recalled again that summer day on the Kings River, fishing with her father. After hauling in his empty line, he pulled off his shoes and waded out to his knees in the slow-moving river. "Come on," he'd called to her. "Don't be afraid, Sweetheart. There's nothing in here that can hurt you. It's no different than swimming in that silly pool at home, just bigger, is all."

They swam and splashed each other, then floated on their backs, drifting with the current. When they finally crawled up the muddy bank laughing together, they were startled to see how far they had traveled, the abandoned poles and bags resting back where they'd first waded into the green water.

Bernie shivered at the memory of the chilly water, but smiled sweetly at the image of her dad's sunburned nose, red and sore for days. Those were the times when they were a family that sat around the television on weeknights watching *Happy Days* or *Mork and Mindy.* Those were good days. Bernie had always placed the blame for her family's tragic end on the stranger who gave her away when she was a baby, not her father. Maybe if she hadn't been there, it wouldn't have happened. At least she wouldn't have been a part of it. Noni, of course, blamed Bernie's dad. He was the one who pulled the trigger. Then again, maybe no one could ever be blamed; it was just a tragedy.

Lost in thought, Bernie didn't even notice Crystal sliding into the chair across from her until her chirpy voice snapped Bernie back to the here and now.

"It's all set. The Luna deps are going to be November twentieth at the Fiesta Americana Hotel in Mexico City, which, by the way, looks fabulous—beautiful rooms, an amazing pool, and there's even a babysitting service in case you need someone to watch Carlos while you're deposing Mrs. Luna. The zoo is even nearby, something extra, maybe, for Carlos." Crystal was beaming, proud of the amount of attention she had given to all the arrangements. "I have an interpreter, a conference room in the hotel, and I even managed to get you the deluxe suite for half price since you're booking the Lunas' room and a conference room, too. Anyway, you leave here on the eighteenth, so you have the whole day before to prepare with Carlos and Mrs. Luna, get adjusted to your surroundings, and most importantly, seriously, stock up on bottled water." She slapped both palms on the desk and smiled proudly, clearly waiting to hear how great she was.

"You know what?" Bernie spoke slowly, finally meeting Crystal's eager gaze. "I know you worked hard on setting all this up, and it all sounds fantastic, but . . ." She paused, knowing her words were going to send Crystal through the roof. "I think you were right before. I'm not sure going to Mexico is the best thing to do right now. I don't think it will accomplish anything other than pissing Reilly off and running up our costs. I'm thinking we should bring them here, like you suggested."

Bernie watched the dark cloud slip down over Crystal's face, the smile fading, the chin slowly dropping to a smirk of disbelief. "You've got to be kidding," Crystal said. "I spent three days getting this all set up." She released a gasp of air toward the ceiling, appalled at the very idea of undoing all that she had worked so hard to accomplish.

"I'm sorry, but I don't think I want to leave the country right now. It's not a good time for me to be gone." Bernie casually picked up a piece of paper and began reading it over, avoiding Crystal's seething glare. "There are reasons I shouldn't leave. Personal reasons."

"But you said . . ."

She lowered her hand, still holding the piece of paper, and attempted to deflect any brewing contempt for the sudden change in strategy, the waste of time and energy. "I know what I said, but now I want to bring them here. I'm certain we can arrange for whatever Mrs. Luna needs to cross the border. If not, let's contact an immigration guy and get some help. And I want it here in this office, not in Reilly's office." Bernie paused and thought of her trip to Madera, Moochie and Carlos making silly faces together for a camera. "Besides, I think Carlos and his grandmother would rather come here. They have friends here. We can schedule the mediation while they're in town, so it's really much more efficient. One trip instead of two. No need to piss Reilly off any more than he already is."

"Terrific. I love to do things twice. I wouldn't want to actually get caught up with everything else you've been piling on me like crazy. I'm buried."

There were times when the closeness that develops through years of working together becomes confusing, a blur of crossing imaginary boundaries long ago established. It would not be the first time she pissed her secretary off, and it wouldn't be the last. "Come on," Bernie reasoned, "you don't have to do anything but move the darn thing from Mexico to here. Everyone other than you and the hotel manager will be happy about that change. I'm the one who has to actually take the deposition, and I'm the one paying all the bills right now, so I get to change my mind." Bernie turned away to her computer screen to end the conversation.

For the rest of the day, Crystal would only speak to Bernie when absolutely necessary, and then it would be excessively polite and controlled, as if the two women hadn't spent years sharing long lunches, popcorn breaks, and hours of courthouse gossip. Bernie's flurry of activity had fallen onto Crystal's plate, and that plate was overflowing with tasks and brewing anxiety.

Bernie closed her office door, shutting out the sounds

of telephone calls and Crystal's fingers striking her keyboard as she worked to undo all she had done. She sat at her desk, eager to share her weekend discovery with someone who would actually be excited about it. She fumbled through the black bag resting at her feet until she found the green folder she searched for, the folder with Don Fielding's contact information. He answered on the second ring, and the sound of his voice surprised her. "Oh, hello," she said, "I didn't expect you to answer the phone yourself."

"Who is this?"

"I'm sorry. This is Bernadette Sheridan," she said, her voice automatically shifting to her professional tone. She sat up straighter and switched the telephone to her left ear, freeing her right hand to grab a pen and jot notes down while she talked.

"Oh, Bernadette, hi."

"Hi Don, and call me Bernie, everybody else does." She took a moment to run her fingers through her hair, letting the sides drop back down around her ears, hiding them from the kind voice on the phone.

"Pardon the noise, but I'm actually at Lowe's right now. I'm helping Lance, my uncle, with a fence today." A rumble of echoes could be heard in the background, as if he stood in a long, hollow tunnel.

"Ahh . . . I get it. This is your cell phone number."

"Yeah. It's the only phone I use right now, since I'm not really settled anywhere just yet."

"Well, I just wanted to give you an update on the Luna case." A twinge of excitement crept over her and she couldn't help but smile as she spoke. "I went out to Madera over the weekend, to the Lunas' old house, and picked up a box of papers and other odds and ends that their housemate gathered up. I'm still sorting through everything, but it looks like I have a couple of things that might do us some good." She paused a moment. "Believe it or not I have Western Union receipts from Rogelio to his mother. Can you believe it? Actual receipts. It just doesn't get much better than that."

"How many you got?"

"Just three, but that doesn't mean that's all there is or all that was sent. He wasn't keeping a record or anything, but it's evidence to support Mrs. Luna's claim that her son sent her money that she relied on. We can subpoena the store's Western Union records to see if there were more from that location, and she will testify about the amounts and possibly have bank records to verify the deposits, but to tell you the truth, I just didn't really expect to find anything this good out there."

"Well, that's great work, Bernie. Makes my job easier."

Bernie could feel him smile and pictured him strolling through the maze of hardware and tools, scanning the racks of nails and bolts while he talked on the phone, probably nodding hello to everyone he passed, a lock of his black hair falling into his eyes, him pushing it away. "So, do you want to come by the office and take a look? Or I can just have Crystal copy them and put it all in the mail, if you prefer."

"Hmmm. Can you hold on one second?" She listened to him chatter with the clerk and the rustling of a bag. "Okay. I'm back. Listen, I have to finish this fence today. They have a couple of dogs that are stuck inside right now, and my schedule's pretty tight the rest of the week. Actually, I'll be out of town for a few days after tomorrow, and I have a couple of appointments already set up. What about this evening? Can I get them later on today?"

"How late? I usually head home by six. If it's after that, I guess . . . I guess you could come by my house. I can take the copies home with me." As soon as she said the words, she thought about the state of things when she left that morning, dirty coffee cups and cereal bowls scattered along the kitchen counter and the mountain of old newspapers and catalogues that cascaded from the coffee table to the floor.

"If you wouldn't mind, that really would work out better for me. It's going to take me the rest of the afternoon to get this done. How about seven o'clock? Is that too late? I don't want to impose on your family time."

"No, that's fine; I live alone," she explained. "I'm on Brown, just west of Van Ness, between Clinton and Shields. Do you know where that is?"

"Sure, I know that neighborhood well. Christmas Tree Lane, right?"

"Right. Well, it's a little south of that, but same street. I'm at 3618, a little white house with a red front door—you can't miss it. And my car's in the driveway, a green Outback, you'll see it."

She hung up the phone and picked up the green file folder to fan herself. She wasn't particularly stressed, and she certainly hadn't been drinking any red wine, but she felt the familiar warmth spread all the way to the tips of her ears. Nervous energy raised blood pressure so she took a deep breath, inhaling slowly, willing her body to relax.

When Bernie took the Western Union receipts out to Crystal for copying, Crystal was on the phone with Reilly's office, explaining that the depositions could be taken here after all, that Ms. Sheridan had a family situation that prevented her from leaving the country. Her sincerity was believable and her manner friendly, but professional. Bernie moved on to the workroom. She wasn't completely helpless —she could work a copy machine.

With copies and originals of the receipts and photos in hand, Bernie left the office earlier than usual that afternoon, leaving Crystal to lock up. She wanted to tidy up at home, at least stack the dirty cups and bowls into the dishwasher before Don Fielding showed up at her door.

Adding a built-in dishwasher was the first improvement she had made to the house since taking ownership. "Why do you need that?" Noni had asked on one of her rare weekend visits, her face pinched into a tight knot. "There's just you. You can't wash a cup and a bowl?" Bernie smiled when she thought of the old woman in her scooter, opening and closing the door, listening to it click, pulling out the racks, pushing them back in. Even with the new Maytag, Bernie usually just left dirty dishes in the sink and on the counter until there wasn't a clean cup in the cupboard for her morning coffee. Only then would she open the door and arrange a week's worth of dishes in the racks, her lazy habits hard to break. Noni had spoiled her for too many years, doing everything for her, cooking, cleaning, laundry and dishes by hand, fiercely scrubbing pans until they shined like new.

Bernie rinsed a handful of forks and spoons before dropping them into the plastic silverware basket one by one, clattering and slapping into each other. Whether it was doing dishes or photocopying faded receipts for money sent across the border, she kept moving. It was a physical effort to avoid dwelling on thoughts of the woman who gave birth to her, the letter that was on its way to her, a growing curiosity that swelled by the minute. She focused on the Luna case, the weather forecast, folding laundry and taking out trash, moving seamlessly from one project to the next. But a stream of questions constantly invaded her thoughts, stopping her cold in the middle of the task at hand. Did her birth mother have big ears and thin hair, too? Did she snort when she laughed? Did she and Bernie share some odd facial expression that would defy explanation since they had never been together during her childhood?

Whatever loomed ahead, Bernie surmised, could in no way be worse than anything she had been through already. The difference now was that she controlled the course of action; she decided what would and would not transpire. Finally, Bernie reminded herself that her quest was purely to discover more of her own life, not to kindle some new maternal relationship, regardless of what her birth mother wanted. This was up to her. For the first time, she realized there was a chance she might have some answers to some of those difficult questions that had often haunted her in the past.

Since she was thirteen years old, Bernie had clawed through a dark web of speculation about the mother who raised her, Mom, wondering what she'd done to make Dad so angry that day. It didn't matter if she was reading the story about the fire in the mountains, driving down the highway to look for evidence, listening to music, or going to the bathroom, her brain could veer off course into dark, uncharted waters. Some unseen impulse in the recesses of her brain would take control without warning and then boom, she would suddenly look around and realize she was ten miles further down the highway, or she was turning a page she couldn't recall reading. Lost in her own head, she called it.

As the dishwasher began to thrum and whir, Bernie contemplated what to say if and when she actually met the birth mother. Words were unconsciously coming together, like a negative in a developing solution, the blurry image slowly becoming clear, taking shape in a dark room. She would, she decided, tell her everything, every painful detail of Bernie's childhood. She should know the truth of Bernie's past if she wanted to know her now. Honesty, she thought, was the best course of action. It was too late for playing games. She wanted truthfulness from her mother, and she would give it in return.

Bernie ran a damp sponge along the countertop and moved on to clear the coffee table as best she could, grabbing an armful of old papers and tossing them into the recycle bin, wanting things to look as nice as possible when Don arrived. Though she barely knew the guy, he intrigued her, and it wasn't just that she liked his messy hair. He seemed so pure and tranquil. He's a numbers guy who plays music and likes to fix things up, all normal enough, but there was another layer to him that she couldn't figure out. Whatever it was, he was certainly different from most of the other people she dealt with. Bernie wondered what he would do if he were in her shoes. No doubt he would celebrate finding out his birth mother was out there, eager to see him after so many years. Of course, he hadn't lived through the nightmare of losing his family in one violent moment. Still, she doubted he would be bouncing around like a bee in a field of wildflowers, bumbling from one bloom to the next then back again. A nervous Nellie is what Noni called her when she got like that.

The house was finally presentable for guests. Shutters drawn, lamps glowing softly, and the air conditioner humming softly though a hint of autumn hung in the air. Bernie didn't care if her PG&E bill went through the ceiling; she liked to sleep with the weight of thick blankets about her, so she kept the thermostat set at sixty-four degrees. Just as she was dragging a brush through her hair, trying to ignore the new strand of grey corkscrew at the top of her head, she heard the clang of the brass door knocker. A nervous flutter in her stomach surprised her as she hurried to answer. It had been a long time since she'd heard that sound.

"You found it," she said, pulling the door open wide to let him in.

"You give good directions, and the red door's easy to spot," he said, giving it a light tap with his knuckles as he passed through.

"Come on in." Bernie led the way through the living room to the small alcove dining room off the kitchen. She had neatly arranged the original receipts along with an envelope of copies she had made for him that afternoon. "Have a seat. I use this table for work more than actual dining, so make yourself comfortable." She pulled one of the chairs away from the table as she passed, then stopped before sitting down herself. "Actually, I never use it for dining. Can I get you something to drink before we start? Let's see, I have diet 7-Up, water, Corona, and," she held up her half empty glass of red wine "an open bottle of cheap Pinot."

"A Corona sounds good." He sat down slowly as he gazed around the room, again turning his attention to the walls and ceiling that surrounded him. "This is a great house, too, like your office. I love the ceiling," he said, pointing to the swirls of plaster that rounded gently up from the walls, looking a bit like a frosted cake.

"Yeah, me too. I actually grew up in this house, so I've lived here most of my life, well, since I was thirteen." Bernie took an extra minute to slice a lime and poke a small wedge into the mouth of the open bottle.

"Really? That's amazing."

"It was my grandmother's house." She set the cold beer down in front of him, then slipped into the seat across the table. "Now it's mine."

"Did you live with your grandmother?"

"Yes, after my parents died." She reached into the box and pulled out an envelope, avoiding his eyes, hoping to stave off the inevitable look of pity.

"Oh," was all he said, nothing more.

She reached up and combed her fingers through her hair, grabbing a handful and letting it fall, a practiced illusion of calm that expertly caused the entire mess to frame her face and cover her ears. "Like I told you, my folks died when I was young, and I came to live here with my Noni." Her head dipped to the right, and she raised her shoulders, suggesting it was no big deal.

"That must have been tough. How old were you?" he asked, his words full of compassion, but not pity.

"Thirteen."

"Oh, you already told me that; I'm sorry."

"It's okay. Anyway, I still love this place. It feels safe." She picked up the receipts and held them out to him in a weak attempt to change the subject from her life to work. Don didn't notice her efforts and continued the conversation.

"This kind of explains your interest in my adoption story. I have to tell you, I've been thinking about that conversation a lot, trying to figure out what was really going on there. Did your grandmother adopt you? Is that it?"

"No, she was my guardian." Bernie gave a slight smile, recalling the office interview, imagining what he must have thought of her probing questions about his past. "But," she continued, "to be fair, since I've pried into your childhood, I should add that my parents, the ones that died in the accident, were my adopted parents. They adopted me. Noni is my adopted mom's mom." She lifted her glass and took a sip of the dark wine. "Guess you could say I was kind of adopted twice."

"I didn't mean to pry." He gave his head a gentle shake, and his black hair fell down over his eyes, prompting him to brush it back with his long fingers.

Funny, Bernie thought, *he's trying to tuck his hair back behind his ears, and I'm trying to keep mine covered*. She felt the flush of red wine and smiled, wishing she'd opted for the beer. "You didn't pry. It was a long time ago and I offered the explanation. And, in case you think I'm afraid to move out, I didn't always live here. I had my own place for a long time."

Bernie knew that in a modern world where you rarely found people living in the same city of their birth, living in the same house for twenty-five years was peculiar. "Anyway, eventually Noni went to live at the Nazareth House, and I moved back in here."

"What's Nazareth House? A nursing home?"

"Sort of. It's, I think the official term these days is senior residence." An old worry plagued her. Despite Noni's insistence on the situation, she still felt a painful guilt about moving her to an old folks' home. When she was a child, her Girl Scout troop had gone to sing Christmas Carols at some place out in the country that smelled like dead flowers doused in urine. Her mother had made her promise to never put her in one of those awful places when she got old, never imagining the alternative to living to a ripe old age. Bernie had dutifully vowed that she'd never do anything like that, not ever.

"I tried to get her to stay here, in her own home, get her some in-home care, but she wanted to live at Nazareth. It's actually pretty nice. Not like those places you read about in the news, you know, old people left dirty and hungry with oozing bedsores."

"I'm sure it's wonderful," he said, nodding in approval.

"It really is," Bernie added, still feeling the need to affirm her actions. "She gets to go to mass every day—that's important to her—and she has her own little community of friends that she hangs out with. It's a little like high school sometimes, the way they argue about petty stuff. It's pretty funny. And she has help getting around. Her hips are shot."

Bernie surprisingly felt free to chat rather than simply dive into the work. She told Don about the time she and her friends got caught skinny dipping in the pool at Fresno High, about fishing with her dad on the Kings, Sunday dinners with Noni when her folks were alive, how she hated those days, but now thought of them often. Simply handing over the documents and sending him on his way might be less complicated and faster, but it had been a long time since she'd just sat and visited with someone in the evening. She'd forgotten how much she enjoyed company and conversation, drinks after work, so to speak. That was the one part of being single and living alone that was tough; there wasn't anyone to just talk to about nothing at the end of the day.

"So, back to why I'm here; Noni went to Nazareth and I moved in here. Now, she's the one that comes here for Sunday dinners, but not every week. It's too hard getting out."

"That's too bad," Don said. "I know what it's like when your hips go. My father-in-law had a hip replaced last year and it never took. Said he'd rather die than go through that again, so he struggles."

Bernie flinched ever so slightly at the words father-in-law. "Oh, for some reason I didn't think you were married, but I don't know why. I hope I'm not keeping *you* away from home at dinner time." She suddenly felt a little foolish about her fascination with his hair.

"Well, I'm not. At least not anymore. I went through a divorce last year and moving here and starting over in a new city with a cabin in the mountains to take up my time seemed like a good idea. A fresh start."

"Oh, I'm sorry. I know what that's like too."

"Are you divorced?"

"No, not technically. We weren't ever really married."

"Same difference."

"At least we didn't have kids. Do you have kids?" She knew he had not mentioned children before, but perhaps it just hadn't come up.

"No. Just a cat. She kept the cat." This time he took a minute to drink from his bottle, taking two or three big swallows. "So, if it's really not prying, and we're getting to know each other better—which is really nice, by the way, since

I'm still fairly new back in town—how'd your parents die? You said they died in an accident, but I don't think you ever explained what kind of accident. Was it an automobile accident?"

The question startled her. People often told Bernie that her pale grey eyes seemed to flash blue at certain times, usually if she wore something blue or if she was surprised or angry; she would bet good money that they shined cobalt at the moment. She hesitated, unsure of what to say, to lie or tell the truth.

"I'm sorry," he said. "My overly curious nature. Never mind, but, if you'll recall, you asked me a lot of personal questions. For the record I, too, can be direct."

"It's alright. It just caught me off guard; yes, they died in a car accident." She wondered why she still felt the need to lie. It wasn't like she was back in her plaid skirt and white blouse at St. Helen's, the girl whose parents offed each other as Jason Grodin had so nicely put it. When she transferred to the new school near Noni's house, she decided a fiery car crash was better than telling people the violent truth of a murder-suicide. Noni went along with it, told her she could make up anything she wanted if it made life any easier. Later, she just said they died in an accident, telling herself that's what it was, really. An accident. All these years later, the one thing she knew from the box of news clippings under her bed was she wasn't alone. Those awful things happen every day, but usually to other people.

"That's terrible. Wow," he breathed, "no wonder you're into this Carlos case so much."

"That's what my secretary, Crystal, says. Only she made a point of explaining how different the whole thing is because I'm white, and my parents were white Americans, and Carlos is just a poor Mexican kid whose parents were field workers, so he's not worth as much." She waved her hand, whooshing away the offensive argument.

"Unfortunately, she makes a good point as far as the numbers go with a jury."

"Not if I can help it." The room began to darken as the last bits of sunlight faded away. Bernie reached behind her and turned the dimmer switch up so that the overhead light grew brighter, another one of her small improvements to the old house. "Their lives were just as valuable to that little boy."

"It must have been hard growing up without a mother," Don said calmly. His hands folded into one another in front of him, resting easily on the table, not holding onto his drink like most people would do in a new environment, clutching onto a safety net, even if that net was only a bottle of beer.

"I had a good mother for a long time and then I had a really good grandmother. And as you can see," she waved her open hand about the room, "it all turned out okay. Different than I would have wanted, but okay." Bernie finished the last swallow of her wine and set the empty glass on the credenza behind her, a symbolic gesture to end the topic of her life as a matter up for discussion.

"Yes, I can see," he agreed.

His simple response was perplexing. Bernie did not want to consider what he might see beyond a house and furniture, so she reached down and picked up the nearly empty cardboard box and placed it at the end of the table near the stack of papers already laid out. "This is the box of papers

I got from the Lunas' old house. I'm still going through it, but there didn't appear to be any more receipts. The rest is mostly junk mail and I don't think most of it matters to you for your work, but I thought you might want to see some family pictures." She rustled around and lifted out a handful of papers and envelopes she had already organized.

"Of the Lunas? Oh absolutely. I'd like to see what they looked like. It adds a whole other dimension to the job if I have an image, a face, in my head." He reached across for the small stack of photographs that Bernie held in her hand.

She handed him the photos, her gaze fixed on him to watch his response. "We have the whole family there." His words resonated with her. A whole new dimension. How would a photograph of her birth mother affect her?

"Cute kid." He looked into the photo and returned Carlos's frozen smile as if he was in on the secret and knew the source of the child's playful grin.

"Those photos and the Western Union slips really make this case strong." Confidence ran through her as she watched his face light up, his head nodding up and down.

Don shuffled through the few photos, then turned his attention to the receipts, still holding onto the pictures, not ready to let those faces go. "Looks like he sent his mother five hundred bucks three times in five months from these; not a huge amount, but it's something solid."

"Right. Naturally, I'll argue that he sent similar amounts of money regularly, probably monthly. We simply don't have all the receipts."

"Perhaps. He probably sent four or five grand a year. It's not huge, but it's something." He tapped the receipts with his fingers and sat back in his chair and looked down at the photos again, examining the image closely. "What else you got in there?"

Bernie watched the man across the table, carefully measuring her next words, wanting to make her point without manipulating his work or sounding arrogant. "Well, your job is to build those numbers up. Make them bigger, not smaller. Even if the evidence is incomplete, I can argue the assumptions."

"I'm simply speculating," Don said, returning her gaze. "And I'm giving my honest reaction to what we have for right now. This is all very preliminary, but I won't lie. I never lie. That needs to be clear."

"I'm not asking you to lie," she countered, straightening her spine with each word. "That would be unethical, but in this case, we need some hard damages for these folks. I need to prove they were worth more than a few receipts, that their lives had real value, and I need you to help me do that." His tranquil demeanor she found so appealing ten minutes ago grew annoying and a twinge of irritation at his nonplussed attitude jabbed her in the gut.

"And I will, Bernie, but you should be careful not to project what isn't there. It's better to be cautious with expectations."

"I just want to make sure we're on the same page. Let Reilly worry about tearing the case down; that's his job."

"I've heard about him. Stuart Reilly."

"Yes, his reputation proceeds him."

"I actually had a call from him today. He wants me to look at a case for him. Not this one. Don't worry, I made sure of that."

"Well, good luck. He's not the easiest guy to work

158

with." Bernie shook her head in disgust, but Don wouldn't notice. He had picked up the newspaper that was pushed to the side of the piles of letters and receipts, unfolding the front-page section to find half of it gone.

"What was this?" He held the cut-up page in front of his face.

"Oh, I cut out the story about the woman who set fire to the Sierras." With another flippant wave of her hand, the news article became a meaningless event, nothing for anyone to worry about.

"You know her?"

"No. I just, well, she wrote a letter to the judge. And, it was a good letter, so I cut it out."

"Oh yeah? What'd she say?"

"Well, she was looking for leniency, so she tried to explain how no matter how good your plan is, things happen that blindside you. Life veers, you know. Tragedies happen, stuff like that."

"Kind of like 'shit happens'?" He folded the paper back up and chuckled at his own joke.

Bernie offered a weak half-smile, not entirely sure he wasn't poking fun at her. It didn't seem like the kind of thing he would say.

"Maybe a little more than that. I guess the letter struck me because of what I do for a living. I see people every day who are trying to resolve some life-altering problem that landed in their lap out of nowhere, so to speak."

"Yeah, but sometimes good things fall in your lap too."

"Well, they don't seem to happen as often or affect us so much as the bad things do."

"Oh, I disagree. I think they happen all the time. I just don't think people pay much attention to good things. We expect good things to happen, so we don't even notice when they do. But with misfortune, we're shocked and scream about how unfair it all is. We give it all our energy."

"So, are you some kind of positive thinker with a set of daily affirmations or a mantra that you chant every morning?" An easy grin formed as she imagined the man looking into the mirror, telling himself life was good, and he was good enough, darn it.

"I do think positively; I'm not ashamed of that." He returned her sly grin, his eyes nearly closing and the same shock of hair flopping into his eyes. "You should try it." He inhaled deeply, then added, "Hey, bad things happen to all of us at some time or other; you just have to learn to leave them behind."

"So, did you leave a pack of trouble back in Seattle?"

"A little here, a little there." He laughed again then swallowed the last of his beer.

The chatter stopped as he pushed the paper aside and returned his attention to the photos that allowed him a snapshot glimpse into the life of Rogelio and Lucero Luna, the young couple who made their way to America where they worked and slept and dreamed of a better life for their little boy, Carlos.

"Want another one?" She was already standing next to his chair, holding her empty glass in one hand, picking up his empty bottle with the other.

"Hmmmm. I should probably get going, but okay." He looked up at her and nodded eagerly, "just one more."

"Want some crackers or something?" Bernie headed

for the kitchen and fresh drinks while Don continued gazing at the pictures as if he knew the subjects, studying their faces intently.

"That sounds good. I haven't had dinner yet."

"Me neither, but I don't usually do much for dinner other than crackers or leftover lunch, unless I'm in one of my cooking moods. Then I usually end up taking most of it to Noni and her friends. I don't know how to make just a little bit of spaghetti."

"Well actually, I'm starving. What do you say to forgetting the beer and crackers and we go get some dinner?"

Bernie paused, then quickly returned the cold bottle of beer back to the fridge. "Dinner. That sounds fantastic. How do you feel about Thai food? I bet you like Thai food, and there's a great place not far from . . ." Bernie gasped mid-sentence and blinked slowly. "Oh God, I didn't mean you must like Thai food because you're Asian."

"I love Thai food, and for the record, I'm Vietnamese, Bernie, but my family is actually Irish, and my ex-wife is Greek, so Thai food was rarely on the menu."

"I'm sorry, it's just . . . I don't know. It came out so white and weird and racist, but I really meant that because you seem so Zen, so calm, and I think of Thai as . . . You know what, never mind, my whole foot doesn't fit in my mouth; chalk it up to a bad batch of Pinot or just ignorance. Either one works. God, I really thought I was more enlightened than that."

"Don't worry about it, really. I love Thai food. There are worse things than being called Zen, I guess."

"I'm sorry. For what it's worth, everyone thinks I'm

shy because my face turns bright red when I get embarrassed." Bernie laughed freely, knowing her cheeks were on fire. "Like now. I'm not the least bit shy, but I am humiliated. This shade is humiliation red."

"You have a great laugh; your whole face lights up, and I don't mean that it's red. You should laugh more."

"I laugh plenty." Bernie cast him a shy smile, embarrassed by the compliment. She grabbed her purse and keys, then remembered the copies. "Better take this," she said, handing him the manila envelope. "Copies of the receipts and some other things I thought you might need. I'll drive."

"Thanks." Don tucked the envelope under his arm and made his way outside to wait for her beside her car. When he opened the passenger door, another envelope dropped out. He picked it up and sat it in his lap while he reached behind him for the seatbelt buckle. "This fell out of your car," he told her, holding the envelope up for Bernie to see, but she was already backing out of the driveway and merely glanced at it.

"Oh, thanks. It's probably nothing, but hang onto it, I'll look at it later."

The restaurant only had six tables, and three of them were empty. They sat sipping hot tea, waiting for their mango salad, pad thai noodles, and spicy shrimp and vegetables.

"See? Isn't this Zen?" she asked. Both Bernie's elbows rested on the table, a small cup of tea cupped in her hands.

"Very," Don answered, then sipped from his cup.

"Have you been doing any fishing?" she asked. After all her frenzied efforts at the office, her tired body succumbed to the peaceful aura of the restaurant and the warmth of the hot tea. She felt relaxed.

"That's what I do all weekend. I like to go early in the morning, before the sun is even up."

"That's the best time of day—the crack of dawn. If nothing else exciting happens, you can still say you watched the sun rise. I remember going fishing with my father a few times. I loved that."

She sipped the tea and again recalled her father sitting next to her on the bank of the river, the rising sun turning the dark water to gold, its flow and rhythm the only sound, their silence more comforting than any words could have been.

"It's pretty great. Hey, you want to go up with me, try your luck?"

"What? Go to your cabin with you?"

"Sure. I'm going up Friday evening, coming back Monday morning early."

"No, no, I can't do that." Her back stiffened and she sat taller in her chair.

"Why not?"

"I have too much to do, for one thing. For another, I hardly know you well enough to spend a whole weekend in a cabin with you. And I have stuff going on. Family stuff."

"Sounds like a good reason to go fishing."

"What? Family problems or work?"

"Both. Look, there's plenty of room. It's an old A-frame with a loft for the master bedroom and another small room downstairs. I'll even let you have the loft for privacy."

Bernie knew it wasn't the hot tea that sent the splash of red up her neck and back to her ears. "That's too, I don't know, weird," she said, again relaxing her elbows on the table. "I hardly know you."

"I'm not asking you to sleep with me. I'm asking if you want to go out on the lake and catch some fish, maybe take a hike, sit and read a book or your files while I do some work on the roof."

"You are direct," she said, flinching at the notion of sleeping with the man across the table. It was out of the question, no matter how intriguing it seemed, no matter how much she liked the way he moved and spoke and smiled and laughed. Theirs was a professional relationship.

It had been a long time since Bernie had shared her bed with anyone, and the more time that passed, the more she convinced herself she simply was not all that loveable, at least not romantically. She was attractive enough; that wasn't it, but she had convinced herself that that kind of life was not meant for her. She planned to live the last half of her life uncomplicated, without feeling her body entwined with another, without a *better half*. She told herself time and again that she could be happy without quiet whispers in the night, warm breath on the back of her neck, or gentle fingers stroking her skin. Still . . . she wished she knew *real* love, at least once.

"And you're not?" he said, interrupting her private thoughts. He leaned back in his chair and watched her. The intensity of his gaze made the hair on her forearm stand on end.

"What?" For a brief moment, Bernie feared he had read her thoughts, and knew her secret dreams, and even worse, her heart-aching loneliness.

"Direct. Bold. Don't you think you're a bit bold? It's not a bad thing, you know."

"Yes, I prefer direct and honest, but I never said I

thought you were asking me to sleep with you. It's that spending the night in someone's house that you hardly know is awkward."

"You wouldn't think that if I was another woman."

"Yes, I would."

"You would not."

She liked the way he challenged her without being a bully. He wasn't at all like Randy, her sullen ex-boyfriend who had taken up five too many years of her life. By the time he moved away, she was emotionally drained and too uninterested in the whole idea of love to pursue a new relationship, so she never did. "Well, regardless. I really do have some family stuff to deal with."

"Okay, but you'd feel better about everything if you'd breathe some mountain air."

"Next time," she said.

"I'll hold you to it, but it will be a while; winter's coming. I'll be closing the cabin this weekend."

"Right now, I'm so stressed out I think I'd scare the fish to death. I wouldn't need a pole."

"You're probably right. You kind of scare the hell out of me sometimes."

"Ha, I doubt that," she said, forcing a closed mouth chuckle, not a real laugh, not the kind that pops out freely and bounces around in your head and heart long after it's faded. That kind of laughter was rare. For a moment, the two sat quietly, sipping tea.

Just as the small silence began to feel awkward, the quiet server, her hot pink dress gently clinging to her thin frame, placed a large platter down on the table between them. Sliced mango and pink shrimp were piled on a bed of bright greens. Chopped peanuts covered the steaming pad thai, and the shrimp with vegetables plate was full of plump prawns. It all smelled delicious. The awkward fishing invitation was quickly forgotten as they filled their plates.

For the next hour, the talk centered around food, the preference for peanut sauce to chili sauce, the perfection of the flavors and texture of the pad thai, and eventually it turned to the best restaurants either of them had ever been to.

Don talked for ten minutes about a chicken fried steak he'd had at a place called Threadgill's in Austin. He described the crispy coating over the tender steak, the creamy mashed potatoes and gravy. Bernie argued there was no way it could be as good as the Chinese food she'd had in Wexford, Ireland. She'd spent six weeks traveling around Europe with a friend while she was in college and they vowed to try Chinese food in every country. Emerald Gardens, tucked away in the corner of a small Wexford lane was, hands down, the best food on the planet. Their banter about meals eaten in exotic and remote places would be interrupted to rave about the platters of beautiful food in front of them, offering praises to the server as she filled water glasses, promising her this was the best food they'd ever had anywhere.

"Funny," Bernie said, feeling full and contented at the end of a good meal with good conversation, suddenly more comfortable talking to the dark-haired man across from her than she'd been in a long time. "I can imagine you with a fishing pole, or on a witness stand, or in front of a classroom, but I don't really see you playing music in a rock and roll band."

"Why is that?"

"I don't know; you seem too calm or, I don't know, quiet, for that kind of thing." She leaned closer. "I will definitely not say Zen."

"Ha," he said, amused. "You can say Zen; just don't say I'm a bad driver."

"Ouch," she said.

"Seriously, I can get pretty loud, but not all of our songs are loud. Tell you what, when I get back from my trip up north, I'll bring you a CD."

"You have a CD?"

"Oh, just a demo, nothing you'd get at Rasputin's."

"Still, that's impressive. I'd love to hear it."

"I'll bring it by and maybe we can go to lunch." He watched her closely as he spoke, his gaze focused on her alone. "I like you."

Bernie felt a slight involuntary flutter deep within her chest at his hint of a lunch date. He could just as easily have dropped the CD off in the morning, but he wanted to have lunch with her. She pressed her lips together, and nodded her head. "Yeah, sure, just give me a call when you get back, we'll set something up."

When the server laid the check in front of Don, Bernie tried to grab it away from him, her customary strong will kicking in. "This is official business; I'll get it."

Don held the check up and away from her. "No, I invited you, remember? It's my treat."

"This isn't a date." With an outstretched hand, she refused to give up, refused to give in.

"You're difficult," he reasoned, then leaned back and peered at her through narrowed eyes, as if he were examining a Picasso, trying to make sense of the crazy patterns of color and shapes before him. "Let's split it," he finally said, and handed her the bill.

"Deal." When Bernie reached into her purse for her wallet, she saw the envelope Don had found earlier in the car. She looked at the return address and quickly used a clean chopstick as a letter opener. "This doesn't look good."

"What's that?"

"It must have slipped out of the box when I loaded it in the car. It's to Rogelio and Lucero Luna from the INS."

"Immigration?"

"Yep. And it's in Spanish, of course. My Spanish is pretty limited, good enough for a small conversation, not for legal paperwork." She held the white page in both hands as if she were afraid it would fly up and hit her in the face if she didn't hold it back.

"Let me see it; I know a little Spanish."

She passed him the letter and watched his face, grimacing and twisting, biting his lip as if he was in pain. "Is it the translation or what it says that's making you look like that?"

"I can't be certain; you'll need to have someone interpret for you, but it looks like they were denied residency status, or something like that.

She snatched the letter back from him and studied the letterhead and signature, the only things she understood completely. "Well at least it proves their plan was to remain here, to raise their child here where he is a citizen."

"Look, maybe I'm wrong. One wrong word can change everything."

"I'm not even sure what effect this could have, but I really want this one to be as seamless as possible. I don't want any surprises with this case. Carlos is special."

Don pressed the palms of his hands flat on the table and slowly exhaled, dropping his head slightly to his left shoulder, again closely examining the woman who sat across from him. "There are always surprises, Bernie. You know that better than anyone, and it's still going to go well, no matter what this says. Two people are dead because of a negligent driver and a child is left without parents. Nothing changes that."

"That's true." Bernie pulled two bills from her wallet, a ten and a twenty, and tossed them onto the table. "Still, experience tells me to be aware of Reilly. I don't want him to have any extra ammunition to weaken my case. I objected to every interrogatory that asked for the Lunas' legal status, since citizenship isn't required for access to the court system, so he's probably looking for this very thing."

Don placed a twenty and a five on the table and handed her a five. "Change," he said. "Can you believe how cheap the bill was?"

Bernie stuck the five-dollar bill in her wallet and headed for the door.

"You're right," she said as she backed out of the tight parking space.

"About what?"

"Life is all about surprises," she added pensively.

"You're a tough one to figure out, Ms. Sheridan."

"I've heard that before. Many times, in fact," she added. The faces of past therapists and counselors flooded her memories, haunting images of the days when Noni worried about her bouts of sullen moodiness, rebellion, and anger, always followed by tears and regret. She glanced over at him, expecting his gaze to be fixed on her, but it wasn't. He was looking out the window, up to the sky.

"Well, that just makes you interesting." He kept looking to the sky, as if searching for a lost star or lonely planet.

"What are you looking at?" she asked.

"The stars. It's so clear tonight. A couple of weeks ago, I was driving out on the north end of town and got lost. I had no idea where I was, so I pulled over to the side of the road, found the north star, and navigated my way back home."

"The true GPS system," Bernie said. "That's brilliant."

"Exactly. And you're pretty brilliant yourself. You impress me."

Bernie ignored his compliment. "So, when do you meet with Reilly?" she asked.

"Tomorrow, actually. He has a quad case, sounds interesting." He turned back toward her and away from his search of the heavens.

"He's a bulldog and an ass, but he wins most of his cases, so he's a good client for you to land."

"I've worked with his type before."

"With Stuart Reilly, it's all about winning; nothing gets in his way. Nothing." Even in the darkness of the small car, Bernie could feel him watching her, questioning her.

"You care about winning too," he added.

"Of course I do, but my clients deserve to win. I don't represent big insurance companies and big corporations. I represent people like Carlos Luna and his grandmother. Real people with real damages."

Don tapped his index finger on the dashboard as if punctuating some private thought, something he didn't care to share quite yet. Talk of travel and hints at sharing a cabin were left at the restaurant. As they drove, they spoke of Carlos. Don was curious what she knew about him now, how he was doing with all the changes in his life, if he was happy where he was.

"I don't really know for sure, but I think he'll be happy to come back here for at least a visit. He has a friend, Moochie, and I think he'll like seeing his buddy again." For the rest of the short drive, she told him about Angelica and Moochie, their little house in Madera, her fear that people might want to take advantage of the little boy for his money, and finally how much she wanted to protect him from any more tragedy, even though she knew that was impossible. Life was full of tragedies.

Bernie was still talking about Carlos when she pulled her car slowly into the driveway and turned off the engine. With the turn of a key, the car was silent and dark. No engine turning, no dashboard lights, no sound. It may have only been one second, but for that one second, they sat side by side in her car in her driveway, just breathing, as if they would be there forever, their hands nearly touching. A second more and the silence would grow uncomfortable, but for a short time, it was one of the nicest moments Bernie had experienced in a long time.

Don spoke first. "Well, I'd better get going." They opened their doors and stepped out of the small car and into the darkness. Bernie moved around the front end toward her front door and Don moved toward the back of the car, headed for the curb.

Bernie stopped at the front steps and turned toward him. "Thanks for coming by and getting those papers. Let me know what you come up with."

"Absolutely. And you let me know how things go with that INS thing. It might be a form letter."

"Yeah, we'll see. Good night. Oh, and good luck with Reilly tomorrow."

"Thanks; I'll call you about lunch next week."

"Right, next week." As Bernie closed the door behind her, she realized that she hadn't thought about meeting her birth mother or worried about Noni for hours. She had always been able to bury herself in work and block out problems, but she had never been good at just spending time with someone for any length of time without some straying to the darker corners of her mind, peeking under rugs for some mite of trouble to lure her attention away from the moment at hand. She had to admit, the dinner was business related, but not completely. She liked Don Fielding better than she'd liked anybody for a long time. No matter what, he really was Zen, and that was a good thing.

* * *

The next two weeks were filled with a haze of phone calls, dictation, and endless research. *Stay busy*, Bernie told herself. Don called to say he had a report ready, one she would like. He was going to be away for another week unexpectedly, and she tried not to think about him or their lunch date. Noni called to see if she had heard any more from her Social Services lady. Bernie honestly answered no, then lied and reassured her grandmother that there would be no more contact; she had put an end to it. The whole affair would only cause Noni to worry more than she did now. Bernie regretted ever sharing the details of Joan Bennett's phone call about a lost mother searching for her. Whenever she weakened and dared to explore the idea of the image of a woman with her eyes and mouth, a twenty-years-older version of herself, she would charge into the file room, pull another case from the shelf, and delve into it like a hungry viper.

Starting with the As, Bernie methodically worked her way through the alphabet, dead set on bringing every file current, calling opposing counsel and insurance agents, negotiating settlements, writing firm and compelling demand letters. She had even talked to the Lunas' former employer, confirming what she believed all along. The hard-working couple could have worked for him for as long as they wanted. He liked them. She called Angelica to ask about the INS letter. Angelica knew about an immigration attorney her friends had been to and was sure they had the papers the lawyer needed, and, of course, she had been the one to introduce them to that lawyer, too. She knew many people who had used him before.

It didn't take much effort for Bernie to arrange for a formal letter from the immigration attorney confirming he had agreed to represent them and that he was confident he would be able to get the Lunas permanent residency. In exchange, Bernie promised to pay him his unpaid fee, though she doubted he had done any work for no money, certain he had received in advance a generous retainer. But she was in no position to argue with him. He would be deposed, no doubt, and whatever he said under oath was what she and everyone else would believe.

Crystal was too busy trying to keep up with the flurry

of work Bernie generated to even stop and complain more about her boss's constant buzz of productivity. She too was coming in early, staying late. Despite Bernie's relentless effort to bury herself in other people's problems, she would still catch herself off guard and worry about her own situation. When the flush of heat flashed through her, Bernie wondered if her mother's neck and chest also burned when stressed or overheated. Had her letter yet reached her mother? And in stray moments between work and worry, she caught herself wondering what Don Fielding was doing at that very moment. Was he working in an office somewhere or still closing his cabin? Was he fishing on some river bank or out on a boat? And, she wondered, did he ever think of her in the middle of the day?

Outside, November swirled about the old Gordon Home in a flurry of orange and yellow leaves that skittered down empty streets as the sky grew dark with a promise of rain. When Bernie was a child, she would help her father rake massive piles of leaves out to the road where he would set them on fire. They would stand back and watch the flames dance in the air while the dead leaves crackled and hissed. Bernie loved the smell of smoke and the heat of the fire in the cool evenings as she pedaled her blue Schwinn up and down the block. She wished it was still legal to burn leaves in the street, to breathe in those lost days one more time. Bernie sat at her desk, eyes closed, imagining her dad's voice telling her to step back a little bit more, feeling his hand firm on her shoulder, gripping her tightly, when Crystal opened the door and ended the fading memory of her father.

"I don't think I was supposed to open this." She held the official-looking letter out for Bernie.

"What is it?" she asked, but Bernie already knew. She should have told Crystal not to open anything from Social Services. She just didn't think.

"It's from Joan Bennett. She sent a letter from your . . . your birth mother. I'm sorry Bernie, I just thought it was business. I didn't read the letter." She looked nervous, then added a slant confession that she did: "I didn't know you were adopted."

Bernie could tell she was struggling, wanting to ask more, not sure if she should dare. "It does say personal and confidential in big red letters." She held the envelope up and pointed to the stamped warning.

"A lot of mail says that. You always told me that just means open me first."

Bernie smiled and remembered how she had instructed Crystal to ignore those stamps when she had represented an inmate at San Quentin. He sent her mail constantly, all of it marked personal and confidential. Crystal was right. That's what she'd told her to do.

"It's okay, don't worry about it. I'll tell you all about it someday." She watched Crystal turn for the door, then stopped her, feigning lack of interest in the letter that she held in her hands, a letter from the woman who gave her life. "When are the Lunas getting in?"

"A week from Saturday. I spoke to Angelica Corona this morning. She called to tell me that she's picking them up at the airport, and they're staying with her. She also said Mrs. Luna plans on staying with her until the case is over, through the holidays. I told her we'd be happy to pay for a hotel, but she said Mrs. Luna preferred staying in her home, where Carlos and Moochie could play."

"I figured that. Of course, you can bet Angie Corona will be keeping a tab for when this case settles, so let's offer her expenses in advance. No one does something for nothing these days."

Bernie laid the envelope down on her desk and placed her hand over it protectively. She could feel her pulse quicken and breathed deeply, willing her heart rate to slow, relaxing her jaw, her eyebrows.

"I'll call her tomorrow and work something out."

"Good. Good. Hey, can you close the door on your way out. Thanks, Crystal."

It seemed fitting that the weather had turned chilly for this moment. She picked up the letter and moved to the red sofa. She grabbed her jacket and draped it over her knees like a blanket, hoping the warmth would stop her from trembling.

Ten

1968

"Are you awake? Can you hear me?"

Juicy opened her eyes. The nosey social worker was back before she'd had a chance to figure out how to get Ginny and escape. The drugs made her drowsy, and she'd fallen asleep again. "I'm not giving you my baby," she said flatly. "I can't do that."

"Okay, I thought that would be your answer, and she's your baby, so, for now anyway, it's your decision. But let's talk about your options." The heavy woman pulled the green vinyl chair from the corner closer to Juicy's bed and sat beside her, hands neatly and unnaturally folded in her lap as if waiting for one of the nurses to serve her chamomile tea. "I want to make sure you completely understand your situation, and Ginny's situation."

"Look, I told you what happened. What more do you want?" Juicy's voice was hoarse and raw. Everything hurt; it even hurt to talk, so how the hell was she supposed to get up and find Ginny without causing some kind of commotion?

"Yes, I know you've been through a terrible ordeal. I'm afraid there's a bit of an investigator in me, so while you were sleeping, I took a drive out to a bar, Fat Betty's. It's not too far from here, has quite a reputation. I even talked to Jimmy, the owner. His story about last night was slightly different than what you told me."

"He's not going to say anything to make those guys

mad. They go there all the time. He knows they'd kill him in a heartbeat if he said anything."

"Yes, I figured that out for myself. But Jimmy also mentioned that he'd seen you in there a couple of times before. He mentioned how funny it looked when you were pregnant, riding on the back of a motorcycle."

"So?"

"He seems to believe that you were, well, more of a, shall I say, 'willing participant' in what went on in that trailer, that you were in the bar drinking with Freddie for some time . . . with the baby, too—that you even had her up on the bar in the baby seat. He has your baby seat, by the way; you left it behind."

"It was just a beer. I hadn't been out for weeks." Juicy refused to respond to her mention of the baby seat. She knew where he'd found it, tucked under the table of that hellhole trailer, right where she had left it.

"Yes, I know what it's like with a new baby. I'm just not sure that taking a newborn to a biker bar is such a good idea, but again, that was your decision to make. You're the mother. It's the rest of the story that causes me such difficulty."

Juicy turned her head away, focusing again on the fading watercolor of escape. "I didn't have any choice," she muttered through clenched teeth. Why did she tell this awful woman anything? What was she thinking? It had to be the drugs. She wanted the IV out. No more drugs. She needed a clear head.

"What Jimmy said was that you took Ginny out to the trailer with you and that on the way out there, you were laughing and seemed to be having a good time. Is that what really happened?"

"That's a lie." Juicy slowly turned her head to see her adversary sitting calmly, a phony sympathetic grin on her plump, round face. "I went *willingly* because I didn't have a choice. When I first went out there, I thought it was just going to be Freddie and me, that we were going to, you know, be alone. He didn't tell me the rest of his plan until we were back there. What else could I do?"

"There's something else, something you didn't tell me. It seems the doctor smelled alcohol on the baby's breath, so they ran some blood tests. Why did that baby have alcohol in her system?"

"Oh God," Juicy moaned. "I can't believe this."

"Did someone put liquor in her bottle? The hospital has the bottle, by the way. You brought it in with her things last night."

"Why won't you just leave me alone?"

"You know I can't do that, so why don't you just tell me everything?"

"Why should I? You seem to have it all figured out."

"Don't you see what a predicament your situation puts me in, as a representative of the state? My job is to look out for the child, not you. What's best for the child has to come before what's best for the mother, even if she's injured, even if she's been abused, even if she says she loves her baby. Just like I have to do what's best for my own daughter, even when she doesn't know what that is; I have to figure out what's best for your daughter too."

"But I love my baby."

"Of course, you do. The sad truth is that sometimes I have to remove children from their mothers for their own good. If I think there is even a chance that baby might be in danger, I have to take her, even if her mother loves her more than anything." She leaned her head toward the injured mother, peered directly into her sad, grey eyes. "Don't you see that?"

"I can see you're trying to fuck with me." Juicy felt trapped, tied down by an IV cord, weakened by sore limbs and sedatives.

"I'm trying to give that baby a better life than living with a bunch of Hell's Angels and rapists."

"They're not Angels." Juicy forced her legs over the side of the bed and managed to sit up. Her head was spinning, but she would get out of there. She would get her baby and go. No one could stop her.

"Well, that's an understatement." She offered Juicy a hand to help her stand, but the gesture was ignored.

"You know what I mean."

"I'm trying to. Really, I am. What it comes down to, as far as I'm concerned, is you basically have three choices. One, you can tell the police what happened, so they can do their job and not waste their time chasing some phantom rapist who doesn't exist, change your life, and somehow manage to support and care for an injured baby. It's a big job, and the going to the police part is probably very dangerous, but you can do that. Maybe those men won't come after you or that sweet girl with a broken arm. Or two, you can keep lying to me, yourself, and everyone else, and continue to endanger that baby and see her hurt again, or, God forbid, worse, and eventually lose her to an overburdened foster care system where she might be shuffled from home to home for months or even years. Or three, you can make that hard decision to do what's best for her right now. You can say, I'm not ready to take on this responsibility. You can say, I love her so much I'm going to give her up. You can give her the life she deserves and in turn, give a young couple the life they deserve, the life of a family. You can save your little girl from a life of drudgery and despair. It's all up to you."

The social worker rose to her feet and paced as she continued her dissertation, occasionally pausing to press her fingertips together, bring them up to her lips as if saying grace at dinner.

"An innocent child doesn't deserve to be stashed under a dirty kitchen table while her mother takes on an entire motorcycle gang. She doesn't deserve to be fed a bottle spiked with whiskey. She doesn't deserve to be tossed from a car like a bag of garbage. She doesn't deserve to have a broken arm, cuts and bruises at four months old. She deserves a home with two parents, decent parents, who will love her and each other more with a child in their home."

Like a Pentecostal preacher begging his congregation to see the light and turn to Jesus, she pleaded her case, knowing just when to pause for a heart wrenching moment, allowing the flock to feel the weight of all that sin. A moment to be persuaded. Another moment to drown in years of guilt, to wallow in them to the point of tears. Her voice softened, and she lifted Juicy's trembling fingers into the palm of her soft hand. It was the final desperate altar call, the helping hand of a loving God who has the power to destroy in a bolt of lightning or rumbling earth. "Do what's best for that baby. I will help you. I will help her. If you'll just let me. Let me help you. Otherwise . . ." Her voice trailed off, leaving the alternative to Juicy's own imagination.

Juicy gritted her teeth, laid back down on the bed, and began to cry. Her moans were like a sorrowful song, a grieving mother, a wounded animal trapped and dying. "But I love her. I love her more than anything in the world. You don't understand."

"Then give her the life she deserves. Give her to a stable couple who will give her every opportunity and privilege possible. They will give her what you can't, and you will give them more than you can imagine." She reached out to take Juicy's hand, but the girl jerked it away again, repelled by the touch that had once comforted her.

"The thing is, Julie—that's your real name, I found that out, too—I'm in a bit of a predicament. Like I said, I have to do what's best for the baby. And knowing what I know, I'm not sure that sending an infant with a broken arm off to live with the very parents that caused that injury is best for her."

"I told you it wasn't my fault."

"How you see it, I'm afraid, is not what matters. What matters is that it happened, and it happened while she was in your care. And if you were to leave here with your baby, where would you go? Back to your house? Where all your things are, I would imagine, and that is also where Freddie is. Freddie, the baby's father, the man who fed you to the wolves and tossed his baby out on the road. The one you're not willing to press charges against. So you go home and he's there, and he's sorry, full of promises to change, to be better. What then? What will he do next?"

"I'll figure it out."

"Meanwhile, what about Ginny? She needs medical attention, food, clothing, care. You also need to heal. I see these kinds of cases every day. You won't make it on your

182

own. Not with a baby, you won't."

"I can't just give her away."

"I know it's difficult. But trust me, you'd be making the greatest sacrifice for your child."

"Go away."

"I'll go away. But, you should know the police are in the hall waiting to talk to you. I asked them to let me have a word with you first. You see, I wanted to give you an opportunity to do the right thing. If you persist in lying to the authorities, I will assume your intention is to protect Freddie and his gang and place Ginny at risk, in which case I'll feel duty bound to inform them of the true facts and remove her from your care while the matter is being investigated."

"You can't do that."

"Oh, but I can."

"This is blackmail."

"No. Blackmail involves money. But perhaps we should talk about money. Do you have any money?"

"You know I don't."

"Well, I know this is highly unusual, but I have been told by the parents looking to adopt a baby that they would be willing to pay a bit of a bonus to the mother for her struggles. I think they said they had ten thousand dollars for that purpose. That would give you a nice start. Enough to start fresh somewhere new. If you get far enough away from here, you might turn your life around."

"So," Juicy sniffed and dabbed at her eyes with a corner of the sheet, "what you're saying is you're going to take her away no matter what, but if I let these people adopt her, you'll give me money?"

"Basically, yes."

"Who the fuck are you?" she screamed. "Why are you doing this to me?"

"I'm someone who tries to solve problems." Her spine stiffened, and her chin lifted defensively, ready for any blows the girl could manage. Her terse words shot out rapidly, leaving no room for interruption. "I'm someone who is in a position to help you, to help Ginny, and to help a man and woman who want children, but can't have them. I'm someone who can see that you are hurt, young, poor, and in a volatile relationship, a relationship that should not involve a baby, a relationship that could end in a bigger disaster than this. Give yourself a future. Give Ginny a future. I'm someone who can make that child's life better than you possibly can."

The room fell silent. Juicy drew her knees forward and squeezed them hard, ignoring the pain that shot through her back and stomach, digging her fingers into her flesh, then covered her face with her hands. Finally, she reached for the pink plastic cup on the rolling table, took a sip of water and a deep breath. She licked her chapped lips and brushed a lock of hair behind her ears.

"How soon could I get the money?" She choked on the words and her face and neck flushed crimson. "If I do this, I need to get far away from here. And I have to go now."

"I can give you the money tomorrow. In cash, of course."

"And you know these people?"

"Very well. I know them very well. Your baby will be in an excellent home. She will be loved and cared for."

"Can I meet them?"

"I don't think that's a good idea. You should know as little as possible. I can take care of the paperwork, but it will take a couple of days. Meanwhile, I can put you up in a hotel, under my name. No one will find you."

"Oh God, I can't. What kind of mother just sells her baby?"

"You're not selling your baby. You're giving her a better life and her new parents are simply rewarding you for your courage. It's a noble thing."

No words came out, only a shattering sob as she nodded her head quickly, wiping her nose with the back of her trembling hand. She had agreed to the unimaginable. There was nothing lower than where she had fallen in two short days.

"You're doing the right thing."

"What about the cops?"

"You still have to talk to them. Whatever you tell them is up to you. If it were me, I'd tell them the truth, whatever that is."

Juicy nodded again, her head heavy in defeat. "I want to see Ginny one more time. I have to kiss her good-bye."

"I don't recommend it," Isabelle said, eager to set things in motion, "but I suppose that can be arranged. Pull yourself together, and I'll let the nurses know that you want to go see her."

When the door closed and Juicy was finally alone with her decision, she turned her face to her pillow where she cried and sobbed uncontrollably until a startled nurse came in to calm her, offering her an injection to ease the pain and anxiety. She was the lowest of low, the worst possible kind of whore. What happened at Fat Betty's was nothing compared to what she did in this very room. She watched the nurse inject the drugs into her IV and waited for the drugs to carry her away. The edges of the room softened as her eyes grew heavy, and then it was easy to breathe. There was no pain. There was nothing.

Eleven

2005

Bernie gently pressed the letter to her chest. She closed her eyes, leaned her head back and tried to imagine the woman who had sat and written the words, words meant for her. The sudden lump that rose in her throat and the tightening of her stomach confused her. In her hands, she was holding the same paper that her birth mother had held only days before. She was preparing to read a message from the woman who had carried her in her womb, the same woman who had brought her into this world, but given her away as an infant. For years, she had blamed this stranger for everything wrong in her life, but now she was as giddy and nervous as a schoolgirl receiving a note from the boy across the room.

Bernie reminded herself that she simply had unanswered questions and wanted information from her mother, not some melodramatic, tear-filled mother-and-child reunion. She didn't need a mother at this point in her life. Twenty-five years ago, when the only mom she'd known was taken away, she needed a mother to hold her and love her through the pain. Noni did that. Noni was the one who cared for her as a mother. Her fingers lightly touched the paper, feeling the words before reading them.

The stationary was a pale pink with a single long-stemmed rose across the top. *Pretty*, she thought. Bernie studied the handwriting, an even cursive in blue ink that flowed slightly to the right, flawless and beautiful, just like she'd been taught in third grade. These letters could easily be the same example of cursive handwriting that floated around the classroom near the ceiling, which meant the writer's penmanship was similar to her very own script. Was there some genetic connection in handwriting styles? Or, did they both just follow the rules of cursive prescribed by some unknown handwriting authority?

And finally, forcing herself to breathe, she allowed herself to read the message that, she cringed to admit, she had been waiting to hear all of her life.

My Dear Bernadette,

I can't begin to tell you how happy I was to receive your letter. I thank God for answering a lifetime of prayers.

First, let me tell you that your name is beautiful—though it's not the name I gave you when you were born. It's much nicer than the name I gave you. I guess it was only right that your new parents gave you a new name to go with your new life. By the way, my name is Julie Randall. I don't think you were told that before. The agency is very cautious about giving out details like names, but I want you to know as much as you want to know. I'm sure you want to know things like why I gave you up, who your father is, where you come from. I hope we can meet someday—I'd like to answer all those questions for you, and then maybe you will understand why I let you go. Believe me, it was the hardest thing I ever did, and the only way I got through it all these years was telling myself how much better your life was with other people. From the little I know, I believe it must have been. There is so much I want to say, but I will wait, hopefully, until we meet face to face.

For now, I just want you to know that I have thought of you every day and prayed to God that you were healthy and happy in your life, wherever that may be. I also hope that your arm didn't give you problems as you were growing up. The last time I saw you, you had a hurt arm. And in case you're wondering where I live or anything like that, I'll let you know that for the past thirty-five years I have been living in San Rafael, just north of San Francisco, not too far from you. I work on the Golden Gate Bridge, in one of those little booths, collecting tolls. Some people might think that's a boring job, just taking money from strangers all day, but I've always liked it, looking out over the bay, watching people in their cars, wondering where they're going, wondering if some woman handing me her dollar could possibly be my Ginny heading off to work in the City. That was the name I gave you—Ginny. My husband, Gregory, works for the Post Office and we have two children, Andrew and Lynette. Drew is 30 and Lynette is 28. They know all about you, and they actually helped and encouraged me to try to find you. They would like to meet you someday.

Joan Bennett said she prefers that we first meet in her office, but I think we should do what is easiest for you, whatever you want. I would like that very much, but if you're not ready for that, I understand. I've waited thirty-seven years. I can wait a little longer.

Bernadette, I truly hope your life turned out as wonderful as I hoped and imagined it would. And more than anything, I hope we can meet one day very soon, very soon. I know I don't have the right to expect you to call me your mother; you have another mother who I'm sure loves you more than anything, and I don't want to interfere with that, I don't have any right to, so why don't you just call me Julie.

> *Sincerely and with love,*
> *Julie*

Ginny. Her name was Ginny? Bernie let the page fall toward her and closed her eyes tight as she searched the recesses of her brain for any recollection of that name, some familiar sound. Ginny, Sweet Ginny, Ginny Baby, Ginny Love, Ginny, Ginny.

Some people claimed to remember the trauma of birth, or nursing at their mother's breast. If she really concentrated with all her might, maybe that name would bring some suppressed memory to life. Maybe she would feel something for this woman other than curiosity and an abiding anger confused by loneliness and loss. She closed her eyes and whispered the name quietly, "Ginny, Ginny, Ginny," but the only thing she felt was utterly ridiculous. She knew it was ludicrous to try to remember her life as an infant, and it was even more foolish to believe she might have some kind of a relationship with this woman after thirty-seven years. And, she reminded herself, it didn't matter that Julie couldn't know the trauma that what would happen after she gave away her baby. The simple truth was that Bernie's tumultuous childhood all started with Julie Randall's decision to give her up.

Bernie read the letter through one more time. What did she mean about her arm? No one ever mentioned anything about her being hurt before. Did someone abuse her? Was her mother the one who had hurt her? And how on earth do you walk away from a baby who is injured? With her right hand, she examined her left arm, squeezing and probing from the wrist to the shoulder. She repeated the examination on the right. With eyes closed, she struggled for any past hint of arm pain, an ache in the winter cold, perhaps. Nothing. There was no hint of some lingering trauma that she could detect.

By the time she opened her eyes to read through the letter a third time in search of more clues, again lingering over the name Ginny, the unsettling wave of sentimental curiosity slipped away as the familiar antipathy pulsed silently through her veins. Her thoughts ran wild. *She hopes my life is wonderful? She's living in Marin County, for Christ's sake. I've been to Marin County many times. No one who lives in Marin County suffers. And she's had a family all these years. A real family with a husband, kids, and probably a fucking dog, too. A golden retriever named Lad or Jake. What the hell did I give her my name for? It's not like she won't be able to track me down now. A lawyer with my name can be found in six seconds on the internet. Now she'll be bugging me forever. I can't exactly go into hiding or change my name. Damn. Damn. Damn.*

Bernie forced herself to move off the couch. Her legs and arms felt weighted and heavy as she circled about the small room, unsure what to do with herself for a moment. Her neck and chest were a mottled splash of scarlet, warm with emotion. She should be working, doing something other than this. But for too many years, an unbearable pain had been hers and hers alone. Noni felt it, too; she knew that, but not like her. Even Noni didn't know what it was like to lose your mom and dad in one shattering blow, one black, gut-wrenching blow that still sent her reeling when she dared to think of that day. For some reason, the letter from Julie Randall caused that old wound to open, raw and painful.

Bernie had invested years imagining the rage and fury that consumed her father that afternoon, fretting over what could possibly have driven him to that level of hatred and despair for her mom. He'd been angry for days, but something happened that day that twisted him beyond the threshold of control. He snapped. He snapped hard and lashed out at his wife in a violent rage. What did he do the moment he saw his wife stumble and fall to the bottom of the stairs? Did he cry when he saw his wife's dark blood pooling around her, soaking into the mound of dirty clothes she carried, clothes that never made it to the laundry room? Bernie imagined him turning slowly away, moving to their bedroom, sitting on the edge of the bed, his face frozen in terror, his hand trembling uncontrollably as he lifted the weapon to his own head.

This was Bernie's private hell, imagining the details of that day. It had consumed and haunted her for too many nights of her life. It only seemed fair to share a piece of that hell with Julie Randall, to let her know that Bernie hadn't had the perfect life she imagined for here when she walked away. After all, while she was learning to breathe, eat, and sleep without her mom or dad, Julie was calmly taking quarters, gazing over the San Francisco skyline, probably planning to cook meatloaf or spaghetti for her family. It just might upset her perfect nuclear family living in fucking beautiful Marin, but that was how it had to be. Or at least that was how it was going to be. Julie was going to know what she had done to her child. An arm injury was nothing compared to what came later.

The office seemed too cluttered and close for her to

think. There was plenty of work that had to be done, but she needed to get out, to breathe, to clear her head. She thought of running to Noni, an old habit, showing her the letter, but she wasn't ready for that scene, and she didn't want to upset Noni again. She wanted some time to be irrational and pissed off, and she wanted some time for this to just be her problem.

Bernie grabbed her purse and headed for the front door, calling over her shoulder as she walked out, "Crystal, I'm leaving for a couple of hours. I have something to do." She would drive, just drive. There was something about being behind the wheel, alone, yet not really by yourself. There was a comfort on the road, sitting close to other people, even though those people had no idea of what was going on in the car next to them that made her feel better. She would first take the freeway, play the stereo really loudly to drive away any thoughts other than the pounding drums and screaming guitars. She would sing along and drive until she felt like turning around. Music and driving was good therapy.

"Are you okay?" Crystal asked, jumping up from her desk. "I thought you might want to talk about . . ."

And the door slammed.

As Bernie was opening her car door to leave, the familiar red Toyota pickup pulled into the parking stall beside her. Before the engine was even off, he was opening his door and talking. "Darn, looks like you're headed out. I was hoping we could visit a minute, have that lunch we talked about." He reached in and grabbed a large white envelope. "I also have some engagement letters for you on some of those cases you've been sending over. Thank you, by the way."

"Oh, yeah. Well, you can leave those with Crystal and

I'll mail them back signed." She tossed her purse onto the passenger seat as she spoke, irritated at his unannounced appearance. "You didn't have to hand deliver them. And you were supposed to call, remember?"

"I know that." He flashed a mischievous grin and dipped his chin a little, as if he were trying to be coy. "I should have called first, but I was out and thought maybe you were free today." He looked up at the dark November sky then at his watch. "Wow, you can't even see the sun; I now have no idea what time it is. It might be dinner time for all I know."

"It's around noon, I think." Don's confused smile was annoyingly contagious. Bernie offered a small grin despite her foul mood. "I'm afraid I wouldn't be good company right now. Maybe another time."

He shoved his hands in his pockets and scrunched his shoulders up as a gust of wind swept over them, making him look like a shy fourteen-year-old boy asking a girl to go to the dance. "You sure?" he asked, his voice gentle and concerned. "It might do you some good to have some company. Some food."

Even through her self-induced hysteria, Bernie felt a tug in her chest and one corner of her thin mouth turned upward. She liked him. Despite the rush of wind that whipped around the old house, a warmth spread over her, but it wasn't her flashing temper or burning anxiety that quelled the chill. This was how she felt the night they'd had dinner, sitting quietly in her driveway. It had only been a brief moment, maybe ten seconds, but it was a nice ten seconds. She wanted to know Don Fielding better, much better. They could be friends, but nothing more, she knew. There was no room for anything more in her life. She had managed this long on her own, why complicate her life more than it was? She started to shake her head no and offer another string of reasons why she couldn't go, only to realize she was once again letting some woman who she didn't even know, who she was only connected to by some biological phenomenon, rob her of a small measure of happiness, even if that happiness was no more than a bowl of lentil soup at Joby's Place. She reached inside and retrieved her purse and closed her car door.

"Okay, but I need to be back in an hour. I have a lot going on. You drive."

"One hour it is," he said, and hurried over to the passenger side of his truck to open the door for her.

"You don't have to get my door," she said.

"I was taught otherwise," he answered, holding the door open wide.

Bernie smirked slyly as she edged past him.

The two-seater cab was considerably smaller than the interior of her Subaru, forcing them to sit closely, their bodies nearly touching. "How would you feel about lentil soup?" she asked. "There's this little place not far . . ."

"Way too healthy on a day like this. Besides, you look like you need a serious break, so just sit back and relax. I know a great place. You're going to love it." He looked over at her as he turned the key, his body leaning forward into the steering wheel.

"You open my door and then decide what I want to eat. Are we back in 1955?"

"Sorry. If you'd rather have soup, we can go to your place. But, if you recall, you chose the restaurant and drove the last time. I'm just reciprocating."

Bernie smiled. "Well, I didn't open the door for

you."

"True. You owe me that one."

As Don slid the gearshift knob to reverse, his hand brushed the side of Bernie's leg. His touch seemed electric, as if a shockwave flowed through her leg straight to her heart. She wondered if it was intentional and waited to see if it would happen again. Even after the truck was cruising in fourth gear, Don's hands busy on the wheel, she could feel the warmth of his touch on her thigh. Like most events in her life, she felt things long after the experience. She had learned to keep those feelings to herself, tucked away and private. It was safer.

"Where we going?" she finally asked, a bit alarmed that they were headed in the opposite direction from all the restaurants she knew. They were heading toward the land of cemeteries, the zoo, and a couple of dilapidated liquor stores. She'd been to all three more than once, but never had she ventured to that neighborhood for lunch.

"Don't worry, you'll love it." With the push of a button, the small cab filled with music, loud rock and roll. Just what she'd wanted.

"Oh, Tom Petty. I used to love that song."

"Very good, but that's not Petty." He turned the volume down before going on. "It's actually my band." He looked over at her and added with a wide smile, "That's me singing backup, playing the bass. Hear that? Listen." He sang along, "Take it easy baby, make it last all night." He tapped the wheel with his right index finger.

"You're kidding." Bernie felt her grim demeanor lighten at the sight of him beaming behind the wheel, unashamed to show off his talent. It made her happy to simply watch him sing, his head nodding to the rhythm.

"Why on earth would you quit doing that to come to Fresno and do fancy math for lawyers? No cabin is worth how much fun that must be."

"Well, I didn't, exactly." He turned the music down, but not off. She could still hear him, the perfect harmony of a backup singer.

"What do you mean?"

"Well, I didn't want to seem like a flake before I got everything settled, but I found another band as soon as I got here, actually even before I moved here. This is the new band." He nodded toward the stereo, his eyebrows pointing the way. "I've been playing with these guys for about seven months now. We recorded this CD last week. That's part of the reason I haven't been available for the past couple of weeks. We put a lot of time into rehearsing and then recording."

"Wow. I'm impressed. You guys sound really good." She jutted her lower lip out and nodded in approval, feeling a twinge of excitement for her new friend, even though it had nothing to do with her. She envied those people who did things just because they loved it—painters, singers, musicians, dancers. She couldn't really think of anything that she did just because it made her feel good, just because she loved it. At that moment, she wasn't quite sure if she loved to do anything. "So that CD you were talking about, it wasn't even done?"

"No, I have the old one, too, but it's not as good as this one. I wouldn't lie to you, Bernie."

His vow of honesty struck her; he seemed so, well, honest. And, his promise of truth seemed to involve more than a musical recording. She believed him. If she had some talent, like music or painting, she wondered, would she have been happier, less jaded? Would she be more like Don, at peace with his life?

"So, what do you call yourselves? Your band has a name, don't they?"

Don didn't answer right away; he was watching traffic. A motorcycle cop stood in the middle of the intersection ahead, one hand held out to stop them from passing through the green light, clearing traffic for an approaching white hearse followed by a long line of cars, their lights on in a solidarity of mourning as they made their way to one of the cemeteries that dotted the landscape. Don downshifted as he slowed the truck to a stop. Bernie instinctively pulled her knees away from the gearshift as he gently maneuvered the black ball, avoiding the possible touch she refused to admit she wanted. He shifted the gear to neutral, prepared for a long wait.

"Don't laugh," he said. "It's a little odd, but we call ourselves The Night Shift."

Her thoughts wandered away from band names as she studied the faces of the passing mourners. *Who died*, she wondered. *Someone old who had lived a good, long life or someone who was only getting started on a long list of plans for the future? Who was the deceased to the man and woman who stared straight ahead out the windshield of their white BMW, no sign of conversation between them? What about the family behind them in the silver minivan, two kids in the backseat, their mother turned back toward them? Who died?* She remembered riding in the back of a long black limo, Noni crying softly, an old handkerchief twisted in her fingers, holding Bernie's small hand next to her, where she sat frozen, unable to speak or cry.

"So, do you like it?" he asked.

"What?" His voice pulled her back to the present, to the living, to sounds of music.

"Our name, Night Shift."

"Night Shift? Yeah, I do, but why that? It sounds very, I don't know, eighties." She turned toward Don, away from the funeral procession and sad faces. He seemed oblivious to the caravan of mourners. He was just waiting for traffic to clear, keeping a safe distance from the passing sadness.

"Well, we do play a couple of eighties numbers, but really the thing is we all have day jobs, and this is what we do for fun nights and weekends, our night shift." His fingers drummed the steering wheel.

"I thought you said you spent your weekends up at Huntington fixing up your cabin?" There was a familiar edge in her voice, always on the lookout for inconsistencies.

"I do. I'm just not always alone. Sometimes, we all go up and rehearse up there, do a little work on the place, then we might even play a gig at Trapper's, a bar at Shaver."

"Wow, you never mentioned any of this before." She realized she had pegged him all wrong, imagining him alone, sitting in an old rocker reading books by the fire, sipping a brandy, a fluffy dog at his feet. She struggled to replace that image with a bunch of musicians drinking beer, playing together in a dark bar, surrounded by drunks and eager girls who always like the lead singer the best, but a date with anyone from the band would do.

"Like I said, I was afraid you wouldn't take me seriously as an expert if you thought I was more interested in playing music. It's not that I lied, I just left that part out. I'm telling you now because, well, I'm not trying to get work from you; I'm trying to get to know you and let you know me."

"So," she said, "when you were trying to get me to go up to your cabin, would I have been staying with the guys from Night Shift?"

The procession finally ended, and the cop sped away. Don moved the truck into first gear, glancing over at her as he pulled away from the light, a flicker of a grin appearing. His voice was gentle, almost a whisper. "Oh no, no, no. I'd never put you through anything like that." His smile broadened as he added, "at least not on your first trip."

"Well, thanks for that, at least." For a moment, she just listened to the music and tried to pick out Don's voice from the mix of harmonies.

"So, you're a Tom Petty fan?"

"I guess so, sort of. If we're being honest, I'm really more of a Joni Mitchell fan. I love her." Bernie couldn't help but think of how she would drive Noni crazy playing *Ladies of the Canyon* over and over again. She would pick the needle up from the spinning record to play "Circle Game" four or five times in a row, her squeaky voice singing along, full of raw pain, conjuring up the memory of her mother.

"Ah, Joni is the Queen. What's your favorite song?"

"'My Old Man,'" she lied. "Okay, that's not true. Confession: I really love "'Circle Game'". Bernie watched him nod slowly, a smile on his face.

"It's a beautiful song. My mother used to play that when I was a kid."

"Sounds like you have a good mom." Bernie hadn't listened to the song in a long time, but she could still feel the raw comfort it had given so many years ago. "That's life, a circle game, the past, the present. We can look back, but we can't go there. Children grow up and it goes on."

"I never gave it that much thought, but you're right."

Bernie looked at her side window, considering how much thought she had put into Joni's lyrics, how they saved her in some small way.

"We're here," he said as the truck pulled into the parking lot of the Triangle Drive-In, a holdout from the days when drive-ins were the hangouts for high school kids out cruising Belmont on a hot summer night.

"I didn't even know this place was here," Bernie said. "How'd you make this discovery?" She knew that most folks would speed past a place like this with no temptation to venture inside, preferring the familiar menus of McDonalds or Burger King. But not her. And apparently not Don Fielding. "How have I never seen this place? I mean, I come out this way pretty often."

"This place has the best burgers and fries in California. There's a better place in Arizona, but that would take more than an hour."

She opened the door herself and slipped out of the truck into a blast of cold wind. She pulled her jacket tight around her and hurried to the front door. Don was already there holding it open for her to rush through. They settled into a booth of red vinyl seats around a chipped Formica tabletop.

"This *is* fun," Bernie said, looking around the half empty dining room. Other than a woman having lunch with her son, a kid about ten years old with what seemed to be a fresh cast on his left arm, no names yet scribbled on the clean white plaster, the other diners were men, men who looked like they worked hard for their money, their skin tough and brown from too much sun, their hands thick and calloused.

Most of the men Bernie saw during her days seemed artificially sleek and polished, their muscles developed from a challenging workout at the gym, not from hours of manual labor. Her dad was neither of those types. She couldn't recall him ever worrying about his body, watching what he ate, running laps or lifting weights. He just was what he was. He always looked the same to her, ageless. Her mother was the one who worked hard at looking good, applying makeup and fixing her hair before going to the market, skipping meals and smoking lots of cigarettes to stay thin. Neither of them would ever grow old. She wondered if Julie Randall was beautiful like her mom.

They sat across from each other, their eyes focused on the plastic menus, examining the choices of burgers, sandwiches, and foot-long chili dogs when the waitress scurried over with her pad and pencil, ready to write. "Can I start you off with some drinks?"

"Yeah, I'll have a diet Coke," Bernie said, not bothering to look up, her eyes still fixed on the laminated menu.

"Wait a minute," Don said. "Get a chocolate shake or a lime rickey. You can have a diet coke any old time."

"You have lime rickeys?" she asked, her voice raising with a hint more excitement than she expected. "I want one of those." Her eyes opened wide, grey with a splash of blue, and a happy grin spread across her face as she looked over at Don. "I haven't had one of those since I was a kid."

"They're the best," Don added. "Make that two lime

rickeys." He turned his attention to Bernie. "Are you ready to order? I know what I want, but take your time. I'm in no hurry to get back."

"What are you getting?"

"Cheeseburger and fries. It's ridiculous it's so good."

"Okay, I'll have that, too, but no mayo. I hate mayo." She looked at the waitress and with all earnestness she could muster said, "Please, I don't think I could handle it if my burger came with mayo or Thousand Island or any other strange sauce. I don't want anything on the bun. I'll add my own mustard and ketchup."

"No problem," the young woman added and hurried away.

"'No problem,'" Don mimicked. "Everyone says that these days. 'No problem.' Whatever happened to, 'Thank you,' or, 'Yes, I'll be right back with those drinks,' or 'Absolutely,' or anything at all. All you ever get from anyone today is 'no problem'. It used to be 'have a nice day' that drove me nuts, but now it's 'no problem'."

"You're a strange man," Bernie said, "nice, but strange."

"Oh, you're just getting to know me," he said. "What's sad is that I'm still trying to impress you and destroy my illusion of Zenness with rock and roll and greasy fries."

Bernie grinned at his jab at her comment about him being Zen.

The eager server brought their lime rickeys and sat the drinks down before pulling two straws from her apron pocket. "Your burgers will be right up," she said then bounced over to drop a check on the table of two men in blue work shirts, their names embroidered above the pockets.

"So, what's happening with the Carlos case?"

"Well, mediation is coming up next month, before Christmas sometime, you know that. I will need you there to work out any settlement matters."

"Yeah, Crystal called and told me about it. Don't worry; it's on my calendar. I'm just curious if there's anything new going on."

"Actually, Carlos and his grandmother are flying in next week. Their deps are coming up soon. And if I'm not mistaken, your deposition is being scheduled as well as the driver that hit the Lunas. Right after depositions, like the next day or the next week, I think, is mediation, and hopefully we'll settle there. If not, we go to trial sometime early next year."

"I'm sure you'll settle." He paused to take a sip from his glass, not bothering to use a straw.

Bernie slipped the straw down into the ice and pale-green liquid and took a long drink. "Oh, my God, that's so good."

"Because it's the real deal, a genuine lime rickey, not just a Mountain Dew with a cherry tossed in." Don wiped his mouth with the back of his wrist before reaching for his unopened straw. He looked out over her shoulder to the outdoors. "It's starting to really come down hard out there. That sucks for those people headed out to the cemetery," he said.

"I don't know, rainy days and funerals kind of go together." She was a bit surprised at his comment; he hadn't seemed to even notice the procession earlier as they sat and waited for the long line of cars to pass. "It's just the atmosphere for how they feel."

204

"Are your folks buried around here?" He pulled his straw from the wrapper and slowly lowered it down into his glass, his gaze shifting from the glass to Bernie, back to the glass, and back to Bernie.

"Yeah, over in St. Peters, a bit farther out." She tried to seem unfettered by his question, but the very mention of parents reminded her of the dilemma tucked away in her pocket. She also knew how uncomfortable the whole subject of her dead parents was for people. They want to know everything, but they don't really want to ask. There was an odd sort of pleasure in watching some of them squirm, but ultimately, she ended up feeling like some strange creature in a freak show, so she told them lies, lies to make it easier for them to take, easier than the truth.

"I take my grandmother out there sometimes. She likes to take flowers to my mother's grave on her birthday and holidays. Christmas, Easter, Mother's Day."

"Just for your mother? What about your father?"

"My father's parents died years ago; I barely remember them."

"But don't you and your grandmother visit both of their graves."

Bernie wanted to change the subject and wished the food would arrive. They did really well when they talked about food and work. "Sure, they're buried right next to each other, but, Noni, my grandmother, is my mother's mother, so she's just more emotional about her daughter." She paused for a moment, then added, "She's never really gotten over it."

"I used to come out here when I was in high school. A bunch of us would pile into somebody's car and head out to the Oddfellow's Cemetery late at night. There's this grave out there that's a bed. An honest-to-God concrete bed, full sized I think, pillows and all." He picked up a pack of Sweet N Low and studied the small print before flipping it back and forth between two fingers. "We'd drink a few beers then dare one another to lay down on top of it for like ten seconds or something, I don't remember exactly, but not very long. Then we heard about some girl getting killed out there. They found her body stretched out on the bed." He shook his head from side to side, as if he was still trying to erase the memory after thirty years. "We didn't go out there any more after that. Too creepy."

Bernie looked toward the ceiling and squinted her eyes as she searched back through her memory, back and back, summoning the details of violent and passionate crimes, her specialty. "I remember that," she said. "It was her boyfriend who did it. He found out she was going to break up with him, so he strangled her, or stabbed her, I'm not sure about that part. Anyway, he killed her and then took her out to the cemetery and left her there on that bed." She looked at Don and could almost feel the blood draining from his face and the slight parting of his lips as he listened to her tell of a murder that happened more than twenty years before. "Another crazy love story gone awry," she said. "It happens every day, you know."

That was one of the first articles she'd snipped away from the rest of the daily news. Noni was the one who spotted the story, eagerly carrying the paper to her while she sat doing homework at the kitchen table. "There's one for you," she'd said, "cut that one out." She handed Bernie the kitchen shears and stood at her granddaughter's side, watching her with peculiar excitement, as if she had given her a cherished gift that she couldn't wait to see opened. Bernie cut out the gruesome article and carried it to the Capezio shoe box she first used to store her collection of death stories, while her grandmother proudly took the sliced-up paper back to her spot on the red velvet sofa.

"You know, I probably still have that newspaper article, if you want to see it. I cut it out for some reason; I guess because it was local, and she was about my age, I don't know." She realized she had said too much, mentioning the saved news article buried in a plastic tub beneath her bed. "Anyway, I always wanted to see that grave; maybe you can take me by there."

She watched his expression fill with the familiar pain of sympathy, the slow tilting of the head, the slack jaw. She hated that look.

"What happened to you, Bernie? Why are you so, I don't even know the word, jaded isn't exactly it, sad, I guess, but in a twisted, grim kind of way. You're the successful lawyer one minute, even fun now and again, then, I don't know, bleak or something; I can't figure you out yet. Why are you so sad?" His dark eyes were clear and focused as if he could find the answer if he looked hard and close as she answered, rendering her unable to lie under such a persistent gaze. With one finger, he lightly touched her forearm.

Before Bernie could tell him she wasn't sad, the nervous waitress finally appeared with a plate in each hand, a juicy burger smothered in melted cheddar resting on a French roll with half a plate of golden crinkle fries. She set one down in front of Bernie, the other in front of Don.

"Can we have some ketchup?" Bernie asked, grateful

to retreat to safety of discussing the content of lunch, a half-pound of meat on white bread with a side of potatoes fried in vegetable oil.

"No problem," the girl said, pulling a bottle of ketchup from the table behind them and setting it between the two plates before spinning on her heels and heading fast for the kitchen.

Bernie looked at him and smiled weakly, urging the somber mood to shatter, "Your favorite response," she said, then lifted the bun to a thick spread of creamy mayonnaise. "Ugh, it's ruined," she moaned and dropped the oily bun back down onto the plate, knocking her knife and fork clamoring to the floor in the process. "Now I'm sad."

"Wait a minute, wait a minute, don't get excited, don't have a conniption, this one's yours. There's nothing on it." Don reached over and pulled her plate toward him, replacing it with his own. "See, good things happen; like this burger."

Don slapped the label on the ketchup bottle to get it flowing. "You know, speaking of clipping news articles, I meant to ask you if you saw the follow-up article about that girl who set the fires in the mountains."

"What girl?" She picked up a French fry and folded it into her mouth. It was almost too hot to eat, but a quick sip of lime rickey solved the problem.

"Remember, the story you cut out. She had written a letter to the judge that you liked, so you cut it out."

"Oh, yeah yeah yeah," she said, happy to talk about other people's traumatic situations rather than her own. For a moment, she had worried this would turn into another struggle for information about her private life, and like he said, not mentioning something is not lying. She really didn't want to lie to him.

"Well, she stole it. She got that whole spiel from some novel; apparently she's a plagiarizer as well as an arsonist."

"You're kidding."

"Nope. Someone read the letter and recognized it. I meant to call you and ask you if you'd seen the story. See? You can't believe everything you read."

"And, the world is full of liars. Everybody lies sometimes." She didn't care that the story was stolen. She didn't care that someone wrote those words as a piece of fiction. They still rang true for her and she would keep them tucked away with all the other rueful tales.

They each took big bites and for the next five minutes, the only thing they talked about was their lunch, the preference for crinkle fries to shoestrings, occasionally curly fries, but not often, the perfection of the burger, the bun, and the unmentionable fat and calories they were consuming. And finally, all they could do was moan in pleasure as their bellies filled.

"Boy, it's really coming down now," Don said, swirling a long fry into his ketchup, while the rain slapped against the wall of windows.

"Yeah, it's dark. It's like it's nighttime in the middle of the day." Bernie had stopped eating and pushed her plate to the side to keep from finishing the last handful of uneaten fries.

"Hey, I have an idea." Don leaned forward, as if he were about to share a secret. "Let's play hooky this afternoon. We'll get an old movie, build a fire, and just hang out. You can call in well." He smiled at his own joke. "You know, instead of sick."

"I get it. But, I can't do that. Geez, I've been gone too long already." She looked at her watch and realized it had been over an hour since she left the office. "Crystal's probably freaking out with this weather. We have an office ghost, you know."

"A ghost?"

"Yep. Old Mrs. Gordon roams around upstairs while we're working. Floors creak, doors slam mysteriously. And, occasionally she steals files. But she always returns them. I think she just gets bored, so she messes with things."

"You don't really believe that do you?" He seemed amused at her ghost story.

"I don't know. There have been some pretty strange things, but no, I don't think it's a ghost. I think it's a busy office and sometimes I don't remember where I put things and it's an old house that creaks and groans, and sometimes doors catch a draft of air from below and swing closed. But Crystal is afraid of Mrs. Gordon on rainy days. I need to get back and protect her."

"Oh, come on, she'll be okay."

"No, not today. Like I said, I've got a lot going on, and I need to work." It was tempting to avoid dealing with the message from Julie Randall. But she was the one that had sent the first letter, and she needed to plan her next move.

"Alright, go on, be responsible."

"Rain check," she said, then added "since it's raining."

"No problem," he answered, drumming his fingers on the table, *pa dump um*, a jab of comedy backbeat with a teasing grin.

"You know what we could do for a bit of fun, if you don't mind. On the way back, will you take me by that grave, the one that's a bed? I'd like to see it. What's a few more minutes?"

"Sure, I'll take you there. If I can find it; it's been years." He raised a finger to the waitress, signaling her to bring the check.

Twelve

1968

Juicy looked down into the crib and let the tears roll down her cheeks. How could she have let this happen? Her baby's right eye was swollen and purple, and the right side of her head was covered with a large gauze bandage. Her little cheek had scratches and abrasions, freshly cleaned and shiny with some antibacterial ointment. The worst thing was her tiny right arm sealed in a plaster cast, bound with a sling to keep her from flailing it about. She slept now, her breathing heavy from exhaustion and probably pain medication, but Juicy remembered how she had screamed in agony, how she'd picked her injured baby up so fast she'd probably hurt her even more, the dirt and blood that stuck to her scalp. What kind of mother lets her baby end up like this? Mrs. Fiero was right. It was her fault.

A nurse remained in the room with her, silently writing notes in a chart. Juicy could tell by the way the woman peered over at her that she blamed her, too. The nurse would know this was all Juicy's fault and that she was giving her baby away to someone who deserved to be a mother. Juicy could feel the shifting eyes that studied her from head to toe before looking away and the flash of a phony smile.

"Will she be okay?" Juicy finally asked. "I mean, her head is hurt. Is that serious?"

The nurse turned away from her paperwork and moved alongside Juicy. "The doctor seems to think she'll heal quickly. You know, those little bodies can handle more than we think they can. They're small, but they're strong and resilient."

"I'm so sorry," Juicy whispered, stroking her baby's chubby leg. "I'm so sorry. For everything." She looked at the nurse closely, her eyes pleading for mercy, though she herself didn't feel she deserved the kindness she sought. "Can I hold her? Please, just for a moment. Please. I won't hurt her."

"She's very tender, but you know that." She looked toward the door, as if she expected someone to walk in. "Okay, what I want you to do is sit in this chair." She nodded toward the green vinyl chair in the corner. "I'll hand her to you. You don't seem too steady on your feet, and I'd hate for you to fall down with her in your arms."

Juicy sat and watched the young nurse gently lift the sleeping child from her bed and hand her over to her waiting arms. Her body was warm and heavy with sound sleep. She smelled different, the scent of Phisohex instead of Baby Magic drifting from her head. Juicy closed her eyes and tried to take in every detail of her daughter, imagining her in six months, six years, going to school, riding a bike, falling down and running to her with teary eyes and skinned knees. She tried to give her all the love in one moment that she would need a lifetime to give. She wanted her to have a life filled with birthday parties, swing sets, Barbies, Easter dresses in the spring, and mugs of hot chocolate on cold winter nights. She wanted her baby to have two parents that loved and cared for her as much as Juicy did right now, but parents that could give her things Juicy could not, parents that could pamper and spoil their baby in every way. God knows she wanted to do that herself, but that vicious social worker was right. She would probably just end up screwing this little girl's life up, too, like she had her own. She was a loser, a monster, a fuck up. She had shoved her baby under a table while she screwed a bar full of disgusting men, and why? Because her boyfriend told her to. Because he stole a little bit of money from his friends and he'd rather give her up than face their wrath. Her life had been shattered for a measly hundred and fifty-five dollars. She didn't deserve to be loved by this child, or anyone, for that matter.

Juicy rocked back and forth in the stiff chair and gently placed her lips onto Ginny's soft hair. Little curls wisped around her ears and at the nape of her neck. "You're too beautiful for me," she whispered, breathing in the scent of the sleeping child. "I'm going to give you something better than me." She kissed her small forehead and lightly touched her soft skin, running her fingertip down her nose. The baby stirred and let out a little cry. "Shhhhh," she said. "Sleep, little Baby Girl. Sleep."

Tears welled in Juicy's eyes and one spilled onto the baby's head. "Don't ever think I didn't love you, please. I do love you. I do." Juicy rested her cheek lightly against the baby's forehead and closed her eyes again. "I'll never forget you, Sweet Ginny. I'll never forget you." For a long time, she quietly rocked and held her, careful not to hold her daughter too tightly for fear of hurting her any more than she already was. She folded Ginny's tiny fingers around her index finger and swore she'd remember the way that felt and looked for the rest of her life.

"Ma'am, she really should be back in her bed." The

nurse touched Juicy on the arm and bent close to her. "Why don't I take her from you now?" She slowly slid her hands under the baby's neck and bottom and lifted her out of Juicy's arms. "Here we go, Angel, back to bed."

Juicy sat in the chair, her empty arms frozen in the curve of a sleeping baby. She wept silently, but her arms would not move. She could not lift a hand to wipe the tears or reach for a tissue. The tears ran down her cheek, and her chest heaved and shook uncontrollably as snot ran from her nose and onto her lips. Still, she could not move her trembling hands. The nurse came to her, placed one arm around her shoulder and another firmly on her forearm. "Come on, Honey. She'll be fine. You need to take care of yourself now." She guided Juicy up from the chair and placed tissues in her hands, then physically lifted the weeping woman's hands to her face to wipe away her tears. The kind nurse gripped Juicy's arm, keeping her steady, keeping her upright and connected to another human being.

Slowly, Juicy regained some control and the nurse let go of her, allowing her to stand on her own. Juicy moved close to the crib, placed one hand on her baby's chest and said one last time, "I love you, Baby Girl. Good-bye for now."

Thirteen
2005

Bernie leaned back in her chair and watched sheets of rain lash against her window. The letter from Julie Randall rested on top of the Luna file. She needed to put the intriguing letter and the lunch she enjoyed with Don out of her mind and get to work. It was time to focus on building a list of probing questions for Thursday's depositions, not wallow in daydreams and fantasies.

The downpour outside offered a few minutes of distraction to allow everything from the day to settle and dissipate. For years, the most exciting things in her life were the battles of her clients, taking on their struggles as her own. She'd worked hard to keep a safe distance from the dangers of intimacy. Now, it seemed the threads of her carefully stitched cocoon were being stretched to the limit. Any minute now, one weak spot would snap and the whole thing would unravel and fall apart. There she'd be, naked to the world. Everyone would know she was just as scared and lonely as they were.

It seemed ironic that Julie Randall and Don should both drop into her life at the same time, the same day, even. It was too much, she reasoned, but she wasn't ready to turn either one away. Julie Randall was still a mystery, and the more she learned of Don Fielding, the more she wanted to know. The only thing to do was turn the page, keep digging at what was and what might be. A flash of lightning lit the dark sky, thundering loudly.

Don had inched his small truck through the gloomy

cemetery then parked along the curb next to the old concrete bed, its pillow and comforter immune to the pounding rain and howling wind. It stood solid and cold, an image of rest in a garden of headstones and brass name plates.

"It's just like I pictured it," Bernie said.

"It's creepy, isn't it?" Don said.

"I don't know. I guess if I wanted to be buried, I might like the idea of having some unique marker, but I don't like graves. I want to be cremated."

"Me too. Or just tossed in a hole, earth to earth," he said.

"You mean dust to dust."

"Yeah, sort of, but I like the idea of turning into rich dark soil, the kind that grows good tomatoes. People are always getting rid of dust."

"Hmmm. I never thought of it that way. I think you're right. Earth to earth."

There was no witty banter, and when they spoke, they spoke in hushed tones, respectful of the company of the dead. Inside the small cab, the windshield wipers chided their idle time, swoosh . . . slap . . . swoosh . . . slap, while the rhythm of raindrops and a hum of the engine filled in a backbeat. For a long while, they sat quietly, almost reverently.

Turning into garden soil. Bernie liked that. Her father liked to garden. He took a week off in the spring, her spring break, and together they would plant zucchini, tomatoes, bell peppers, and eggplant. All summer, her mother would plan meals around their homegrown vegetables. She would send Bernie out to the garden with a basket and tell her to pick their dinner. From that basket would come pots of Ratatouille, spaghetti, sliced tomato sandwiches, and fresh salsa. It was all delicious. She wished her mom and dad could have turned to earth. They both would have liked that. She wished they were at home eating a plate of ratatouille right now.

It was the mother she didn't know, the one who wrote to her on pretty pink stationary, that confounded her. How different her life would have been if only Julie had not given her away. After years of blaming an unknown woman for her traumatic childhood, Bernie realized that her simple criticism might be faulty. That version of truth was now muddied with words on pink paper. Julie was out there, a real person, a woman who collected bridge tolls, a mother to two other people. Bernie bit her lower lip as she gazed out at the steady rain pelting rows of headstones and monuments. She couldn't help but think of her first ride in a limousine, a slow drive to a different cemetery twenty-five years earlier.

Staring out the window at the field of buried lives, dozens of dead mothers and fathers, Bernie wished she could talk to Don about her struggling emotions. She wanted to hear what he thought of her "if not for her" reasoning and the potential to actually meet her birth mother. Would meeting Julie Randall be opening a Pandora's Box of trouble, or would Bernie get insight that would choke out some of those burning embers? Maybe Don would see things only an outsider can see.

* * * *

Crystal knocked on the door as she walked in, disrupting Bernie's daydream. "I'm getting ready to go, thought I'd better check if you need anything."

"Oh, no. I'm set." She tapped the stack of files in front of her and slipped the letter into her desk drawer. "Did you get a court reporter for tomorrow?"

"Yes. I confirmed with everybody; they'll be here at 10:00."

"Good job." Bernie knew she didn't even have to ask if Crystal had done these things. It would always be done before Bernie ever thought of it. But this was their ritual at the end of each day, and this was the kind of comfort that kept Bernie's world in order, as she liked it to be.

"Are you going to work late here or take that stuff home?"

"Oh, I don't know. I think I'll stick around for a bit, wait for traffic to die down."

"Are you sure you don't need anything? I'm not in any hurry tonight."

Crystal wanted to talk to her, to get her boss to confide in her and share details hinted at by the confidential letter. Bernie knew that. She knew Crystal wanted to know about Julie Randall, the lies, the truth, or whatever the story was. But to tell Crystal now would be to snip that last thread, and she wasn't ready to be standing emotionally naked in her office on a dreary rainy night. *In time*, she thought, *in time*. But not now, not tonight. "Nope, I'm pretty well set. You go on home."

"Okay. Well, good night then. Don't forget to set the alarm."

Bernie sat and listened to the storm rumbling outside, gusts of wind and steady rain. Occasionally, a roll of thunder would sound in the distance. This was her favorite kind of storm, loud and full of electricity and power. Even as a child, she wasn't afraid of the howling wind and shafts of lightning. She would wrap a blanket around her shoulders and lie down next to the sliding glass door to see how black the sky could be, waiting for a flash of light. Her mother used to tell her she was a natural-born weather girl, but Bernie knew even then that she wasn't perky enough for that job. She picked up a pen to draft an outline of questions for the following day just as a loud crack of thunder rumbled through the house, followed by a sudden blackness.

"Shit," she said. She sat motionless for a moment, waiting to see if it was a blip of some kind, a dark pause to be followed by a sudden flash of light and buzzing electronics. But the room remained pitch black, no light anywhere, the constant rain the only sound. There was no telling how long it would take PG&E to get the lights back on.

"Shit, shit, shit," she said again, realizing the situation was far beyond her control. The universe was clearly making all decisions for her these days. No work would be done in a cold, dark office; she had to go home. Even if there was no power at her house, there she had candles and a fireplace. Bernie reached down and fumbled for her purse and keys, wishing she kept a flashlight in her desk instead of in the supply room. She pulled her jacket on and felt for the file she was working on, but opted to leave it behind. She could prepare for a driver deposition blindfolded, which it seemed she was. She inched her way out from behind her desk and moved slowly toward the door.

Bernie closed her eyes to navigate the dark office, measuring her steps, estimating the distance between her stretched-out arms and the wall, the door, the fragile lamp on the end table in the waiting area. She was comfortable in the self-inflicted blindness. Even as a child, when a full bladder woke her from her dreams, she would slowly inch her way down the dark hallway with her eyes tightly closed to the darkness of night. Only when her hands could feel the doorway and then the light switch would she open them to the light.

She opened the front door and her eyes as she stepped out onto the porch where sheets of rain blew under the shelter and stung her skin. She turned and locked the door and realized she had not set the alarm. How could she in the dark? She thought of giving it a try, feeling the numbers, her fingers moving rapidly and automatically without the need of sight, but the cold wind was slicing through her; she just wanted to get home. The darned thing probably didn't work in a power outage anyway, not to mention that it was too cold and wet for thieves and prowlers to be scurrying about. "Keep an eye on things, Mrs. Gordon," she called from the bottom step, and with her head down and her coat pulled tightly around her, she hurried to her car as fast as she could.

The steady stream of headlights splashed off the roadways as traffic stalled and stopped at every intersection where drivers struggled to take their turns without the aid of signal lights. Left to their own will, there was uncertainty and hesitation about when to move forward, when to yield. The rain had eased off and now fell only lightly, but the city was waterlogged after the day of cloud bursts and downpours. Bernie listened to the slapping windshield wipers and again thought of Don and their visit to a stranger's grave, a concrete bed with ruffles and a pillow for headstone. *That man is entirely comfortable in his skin*, she thought. Why his wife divorced him, Bernie could not begin to imagine. "Mrs. Fielding," she said to no one, "you must have been crazy to let that one get away." She must have found someone else, Bernie reasoned. Don was smart, creative, gentle, and kind. It had to be the wife. No doubt she broke his heart.

It wasn't a Friday, but on such a black and bitter night, Bernie felt compelled to drive to the Nazareth House and the comfort of Noni, even if it was a brief visit. Guilt consumed her. She had stayed away from the old folks' residence for nearly three weeks. Of course, she had called, complained to her grandmother about an intense workload, and made up a story about a terrible head cold that she didn't want to share. But the truth was she didn't want to talk about Julie Randall or lie about the letter she had sent or the one she carried home in her purse. The trip to the cemetery had reminded her of how much Noni had given up for her, how much she had now because of her grandmother's endless hovering. Two blocks away, there was electricity; the traffic signal blinked from green to yellow to red, and beyond that the mission-style residence seemed to glow in the night.

Sister Rose was in her office and Bernie nodded to her as she passed the open door.

"Bernadette," Sister Rose called. "Can I speak with you for a moment?"

Bernie turned back at the sound of her name and leaned into the administrator's doorway. "Hi Sister Rose."

"Good evening, Bernadette. Come in and sit down, please." She stood and motioned toward a rust-colored Queen Anne chair near her desk.

"I'd better take my coat off; it's pretty wet out there."

"Yes, I'm surprised to see you here."

"I was on my way home and thought I'd check in on my grandmother. See if she was okay in this storm." Sitting in the small office, faced with a large crucifix on the wall and a statue of Mary on the desk, reminded Bernie of her days at Saint Helen's School. She had given up on church years ago, but the rituals, prayers, smells, and symbols were etched in her brain forever. Noni had made sure of that.

"I'm glad you did; I've been wanting to talk to you." The plump sister smiled weakly. "I'm worried about your grandmother; she's not been herself lately."

"What's wrong?"

"It's been going on for several weeks now. She's withdrawn and unusually cranky, which isn't like her at all. For one thing, she yelled at Lolly Granger and told her to never enter her room again. They have been friends for a long time, even before coming to Nazareth House."

Bernie felt a stab of guilt, sudden and sharp, just under the ribs. "You're right; that doesn't sound like her, but she did complain a few weeks ago that Lolly had taken her favorite candy or something silly like that. It could just be a petty squabble. A bit of kid stuff, you know." She reached into her purse for a handkerchief and dabbed at her face, still damp with rain.

"It's more than petty squabbles, dear. She has not been to the dining hall, preferring to eat her meals alone. That is one of her favorite times, socializing with the other residents at dinner." The kind Sister was concerned, her familiar smile nowhere to be seen.

"I had no idea." Bernie tried to think of the last phone call she had with Noni. Was it Monday? Tuesday? She wasn't sure. Noni was quiet, but Bernie didn't think much of it at the time. She knew what the problem was, and, as usual, it was all her fault.

"I called the doctor in to make sure it wasn't a flu or something, and he examined her, but she is fine physically. I asked Father Milton to speak to her, and—this is what is most troubling—she refused to see him. She told him she wasn't in a mood to talk. Until this started—well, you know—your grandmother never missed mass if she was well enough to go. She has not been for several days and she is not sick. Do you know what is bothering her, Bernadette? Can you help us?"

"I . . . I think I know, and, look, don't worry, Sister Rose." Bernie scooted forward in the chair; she'd heard enough. "It will be fine. I'm going to go talk to her right now. It will be fine." She stood and held her hand out to the nun, who gladly took hold. "Thank you, Sister, for letting me know. I'm going to take her home for a weekend soon. For Thanksgiving. That will boost her spirits." With the flash of a sincere smile, Bernie hurried out of the nun's office.

It was her fault. She should never have told Noni about the phone call from Joan Bennett and her birth mother's search to find her long lost child. She should have told Joan Bennett to go away the first time she called. She should have known how upsetting all this would be to Noni and never breathed a word about it. Noni had spent years making sure Bernie understood what a wonderful mother she had, wanting her memory to live on as the only mother Bernie had ever needed, the one she loved. It was Bernie who had fought to remember her father, a good man deemed forever unmentionable in one failed moment. But her mom, Noni's daughter, Noni's greatest loss, should not be replaced by a stranger who had abandoned her, no matter what the reason, no matter how many years had passed.

Bernie peeked into the room. Noni was sitting in her motorized chair at a small table staring at a pink plastic tray of food, mostly untouched. For the first time, she looked old, really old. "Hi-ya Gorgeous," Bernie said, tapping lightly on the door frame.

"Bernadette. What's wrong? It's not Friday, is it?" Her sad eyes seemed to light up at the sight of her granddaughter. "You're all wet, you've been out without an umbrella again, haven't you?" She pushed a switch and her chair eased away from the table in reverse before moving toward her visitor.

Bernie stroked Noni's thin grey hair and kissed her on the forehead. "I just missed you, and I was feeling better, so I thought I'd stop by. Whatcha eatin'?"

"Oh, it's just some chicken and broccoli, not very good tonight. Or perhaps I'm not hungry; do you want it?" She reached her hand out for the tray only to have it intercepted by Bernie.

"No, I'm not hungry. I had a big lunch today." Bernie kissed the thin hand, felt its warmth, the thin skin barely covering the dark veins.

"Well, if you get hungry, it's there." She pulled her hand away and touched her lips, as though she feared there might be food or a bit of drool, the slight tremble betraying her advanced age.

"Noni, you seem kind of down. Are you okay?" Bernie scanned the room, looking for signs of change, but it all seemed the same. It was Noni that was different, smaller, as if a slow leak was draining her spirit away.

"I'm fine, just a little tired. Did that silly woman, Lolly, call you, or something?"

"No, why? Did something happen with Lolly?" The glint of anger made Bernie smile; that was the Noni she knew and loved.

"Oh, I caught her with her greedy fingers in my candy dish, so I told her to stay out of my room. She got mad and went and told Sister that I was mean to her." She rolled her eyes and flung her hands up and down. "She even sent the Father after me."

"Well, don't worry about it. She'll get over it." Bernie offered only a weak smile; she had never seen her grandmother's eyes seem so cloudy, set in dark circles and heavy lines. She seemed frail, as if a good squeeze would crumble her into a pile of sawdust. "I thought you should know that I thought about the call from that social worker, you know, about the woman who thinks she's my birth mother?"

"Oh." Her trembling chin lifted slightly at the mention of birth mother. "Are you going to see her?"

"You know, I don't see any reason to change things now, not at this point in my life. I had the best mother and grandmother anyone could want." She wanted to say father too, but she knew that would only release more turmoil. "I don't need to know anything about why this woman felt the need to give me away. It would just bring up more problems and issues than I care to deal with. I think it's better that I just remember Mom. She's my real mother. Besides you, that is." She moved closer to Noni, stood beside her chair, bent down and wrapped her arms around the fragile shoulders, pulling her close to her, kissing her head. "You were like a mom to me, too. Hell, Noni, you've been my mother, father, grandmother, sister, brother, friend, and sometimes even God to me. I think that's enough for me." She kneeled down and looked closely into Noni's eyes. "I love you, Noni. Please take care of yourself. Please don't give up on me."

Noni reached up and patted Bernie's arm. "Bernadette, I don't deserve you."

"I know, you deserve better." She got up from her knees and took her place in the seat of faded roses.

"Did you go to work dressed like that?"

"Yes, why? What's wrong with my outfit?" She looked down at her khaki canvas pants, big pockets along the side, perfect for holding her cell phone and PDA, and her chocolate turtleneck, soft and warm on a rainy day, her feet tucked in leather clogs. "It's cute. And comfy."

"But you're a lawyer. You should be wearing nice suits to work. When I was a working woman I bought my suits at I. Magnin." She smacked her lips together. "Downtown. Too bad we don't have that store anymore. I could take you to shop there, get you some nice business suits to wear."

"Oh, Noni, you're too much."

Bernie curled up in the comfortable rose-patterned chair, ready for a long visit. She would not jeopardize Noni's health with her childish curiosity. It was her turn to be there for Noni, to sacrifice for her. "Hey, Noni, guess what."

"What?"

"I met a guy." Bernie knew the one subject that would cheer her grandmother, the hope of Bernie with a family. Noni was always interested to hear about Bernie's personal life, eager to know if she had a boyfriend. Of course, no one was ever quite right, and there would be endless hours of finding fault with whoever Bernie mentioned, but still,

Noni wanted to see her granddaughter settle down, have a family, a fairytale ending.

"Oh, now that's news. Who is he?"

"Well, he's just a friend right now. But, let's say he's a friend of special interest. And he's kind of cute."

"Is he a lawyer?"

"No, an accountant of sorts. He's an economist. And a musician; he plays guitar and sings in a band." Bernie knew that would get a rise out of her.

"What?"

"He works as an economist, but he also plays in a band on the side."

"Oh, Bernie. He's a big kid. Those are the ones who don't know how to grow up. Be careful with that one."

"I'm careful, Noni." She could see Noni returning to her old self, doting and worrying over her, shaking her head, grinning ever so slightly, a hint of mischief in her eyes.

"What's he look like? Is he tall, dark, and handsome like Clark Gable? You know he's my favorite. Clark Gable." Noni lifted her eyes to the heavens and smiled sweetly with the mention of the movie star's name.

"Actually, he's Vietnamese so he doesn't look much like Clark Gable, but he's dark and handsome. He's not really tall, but tall enough." She scrunched up her nose trying to recall how tall he actually is, shook her head in confusion, then dragged her fingers through her wet hair. "I think we're the same height. I haven't been close enough to check that out. I definitely have a bigger butt."

"What?" She feigned exasperation. "Bernadette, shame on you."

"All I know is that he's different from most other men

I work with. Most lawyers are just jerks. Like me." Bernie flashed her eyes and smiled brightly, working to entertain the old woman.

"Phhhhhhhh. . ." Noni chuckled and wagged her index finger at her granddaughter.

"I told you, he's just a friend right now, and I do like him. I mean I enjoy his company; we've had a couple meals together is all."

"Hmmmm Hmmmm." She nodded knowingly, as if she had heard this speech a hundred times, which she had over the years.

"I was thinking I might bring him to meet you sometime, or even better, have you come home for Thanksgiving weekend. He can come over and meet you then." Bernie was making plans and creating a friendlier relationship with Don than existed as the words left her mouth. She just wanted to cheer her grandmother up, give her something else to worry about other than the possibility of a strange woman coming in to steal away her dead daughter's memory.

"What's this short friend's name?" Her wry sense of humor was showing itself at last, and Bernie smiled.

"He's not short, just not *tall*. His name is Don Fielding. Sounds so sophisticated, like a movie star name."

"Well I hear a lot of movie stars aren't as tall as they seem. I think Frank Sinatra was a shorty."

"Yeah, well, Don's not a movie star like Frank and I don't know how tall he is, but he's around my height, so enough about how tall he is. Here's what's interesting. He was adopted, too. I guess there's some kind of adopted radar out there or something."

"Does he know about . . . about your. . .?" Her smile vanished, and her hands shook as her fingers fumbled with the fabric of her dressing gown, twitching and plucking at the folds.

"No," Bernie answered calmly, wanting desperately to hold on to her grandmother's hands to keep them still, but she knew better. She knew the constant movement helped control the involuntary tremors. "He knows my parents died, but I told him they died in a car accident. It's just easier to say that, Noni. No one needs to know what really happened."

Noni nodded her head and looked out the window at the darkness, where the rain continued to fall. "It's bad out there. You better not stay long tonight. You can come back Friday."

Bernie sat with Noni a few minutes more, told her about the lights going out on the other side of town, about the lime rickey she'd had at lunch with Don, about the stacks of files she'd been going through, and a little bit about her favorite case these days, the Luna case. The image of Carlos and Moochie grinning into the camera continued to haunt her. Two little boys having fun, innocent and unprepared for the harshness of their futures. She wished she could spare them, freeze them in the moment and joy of the flashing camera.

Bernie gave a gentle hug to say good-bye. "I'll be back on Friday and then on Wednesday to pick you up. I want you to spend the whole weekend with me, help me cook a big meal."

"That would be nice, but I don't want to be in your way."

"That's impossible. Now, get some rest, and make up

with Lolly." Bernie kissed her grandmother's hand and left the old woman happier than she'd been earlier that evening. She was confident that Noni would be back in the dining hall at breakfast, sitting with Lolly and the other women, sipping Earl Grey tea, bragging about her recent visit with Bernadette, her granddaughter the lawyer, who was taking her home for Thanksgiving weekend. Under the table, she would slip Lolly a caramel, and their tiff would be forgotten. *Old children*, Bernadette thought.

It was eerie driving down her familiar street, the houses dark except for the occasional glow of candlelight and the reflection of her car lights on the wet blacktop. There were no streetlights, no porchlights blazing as beacons for the weary traveler searching for home. She pulled into her driveway and made a mad dash through the rain for the front door and managed to get the key in the lock with little trouble. She'd been unlocking that door for most of her life; she didn't need a porchlight to feel the key slide in, to turn the key left and give a slight push and hear the brass knocker rattle as the door gave way.

Inside her home, she knew exactly where to find a box of matches; candles were everywhere. She lit votives on the coffee table, a hurricane lamp on a hallway table, and long tapers in Noni's crystal candlesticks on the dining room table. Everything glowed and glimmered in the flickering light. She sat on the sofa, rested her head back, and watched the shadows dance along the ceiling and against the folds of window curtains. She didn't care if the lights ever came on. She could see everything so much better in the dancing shadows of candlelight.

At some point, sleep took over. A telephone ring

woke her from her brief nap, still sitting up on the sofa. A ringing bell piercing her dreams.

"Bernie?"

"Hi Don." She knew his voice instantly, no need to ask who was calling. For a moment, the irrational fear occurred to her that he knew she had talked about him to Noni, that he knew she had invented some sort of affair or relationship to get the attention of a troubled old woman away from fears of a searching biological mother's ability to destroy the memory of her own daughter. Bernie blushed at the possibility of his knowing.

"Hi, I hope I'm not bothering you, but I thought I should check on you. I drove by your office a few minutes ago and all the lights were on, but your car wasn't there. Anyway, I just thought I'd make sure everything was okay."

"Oh, you know what? The power went out, so I left in the dark. It all must have come back on. What time is it?"

"It's about seven, maybe a little after."

"It's early. I dozed off for a bit. I guess I can blow out these candles and turn the lights on."

"Yeah, the power's back on your street, too."

"How do you know that?"

"I'm out front."

"What?"

"I'm in front of your house. I'd gone by your office to drop off the CD; you forgot it, and you weren't there, so I headed this way on my way home."

Bernie opened the front door. Don was parked at the curb, looking in her direction, the phone still held to his ear. "I guess it would be rude not to invite you in."

"Well, I don't want to bother you."

"Come on in," she said and flipped on the porch light, then the lamps on the end tables. The room was well lit by the time he came through the front door and saw Bernie blowing out the candles on the dining room table.

"It smells good in here," he said.

"It's the candles; they're scented."

"Hmmmmm. . . it smells like freshly baked cookies."

"It's definitely the candles. Have a seat." Bernie took his jacket and flung it over the back of a dining room chair and hurried out of the room. "It's also freezing in here, let me turn the heat on."

"You should put a gas insert in your fireplace," he said. "They're not as warm as a wood fire, but gas is cleaner and easier to start."

"Yeah, I think I'll do that this year. I've slowly been doing little things to bring the house into the twenty-first century."

"Here you go," he said, holding up the plastic CD case from the car. He sat perched on the edge of the sofa and held it out to her. "I forgot to give it to you at lunch."

"Thanks. I didn't expect company, so excuse the mess." She took the disc and nodded toward the scattered newspapers and coffee cups on the dining room table.

"Been cutting out any more articles?"

"Not today."

Bernie examined the small plastic CD holder that featured a picture of the band standing next to a white pickup truck on some dirt road. "Wow, look at you," she said, running her finger over the image of Don, nodding her head slowly.

"I hope you like it," he finally said.

"Well, I'm impressed." Bernie set the CD on the small

bench near the door beside her handbag, so she would remember to take it with her to listen to while she drove to work. She looked toward Don, still perched on the edge of the sofa, ready to stand and leave at any moment. "Can I make you a drink? Or maybe some tea?"

"I don't want to impose; I'm sure you're busy."

"Actually, I'm not. I was going to work, but I left in a hurry and didn't bring any files or work home, so . . ." She finished the sentence with a brief wave of her hand. "And I'm still full from lunch, so I wasn't going to have any dinner, so a cup of tea might be good."

"Okay, a cup of tea, then I'll leave you to your quiet evening."

He followed her into the kitchen and sat at the kitchen table while she filled the tea kettle and pulled ceramic mugs from the cupboard. "I went by Nazareth House and saw my grandmother on the way home, so I haven't been home all that long. I sat down on the couch and dozed off for a bit, but I must have only slept for a couple of minutes."

"And how was your grandmother?"

"Oh, she's been a little down. I think my visit was good for her. I'm bringing her home next week for a few days, for Thanksgiving."

"Great. Will you have other family here?"

"No, it's just us. It's always just us as far as family goes."

"Really?"

"Yep. Since my folks died, and that was more than twenty years ago." She leaned against the counter and realized how sad that must seem to others, two women alone in the house on holidays. "But it was rarely just us when I was younger. Noni always had some neighbor or friends join us. She liked to cook for crowds of people, big plates of pasta, fat meatballs."

"My family's pretty typical, I guess, kids and cousins, too much food."

"Are you the only one that's adopted?" The water began to sizzle, and Bernie watched for the steam.

"Yes, but I have a brother and a sister. They're both married; my sister has a couple of kids, Josh and Lindsay. Josh is six, and Lindsay's nine."

"Do they live here?"

"My brother's in San Jose, works for Apple, but my sister lives here. She teaches fourth grade over at Wilson School."

The kettle whistled softly as Bernie lifted it off the burner. She slowly poured the hot water over the tea bags, then lifted a couple of spoons from the silverware drawer and paper napkins from the pantry. "Do you want sugar, or I might have some honey?"

"Sugar is fine."

Bernie watched him slowly stir his tea. This was the second time they had shared a cup of hot tea, she thought. She held her cup close to her face and blew gently, feeling the warmth of the steam drift over her. The rain continued to fall outside, a steady rhythm, soothing and tranquil after the earlier downpour. "This is nice," she said. "I'm glad you stopped by."

"Me too."

"I have a strange question for you," she said, lifting her cup to her lips. She took a small sip, allowed the warmth to spread through her.

"What's that?"

"If you had a chance to meet your real mother, I mean your birth mother, would you?" she asked, now cupping the warm mug in both hands.

He looked at her for a minute before answering. "Sure, but I have met her. I don't really remember her, but I lived with her for five years. Why do you ask? Did your birth mother contact you?" Don took a small sip of tea, but his eyes never shifted their gaze away from her.

An odd weight she'd been feeling below her ribs seemed to spread up through her chest and down her arms, making her fingers feel heavy, almost numb. "I guess that was a pretty obvious clue, huh," she said, amused at her own transparency.

He nodded. "How do you feel about that?" he asked, his voice measured and calm.

"How do I feel? It depends on the minute. I kind of hated her for a long time for not wanting me. I wanted to meet her just to tell her so, but then, when I actually got word that she was really out there, I became . . .I don't know . . . curious, I guess." She paused to take another sip and allow herself time to compose her thoughts before saying more. "I even sent her a letter, well I sent a letter to the social worker that called me. And then I got a letter back."

Don sat quietly, his thin legs crossed, stirring his tea, never taking his eyes off her. He simply listened.

"Anyway, I was thinking about meeting her, but now I'm not so sure that's a good idea. I know enough just from the letter. I don't really need to know why she gave me up. Clearly, it's bothered her over the years, but now she knows I'm okay, and I know she's okay, and that's really all that's necessary. And I don't really hate her so much anymore, so the letter was a good thing. No one should live with that kind of bitterness in them; it rots you from the inside out. Anyway, I'm not sure I want to open old wounds at this point in my life."

After a long moment of comfortable silence, the patter of rain on glass, the soft sound of the spoon lifting from his cup then resting on the saucer, he spoke. "Only you can make that decision, Bernie. No one can figure all that mother-child stuff out for someone else, and I'm certainly not the one to give you advice. I mean, I was adopted, but it's different. I know where I came from. I know why I was sent away, what my story is. None of that is a mystery for me, and I was raised by good people who wanted me to understand who I am, where I came from. That was not the case for all of those kids taken out of Vietnam, not at all. I was fortunate to be placed with my family. And I don't think my birth mother is still alive, or I would have probably heard from someone by now."

Bernie gave him a puzzled look, touched her hair lightly, but didn't say anything. He had, Bernie believed, a very old soul, ripe with tenderness. It was there in his voice, gentle and clear, in his eyes, honest and true.

"There are many, many people from Vietnam living here now, and they frequently have word about relatives and family still living back home. But you, your situation isn't like that. There was no one to tell you anything. Do you mind telling me why you're not interested in meeting her? Why were you so upset about being given up for what I'm sure she believed was a better life?"

Bernie considered lying, just making up some poppycock story about having second thoughts, but it was raining, and the house was warm, and they were sitting at her kitchen table having tea and good conversation. Such a time called for truth, at least some measure of truth for this man.

"I told you I went to see my grandmother, Noni, tonight. Well, I told Noni about the social worker, about the call, the day I first heard from her. I've pretty much avoided visiting her since I shared that news. I didn't want her to know that I'd sent a letter to my mother, and I've never been very good at keeping things from her, so I've been distant. For some reason, it seemed like a betrayal to everything she's been to me. And a betrayal to my real mom who raised me. When I showed up at Nazareth tonight, they let me know what a sorry state she's been in. Sad, angry, unhappy, you name it." It felt good to finally share some of this burden, as if the words themselves took a heavy weight from her thin shoulders.

"And you think it's all because you told her about your mother looking for you?"

"I know it is. I'm all she has now. I think she's afraid that this other woman will come in and I'll forget all about Mom. You see, my mother was her only child. It nearly killed her when she lost her, but she had me. It would be like losing another part of her if someone else came in and took Mom's place as my mother. I know that seems strange, but I know that's what it is. I can't ever do anything that would hurt Noni. She's given up everything for me, and well, I just can't." She shook her head no, convincing her own self as she spoke, and gazed down into her cup, half empty.

Don reached over and rested his hand on her forearm. "You don't have to do anything, Bernie. But I think you should give everything a little time. Don't close the door just yet. Put everything on hold for a little while; let it all be

238

for a few weeks. Wait until after the holidays." He gave her arm a light squeeze.

"That's what the social worker said in the very beginning." Bernie slowly moved her arm away and sat back in her chair, holding her cup by the fingertips of both hands, as if she were praying.

"It's good advice."

"Yeah, I know it is." She tilted her head back to gaze at the ceiling, another blank page. "I know it is."

"If your parents hadn't died, how do you think they would feel about you meeting your biological mother? It's pretty common these days, adopted children and parents finding each other, especially with all the internet searches. Would they have cared?"

"Gosh, I never thought about that. My dad would have been okay with it; I think he might have even tried to help me find her if I wanted to. He was really a great guy, most of the time." She wanted to cry at the sound of those words. *A great guy*. No one ever considered him a nice guy. He would always be remembered as some sort of monster, the monster who killed her mother. "My mom, I don't know. She was very beautiful, but not a terribly warm person. She might have seen it as some kind of insult or threat to her place in my life, in some way. My dad always complained that she was spoiled because Noni did everything for her. And Noni always bought my mom anything she wanted if she could afford it. I guess it was the same way with me and Noni. I was spoiled, too. But I don't think my mom would have liked sharing me, if that makes any sense. She used to tell me that they loved me more than parents who had their own babies, because they chose me, that I was a gift."

Don smiled and slowly shook his head. "Funny," he said, "my mother said something like that, too. I guess they give a bit of instruction with the adoption kit."

"Adoption kit?"

"Yeah, the kids' version and the adults' version." He grinned so wide his eyes nearly closed. "What did your dad do for a living?"

"He was a cop, a deputy sheriff, actually. My mom used to be a secretary, worked for a lawyer." She paused to look at him, raising one eyebrow to acknowledge the similarity with her own life. "She quit after I came along, but I think she might have been thinking of going back to work. Her old boss, I can't remember his name, had called a couple of times right before they died. Funny, I'd forgotten that until just now."

Don only nodded, not asking anything further, not offering any comments about law being a family trait, not asking if that background influenced her decision to go into law. She appreciated his silence.

"In the end, it doesn't really matter what they would have thought; they're not around."

"I'm sorry. I bet this is a hard time for you; the holidays and all."

"I'm used to quiet holidays."

"Look, I don't want to presume to tell you what to do; you have a lot to consider with your Noni and everything, but, like I said, it's probably not a bad idea to wait until after the holidays to do anything. All those Christmas lights and carols can make people overly emotional and sentimental. Then you wake up and it's February."

"All true."

There had been more than enough personal discussion for one day, for both of them. Sensing it was best to move to nonthreatening banter to end the evening, Bernie swallowed the last of her tea and shifted the conversation to favorite bands. Of course, they both loved the Beatles—who didn't? When Bernie asked him his favorite song, Don was embarrassed to admit that one of his all-time favorites really was "Stairway to Heaven," and he confessed to going to the music store every day after school to play it on the expensive guitars. She admitted to being a folky, loving nothing better than turning up the volume for Simon and Garfunkel or Mamas and Papas in the car, singing loudly while she drove, even harmonizing. Yes, she could harmonize, too. And no, she wasn't ready to try a duet with him, so don't bring a guitar to the office and expect to share a round of Kumbaya. They filled the kitchen with a sound that had been missing for too many years -- laughter.

Don finally rose to his feet, carried his cup to the sink and announced it was time for him to swim home. Bernie walked him to the door and watched him jog to the curb where he turned and tossed a final wave. After locking the door, she peeked through the rain-splattered window to watch his red taillights slowly disappear around the corner. It had been a long day; she was happily exhausted.

The rain stopped sometime after midnight. Bernie had finally drifted into a deep sleep, her mind and body escaping to a pleasant void. She had tried to go to bed early, as soon as Don left, but sleep wouldn't come. She tossed and turned, went through her relaxation mantra, but her wild imagination was racing on, refusing to rest. After only an hour or so of sleep, she was wide awake again.

It was actually his idea, indirectly. Internet searches. She gave up on trying to sleep, pulled on her tattered chenille robe and staggered to her desk in the spare bedroom. The light of the computer screen cast an eerie glow in the dark room. First, she googled the name Julie Randall. One point three million hits, even a movie star with that name. She would have to narrow the search, maybe by location, but first she googled the name Don Fielding. Over one point seven million hits. *Better than Julie's*, she thought. She modified his name search to only images. A page of thumbnail photographs appeared. She scanned the images then clicked over to page two, then page three, and there, on the third row down, was the Don Fielding she knew.

It was a headshot from his university faculty page, and he looked very intelligent in his sport coat and collared shirt. She looked on, and there was a picture of him sitting at a dinner table, his arm around a pretty blonde woman. *That must be Mrs. Fielding.* Again, she wondered why the two people who smiled so openly at the camera would have ended their marriage, and again assumed it be the wife's fault. Don was so nice, so compassionate and pure, almost too good to be true; it had to be the pretty wife. Still, she had learned to question everything, and this divorce of his nagged at her, especially now that the ex-wife had a face. She didn't want to be caught off guard again, caring for someone only to have the rug yanked out from under her. She had had enough of that. She knew how to get the scoop on some things, especially if there was a court file involved. Public records, she reminded herself. And she was the public.

The next search was not for Julie Randall; that quest was forgotten. Bernie looked for paralegal services in Seattle and quickly picked one with a catchy name, A Legal Connection. In two minutes she had crafted a short email to the agency. *Please obtain a copy of the dissolution file of Don Fielding from the Seattle Superior Court,* she wrote. *The wife's name is unknown, but the matter would have been resolved in the last twelve months.* She gave her phone number and asked that they call with any questions and to let her know the fee. Bernie ended the memo with a reminder that the request was to be confidential and asked that the file be sent via overnight mail; she would gladly pay the extra expense. She hit the send button before she could change her mind, and it was done. Suddenly, she felt like she might be able to sleep.

****

When Bernie arrived to work the next morning, Crystal's raised eyebrows and chastising glare told her she had done something wrong.

"What?" Bernie asked. She stood by her secretary's desk, empty cup in her hand, eager for a cup of hot coffee on a chilly morning. "Am I late for something? I thought my calendar was clear this morning, so I took my time." She took two more steps toward the small kitchen before Crystal rolled her chair back to follow her, pulling earphones from her head, rising from her seat.

"You're not late for anything, Bernie, but you left every light in the place on and forgot to set the alarm again. You're just lucky . . ."

"Ach," Bernie interrupted, holding her hand up, smiling, ready to end the lecture. "The power went out on me. I was sitting in the dark, so I grabbed my purse and left. I could barely find the door, let alone mess with the stupid alarm."

"Oh." Crystal sat back down, took the dangling earphones in her hand and shrugged her shoulders. "Sorry."

"So, good morning, Crystal." Bernie dipped her chin slightly in a formal nod to a fresh beginning.

"Good morning, Ms. Sheridan." Crystal smiled and returned the bowed head greeting.

"Coffee ready?"

"Of course."

"And are you chomping at the bit to hear about that letter from my real," she paused a moment to consider the meaning of *real mother* and changed her choice of words, "my biological mother?"

Crystal's eyes opened wide. "Absolutely. But only if you're ready to share. I don't want to seem nosey."

"Get your cup." This was a much better beginning to a day. She would tell Crystal what was going on with Julie Randall, even her decision to forestall any further contact. The relentless assistant, who would spend two hours searching for a thirty-seven-cent error in the checkbook would figure it out eventually, or waste countless hours snooping through Bernie's briefcase, drawers, and personal files searching for the "confidential" letter or some hint about the content of that correspondence.

Opening a closed door to allow a peek into your tidy entryway and living room can often satisfy the hunger of a curious neighbor. Bernie had learned that long ago. A nicely painted wall, complete with a gold-framed mirror and a beautiful painting, separates the polite visitor from the spare room, the space no one is allowed to enter, where twenty years of junk lays hidden from view, surrounded by deep layers of angry mold and black dust.

Fourteen

1968

Juicy sat on the edge of her bed, motionless, numb with fear. The social worker had been standing outside the nursery door when she'd left there, and she wasn't alone. She was talking to a cop and some other woman, probably a cop, too. Oh God, she'd never get Ginny away from here, not now. Like a fool, she'd given into that pushy woman, signed the papers, and now she would take the money, too. They were right; she didn't deserve to be a mother. She was the one to blame for this nightmare. Ginny should be with real parents, a mother and father who wouldn't hurt her. She deserved a better life than Juicy could ever provide.

"Julie, are you ready?" Mrs. Fierro entered her hospital room with a proud smile across her round face. She had won this battle, and the spoils were hers for the taking. Her hair was swept back into a stylish French twist, a strand of pearls around her neck to compliment her fitted emerald green suit. All she needed was a pillbox hat and she could be on the cover of Life magazine, the professional woman of modern times.

Julie had never known anyone like her, so smart, the kind of woman who can look you in the eye, smile sweetly, tell you how much she cares about you, drape a loving arm around your shoulder while using her free hand to slice open your belly and deftly remove a kidney, leaving a poor soul weak and bleeding, a vital organ suddenly missing, a pool of red blood spreading at her feet. It would hurt, probably for a really long time, but it wouldn't kill you—at least not right away. You can learn to live with only one kidney, adjust to the loss, but you never forget about it. The scar remains, a constant reminder of the susceptible nature of living without a part of you, a piece of your very being, gone forever. Julie prayed it wouldn't be forever.

"Yes. Do you have the money?"

Fifteen
2005

There it was, right in front of her. How could she have been so wrong? It had not taken the Seattle paralegal service even a week to retrieve the file and express it to her office. Cassandra Fielding had been the one to file for divorce, just as Bernie had imagined, but it wasn't because she had a lover. Don was the cheater. She put it all in a sworn declaration, thinking that would make the court want to award her a generous lifetime of spousal support. Her tactic didn't seem to work, but Mr. Zen-and-Light, wise and peaceful in all things, multitalented and intelligent Don Fielding who swore he never lied, was, as it turned out, a phony, a liar, and a cheat. Just like everyone else.

Bernie closed the file and stashed it in her personal files drawer, where she kept every billing statement and piece of correspondence from Nazareth House, and the copies of Noni's bank statements and Social Security check stubs. No one, not even Mrs. Gordon, cared to look at those records, but she made sure she kept track of everything, just in case. She knew Don would call soon; if not today, tomorrow. Their times together had been nice. There was certainly a mutual attraction between them, but now, Bernie knew, she would not allow anything more to develop. No romance loomed in her life, contrary to what she had led Noni to believe. She reached into her purse, pulled out the letter from Julie Randall, and shoved that in with Don's divorce file. The best course of action was to stay busy, pushing the files, pushing Crystal, working at the intensity she did when she first started practicing law.

"Bernie," Crystal's voice came through the speaker phone. "I have Glenn Carpenter on the line. He's calling about the Richardson file. Do you want to take it?"

"Yes, and can you bring me the file? I sent him a demand letter last week so he might have an offer."

"Sure, I'll put him through."

The file was on her desk in less than a minute, and in another ten she had settled the Richardson matter for ten thousand dollars more than her clients had hoped for. She was on a roll, pushing the cases to a fast close, demanding resolution and big money for her clients. This was what it was all about; she had to remember that. She was there to put some cash in the pockets of folks who'd been damaged and more than a few dollars in her pockets, too, in the process. This was what she was good at, and it was very satisfying work, despite what people said about lawyers being greedy sharks. She didn't need a relationship with a man, or even a mother, to be happy. One settlement and she was smiling clear and bright. That meant she was happy, didn't it?

Feeling light and joyful, Bernie placed a call to Joan Bennet and advised her that she wanted to postpone indefinitely any plans to meet or correspond further with Julie Randall. Bernie explained that she was dealing with her grandmother's health problems and that she couldn't handle dividing her emotions during this crucial time in her grandmother's life. Bernie simply said she was sorry, but her grandmother deserved her full attention for the time being. Ms. Bennett was exceedingly sympathetic, gracious, and compliant with Bernie's request. She would talk to Julie Randall and let her know about the current situation.

"I'll diary this file for sixty days and give you a call to see how things are going," Ms. Bennett told her.

"Sixty days," Bernie said, wishing she could tell the woman it might as well be sixty years, the meeting would never happen. "Sixty days is fine."

Knowing she would not have to deal with her personal situation for the next couple of months was liberating. Thoughts of actually meeting Julie Randall faded to a hazy mist, like a vivid dream you try to recall in the light of day, only to capture flickering images. It didn't matter if Julie Randall had a million freckles down her arms and legs and cheeks that flamed red, or if her ears stuck out like sailboats. Those childish thoughts were packed away, just like the tragic stories under the bed, where they would age and eventually crumble.

"Bernie," Crystal's voice was again coming through the intercom.

"Yes, Crystal?"

"I have Don Fielding on the line, shall I put him through?"

Bernie started to put him off, hoping to avoid contact for a while longer, but she was on a mission to put her life back in order and the sooner it was done, the better. "Sure, and when I'm done, let's jam through that stack of mail and get out of here early today, go home and bake pumpkin pies or something."

"Sounds good."

Bernie picked up the phone, her fingers automatically lifting her hair from behind her ears, combing it in place as if he could see her through the receiver. "Hi Don," she said, her voice intentionally rushed, as if he was

250

interrupting. "What's up?"

"Hi. I wanted to see if you were free for lunch today."

"Oh, I'm sorry, I'm not. I have a deposition in Merced at two o'clock. I'm leaving in a minute," she lied.

"Okay, well, how about dinner?"

"No, that's not good either. I'm picking up Noni tonight and bringing her home for a couple of days. Tomorrow's Thanksgiving, remember?"

"Oh, don't I know it. Even now, members of the Fielding clan are racing up and down the state to get here."

She could hear his smile and bit her lip at the very idea of sitting around a table surrounded by cousins, parents, brothers, aunts, and uncles, passing plates filled with sweet potatoes and thick slices of turkey. "Listen, I'm pretty busy," she said, urging a quick end to the conversation, "so how about we talk next week?"

"Well, first, real quick, I wanted to invite you and your grandmother to join us for dinner. It's a bit late, I know, but on the chance you don't have plans. . ."

"Oh, thank you for thinking of us, but I've already got a turkey thawing in the fridge." Bernie wondered if this was his first holiday away from his wife, and pondered where the girlfriend that had apparently broken up his marriage was now. "Okay, it's just a turkey breast, but I'm planning on cooking the whole meal. A neighbor, one of Noni's old friends, is joining us, too. But thanks."

"I know this seems forward, but would you mind if I dropped by for dessert, in the evening? I'd really like to meet the infamous Noni."

Bernie closed her eyes, desperately clinging to what

she knew to be the truth of him, not the character he portrayed. If she had not checked up on him, she would never have found out that he was just another player on the good old boys' team. But, she rationalized, at this point they really were nothing more than friends. Just friends. She could still have Don for a friend. And she didn't have so many friends in her life. There wasn't a judgment in that file that she could see. For all she knew, he was still married. Her judgment wasn't what he needed; he needed one from a Washington court, signed and officially entered. And she needed a distraction for Noni, something more than turkey.

"Are you still there?" he asked.

"Oh, yes, I'm sorry. I was just reading a note that Crystal brought in. I have an important call on the other line." *Talk about good liars*, she thought. "Sure, come by for dessert and meet Noni. We'll eat early, so any time after your dinner is fine." The words just spilled out of her. Her mind was saying no, stay away, this is really a red flag situation, avoid him, but her mouth opened, and out came the words, "Come by and have some pie."

"Great. I'll see you tomorrow."

Bernie hung up the phone and checked the time. If she and Crystal worked through lunch, she could be out of there by two, three at the latest. That would give her a couple of hours to get to the store and stock up on groceries, including whatever she needed to make a pumpkin pie, and still leave enough time to do a quick cleaning job on her house. If the place wasn't spotless, Noni would click her tongue and start dusting from her motorized chair, knocking into furniture and walls, muttering to herself about the need to move back in to be the housekeeper since her granddaughter couldn't seem to manage a little dusting now and then. Cooking, however, was one of the things Noni liked to do when she was home, something she couldn't do at Nazareth House.

Bernie would stack the ingredients on the kitchen table, where her grandmother could happily chop and dice and mix together herbs and spices, creating dishes from Bernie's childhood, filling the house with smells of home. Bernie would serve as the chef's assistant, the extension of arms and legs for those places where a chair on wheels won't take you. Baking a pie would be good for Noni. She'd blame imagined flaws in the meal on her old fingers, weak and trembling with Parkinson's, or her ancient hips that wouldn't hold her up for more than a few minutes at a time. Bernie would only praise her more, begging her to move back home and cook for her every day. This was what they did when Noni came home. This was the life Bernie knew. This was her comfort. Why would she ever feel like she wanted something more?

****

Thanksgiving. The air was crisp and cool after two days of rain. The sight of the Sierra, topped with snow like a dollop of icing, surprised Bernie. It was easy to forget the mountain peaks were right next door, their majestic view clouded by a thick layer of dirty air that nestled in the valley, waiting to be washed away by a good downpour or blown away by a strong wind. She opened the thick folds of draperies wide. "Noni, come check out this view; it's gorgeous."

Noni buzzed across the hardwood floor, still wiping her hands on the red striped dish towel draped across her lap. Dark circles rimmed her eyes, but the halo of sad defeat of recent days seemed to have lifted as she dipped her fingers into a bowl of zucchini, eggs, parmesan cheese, and breadcrumbs, mixing together Bernie's favorite casserole. Neither one of them cared so much about a turkey; there would be turkey, but zucchini casserole was their holiday food.

"In my younger days, we had that to look at every day," Noni said. Her head shook side to side as if she were saying no to a greedy child, at the idea that a peek at the nearby mountain range had become a rare occurrence. Finally, she looked over to her grandchild, momentarily forsaking the picturesque landscape. "What are you working on these days? Anything good?" She loved to hear about Bernie's work, the stories of clients, how they'd been hurt, the details of their injuries and accidents, how her granddaughter fought for them and made their lives better.

"Well," Bernie said, pausing to take a sip of coffee before setting the cup down carefully on one of Noni's old stone and cork coasters, "I have a really sad case, a little boy whose parents were killed in a car crash."

"Oh," Noni said, "You told me about that one. It must be hard for you."

"Actually, I think it's good for me. I can look at this kid's life and see what it can be, despite the circumstances." She proceeded to tell her grandmother more about the case, about the pictures of Carlos and his mom and dad, and how he was now living in Mexico with his grandmother. She shared Crystal's point of view that he would be better off living here with foster parents, getting a better education or some such nonsense, then proudly defended her personal knowledge that the love of a grandmother was far better than anything the U.S. had to offer. Besides, she added, she was going to get Carlos and his grandmother enough money to be able to afford an excellent education and a beautiful home, too, but that would probably be in Mexico, not here. She couldn't imagine the old woman would want to uproot her life completely at her age.

"Oh, Bernie," Noni said, "I'm so proud of you."

"Thank you," Bernie said. "That means a lot to me. I always want to make you proud, Noni."

"So, now tell me about this man you met, the little singer." The old lady's eyes seemed to open wider to completely take in the next bit of news.

"Well, actually, you're going to get to meet him later this evening."

"What? He's coming to dinner? You should have told me sooner; I would have made my rolls instead of those packaged things you bought."

"Relax," she said, laughing at the idea of stressing out over a couple of dinner rolls. "He's just coming over for pie. We baked a pie last night, and it's beautiful if I don't say so myself."

"We only made a pumpkin. Maybe we should have done a cherry or lemon, too."

"Noni, one pie is plenty. And get all those crazy ideas out of your head; he's just a friend, nothing more, not now and not ever. You were right," she lied, "musicians are flaky. I don't know what I was thinking."

Noni smiled knowingly, nodding in agreement, but

still giving her a curious look, as if she doubted everything Bernie said.

"Trust me, Noni, we're just friends."

"I didn't say anything." She clicked her tongue, just as she used to do when her granddaughter would spend an entire day in her pajamas, stretched out on the couch, her nose stuck in some book, not even dressing to come to the dinner table. "Tsk, tsk, tsk."

"No, but you have that look. I know you just as well as you know me. We don't have secrets. Not us."

The old woman turned again to gaze toward the mountains.

Throughout the day, warm smells filled the small house as Bernie roasted the turkey breast and baked Noni's casserole. While her grandmother read the morning paper, Bernie set the table with Noni's wedding china, a glossy white with a silver rim and tiny lavender bouquets along the bottom and top edges. The tablecloth was a deep purple and the napkins were pale lavender, the same shade as the flowers on the dishes. She even brought out the heavy flatware kept in a wooden case in the credenza. Bernie lit tall candles she had placed in Noni's crystal candlesticks, a souvenir of a long-ago trip to Italy, then poured an Alexander Valley cabernet into Waterford glasses. Noni only drank red wine, and now only on special occasions, so Bernie only poured a small amount. To further please Noni, she even dressed for the occasion in shades of fall, wearing a rust-colored sweater over chocolate-brown wool flannel pants. No jeans for her today. Noni, too, had donned her favorite pearl necklace and a handsome suit jacket she had left in the spare room. Bernie helped do up her hair, combing it back like she wore it when she was younger, in a mock French twist. Just when the light began to fade and the temperature outside to fall, the two women sat down to dinner.

"Bernadette, this is lovely, just lovely."

"Thank you. I don't do this often, so it was kind of fun." She didn't mention that the only time she ever sat at this table was to work, preferring the larger space to the small desk in the spare room. Instead of lovely china and goblets of wine, there was usually a stack of file folders and a PowerBook.

"I'm sure your friend will think it's lovely, too."

Bernie raised her left eyebrow at the reference to her friend. "I didn't do this for my friend, who has a name by the way—it's Don, remember?"

"Sorry. I'm sure Don will be impressed." She tucked her chin in mocked submission and smiled coyly.

"Too bad it will all be cleared away by the time he gets here. All he'll see is a stack of dirty fancy dishes."

"We could wait and eat later. It will keep."

"Are you crazy? Now, do you want to say grace?"

Noni offered a blessing as Bernie stared into her empty plate, but on cue, made the sign of the cross and joined in the "Amen." Those old rituals and prayers, tucked in the back corners of her mind, appeared when needed, unpracticed, but never forgotten.

Bernie reached across the table and dished a large spoonful of cheesy zucchini casserole onto Noni's plate; the ceramic dish would be too heavy for her grandmother's trembling fingers to manage. She placed slices of turkey on each of their plates, knowing instantly the piece her grandmother would choose, then passed her a basket of hot rolls. After a lifetime of living under one roof together, she was sure she knew the old woman's every like, dislike, limitation, and strength. When she was satisfied that Noni's plate was complete, she paused for a sip of wine, allowing its warmth to flow through her, calming her before enjoying the first bite.

As she surveyed the table, the dancing light of the flickering candles, the rich colors of holiday food, a familiar sadness rolled over her. It was a quiet sadness that made her appear deep in thought, pensive and intelligent. Bernie couldn't help but wonder what Julie Randall's Thanksgiving table looked like. Was there a crowd of family gathered around? Did they say grace, make the sign of the cross or simply bow their heads? Did they forego prayers and go around the table, each person offering a word of thanksgiving for something good in their life? Did Julie Randall perhaps say she was thankful to have received word from a daughter lost long ago?

But such questions are silly fantasy, she reminded herself. Nothing is to come from imagining a life denied her. There had been many family meals eaten at the table before her; many that were shared with her mother and father, the ones she knew, many with friends of hers, friends of Noni. At family dinners, Dad would sit at one end, Mom at the other. Those chairs were still empty, she and Noni preferring their same seats after twenty-five years.

Don had invited her to his family gathering because the idea of only two at the table seemed a desperate thing, lonely and tragic. She smiled weakly at her need to invent another guest, Noni's friend, a third, so to speak, as if one more diner would somehow make this seem more complete.

She didn't need to make excuses, a table for two, beautifully set, laden with delicious food, was complete enough for her.

All these musings swept through her mind as she savored the roast turkey breast and creamy zucchini. A lifetime of choices and circumstance evaluated in the time it took to take a drink of wine, cover her lap with a linen napkin, and pick up a knife to butter a hot roll.

"How is it?" she asked, knowing it was terrific by the sparkle in Noni's eyes and her soft humming as she chewed. Hmmmmm, hmmmm, hmmmm. She dipped the silver fork into the mashed potatoes then the zucchini, mixing it together in one bite. The two women ate slowly, enjoying every morsel of flavor, sipping their wine, each complimenting the other on her culinary skills.

"Bernadette, where did you learn to make such good gravy?"

"Hmmm, I guess I was paying more attention than you thought." Just as Bernie took a bite of turkey smothered in thick gravy, the telephone rang loudly, piercing the candlelight dining experience.

"Who could that be?" Noni asked, a deep crease forming in her forehead as she jutted out her chin and frowned.

"Oh, I bet it's Don, you know, my friend," Bernie said, emphasizing the word *friend*. She pushed away from the table and hurried to the kitchen and the nearest phone. "He probably changed his mind once he got together with all of his family, didn't want to leave, or something came up."

"Well, more for us then." Noni went on eating, quivering bite after quivering bite.

"Hello," Bernie said, her voice so light and airy it

almost sounded like a song.

"Hi, this is Jerry Duncan from Apollo Alarm. I hate to bother you on a holiday, but the alarm has gone off at your office, and I need to let you know."

"Oh no, did someone break in?" The words now rushed out, anxious to be heard, no longer worried that she sounded carefree.

"What? Who is it?" Noni called from the dining room, sounding irritated at the unwelcome intrusion.

"I don't know that," the man said, "the police are on their way over there now. I wanted to let you know in case you wanted to go check it out yourself. You can wait to hear from them if you want, but someone needs to go and reset the alarm. We can shut it off after the police clear the call, but only you can reset it."

Bernie hesitated, bit her lip. "No, I'll go now. It's my responsibility." She hung up the phone and hurried toward the front closet for her jacket. "Noni, I hate to do this to you, but I have to leave and go check on my office. The alarm went off."

"Was it a burglar?"

"That, I don't know. Listen, you stay and finish eating, I'll be right back." She pulled her jacket close and zipped it up.

"Can I go with you?" Noni was already backing up from the table.

Bernie thought about the hassle of getting her grandmother out the door and into the car. She could walk from the house to the car well enough, but it was a slow process. She desperately wanted to say no, just stay here, I need to move quickly, but instead, she answered, "Of course you can; let me get your coat."

Traffic was non-existent on this Thursday evening. It was the time of day when most people had finished their big holiday meal and were either napping or plopped in front of a television, watching football or old movies. Bernie was turning onto L Street in under ten minutes. Two police cars were parked at the curb, their red lights flashing. Another car was also there, a dark-colored Volkswagen Rabbit. The alarm was still ringing, loud and shrill. One officer was shining a powerful flashlight up and down the sides of the old house, checking the windows. Another officer was back at the curb, talking to a woman standing nervously on the sidewalk alongside her car.

"I'll be right back," Bernie said as she parked in her usual spot at the side of the building. "Stay here."

Darkness had descended completely during the short drive and Bernie struggled to see if she recognized the woman speaking to the officers, but it was no one she knew. She hurried up the steps and used her key to unlock the front door. The alarm was deafening. Shutting off the noise was the first thing she had to do. By the time she pushed the door open, the officer with the flashlight was beside her, blocking her entrance.

"I'm Bernadette Sheridan," she told him. "This is my office."

"Good evening, Ma'am. I'm Officer Watkins; why don't you let me go in ahead of you, just to be safe? In fact, stay out here for a few minutes."

"Oh, sure. I just wanted to shut the alarm off." Bernie backed up a couple of steps, folded her arms close to her chest to keep warm and looked back to the woman and the officers.

She seemed familiar, but her head was turned away, looking down. Bernie leaned over the porch railing to get a view of Noni sitting in the car. She smiled, nodded and waved in assurance that all was okay, then motioned that it would just be a minute.

The officer entered the building and shined his light up and down the stairway, stopping for a moment to examine the stained glass at the top of the stairs, then turned the beam down toward his feet. "And there it is," he said, "just like she said." He bent down and picked up an envelope.

"There's a light switch just to your left," Bernie said, watching him shine his light around the dark room, wondering what he had found on the floor.

And with the flick of switch, the stairwell and reception room were illuminated. He walked through the office and turned the next bank of lights on, slowly moving from room to room, lighting the whole place up as he went, even climbing the creaking stairs to investigate the second floor, the floorboards groaning at the unfamiliar weight of footsteps. Occasionally, Bernie would look back to the officer standing with the woman near his patrol car. When the policeman searching the inside finally made his way down the stairs, he spoke into the small mic clipped to his shoulder. A crackle of static was his response and he repeated louder, struggling to be heard over the still ringing alarm, "All clear in here."

"Can I go in now?" Bernie asked. "That noise is terrible."

"Yeah, go ahead and turn it off." He stepped aside to allow her to pass.

For a brief moment, Bernie feared she had forgotten

the password, but her fingers moved automatically, and the ringing alarm was silenced. "That's better," she said.

"This is the culprit," he said, handing her a pink envelope, the one he had picked up from the floor, just inside the door below the mail slot.

"What's this?" Bernie asked, flipping the envelope over to see simply her name scrawled across the front.

"The woman standing over there with Officer Douglas says she dropped it into the mail slot and the alarm just went off." He used his elbow to indicate the pair standing at the curb, then used the back of his hand to wipe at his running nose, sniffing loudly.

A pink envelope, the size used with personal stationary and greeting cards. This was no hand-delivered last minute motion or official letter. She recognized the envelope and handwriting immediately; it was from Julie Randall, and it was hand delivered. She looked over to the woman standing with the officers, and before she took one step toward them, she knew. It was her. Twenty feet away from her at this very moment stood her mother, the one who gave her away thirty-seven years ago. Despite the cold, her cheeks flushed warm. Her eyes burned for just a moment and her stomach muscles tightened involuntarily.

Oh shit, she thought, *Noni's in the car. Shit . . . shit . . . shit . . . right there . . . this could kill her . . . seriously*. She was suddenly grateful for the darkness surrounding them. The brightness of the house lights kept Noni hidden in the darkened car, the length of the porch and old house the only thing visible from where she sat waiting.

"I'm going to turn these lights off and lock up," Bernie told the officer. She hurried through the door and started toward the back of the office, pausing there briefly, holding onto the back-stair banister, breathing in deeply, then out, in three audible sighs, feeling it deep in her belly, as low as her navel. Another valuable residual from years of therapy and law school, too, she thought, the ability to gain composure and confidence in emotionally tense situations. She imagined a flow of warm water running down her back, her arms, wiggled her fingers, took one more deep breath, then began her journey. A slow sequence of darkness followed as she worked her way back toward the front door, turning off all the lights that the officer had turned on, double-checking to see for herself if anything had been disturbed. She reset the alarm and locked the door behind her. She felt her back stiffen, the sloping S of her spine transforming to a rigid bar before descending the steps to the sidewalk where she would meet the woman who gave birth to her. Bernie inhaled deeply one more time. Just as her fingers moved automatically to set the alarm, her body moved on autopilot, out the door and down the same steps she used every day.

Her heart raced and her legs felt numb as she walked toward the officers and the woman, but still she kept walking, one foot in front of the other, then the next. Once there, if the strange woman really was Julie Randall, her birth mother, everything would change. In a matter of seconds, life could veer as it so often did. She wondered why the alarm had gone off. Had Julie Randall tried to break in and set the thing off, or was this some kind of fated incident? Or maybe it was the handiwork of Mrs. Gordon? She blamed everything else she couldn't explain on a ghost that she didn't even believe in, why not this too?

"Hi," she said to the small group gathered on the

curb. "I'm Bernadette Sheridan." She stood tall, her feet directly under her hips, no waver in her stance, her voice rich with feigned confidence.

The woman standing in the shadows with the officer looked at her; she was biting her lower lip, or maybe she was just licking her lips, but her mouth kept moving. Her pale eyes were a reflection of Bernie's own, but they were a softer, faded shade of grey. Despite the terrified look in her eyes and the lip chewing, she held her head high, her chin set and ready for any blow, as if she knew something bad was coming and was ready for it. Officer Douglas, whom Bernie had not yet spoken to, nodded and motioned for her to move away from the others, to speak with him alone. "Good evening, Ma'am."

"Hello, Officer; so, what's going on?" She swayed a bit now, side to side, pressing down on the bottom of her pockets, assuming an air of camaraderie with the man in dark blue, silently urging him to share his findings, even the smallest bits of information with her.

"I think everything is pretty well taken care of, no sign of forced entry or anything missing, as far as we can tell." The porch light didn't extend as well to where they stood, shrouding the pair in darkness, while the other two remained visible in the light. "I just want to make sure you don't have something to add; it's your business, so you might notice something more than perhaps we did."

"Do you think she tried to break into my office? Is that what really happened?" Bernie looked over her shoulder quickly, getting another look at the person who had dropped the pink envelope in her mail slot; her mother, she was certain of it. Julie stood, returning her gaze, her hands like blocks of lead, hanging limp in her pockets.

"No, not at all. Apparently, when she dropped a letter through the mail slot, the alarm went off. Has that ever happened to you before?"

"Never."

"Sometimes those motion detectors will be pointed in the direction of a mail slot and pick up the motion and go off. It wouldn't be the first time." He used his flashlight to point to the front door.

"Well, it's the first time it's happened to me," she said, her tone now leaning toward agitation, "and I've had this alarm system for two years, so it seems a little odd. I mean the mailman drops mail in there all the time, and it doesn't go off. Why would one letter suddenly make it go off?"

"Well, you might want to have it checked. Perhaps something caused it to move slightly. We just happened to be parked right around the corner when the alarm went off, so we heard it and got over here before any call came through. This woman was getting into her car to leave, so we stopped her. She said she was just dropping off a letter, but we couldn't be too sure, so we held her until we could check things out. If you say it's all okay in there, I'm going to let her take off." He spoke gently, an unusual tone for a big man in a uniform, a gun at his side, handcuffs at his back. "But if you think she was attempting to break in, and things seem disturbed, tell me now, and we'll take her in. I ran a check on her license; she's clean."

"Uh-huh."

"Do you know her?" He looked over to the woman and his partner, both of them standing and staring in their direction, the woman looking more anxious by the second, now clutching at her dark raincoat, pulling it tighter and tighter around her as if she was freezing or perhaps simply trying to shred it in two across her back.

"Look, I think I know who she is. If I'm not mistaken, she's my . . ." Bernie looked back over to the side of the building where her car was parked, the streetlight providing an outline of Noni sitting and waiting, watching everything, "she's my . . . her name is Julie Randall, right?"

"Yes ma'am."

"Go ahead and let her go," she said. This was one of those times Bernie wished she was a smoker; it would give her something to do with her hands, her nervous energy. She could inhale deeply, exhale slowly, flick ashes, grind the half-smoked butt out in the pavement, blow a wild cloud of smoke in the air, and look tough. "She's an old client."

"That's what she said, that she was a client."

They moved back to the other pair and he said something quietly that Bernie couldn't hear. "You have a nice Thanksgiving; what's left of it," he said louder, but it wasn't clear if the message was to her or Julie or both of them.

"You too," Bernie answered. Julie simply nodded in agreement.

They watched the two officers confer briefly before climbing into their separate cars. Bernie was quickly considering her options of how to handle this awkward and difficult situation. A weaker person, someone like Crystal, or a guest on one of those sappy daytime talk shows, would dissolve in a puddle of tears, reach out for her long-lost mother, wrap her arms around her, and promise a lifetime of love and devotion from this day forward. Not her, not now. The only person to whom she owed a lifetime of love and devotion was shivering in the passenger seat of her car, oblivious to the drama that was unfolding right before her. *If Noni knew what was going on, she'd probably have a stroke. She wouldn't like this at all, not at all.*

Julie Randall continued to clutch the bottom edge of her jacket as she took an uncertain step toward her daughter. "Bernadette," she said, her voice hoarse and weak. Bernie wondered if it was fear, anxiety, or simply the icy wind that whipped around the corner that caused Julie to sound so diluted. "I, uh . . ." She lifted one thin hand to her own face, and lightly touched her lips.

Numbness, Bernie decided as she took stock of her own feelings, considering the moment at hand. She was numb, her senses altogether dulled for this huge moment, one she had only dared to imagine for most of her life. But after years of training, therapy, and reflection, years of facing opposing counsel, steeling her emotions to appeal to a judge, a jury, the world; she knew how to perform, to take command of any situation, and that was what she intended to do. Control the situation.

"Look," she said, trying her best to sound sincere, but firm, too. "I know who you are. I don't know why you're here, but whatever the reason, I can't help you right now." Her lips pressed tightly together into an awkward smile that clashed with her shaking head that said no, no, no.

"I never meant to bother you," Julie said. "I planned to be gone before you ever got the letter. I don't know why I'm here. I'm sorry about all this . . ." she jerked her hand about, as if to conjure up the absent officers and the blaring alarm.

Bernie stood motionless, her face a blank slate. She didn't offer back one of those favorites of Don Fielding, the it's-no-problem type answers that soften difficult moments.

She didn't say anything at all. She simply prayed her body would not betray her; that she would not melt or even sway, that she would remain a solid sculpture of ice while she carefully memorized every detail of her mother's face.

The silence between them lingered, awkwardness intensified by Bernie's learned ability to detach from all emotion—no guilt, no love, no hate, nothing. Julie closed her eyes briefly, wincing from unimaginable pain, her daughter's icy response a splash of vinegar on an old, festering wound. It was a look that ultimately moved Bernie to finally speak.

"Like I said, I can't help you right now." Now would be a good time to take a drag on that imaginary cigarette, she thought, it would give her that extra beat in time, make her seem sturdy. She took a deep breath, inhaling only a wash of cold November air, skipping the three exhaling sighs of therapy. She has hair like mine, she noticed, just shorter, and a lighter color. "I asked that social worker, Bennett, Joan Bennett, to call you and tell you to put all this on hold." The wind caught a lock of her own fine hair, lashing it across Bernie's face, but she didn't brush it away. Her gloved hands dug deep in her pockets, the right one fidgeting with the unread letter in the pink envelope. "You really should go home now. There are reasons I can't go into right now." She looked over to her car, to Noni, still there, still watching.

Julie tucked her chin as if to turn away, but her body moved forward, leaning in closer, invading the safe distance maintained by strangers, daring to look closely into her daughter's eyes, her fingers reaching out to lightly touch Bernie's cheek. "You're beautiful," she said, a quiet sob escaping with the words. "I'm sorry." She shook her head vigorously, as though she could shake away the events of the evening, and turned away.

A quick gasp of air escaped from Bernie's tight lips, and Julie stopped to look back. Once again, she examined her daughter's face, searching for something, anything.

"Julie," Bernie said, drawing another cleansing breath, searching for the loose fragments of an unfamiliar lifeline that had been severed long ago. "I have my grandmother in the car. She's elderly, and not well, and I don't want to upset her. You being here would upset her, so that is why I can't deal with any of this right now." Her frame remained a solid fortress, ever aware of Noni's eyes boring in on her, but it was a stronghold built of pumice, crumbling away bit by bit. She was still standing, a bit shaky at the core, but upright. "There are things I would like to say, and I have questions for you, but for now I'm just going to ask you to walk away. One more time."

She couldn't resist the hateful jab; it had simmered inside her for too long. It came out without thinking, one of her quick-witted traits that usually served her well, but perhaps not on this occasion. The minute the words *one more time* left her mouth, she wished she could swallow them up again.

"Of course, of course," Julie answered. Her gaze seemed to drop slowly as she spoke, moving from Bernie's face down toward her feet, but still set on her daughter. "I'll wait to hear from you, then; I really didn't mean to bother you."

"Why are you here?" Bernie asked, again delaying the parting, preventing her mother from leaving. "I thought you had a family; it's Thanksgiving. Shouldn't you be home or somewhere doing all those family things? Cooking. Eating.

Dishes."

"I should be, but I'm not. I talked to Ms. Bennett last night and . . . I don't know." Her face looked drawn and worn, everything seemed to sag with exhaustion, but she smiled a little anyway. "I was standing at the stove, waiting for a pot of water to boil, and just felt like I needed to do something for you right now. Right now, well, right then. So, I sat down and wrote you a letter, put on my coat, told my husband to finish dinner, and drove it down here so that you'd have it as soon as possible." She shrugged her shoulders in half defeat, finding some kind of humor in her rash behavior. "I was halfway here when I realized how foolish it was, then decided that I might as well go all the way. I knew where your office was; I looked it up online. And it was a good drive; I needed some time. You can read the letter, and we'll talk later."

"Are you driving back now?" Bernie noticed a ruddiness in her mother's cheeks and wondered if it was the cold night air or an internal heat that inspired the flash of rosy color.

She didn't answer, just lifted her shoulders and dipped her head to one side; she didn't know. "I'm sure they're fine without me at home, but . . . I'm feeling a bit worn out."

"Well, like I said; my grandmother is old, and I just can't upset her. It's late, and you probably shouldn't drive tonight." Why did she care? The woman hadn't given a thought or care about her welfare since she abandoned her, so why did she care about her driving at night? "There are some hotels not far from here."

"Thank you, Bernadette. If you want to talk later or tomorrow, I put my cell phone number in the letter. No pressure, but if you do . . . I'll get a hotel, and maybe . . . well, if I don't hear from you by noon tomorrow, I'll just go back home and wait there."

"I think you should get some rest and then go home. You shouldn't expect my call; I told you, I can't deal with this right now and Noni, my grandmother, is spending a couple of days with me, so . . ."

"I understand," Julie said. "I'm glad I got to see you even for this little bit." Her body moved toward Bernie ever so slightly, as if she was drawn to her, a magnetic force pulling her closer.

"Good night." Bernie took two steps, then turned back toward her mother. "Hey," she said, again halting her mother's departure, "what happened to my arm? What did you mean by that?"

"The last time I saw you, you had a broken arm; it was in a tiny little cast." Her eyes glassed over with the memory of Ginny lying in the crib, and she rubbed her left forearm to indicate where the break had been.

"How did that happen?" She was good at asking tough questions and tonight was no different. She knew how to get people to give her information, and usually the best method was to point blank ask for it. "Did you break my arm?" she asked. She held her breath, fearing the answer that followed. "Is that what happened?"

Julie walked back toward Bernie, and Bernie knew the answer by the way the woman took a deep breath before answering, pulling together her courage, summoning up the nerve to confess to a difficult truth. She had seen witnesses do this deep breath thing hundreds of times. "Yes and no; it's not what you think."

Bernie shook her head in disgust. "Of course not," she answered sarcastically. "I'm sure you had a good reason for snapping a newborn's arm."

"You weren't exactly a newborn, and it wasn't like that." Her narrowed eyes and rigid body pleaded with Bernie for a chance to be redeemed, to explain. "You were four months old. Four months. And I didn't snap your arm; it was an accident. I got hurt too; we both were injured."

Bernie felt her mind reeling, the ground spinning beneath her. This was never what she had imagined; where was the innocent teenager giving birth to a living mistake, handing the little bundle off to a waiting nun, then rushing home in time for the start of senior year, football games, and prom dresses? She wished she hadn't mentioned her arm. Reality was no match for the easy-life fantasy she long ago created. Another accident, the inherited lie.

"I shouldn't have brought it up, not now, anyway." It was the best response she could muster for the time being.

"Bernadette, please, let me explain just that."

"Not now," she said. "Good night, Julie."

Bernie watched her mother move slowly around her car and climb behind the wheel, looking for any movement that resembled her own. But in the dark, who could tell? Her mother was nice looking, earthy, she thought. She wore silver hoops in her ears and she drove a dark-colored Volkswagen convertible. Was it black or green? Every detail, get every detail, she told herself, wanting to remember it all, bring it out later, examine it piece by piece, word by word.

Bernie's eyes burned and the urge to cry made her stomach churn and spasm. *Stop,* she wanted to scream. *Don't leave me. Please, don't go.* Had those words been ripping at her brain for thirty-seven years, buried deep in her being, unspoken and forgotten? Why did she have to be so cold? Why did she drive everyone away? Why didn't she just bring her home with her and stay up all night asking all those questions that had burned inside of her for all these years? Why didn't she let her explain about her arm? Why, of all nights, did she have to have Noni?

"Bye," Bernie whispered, lifting two fingers hidden safely in her pocket, an unseen gesture of good will, maybe even affection.

Smile, she commanded herself as she hurried to her own car. A big fake smile forced its way across her face, the visual announcement that the field trip downtown was all for nothing, that all was well. The façade she constructed was sturdy and strong, a freshly carved ice sculpture, the image of perfect happiness expertly chiseled in her own likeness.

"Ooooh," she said as she hopped into her seat, slamming her door behind her, reaching instantly for the seatbelt, avoiding the eyes of the woman who knew her better than any other. "It's colder than, what's that you used to say, Noni?" She turned the key and the engine hummed.

Noni chuckled, remembering how she used to make her granddaughter laugh with the silly sayings of her funny husband from long ago, when she still had so much to laugh about. "It's colder than a witch's tit in a brass bra. Your granddad used to say that."

"Nice, Noni. You're such a class act." She shifted the gear to reverse and backed out of the parking spot while warm air from the heater began to fill the car.

"That man had more silly sayings than anyone I ever met; he was from Arkansas, you know. They didn't have much to do there, I guess, but sit around and make dumb jokes." She drifted away to another time, another life, but only for a moment. She was quick to return to the moment, to know what was going on. "So, who was that lady? What happened?" Noni asked.

"Oh, it was just a client of mine. She dropped a letter off in the mail slot and the darned alarm went off." It occurred to Bernie that she used words like "darned" in the presence of Noni. With anyone else, she would have gone right ahead and said what she meant: the damn thing went off for no good reason. "It was nothing; I'll have to have the alarm company fix it. Funny, though, I mean the mailman drops mail in there all the time and no alarm goes off. There must be some kind of glitch in the system." She paused to turn and look closely at Noni, knowing how to change the subject, to get her back to the humor she'd shown just moments ago, away from the events of the last few minutes. "Or it was Mrs. Gordon playing with the motion detector."

"Who?"

"Our ghost. Didn't I ever tell you about our ghost?" Bernie reached over and patted her grandmother's leg, reassuring her, jostling her playfully.

"No. Your office is haunted?"

Bernie drove, chattering like a child caught in the act of doing something they know is very wrong, convinced that if they keep talking, nonstop and fast, somehow their infraction will go unnoticed and praise will replace punishment. *Again*, she thought, *I am blaming a ghost for those things I can't understand.* She rattled on, words tumbling out, while another part of her brain contemplated the ease of attributing all disturbances, annoyances, and troubles on the unseen spirit of a dead doctor's dead wife. "Can you believe it? She steals my files, makes me crazy. Poor Crystal. That ghost drives her to the edge of a nervous breakdown sometimes. It's actually pretty funny, sometimes, to watch her get scared when a floorboard creaks upstairs. I know it's just the old house settling or something, but that girl, she's such a lamb sometimes."

The light at the corner of McKinley Avenue and Van Ness Boulevard flashed red, forcing Bernie to brake to a hard stop, ending her banter. A two-story house on the corner was lit up with red and green lights along the roofline and three electronic reindeer grazing on the front lawn. "Christmas lights. Already," she muttered.

The days were passing quickly, another year coming to an end. Bernie looked over to the car stopped alongside them. There she was. Julie was making a right turn, looking to her left, directly into her car, staring at Bernie and Noni. Only three feet and two panels of glass separated Julie from Noni. Bernie grew silent at the sight of her mother, subdued by the sad confusion passing over Julie's face as she peered into her daughter's car. An artist who discovers her long-lost masterpiece of her own creation damaged beyond repair and not for sale. Bernie offered a weak smile and dipped her chin, a gentle nod from a passing car, nothing more.

Noni turned to see who caught Bernie's attention. "She looks familiar, do I know her?"

"No, it's just that client from the office."

"Oh dear," Noni gasped and turned back toward Bernie, clutching at her belly.

"What's wrong, Noni?" Bernie reached over again to press on her grandmother's leg, this time with worry and concern, not playfulness. "Are you okay?"

"Yes, I don't know what I . . . I think it's just a little gas." She moaned slightly. "It's nothing. Nothing."

"Are you sure?" The light flashed green and Bernie hurried through the intersection, leaving a bewildered Julie Randall behind.

"No, no. I'm fine. Let's go home, and I'll take some Gaviscon or something." Noni's chin seemed to tremble more, and she nervously fingered the air vents, funneling the warm air toward her. "Maybe it's the wine."

The need to chatter instantly faded with renewed worry over Noni's health. "Does this happen often?" she asked her grandmother. "Have you told your doctor?"

"I shouldn't have eaten so much," Noni said, shifting in her seat.

"You didn't eat that much, Noni. Maybe you're getting the flu or something. Should we go to the hospital?"

The conversation now would revolve around medications, diet, and digestion. The nosy spirit of Mrs. Gordon was forgotten and the whole Julie Randall incident would be set aside for another day. Bernie was the only family that Noni had. Julie Randall had lots of family waiting for her at home. Julie didn't need Bernie; Noni did.

Sixteen

1968

It wasn't hard to get a ride home. Juicy simply sat at the counter at the diner across the street from the hospital and made small talk with the waitress. In less than an hour, she'd offered the dark-haired girl who filled her coffee cup again and again, fifty dollars for a forty-mile ride.

The house was dark. Juicy waved good-bye to her driver and jogged across the street and around to the back of the house where she had hidden a key after accidentally locking herself out one afternoon. She had once feared being locked out with the baby inside; the idea of being separated from her for even a moment unbearable. For nine months, Ginny had been a part of her body. They weren't even two separate people. Then she was never farther away than the next room, still a source of nourishment as she nursed her, then bottle-fed her. Now she would have to get used to life without her, the quiet nights and empty arms. She had no idea how long she could go on living with such loss, or even if she wanted to, but for now, she wanted something, and it was inside this dark house.

The smell of stale beer and cigarette smoke lingered from a recent party, evidenced by the overflowing ashtrays and scattered beer cans and bottles. Some of the furniture was kicked over; it must have gotten wild as usual. It was a Friday night, and Juicy was nearly certain Freddie would be gone for the weekend, but she still hesitated to turn any lights on. Her eyes slowly adjusted to the darkness, and she moved on to the one bedroom she had shared with Freddie and Ginny.

The bed was a mess, all the sheets wadded up on the floor, and there were more cans and bottles strewn about. It had been a real party, just a different girl or girls. She wanted to wretch at the thought of what she'd been through, how she had actually thought she'd loved this man who had given her the greatest thing she'd ever known, then managed to take it away in such a short time.

It was there on the dresser, knocked over and face down, the eight-by-ten photograph of her holding Ginny. When Ginny was born, the hospital had given her a certificate for a free sitting at Sears and Roebuck. She didn't have money to buy all the pictures; if she'd known how things would turn out, she would have pawned everything she owned to get every last one of them. This one would have to do.

She stopped by the empty crib, a used model from the Goodwill store. She grabbed the blanket and stuffed doll; she would take those, too. It wasn't much, but she had to have something. She took a pillowcase off the pillow and shoved the doll in, wrapped the picture in the blanket and threw that in, too. She went to the closet and took a clean pair of jeans, then a couple of shirts and sweaters from the dresser, some underwear, and a pair of shoes. She didn't have a lot, so there wasn't much to leave behind.

With the stuffed pillowcase dragging behind her, on rubber legs she inched her way to the garage. Tears fell steadily down her cheeks, but she didn't bother to wipe them away. What would be the point? There were so many to follow. Her strength was waning rapidly in this place. She had to get away, and get away fast.

She knew where Freddie kept the spare truck key: in the old Folgers coffee can of screws and nails that he kept on his workbench. She tossed the packed pillowcase onto the front seat, opened the garage door, then climbed into the very truck that she and Ginny had been kicked out of. The fall hadn't killed her, only ended her life. She didn't want the truck, but she needed the ride. She would leave the haunted vehicle behind at the bus station. The cops would find it in a day or two and call Freddie to tell him they'd recovered his "stolen vehicle." There would be no way to know where she'd gone since she didn't even know where that was. She would take the first bus leaving, and wherever she landed, that's where she would be.

At 9:30, less than an hour after leaving the small house where she had tried in vain to grow a small family of her own, Julie Randall was on a Greyhound bus, traveling north on 99, headed for San Francisco.

Seventeen
2005

Don was waiting on the porch, a bottle of wine in one hand, the other hidden in a jacket pocket, trying to keep warm. Bernie waved to him as she pulled into the driveway.

"That's Don," she sighed, wishing he had forgotten where she lived. The events of the evening had delivered more than enough excitement for her, not to mention Noni, who had barely spoken a word on the drive home. Bernie was worried. "Noni, you're not feeling well; I'm going to cancel this; it's no big deal." She wished Noni would agree with her, say yes, send him away. Then the failed evening would not be her fault. She would merely be acting as a diligent caregiver, a loving granddaughter. But that's not what she said.

"No, I'm feeling better. I'm an old woman, those things happen. It was just a little indigestion, I think. I probably just need a little Mylanta." She fumbled helplessly with the door handle until Bernie made her way around to the passenger side to open the door for her.

While Bernie helped Noni from the car, Don came to offer his assistance, his arm. "You must be Noni," he said, and even though it was dark, Bernie could tell he was smiling. She knew he was smiling so big that his eyes nearly closed and that a strand of his straight black hair was hanging over one eye. He smelled good, like mountain air, fresh and clean, not like a bottle of aftershave.

"That's me. I'm the old woman with bad hips," she groaned, maneuvering herself in the seat, shifting her legs to the outside, "and a bit of an upset stomach." Bernie reached inside and put an arm around her, knowing exactly how to bear her grandmother's weight to get her onto her feet.

"And I'm Don; my hips are pretty good, so can I help?" he asked.

"Yeah, why don't you unlock the door." Bernie reached in her pocket for her keys, singled out the front door key, and handed the keys over to him. "We have this down, don't we Noni?"

Noni didn't answer, simply nodded and pushed herself up to a standing position, leaning heavily on her granddaughter. Together they would walk slowly, slowly, arm in arm, into the house where a motorized chair would assume the duty of weak legs.

The house was warm and still smelled of roast turkey and sweet corn pudding; the dining table was still covered with their elaborate dinner, just as they'd left it. "We had to go to the office," Bernie explained to Don. "The alarm went off." She gave a quick version of the dropping envelope, the version where Julie Randall was simply a client hand-delivering a letter.

"That's better," Noni said, back in the comfort of her chair, independently mobile once again.

"How about I make you a cup of mint tea," Bernie said. "It will warm you up and help your tummy."

"That might be good," she answered, her trembling hand lifted and wavering in the air, signaling to Bernie. "Let Don try some of that zucchini casserole. Heat it up a little first."

"Oh, I'm sure it's delicious," he said, "but I really couldn't eat another bite."

Bernie could easily envision the scene of his

Thanksgiving dinner, a large family gathered around a long table, plates piled with mashed potatoes and cranberry sauce, another table in the kitchen for all the younger ones, the kids' table.

"Well, how about some pie and coffee?" she offered. "Or a glass of wine. I made a pumpkin pie, but I don't know if it's any good. It looks good, but you never know about the flavor until you slice it, so it might be awful. I may have overdone it with the spices." The rambling speech plagued her again, as though the sound of her own voice would drown out the last hour of her life, keep it all at bay.

"I'd love a piece of pumpkin pie," he said, adding a slight bow of his head in submission. "And there is no such thing as bad pumpkin pie."

"Apparently you *can* eat another bite," Noni said, "just not my zucchini casserole."

Bernie flinched at the old woman's remark, but couldn't decide if she was trying to be funny or simply rude. Whatever it was, Don seemed oblivious to Noni's wry jab.

"Actually, I was saving just enough space for dessert. I didn't even have any of my mother's boysenberry pie, a personal favorite, so that I could have pie here with you two."

Good save, she thought. He's charming Noni into liking him, just like he charmed me, like he undoubtedly charms all his women. His boyish smile was infectious and eager, as if the very source of his joy was the sight of her. Bernie felt her cheeks warm with a happy blush, a softer shade than angry red. Her moment of tenderness was brief, tainted by the painful knowledge that he was slick, especially with the ladies, an accomplished player, apparently even with elderly women in wheel chairs. That might be valuable for her in the courtroom, watching him charm a jury, but she didn't need that complication in her personal life.

"Noni, how about you? A piece of pie? You think you're up to it?"

"Maybe a small piece," she mumbled as if sacrificing something, a holy martyr for a simple slice of pumpkin pie.

Don followed Bernie into the kitchen, leaving Noni to herself in the living room. Bernie would make coffee, slice pie and whisper endless apologies about the messy kitchen, her failure as a pie maker, not being there when he arrived, all while her mind raced on about meeting Julie Randall, wondering if she stayed in town and got a hotel, replaying an internal tape of memory over and over, each word spoken, how she looked, moved, how she clutched at the hem of her jacket, how she had driven two hundred miles to stick a letter in a mailbox. Bernie had not yet had a chance to read that letter. It was still tucked in her coat pocket, saved for later reading when she was alone in the safety of her bedroom.

While Bernie and Don tended to the business of dessert, Noni glanced again through the morning's headlines. No one noticed the dark colored Volkswagen convertible slowly passing by the house, making a U-turn at the corner and passing by again.

After quickly clearing the dinner dishes from the dining room table, Bernie relit the candles. They would eat their pie and drink coffee, surrounded by a warm glow of candlelight, and the night would be calm once again. But, despite Bernie's efforts to create a peaceful ambience, Noni seemed distracted and uncomfortable.

"How's your pie, Noni?" Bernie asked, concerned

about her grandmother's obvious distress.

"Oh, it's fine. Fine." Noni's brows were furrowed, and she trembled from head to foot, shaking and quivering as if she was chilled to the bone.

"It's delicious," Don said. "You're a pretty good cook, Ms. Sheridan."

"Thank you," she said, feeling the pink spread across her cheeks once again. "Noni, are you sure you're feeling okay? Maybe the night air was too much for you. I shouldn't have left you sitting in the car all that time."

"I'm fine, really, just tired. I think I want to go back to my place in the morning, though. It's easier for me to get around there, and my bed there goes up and down like a chair." Though she had only eaten two small bites of her pie, she put her fork down and pushed her plate away and sighed heavily.

"Sure," Bernie said, "whatever you want." Clearly, something was terribly wrong, and it seemed like much more than an upset stomach. Noni had been so anxious to meet Don, so happy at dinner, hungry and chatty. She was getting old, Bernie reminded herself, noticing the nonstop tremor in her grandmother's hands and jaw. She tried to remember how old she was, did the math in her head. Noni was eighty-six.

"I'm going to go to my room for a while, if you don't mind," Noni said, rolling herself away from the table. "It was nice meeting you, Don."

"Do you want me to help you?" Bernie offered.

"No, I just want to read a bit." She maneuvered her chair easily across the living room, picked up the newspaper, and rolled down the hallway to her old bedroom. She closed the door, leaving Bernie and Don free to talk.

"I don't know what's come over her," Bernie said, keeping her voice low and away from Noni's range of hearing. "She's not feeling well, I can tell."

"Maybe it's me," he offered. "Did she know I'm Vietnamese? Sometimes that's a problem with older people, the war and all."

"Oh, that wouldn't be it. Noni doesn't have a mean or racist bone in her body. Before she had to take me in, she was a social worker; she loves everybody, well, most everybody. She really is the most fair-minded person I've ever met."

"Bernie, everyone has a racist bone in their body. Sometimes they're little bones and sometimes they're really big bones. Sorry, it's not the issue right now, I know." He paused and sat quietly, his gaze fixed on Bernie. "Maybe she's just tired; it's getting late."

"You're probably right," she said, but she knew that wasn't it. Her instincts were screaming that somehow this had something to do with Julie Randall; it had to be. Everything was fine until that phone call, until they had to leave the house. If Julie made a habit of making unannounced visits to hand-deliver letters on holidays, there was probably trouble ahead.

They sat at opposite ends of the sofa, their bodies angled toward one another, like breathing bookends, occasionally sipping the Italian wine Don had brought along to share. The trip to the office and meeting Julie Randall still haunted her, but the mellow flavor of the wine softened the sharp edges in her mind. While she had initially wanted to send Don away, she now welcomed a bit of time to talk with him while Noni spent some time alone. The proximity of another person was a distraction from the can of worms about to be opened. She knew in her bones that this was one of those times when no amount of planning could control the impending chaos as life simply spun out of control.

Bernie studied the way Don seemed to unfold as he relaxed, one leg crossed over the other so that his left foot rested on his right knee, his long fingers curved around his ankle, his nails cut short and clean, nervously tracing the diamond pattern of his black and red socks. His V-neck sweater matched the color of the wine, a rich burgundy, and his blue-black hair refused to stay in place. Eventually, the electrical currents that had coursed through her body for hours slowed to a more pleasant rhythm, a soft hum rather than steel drums.

"I had a weird night," she finally said, her voice low and confessional. She was sharing a secret, unable to keep this news to herself.

"I thought something might be up. You seemed kind of wired and amped up earlier, and I didn't think it was me." His gaze was intense and curious, inviting her to lighten her emotional burden.

"Remember when I asked you if you'd want to meet your mother, your birth mother, if you could?" Her eyes shifted to the left, then right, searching for the words and the courage to take this conversation further.

"Yeah." He sat up straighter, his foot dropping to the floor to allow him to inch nearer to this new friend, to hear her whispers.

"Well, tonight . . . I did." Just saying it out loud caused a well of unexpected emotion to wash over her. Her eyes burned with a threat of tears. She swallowed hard and willed them away, tightening her stomach, steeling her nerves to any sign of weakness. *No tears*, she reminded herself. *This woman was nothing more to her other than a little shared DNA*.

"You met your mother? Your biological mother?" He could just as easily have been asking if she'd won the lottery, his eyes flashing wider than she'd ever seen, full of anticipation and curious wonder.

"Uh-huh. She's the one who set the alarm off." Bernie didn't respond to Don's excitement; she fought to remain expressionless, took another sip of calm, slowly set the glass down on the end table behind her, and casually combed her fingers through her hair. *Numb*, she thought, again, *I'm numb*.

"So, where is she now?"

"I don't know. I couldn't let Noni know who she was, so I sent her away. It was getting late, so I told her to get a hotel and rest, then go back home in the morning. She lives in San Rafael." She shook her head from side to side. "Can you believe it? She drove all the way down here on Thanksgiving Day to stick a letter in the mail slot at my office. She must be a little nutty. Anyway, I couldn't talk to her about anything right then, not while I'm dealing with Noni." Her gaze briefly shifted toward the closed bedroom door. "Noni would freak if she knew what was going on, and you can see she's not feeling well."

"You're kidding." He seemed baffled by her news, his lips slightly parted, no smile anywhere in sight. "Did you arrange to meet later?"

"No. I told her Noni wasn't well." Sensing his disapproval, she emphasized, "this whole birth mother thing is very upsetting to Noni. She's old, Don. She doesn't need any more to worry about. I can't be dealing with that while

Noni is struggling."

"What exactly does Noni know? How much have you told her?"

Bernie shared with him how she'd gone to Noni after the first call from the social worker, and knew then not to let her know about the exchange of letters. She now needed to put it all on the back burner for a while. "Noni's old; I have to think of her first. It's my turn to take care of her after all she's done for me."

"Okay, but why should your grandmother care if you met your birth mother? It really doesn't have anything to do with her." Confusion seemed to evolve to utter exasperation. "I don't get it."

"Because Noni only thinks of my mother, my adopted mother—her daughter—as my mother. And since my mother's dead, the very idea of someone else taking her place is just too painful; kind of like killing her again. I can't do that do her." She was adamant, convincing herself that she was doing the right thing as she explained her decisions.

"But you're not doing anything to her; you'd be doing something for yourself and for your biological mother too, who, by the way, is obviously alive. I would think Noni would want you to have someone other than just her."

"You don't understand; there are things that happened and . . ." Her eyes closed, "you just can't understand."

"Tell me," he pleaded.

"I can't." The pleasant lull of Italian wine and conversation had passed. Bernie felt pressured to share painful secrets, and that was not going to happen.

"We all have things to hide, don't we Don?" She

hinted at her knowledge of his cheating and lies, the cause of his divorce. "We put ourselves out there like we want people to see us, but underneath, well, there's usually some dirty little secret hiding under the bed, or maybe up in Seattle." She cocked her head, raised a knowing eyebrow and lifted her glass.

"What are you talking about?" he asked.

"I'm sorry," she said, but her back stayed firm. There was no apology in her clenched jaw. "I really think you should probably go." His look of incredulity was unexpected and painful, a familiar knot in her gut. "This was nice and all, but I need to work through some things on my own. And I need to deal with Noni, help her get ready for bed. Still, these are my problems; I shouldn't have gone after you like that. Really, I'm sorry for being rude." And this time, her shoulders and chin fell. She was sorry.

"But what did you mean by that secret in Seattle business?"

"Nothing, forget it." She picked up her glass and swallowed the last bit of wine. She scooted forward on the couch, looked over to him, waiting for him to get the hint, to stand and head toward the door.

"No, you meant something." He stayed put. "You've heard something or seen something, probably about my divorce, right?"

She didn't say anything, her face a blank slate.

"I thought you prided yourself in being direct, not leaving questions unasked. So," he said, "tell me, please, if something is bothering you."

Bernie sat quietly, slowly shaking her head.

Don finally rose to his feet, resigned to her stubborn

silence, her wish for him to leave. "Bernie," he said, "if you want to know something about me, just ask. I'll tell you. I'm not perfect, and I never claimed to be. I also don't feel any need to confess every sin and flaw of my past to you, but if you want to know something, just ask. I won't lie to you." He picked up his jacket, draped it over his arm.

"Okay, I'll ask. Are you divorced? You told me you were divorced; are you?"

"Yes, officially as of November fourteenth. I admit that when we met the divorce was not quite final, but in my defense, I considered that a technical formality. I do not consider that a lie. The reason I've been in and out of town so much is to go back and take care of those last bits of formality."

"Did you get divorced because of another woman?"

He sighed then pressed his lips closely together. "No. I met someone while my wife and I were separated, and it certainly made things more complicated, but it was hardly the cause. But why do you ask? Where are you getting this information?"

"So, where's this woman now?" Bernie's voice remained flat, absent emotion, compelling Don's piqued manner to adjust to her own, from fire to ice.

"In Seattle, I think. Why does she matter? I haven't even seen her in months. And what does that have to do with anything going on here?"

Bernie smiled knowingly and rubbed her left eye with her ring finger, desperately wishing she had not opened this door, wishing she had never invited him over, never shared a burger or a trip to a cemetery, never hired him to work on her cases. This was why it was better not to get too involved with people. It always led to her feeling more alone than ever.

"Bernie, it's an old story, but if you want the sordid details, I'll give them to you. Even though, quite frankly, it's none of your business. My wife worked hard to ruin my reputation during our divorce. I guess it worked since her rumors spread to people I'd never even met at the time."

It was the angriest and most intimate conversation she'd had with a man in years and the only way she knew how to deal with it was to end it immediately. "Don, I don't want to hear the dirty secrets that ended your marriage. Seriously, I think we should call it a night. And maybe we should just stick to business for a while."

Don pulled his jacket on and stood looking down at Bernie. "You've had a rough day, and I'm an easy target. I'll talk to you soon, and meanwhile you think about if you're comfortable being my friend, and I'll think about it, too. It bothers me that you felt the need to dig into my past. That's weird, Bernie. Tell me, is *your* life an open book? Do you want people digging around in your past? I doubt it."

For a long while, Bernie sat in the weighty silence and tried to sort out the preceding hours, yet another example of life going off script, sending the best laid plans into the trash heap. The happy day she had imagined as she and Noni prepared their holiday feast was just that, imagined. Noni was alone in her room, upset about something or not feeling well. Don had gone home angry and the first friendship she'd made in a long time was likely over. Her kitchen was a disaster. And more than all that, she had met the woman who brought her into this world thirty-seven years ago. There was a time when Julie Randall had been her source of life, the very air that she breathed. Now they were strangers.

Any other night, Bernie would have drifted off to bed, leaving the bits of turkey and mashed potatoes to harden on the good china, the leftover casserole to rot on the counter. But the very presence of Noni in the house denied her the luxury of lazy procrastination. She stood at the sink, scrubbing casserole dishes and saucepans, pondering the state of her life and everyone in it, both living and dead, sipping on one last glass of wine. The familiar ache of loneliness spread through her like a heavy weight.

Now that Julie had a face, Bernie found it increasingly difficult to blame her for a rotten childhood. Julie didn't look like the evil person she had imagined; she looked . . . nice. And in the end, Bernie had survived and done well in her life. The stories hidden under her bed were gruesome tales of other nightmares, of horrible deaths, murders and suicides, husbands killing wives, wives killing husbands, even parents killing their own children. Who lived through those stories? Someone always lived to suffer, but did they spend their entire lives consumed with ugly bitterness as she apparently had? Like Noni had? All these years later, and they still only had each other.

The two of them had made a life together, healing from the same wounds, loving fiercely, but hating, too. It was easy for Bernie to say that she would have been spared the shattering blow of losing both a mother and father through a single act of violence if she hadn't been their daughter, if she had not been given up for adoption. But that doesn't mean there wouldn't have been some other horrible thing happen if her birth mother had kept her. Everything would have been different, but she didn't know that it would have been better.

No one could know that.

Julie Randall, nameless and faceless, had served as her maternal whipping post for everything that had gone wrong in Bernie's life for the past twenty-five years. It was easy to blame the unknown. For Noni, that mark was Bernie's father, the dad that Bernie loved more than he could have known. If he'd only known how much she loved him, he wouldn't have done what he did. Blaming her father was almost natural; he was the one who shattered any balance or normalcy in her life. He was the one who pulled the trigger that sent a bullet into his wife, then pulled it again on himself. If he were here, who would he blame? And, Bernie wondered, who does Julie blame? Where does all the blame and shame end? Where does all that anger and resentment go?

It was only after the dishwasher began to hum that she retrieved the pink envelope from her coat pocket. She sat at the kitchen table, unfolded the two crisp pages, and read.

Dear Bernadette —

Joan Bennett called to tell me that you had asked to put our communications on hold. She explained that your grandmother was ill, and I'm very sorry about that, but I'm also sorry that I won't be hearing more from you. I know I'm breaking the rules by writing this letter and bypassing Social Services, but I need to do this. I've waited so long to find you, and now that I have, there are things I need to say. I don't want to wait anymore.

Today is Thanksgiving. I have a house full of people here for dinner, friends and family, including my other children—your brother and sister—but I feel empty and alone. My first-born child won't be here. She doesn't even know me, and it's almost more than I can bear now that I know where you are, now that there has been word from you.

Bernadette, I never wanted to give you up. I loved you more than I had ever loved anyone my whole life. People always tell me I have the memory of an elephant, but they don't know how hard I've tried to forget certain things. Things that happened, bad things, and it seemed like I had no choice at the time. One thing I know is I never wanted to forget you, how much I loved you. In the end, I was sure you would be better off with anyone but me, that you would have the life you deserved if you were away from me. Now, all these years later, I'm not sure. All I can hope is that your life was full of good things as you grew into the woman you are today.

So if you change your mind and feel like you would like to see me, please know I want nothing more in the world than that. My cell phone number is 415-555-2804. I will come on a moment's notice, any day, any time. I hope this doesn't mess things up for me with Joan Bennett, since she's been very helpful and kind, but I've waited too many years to listen to another social worker tell me what to do. This time, I'm following my heart. I left a big piece of it with you so long ago, and I've regretted it every day.

Much love,

Julie

Julie. Bernie held the letter loosely in her lap and thought of the woman who had stood on the sidewalk in front of her office, the woman who drove two hundred miles just to hand deliver a note on pink paper, leaving a house full of people to fend for themselves on Thanksgiving. Her lips softened and parted to a slight smile at the thought of someone wandering through a house searching for the missing Julie: "Where's Mom? Mom? Has anybody seen Mom, I think the turkey's burning?" Did she tell them she was leaving? Probably not, or they would have talked her out of such an irrational act. Irrational. Her mother was irrational, following her heart. Bernie had to admit, she liked that.

It was tempting to call the number, if only to ask if she had stayed in town for the night, to ask her where she was born, who her father was, if her grandparents were alive, and was there a family history of cancer or heart disease. A family history . . . a family history. She wanted to tell her she, too, had a fantastic memory. Did she inherit that? She had so many questions. Why did Noni have to be so difficult?

Bernie turned the lights off, made sure the doors were locked, left the letter on her bed and padded down the hallway to tap lightly on Noni's door. "Noni? Are you awake?"

Noni was sitting on the cushioned window seat, her afghan wrapped around her shoulder, staring out the window into the darkness. "I guess your friend went home," she said, her words weak with age and exhaustion.

"Yeah, but I'm not so sure we're still friends. We kind of had a disagreement."

Noni looked at her. "Bernadette, I only wanted Patty to be happy with Ron. She needed you, and I didn't want her to go away. I love you, Bernadette. If anything happens, promise me you won't forget that." Her chin was quivering, her whole head in a constant side to side tremor.

"Noni, of course I know you love me. You have been so good to me. And what are you talking about? Nothing's going to happen; I won't let it." She sat next to her grandmother and wrapped her arm across the frail shoulders. "You're freezing; let's get you into bed."

With the support of Bernie's strong arm, Noni rose to her feet. Bernie helped her to the bathroom, helped her change into her flannel nightgown, then helped her into bed, tucking her grandmother in as though she was a small child. "You rest now," she said, then kissed Noni on the forehead twice.

Noni closed her eyes for the kiss, then softly said, "Goodnight, Bernadette."

With images of Julie Randall on a cold November night, fists clutching the hem of her jacket, jaw set for any punch, leaning closer and whispering "You're beautiful," Bernie fell into a fitful sleep. The pink letter that had caused all the ruckus was resting on her chest, just over her heart. This was one mess she could leave overnight and hopefully relive in her dreams, a place where no one could see.

The sound of someone calling her name confused her. She didn't move until she heard it again, this time with a crash. "Bernie, help me."

Bernie threw back her blankets and ran the short distance to Noni's room. Noni stood next to her bed, clutching her belly, wincing in pain. "I'm not . . ." she groaned, "feeling well."

Bernie raced to Noni's side and grabbed onto her, trying to hold her up, wrapping one arm firmly about the waist from behind, the other around the front. As she struggled to keep both of them upright, the pink paper seemed to appear from nowhere and fluttered to the floor. Bernie saw the letter falling and wondered how it had stayed in her hand even through sleep, even while racing to her grandmother's side.

Noni groaned louder and doubled over, clutching her belly and Bernie's arm. "Oh, oh, oh, oh, oh God," she cried. The smell hit Bernie's nose before she actually saw the mess at her feet, before the realization that Noni did not simply have a bad case of gas. A splash of loose stools fell to the floor, spattering the letter, dotting Bernie's bare feet and running down Noni's weak legs. "Oh God," she said again. "I'm sorry." And like a child, the old woman began to weep. "I'm so sorry."

Bernie guided her grandmother to the bed and sat her down. In one swift movement she pulled the damaged letter from the dirty mess and ran for the bathroom, repeating over and over again, "Don't cry, Noni. We'll fix it. Please don't cry."

Bernie turned on the shower and situated the shower bench for her grandmother to sit on. She left the soiled letter in the sink and hurried back to the bedroom where Noni sat on the bed, confused and frightened by the further betrayal of her own body.

"Come on, Noni, let's get you cleaned up," she said, again moving in close, offering her shoulder and arms to help bear her weight. She ignored the mess on the floor, the bed, herself. She would worry about that later. She had to get Noni cleaned up and calmed down before anything else. It was her turn to be the caregiver.

Bernie guided Noni into the shower stall. Under a stream of warm water, she lifted the old woman's arms and removed her soiled nightgown, dropping it in the corner of the shower. She used a washcloth and lavender soap to clean her grandmother's delicate skin from head to toe, gently washing her legs, feet, each toe.

Noni repeated again and again, "I'm sorry, Honey," her chin trembling, her limbs weak and flaccid to her granddaughter's touch. "This is so embarrassing, so awful."

"It's okay," Bernie whispered, water running down her own back, soaking her hair, dripping into her eyes. Her own nightgown clung to her skin, drenched and heavy. "Do you think we should go to the emergency? Should I call an ambulance?"

"I don't want to go to the hospital. I think I'm okay now. I just couldn't hold it."

After she had dried Noni thoroughly and covered her with two large bath towels, Bernie pulled off her own wet nightgown and dropped it on the shower floor along with Noni's. She pulled her faded green chenille bathrobe from a hook on the wall and tied it tightly about her as she hurried down the hall to find a clean gown for Noni. She helped Noni into a soft chair and draped one blanket over her shoulders and another across her lap and cooed softly, as if she was talking to a baby, while she dried her thin hair.

It was three o'clock in the morning, the day after Thanksgiving. While the rest of the city slept with full bellies, dreaming of pumpkin pie and coffee for breakfast, Bernie knelt on her hands and knees scrubbing the floor. She pulled dirty sheets and blankets from the bed and carried them to the laundry room. Finally, she helped her frail grandmother into a clean bed, again kissed her on the forehead, again tucked her in. "Noni, you call me if you feel sick again," she said. "Are you sure you don't want me to stay in here with you? I can curl up on the window seat."

"No, Honey, go to bed. I'm fine now."

In the bathroom, Julie's letter still lay in the sink, looking like it had been dropped in a mud puddle. With a fresh washcloth dampened with warm water, Bernie worked to clean the letter. She gently dabbed and wiped, then rinsed the washcloth clean to dab and wipe some more. Eventually, she wiped the letter clean. In the process, the blue ink faded and the paper thinned and wrinkled, but she could still read the loving message. She carried the damaged letter to her bedroom, knowing where it belonged. The safest place for this letter to hide away was in the box under the bed. Julie Randall's words would rest in the company of all those other tragic stories collected over the years.

The pink paper seemed out of place in the pile of yellowing newsprint. Bernie wondered if it would age and yellow along with the others. She hoped not. She was afraid to admit it, but she hoped that it would somehow be the beginning of something new. It might not happen for a while, but the letter was there, tucked in with all that death and sadness. Even if it was a symbolic gesture, there was a power in adding that new message to the mix, placing it at the top.

The rhythm of the washing machine eventually lulled her back to sleep. When her eyes opened, the middle-of-the-night drama seemed unreal. Had Noni really shit all over everything? From some lost corner of her brain, came an image of her mother sitting at the kitchen table, crying. Her sharp edge of memory that others admired sometimes betrayed her, sent her reeling into darkness. Bernie had come home from school and asked her what was wrong. Her mother had glared at her through red eyes that seemed to be swimming in a pool of mascara, black rivers running down her cheeks. "Everything would have been fine," she had cried. "I could have had a real life all these years, but your stupid grandmother shit all over it. She made sure I'd stay, and I did. But not now, not this time. I don't care if divorce is a sin. I want out."

Where did that come from? She tried to imagine what it could have been that Noni had done that ruined her mother's life. When was that? Her mom's hair was bleached blonde, almost white, so it wasn't too long before she died. And in the car, her father was mad at Noni, too, saying he wished she'd never told him. She knew she could never ask Noni what it all meant now. *Damn it*, she thought, *if I'd remembered that earlier, when Noni was stronger, I could have asked her.* She lay there and wondered if Noni knew more about her parents' fate than she'd shared, but that was unimaginable. Noni would have told her anything to help solve the mystery that tormented her, wouldn't she?

She struggled to clear her head, to make order of the messy details that loomed with the day. She wondered if Julie Randall was still in town, where she might have spent the night, if she was having breakfast somewhere. It was Friday, a holiday. She would take Noni back to Nazareth House where she wanted to be. Normally, Bernie would have tried to talk her out of it, to get her to stay the weekend like they'd planned, but after last night, she wouldn't take any chances. There were nurses at Nazareth. They could do more for her there.

By the time Bernie helped Noni into the car to make the short drive back to Nazareth House, it was nearly noon. The air was chilly, but the sun shined brightly from a sky of perfect blue. Noni was feeling better, seemed more like her old self, at least her stomach had settled down, but she still seemed out of sorts and overly nervous.

"Are you sure you're feeling okay?" Bernie asked as she turned the key and adjusted the heater.

"I'm fine," Noni answered, her chin still trembling, her jaw now moving side to side, an old nervous habit from younger days, not the tremors of age. "I don't know what happened to me last night. I think I'm not used to drinking wine anymore."

"Impossible," Bernie teased. "It flows through our veins."

Noni chuckled a little, but her jaw continued to gnaw at unseen terrors, side to side, grinding down the ancient molars in the back of her mouth.

"I'm worried about you, Noni. You seem upset about something." Bernie paused to glance at her grandmother before backing out of the drive. She looked older than eighty-six years old, with the flat, thin strands of gray hair bobby pinned back behind her ears instead of the curls and elegant twist she loved. Bernie reached over and lightly brushed her grandmother's fine hair away from her forehead with her fingers. "We'll get you back to Nazareth and let the doctor take a look at you."

"I don't need the doctor."

"Well, I do. I need to know that you're okay." Bernie drove slowly, careful with her fragile cargo. She worried Noni might feel sick in the car, so she drove slowly, keeping a close watch on her grandmother. Not once did she notice the dark green Volkswagen convertible that trailed her, always a block away, just outside the rearview mirror.

Eighteen

1968

San Francisco. The sky was so bright, it almost hurt. She stared across the bay. Sailboats skimmed along the dark water. And there in the distance, standing guard over the bridge that tugged at the edges of the bay, was Alcatraz. Like her, the vacant prison was haunted by hatred and violence, left to stand empty and alone in view of the City that swelled with life and young love. Like all those prisoners before her, she could see the promise of the skyline, but she would never feel it. She was a walking ghost.

Nineteen
2005

Julie drove past Nazareth House slowly. The statue of the Virgin Mary was there to greet all visitors, her hands open and ready to receive the needy. *Bernadette must be Catholic*, she thought. Of course, with a name like Bernadette, she should have guessed. Her little Subaru was easy to spot in the nearly empty parking lot. At the next block, she turned back around and found a place to park where she could watch her daughter from across the street.

Look at her; she's so good to her grandmother. She must have had good parents, exactly the life I wanted for her. Maybe I should just let her be, wait for her to contact me, like she said. But how can I? It's been thirty-seven years, thirty-seven torturous years away from her, imagining what she looks like, wondering how her day was, if she got what she wanted for her birthday, for Christmas. And now, she's right there, just across the street. I could call out her name, and she would hear me, turn, and look my way.

Julie watched her daughter guide the hobbling old woman through the doors and tried to figure out what they were doing. Bernie had said her grandmother was spending the weekend with her, but she would bet her last nickel that the grandmother lived here at this place, an old folks home for old Catholics. Why else would they be here on the day after Thanksgiving, so early in the day? While she waited, she picked up her cell phone to call home yet again, let them know she was still in Fresno, not sure if she would make it home before dinner. You do what you have to do, Greg had said last night. He knew what this meant to her. Of all people, he knew how she had longed for the day she found her Ginny—no, it's Bernie, she corrected herself.

"I can't believe I'm not tired," she said into the phone. "I'm sure I only slept a few minutes last night, but I'm actually feeling pretty good. I just saw her again."

"Don't push it," Greg said. "If you get tired, get a hotel and rest. Don't get on that highway if you're sleepy."

"Well, first I want to see if I can't talk to Bernie again before I take off. I'm just tired of doing what everyone says, so I'm just checking things out a little bit before I decide what to do, before I give up on this trip." She rolled the window down and let the cool November air drift over her, wishing there were a Starbucks on the corner so she could sip a large latte while she studied the empty parking lot.

"Jules," her husband said. "I'm worried about you. I don't like the idea of you playing private eye, following people around, watching them. I mean, you don't want her to think you're some kind of psycho, like a stalker or something. Come home. We'll figure something else out. I'll help you."

"Greg," she whispered, "I'm not going to do anything stupid. I'm good with people, you know that." His concern warmed her, but this time she was following her own gut.

"Yeah, but you can wait a few more months. Maybe you should just come on home now, or, if you want, I'll come get you. Andy can drive me down, and I'll drive your car back. There's nothing going on here, anyway."

It was one of the things that she loved about him, his endless caring, her living and breathing guardian angel. If it had not been for Greg, well, she didn't like to think of that. She rarely disagreed with him, he was always so sensible and sometimes irritatingly fair, but this was different. This time she needed to do something; she wasn't entirely sure what that was at this point, but she wasn't ready to drive away. That much she knew. Not yet.

"No, let me just . . . hey, I have to go. Bernie just came out and she's by herself. Ooooh, I have an idea." She hung up before Greg could talk her out of doing something foolish.

The reception area was empty. A fake Tiffany lamp glowed over the unmanned information desk, a steaming cup of coffee resting near an open romance novel. On the cover a muscular man with shoulder length hair held a woman close to him, her back snug against his chest, her face turned up toward him, her heavy breasts nearly bared by the plunging neckline. Julie strolled down the hallway, her toll bridge smile leading the way.

"Good morning," she whispered to an elderly woman, her wheelchair parked in the hallway. "How are you today?"

"Who are you?" the woman asked. "Do you work here?" Her face scowled, as if she was ready to pounce with a complaint to anyone on the staff. Her swollen feet were stuffed in thick, white socks resting on metal footrests, a bright yellow sweater draped across her shoulders.

"Oh no, I'm just visiting. I'm a friend of Bernadette Sheridan, and I thought I'd pop in and see her grandmother. Do you know Bernadette?" Julie wished she knew the grandmother's name. This might be difficult if she didn't happen to recognize the old woman she'd seen Bernie escort through the door just moments before.

"Bernie? The lady lawyer?"

"Yes, that's her." Julie moved closer. Bernie. She

liked that better than Bernadette.

"Everyone knows her; Isabelle is always bragging about her; Bernie says this, Bernie says that. Bernie comes here on Friday nights; she brings Isabelle candy sometimes." She let her long, thin fingers lift to her lips, paused deep in thought, and seemed to be considering the situation carefully. "She was here this morning, so she might not come tonight."

Julie smiled and nodded, eager to give a little attention to the poor soul with the hope of getting a little information. "So, are you and Isabelle friends?" Her voice dripped in sweetness as though she spoke to a four-year old.

"Oh yes, we sit together at supper."

"Where is Isabelle's room? Is it near you? I mean, are you two close to each other?"

The wrinkled old woman lifted her hand and pointed to the door down the hall. "That's her room, there. Want me to take you to her?"

"No, no. I think I'll just pop in on my own and surprise her."

"Well, I hope she's not reading her paper. She gets mad if you bother her when she's reading the paper. And don't eat her candy, either."

And with that, the old woman pushed a button and buzzed away. Julie knocked lightly on Isabelle's door and waited for an answer, her thoughts racing. *Should I tell her who I am? Or is it better to make up some story like maybe that I'm a church volunteer or something.* She was still wondering what to do when she heard a voice from inside answer.

"Come in."

Julie opened the door slowly and stepped in

cautiously. There in the bed, her eyes closed, was Bernie's grandmother, Isabelle Fierro. Julie moved closer, a tense smile frozen on her face, clutching her oversized handbag for support. She hoped she didn't look too much of a fright after spending a night in her car. Julie was positive this was the same woman she had seen Bernie helping through the door. And there on the dresser was a large photograph of a younger Bernadette, glancing over her shoulder, her long auburn hair hanging down her back. The perfect senior picture.

"Isabelle?" she whispered. "Are you Isabelle?"

The old woman opened her eyes and blinked twice before a rush of fear and panic swept over her. She moaned or cried, the sound unintelligible, and covered her face with her hands. "Go away," she cried. "Please, just leave me alone." She was almost yelling. "Get out of here."

"Ma'am, I'm sorry; I don't mean to bother you." Julie stepped back. "I'll go." She looked over her shoulder, just in time to see Sister Rose and a young, dark-haired man rushing through the door.

"Who are you?" Sister Rose demanded. "What are you doing to Mrs. Fierro?"

"I just wanted to . . ." Julie turned back to the bed and looked again at the old woman. "Mrs. Who? Did you say Fierro? Isabelle Fierro?" There on the dresser, not three feet from the picture of a young Bernie, was a smaller picture: an older woman, a younger woman, and a little girl. Julie's knees went weak, and her heart rose to her throat. It was her. It all came clear in an instant. The perfect, but childless, couple, the perfect home and yard where Ginny was supposed to be better off, the shrewd manipulation. It was all for herself. Isabelle took Ginny for her own daughter. A lifetime of pain and anguish roared through her brain, a white heat.

"It's you," she growled, hungry for the truth, hungry for vengeance. "You stole my baby for your own self. You tricked me; you lied to me. Why? Why my baby?"

"Go away," Isabelle cried, her face still covered by ancient hands. "It was the best thing for everyone. I just wanted to fix things. How could I know? I couldn't know what would happen. Go away. Go."

"Please, Ma'am, come with me." Sister Rose took Julie's elbow and physically maneuvered her away, toward the door. "Come now, you can't be in here." She looked to the young man. "Jose, take this woman to my office; I'll be right there." She then moved to Isabelle's side, leaned in close, moving the old hands away from her watering eyes.

"Isabelle, what is all this? Hush now," she whispered. "It's all okay now. I'm here, I'm here now. I'm going to call Bernie to come over, too. It's going to be fine."

Julie didn't hear anymore. Her escort was leading her away, away from the woman she had hated for so many years, away from the woman who had robbed her of her firstborn, a lifetime that could never be replaced. Every step she took, the entirety of the situation grew more sickening, the very thought of Bernadette and her devotion to this horrible woman. She would tell her daughter everything. It wasn't her fault; she didn't give up her baby freely. She was tricked and manipulated when she was hurt and sick, when she was in a desperate place. It would be difficult for Bernadette to know the truth, but it had to be done. Bernie had to know the level of deceit that was involved, how her grandmother had taken advantage of Julie at her weakest moment, when she was damaged and broken. She would be here when her daughter, yes, *her* daughter, would arrive to tend to the hysterical old lady. She would wait here and tell Bernie every detail, even the part about that damn trailer. There had been enough lies. It would all be out before this day ended. Today, Julie would really get her daughter back.

310

Twenty

1968

Alcatraz loomed in the distance and a hard wind blew cold. Juicy shivered and held onto the railing. She was weak, exhausted, and every inch of her body hurt, but she liked the sting of the wind, feeling her hair lash about wildly. This was her first trip to the Golden Gate.

The money buried in her bag made her nauseous. How could she ever bring herself to spend it? It was cursed, damned, like her. Somewhere along the trip north, as she stared out the window at the rolling brown hills, ideas came to her. There were options. She could join the other losers of the world and find her peace in the cold, rough water below the famous bridge. There, she could disappear forever. She had made that her first stop. If she didn't have the courage to make the jump, she would head for the park and be a "hophead hippie," as Freddie used to call them. They'd seen them on the news, young people barefoot and dancing in the street, flowers in their wild hair. Freddie had called them a bunch of freaks, said all they did was drop acid and smoke dope all day. Getting high sounded like a fine escape. She would find the people with flowers in their hair and use her money to fill her head to overflowing swirling visions and happy illusions. Her pathetic life was so wretched that a part of her wanted to laugh like a lunatic. It wasn't so long ago that she was just another silly girl who'd fallen for one of the many jerks out there. Two years later, she was a dirty rag not worth saving, someone who used to be a mother, someone who used to have value. She clutched the rail tighter, closed her eyes, and leaned into it, feeling the rough wind, imagining the fall.

"You're not gonna jump, are you?"

His voice startled her.

"Huh?" She looked to see who spoke. Was this guy talking to her? Did she know him?

"You look like you could fly right off of there if you let go, and I wouldn't want to see that." He smiled gently and offered a hand.

"No, I was just, uh, looking at Alcatraz, only wishing I could fly." She stepped to the side, moving away from the stranger dressed in his grey uniform, refusing his hand. A mailman. He was a mailman.

"It's something, isn't it?" he said, giving her space.

"Hmmm."

"Who won?" he asked.

"What?"

He pointed to her bruised face. "Looks like you had a bit of a scuffle, or something."

"Oh, that. It was an accident."

"Looks like it hurts."

She lifted her fingers to her cheek, touched it lightly. "Not really." She turned away, hoping the intrusive letter carrier would keep on walking, but he didn't. Why was he out here anyway? There certainly were no mailboxes along the bridge.

"This is the second-best view in the world," he said. "I come out here sometimes on my way home, like now, just to feel the wind and the sky and the ocean all around me. I just wish I could make the cars go away."

"It's nice." She kept her gaze on the giant rock in

the middle of the bay.

"Don't you want to know what the best view is?"

"What?"

"The best view is just across the bridge, from the headlands, where you can see all this and the skyline, too. Ever been there?" He ignored her cold efforts to avoid him, pressing her for conversation.

"No," she said, her eyes still turned to the old prison and the choppy sea that rocked beneath them.

"Want to?"

"What?"

"See the other view. I'll take you there, if you want." He placed one hand on her forearm. "You look like you need to see the city skyline. It will change your life."

And finally, she turned to face him, to see who grabbed her now. "Really? It's that easy to change a life?" she scoffed.

"It is if you let it. And if it doesn't, you can come back here and look at this one again, and I won't bother you."

He held onto her arm, pulling her and her pillowcase away from the railing, guiding her along before she could even answer. "I'm Greg," he said. "What's your name?"

"Julie." She would never let anyone call her Juicy again.

"You live around here?" he asked.

"No; well, maybe. I just got here." Julie pulled her arm free. She was done with people forcing her to go where she didn't want to go, or do things she didn't want to do, and she was absolutely done with men putting their hands on her.

"I live in one of the houseboats off Sausalito, just up the road. It's my sister's place. She has another room for rent, if you're looking. You should check it out. It's very cool."

Julie kept walking beside him, not certain where she was going or why she went along, but she did.

"You hungry?" he asked. "My truck is in the lot at the end of the bridge. I have a couple of sandwiches I packed for lunch, but I never got around to eating."

"Why are you out here?" she finally asked. "Why are you really walking on the bridge?"

Greg turned his face toward her then looked at a flock of seagulls squawking overhead. "I was on my way home and saw you standing there. You looked a little lost, so I parked the truck and walked back to make sure you were okay."

"I wasn't going to jump."

"I didn't say you were."

As cars sped by, the two strangers walked to the north end of the bridge and over to a red and white Chevy truck. Greg unlocked the door and reached in for his black lunchbox. "There's a bench over there," he said, pointing to the edge of the parking lot. "Come have a sandwich and I'll tell you about Lanie's houseboat. She's a free spirit and lots of fun. You'd like her, I think."

As the wind whipped through their hair, Greg and Julie shared his cheese and tomato sandwiches and a thermos of hot coffee. It was the beginning of a friendship, the beginning of a new life with new people. The road to healing both physically and spiritually was long and never easy, but life on the water allowed her time and space to cry and think about Ginny, the baby she missed so much she wanted to die.

For months, Lanie made her herbal teas and rubbed patchouli oil on her feet, telling her it would heal the trauma of her past and energize her future with love and peace. She taught Julie Yoga and meditation. Greg took her on long walks through the Marin Headlands and Point Reyes, showing her a beautiful world just outside their door. He showed her California poppies, Indian paintbrush and lupine, and said they reminded him of her, wild and beautiful. Eventually, she came to believe that she had done the right thing, that Ginny was living a life she could never have given her. Over time, Greg made her smile again, and then one day he made her laugh again. She never forgot where she came from and what she left behind, but she slowly learned to move on.

Twenty-One
2005

Bernie had not even taken her coat off when Sister Rose called and told her to hurry back, telling her an unknown woman was causing poor Mrs. Fierro to be terribly distressed. Minutes later, Bernie pushed through the doors of Nazareth House, past Sister Rose's office where Julie Randall anxiously waited, and headed directly to Noni's room. Noni first. She composed herself before entering, licked her lips and sauntered over to the chair beside her grandmother's bed. She lifted the hand that hid the old woman's face, took it into her own, and stroked it gently.

"Noni, what are you doing in that bed? Shouldn't you be out there bugging poor Lolly or something?" She leaned over and kissed her grandmother's forehead.

"Bernadette, what are you doing back here?" She blinked several times and tried to push herself up.

"I missed you, I guess." She helped her grandmother to a sitting position in the bed. "Actually, I heard there was a bit of a rumble going on, so I thought maybe I'd come and take care of things, you know, kick a little ass or something." She offered a wry smile and winked at the old woman.

"Bernie, just go home, please." She squeezed her granddaughter's hand. "What I want is for you to not talk to that woman. Just go home."

"Noni, listen to me." She moved closer and stroked her grandmother's forehead. "I know who she is, and there is nothing she can say that will make you any less my grandmother or Mom any less my mother. Okay? You're upset over nothing at all, so I don't want you to worry about her or anyone else. I'll take care of this."

"Bernie, I'm old." Her milky eyes were sunk deep in her frail face.

"Really? I don't believe it."

"I just want you to know I love you. And your mom did, too. I'm sorry for all that happened. I raised a good daughter, a good girl. I didn't want her to go away, I didn't want . . . she was a good girl, a good girl . . . I'm sorry . . ." The old woman was distraught, trembling and rambling.

"Stop it, Noni, stop it. You don't have anything to be sorry for. What I want you to do now is get some rest. You had a rough night and a rough morning."

She watched the old eyes blink slowly and felt the hand she held begin to soften. The nurse had given her some Ativan and it was settling in, nudging her tired body to sleep. She sat there, stroking Noni's forehead until the old woman snored softly. Only then, when she knew her grandmother was sleeping, did she venture down the hallway to confront Julie Randall once and for all. She would put an end to this bullshit. Giving birth to her did not give anyone the right to upset an old woman, especially when she'd been told Noni wasn't well.

Julie sat in one of Sister Rose's guest chairs, nervous and eager to finally tell her side of the story, to let her daughter know the evil that had been done to her, to both of them. She rose to her feet when Bernie entered and started toward her with pleading hands. "Bernadette" she said, panting as though she was out of breath.

"No, sit down," Bernie commanded. "Sister Rose, will you excuse us, please?"

"Of course. I'll be outside if you need me."

Bernie moved to the front of the administrator's desk, leaned against it and faced her mother directly before saying anything. "I'm going to ask that you not say anything at all until I'm through speaking. Is that agreed?"

"Yes." Julie nodded, folding her hands. She would wait, let Bernadette go first, but then she would spill her ugly truths, the only truth that mattered.

"There are things you don't know, that you need to know."

"And there are things you don't . . ."

"I thought we had an agreement. This is my turn; you get your turn when I'm through, and I need to get through this uninterrupted." Her voice was stern and unwavering.

Julie nodded and sat back in her chair, clutching the arm rests fiercely.

"That woman down the hall is more than my grandmother. She took me in and cared for me and loved me when there was no one else in the world who would. You gave me away, and I'm sure you have your explanation for that, I'm sure there were very good reasons, but what you don't know is how that decision affected me. My life."

Bernie took a deep breath and closed her eyes. "I'll just tell you the short version, but it is a story very few people know. When I was thirteen years old, my father, the only one I ever knew, by the way, shot my mother, then seeing what he had done, he had the decency to shoot himself. I wish he'd taken the time to leave a note, to explain why he did such a horrible thing, but he didn't. I have lived all these years with that question unanswered."

Julie's mouth fell open and her shoulders slowly

sunk into her as her eyes filled with tears. "Oh no," she whispered. "Oh, dear God."

Bernie ignored her and continued on with her story. "I lost two mothers before I was out of middle school, but you know who was always there? From day one? Noni. First, you gave me away, and then my dad took away the only mother and father I ever knew."

Julie wiped endless tears from her face as Bernie shared the grim details of her past. It was worse than her own story.

"You see, Julie, despite your reasons, and the terrific life you found after getting rid of your baby, it didn't work out so well for me. I never got the life you imagined for me. I know everyone has their share of problems, but I can't help but think how different my life would have been, how much I might have been spared, if you had somehow managed to stick it out as a mother all those years ago. I can't help but wonder if I hadn't been in the picture that my parents' lives might have been spared."

Bernie glared at Julie, callously watching the earthy woman dissolve to a shameful wreck before her eyes.

"I'm so sorry, so sorry," she wept.

"Noni raised me, fed me, loved me, and I can't allow you or anyone to upset her or hurt her. Especially now. Do you understand?"

Julie nodded, wiping her eyes with the cuffs of her sweater. "I don't know what . . ." her voice trailed off and she sat speechless, motionless.

"Now," Bernie said, "you tell me whatever it is you think I need to know that will make me understand why you have any business at all visiting my grandmother here, particularly since I told you she was in no condition for this type of confrontation."

"I'm sorry; I shouldn't have come. I thought I could introduce myself, and she would want you to know me, that it would make her, I don't know, happy that you could have someone else in your life. Forgive me," she said. All color seemed to drain from Julie's face, making her seem weak and beaten once again.

A flurry of memories, practiced speeches and images raced through Bernie's thoughts. This was her chance to say it all. But all that she could say was "Fine." She could no more attack this woman than she could turn her back on Noni.

Julie nodded and slowly rose to her feet. "I should probably go, leave you to deal with your grandmother."

"Yes, that's probably best for now."

"Bernadette," she gently reached out and took her daughter's hands into her own. "For what it's worth, I never stopped loving you. I never stopped thinking of you, praying for you. And I never wanted to give you up. Never. I remember every moment with you, the way you felt in my arms."

Bernie felt her own fingers tremble, the familiar lump rising in her throat. "Thank you for that."

"May I hug you? Just once," Julie asked.

Bernie pulled back, wary of such contact, but then relented, allowing for a quick embrace. She felt her mother's arms fold around her, her head pressed against her cheek. It was not horrible, not in the least, but it left her feeling off balance and bewildered.

Julie turned toward the door, dejected and heartbroken, her feet scuffing as if they were too heavy to

320

lift off the floor.

Bernie watched her closely. She finally surrendered to a lifetime of curiosity and asked, "Why'd you do it? Why'd you give me up?"

Julie paused, carefully measuring the dose of truth that she would deliver with the new knowledge of her daughter's life, concerned about what too much truth might do to Bernie now. Again, at the mercy of Isabelle Fierro, she sacrificed for the good of her child. "I was young and stupid, not married, of course. We had an accident one night, that's when your arm got broken, and the people at the hospital convinced me that you would be better off with real parents, you know, married, with a home and a swing set in the backyard. I thought I was giving you more than I ever could on my own. I'm sorry for the way things turned out."

"Yeah, well, it's not like you could know." Bernie stepped past her mother and opened the door for her.

Julie reached out for one more touch, resting the tips of her fingers on Bernie's elbow. "Would you mind if I wrote to you sometime? There is more to say. Another time."

"No, that would be fine. I just need to focus on . . . let some of this sink in, you know."

"Yes, I know." Julie walked away, turned back for one more look from the front door and lifted one hand in a wave and disappeared out the door.

Bernie returned to Noni's bedside, where she would sit and listen to the shallow breathing, her body rocking back and forth, back and forth, to the familiar rhythm of her grandmother until they breathed again as one.

For the next three weeks, Bernie visited Nazareth

House every evening, often late in the evening, long after the residents had eaten their communal dinner, but before Noni downed a nightly Ativan and settled in for restless sleep. Bernie's days were consumed with work, the aftermath of the firestorm she'd created during her spell of tearing through stagnant files, breathing life back into them. She had managed to settle half a dozen cases with promises of checks to be delivered before Christmas. It was going to be a good bonus year for Crystal, especially if the Luna case settled for what it was worth, or more.

Crystal would normally be the one to call and confirm appointments, but Bernie did not want their first conversation since Thanksgiving to be at Don's deposition, awkward and uncomfortable in the presence of Stuart Reilly. That was the type of small detail that could nick away at a rock-solid case, diminishing its value by more than a few dollars. She would use a formal call, a call with a purpose, to break the silence and set them back on the proper ground of two professionals who work together, not two overgrown adolescents who flirt and hang out in graveyards on a stormy afternoon. He answered on the first ring.

"Hi Don, it's Bernie." She sat up straight, tugged a strand of hair down over her ears, and bit her lower lip at the sound of his voice.

"Hi Bernie. What can I do for you?"

His impassive tone was precisely what Bernie wanted, professional, polite, free of any hint of a personal relationship.

"I'm calling about the Luna case. Depositions are on Monday and Tuesday and mediation is set for Wednesday. I have your deposition scheduled for Tuesday at 3:00. I'm assuming Crystal cleared that time with you." It was as if they'd never shared a single moment beyond their formal and necessary relationship.

"Yes, she did. It's on my calendar, and I'll be there. Did you still want to meet before the dep and go over the numbers?"

"That's probably a good idea, but I don't think we'll need a great deal of time. Why don't you plan on being here at 2:00, and we'll do a quick review, and go from there?"

"Fine, I'll see you then."

And he hung up. No good-bye, just "I'll see you then." The wave of sadness that rippled through her was unsettling. This was how it should be, she reasoned, professional, void of complications and issues. Her cheeks warmed, and a painful heaviness settled in her chest. It's just the time of year, she told herself. People are always lonely during holidays, wishing there was someone, anyone, to be waiting for them at the end of a long day. She was one of those people. Lonely and alone.

Bernie picked up her pen and began drafting questions and notes for Carlos and Mrs. Luna, the driver, and their expert economist, Don Fielding. She would be more than prepared for Stuart Reilly this time. There would be no surprise video to ruin this one, and she would not be distracted by an encounter with her birth mother or silly romantic notions during the holidays. Force of will kept her writing, kept her working. Her focus had to be completely on Carlos Luna.

A dense fog had blanketed the Valley for days. The bare ash tree stood lonely and cold outside the office where Bernie now flipped through the thick mediation binder, her Bible for the next few days. Crystal had spent hours organizing every piece of evidence to be at her fingertips during depositions and mediation. She paused to study once again the photographs of Carlos and his family, invoking their lives and personalities into the case along with police reports and damage estimates. They were people, not just numbers, statistics, or decedents. They were a mother and a father who had a little boy that loved them, who they loved. As she studied their lovely brown faces, smiling into the camera, her mind drifted to a day long ago, to another son, another tragedy.

She was just nineteen, spending an afternoon at Avocado Lake, where her boyfriend, Keith, was a lifeguard. The old mine pit, deep and cold, was a favorite hangout for locals, a place for picnics and swimming on Sunday afternoons. She was dozing in the sun near the lifeguard stand when a young girl, no more than thirteen, came up crying, her brother and she were swimming, and he disappeared.

Keith dove in and Bernie followed, frantically searching for the boy, knowing every second counted, grateful for the coldness of the water. It wasn't long before Keith dragged the young boy to the top, then pulled him onto shore. Together, she and Keith performed CPR, blowing air into his lungs, turning him over to spit out swallowed lake water, pressing on his chest, pumping his heart for him, blowing air into his lungs. For nearly an hour they pumped life into his young body. They worked with all they had to keep his body alive, waiting and waiting for the ambulance to arrive, cursing and wondering why it took so long for them to respond. Finally, the ambulance crew appeared with a gurney and took over the exhausting job of breathing for another. The two-man crew scanned the crowd as they lifted the boy's lifeless body onto the backboard. The older one gave directions to his partner, his voice in hushed tones, but Bernie stood nearby, listening to every word, her own heart nearly stopping as she listened. "Okay," he said, "make it look good until we get him in the ambulance."

Blood had raged through her exhausted body. Make it look good? Make what look good? Would they try harder if this boy had blonde hair? It was one afternoon, a summer day made for lake swimming, and the world again shifted beneath her feet. She never wanted to forget it. And she never did. Rogelio and Lucero Luna were more than a dollar sign; they were Carlos's mom and dad, and in his eyes, they were priceless. She would not let them down.

Angelica Corona delivered Carlos and Mrs. Luna to the office right on time. Angelica was huge, her unborn baby due any second, but she didn't seem any less energetic. Carlos had grown in the few months he'd been away, a bit taller, but it was his face that seemed to have changed most. *A six-year-old with ancient eyes*, Bernie thought, watching him from where she sat in her private office. He would occasionally glance at her, his gaze dark and intense. Shy and frightened in the unfamiliar space, surrounded by strangers, he focused on the toy Transformer he held in his hands, flipping arms and legs around until the robot evolved into a battle tank, then shifting the tank back to the shape of a warrior robot.

"Carlos, look at the tree," Angelica cooed, pointing to the Noble Fir that Crystal's husband had delivered to the office. Bernie had watched from her office while the handsome couple strung white lights and covered the branches with the blown glass ornaments Bernie had collected over the years. It was the first year she didn't join in the small office ritual, choosing instead to ignore the holiday altogether, or at least as much as she could. The tree took on a different light through the dark eyes of the six-year-old boy sitting on the couch.

Carlos muttered something, but Bernie couldn't quite make it out, not sure if his words were in Spanish or if he was just mumbling.

Angelica answered him, her voice loud and clear. "Aaah, Moochie has school, mijo. You'll see him when you get home. Later, mijo, later." She then turned to the older woman who sat in a chair across the room, out of Bernie's line of vision. "Señora Luna, mire el árbol hermoso."

The old woman answered in Spanish, her speech too fast for Bernie to translate, even in bits. Carlos added, "Abuela, mire mi robot, my Transformer car."

"Carlos," Angelica chided in her singsong voice, "Spanish or English only, please. No Spanglish." She leaned close to him and stroked the back of his head. He didn't resist her touch, even let his head fall toward her, against her bulging belly. "Your mama did not like mixing up the words; 'one or the other,' she used to say. Remember? And besides, while you're here, practice your English. You need Spanish and English to get a good job someday, no matter where you live. Eh, mijo?" Her fingers ruffled his hair playfully. Carlos nodded and gave her a sly grin, clearly happy to be petted and teased, his smile revealing a gap where his front teeth used to be.

Bernie closed her binder, stood, and prepared to move to the conference room and meet with her waiting clients. She was near the door, but stepped back out of view and waited at her office door when she heard Angelica speaking again to Carlos, curious to hear what the woman had to say, somewhat fascinated by the way he seemed to soften at her touch.

"Do you know what Lucero means?" Angelica asked the boy. "Your mama's name was Lucero. It means 'brightest star of the morning.' So now your mama is the brightest star, up there looking out for you all the time. We just can't see her right now because of all the fog, but she is there. She is there." She leaned over and kissed the top of his head then gave it a rough rub of her hand, tough love this time. Bernie then watched her point toward the sky and repeat her words, this time in Spanish for the benefit of the grandmother.

Bernie smiled at the soft words, surprisingly poetic. It was only when she stepped into the waiting room that she got a full view of Mrs. Luna, frightened in this strange land of lawyers and phony smiles, clutching a small brown purse close to her, a sign for every petty thief worth his salt that every bit of money the poor woman had in the world was tucked inside that little bag. A wave of compassion washed over Bernie for the painful loss the woman had suffered, the loss of her son and his wife. She wanted to do all she could to give this family a little justice, even if it was in the form of a check.

"Buenos dias, Señora Luna, Carlos." Bernie reached out to take the hand of Mrs. Luna, gave it one slight squeeze then turned to Carlos for an exaggerated up and down shake that made him tuck his chin and stick his tongue out, rolling it across his bottom lip. Finally, she looked toward their friend. "Hi Angelica," she said, "nice to see you again."

The suspicion that she had harbored last summer, that Angelica was a gold digger, had vanished. Watching her with Carlos, imagining her and Lucero sharing a cup of coffee at the end of a long day, caring for one another and each other's boys as their own, had remedied that false assumption. It occurred to her that the friends of her own parents, those men and women who had been to her home, whose homes she had visited, had vanished from her life too. Was it Noni that kept them away? Was it the short distance she had moved, or just living with the older woman that made them feel unnecessary in the life of the little girl whose parents were dead? Did they still think about her?

In the short distance of moving from the reception area to the conference room, the future of Carlos Luna loomed before her eyes. He would have money; she was certain of this case as much as ever. His childhood, however, would be very different under the care of his father's mother than it would be in the care of his mother's friend, sharing a room and toys with his own friend, Moochie, while sharing a home with the family he had known with his own parents. She and Carlos weren't alike at all, but she wanted him to have the best life possible, as she had been given.

"Angelica, a formal interpreter will be here in about an hour for the depositions, but if you wouldn't mind, perhaps you can help me out until then."

Angelica couldn't show more teeth if she tried. "Oh yes, Mrs. Sheridan. Yes, I can help." She strutted behind Mrs. Luna, her stomach leading the way, and took her place at the head of the long table.

By late afternoon, Stuart Reilly had completed his depositions of Carlos and Mrs. Luna. The questioning was short and sweet, an unusual style for the pompous lawyer who liked the sound of his own voice. Little orphan boys with meek voices were tough opponents for the starched gentleman to victimize, and there was little information to be gained from prolonged interrogation. The grieving grandmother from Mexico who spoke little English proved to be no easier for the defense counsel. There was nothing there to crumble but the truth of a bad situation. The only potential target or weak link was her economist, Don Fielding. Reilly could only hope to limit damages.

Bernie reconsidered the short prep time with Don. She now hoped he might be able to meet with her that night, so that she could share with him the events of the day, nail down the numbers as well as the personalities of her clients. During an afternoon break, she had Crystal call and ask him if it was possible for him to come at the end of the day. He agreed.

Just before five o'clock, Bernie heard Crystal buzz him in and offer him coffee, even though the pot was already emptied and clean, ready for the next morning. Bernie took a deep breath, gathered her legal pad full of the day's notes and reached for the mediation binder only to discover it was not there. Everything she needed was in that one binder: photographs, accident report, mediation brief, and the impressive damage charts Don had prepared. Certain she had brought it into the office with her after the depositions, she searched under every slip of paper, in every drawer, under her desk. Nothing. "*Shit,*" she whispered. "*Where the hell can it be?*" *Shit*.

"Crystal," she called, forcing her voice to sound light, unworried or untense. "Do you have the mediation binder out there by any chance?"

"No, I'm pretty sure you have it."

Bernie walked around her office, checking to see if

she had set it down someplace out of the ordinary. But it wasn't there. It didn't matter if she could recall every detail in the binder, she wanted to have it with her during this meeting, a physical crutch, but she didn't want to keep Don waiting. She had to see him. It was important to prepare him for what would undoubtedly be a difficult day. There was no choice but to resume her search for the missing binder after her meeting with Don.

She paused on her way to the conference room to tell Crystal to go ahead and go, leaving her and Don alone in the big old house. Don stood up when she entered the room, just as he'd done the first time they met.

"Hi there," she said. "How are you, Don?" A smile appeared involuntarily. He had cut his hair shorter, above his ears on the sides and above the eyebrows at the front. Bernie couldn't decide if he looked older, more businesslike, or younger, like a college kid who had just removed his black, horn-rimmed glasses, striving for a cooler look. "You got a haircut, I see."

"Yeah," he rubbed his hand across the back of his neck. "I'm still trying it on, I guess." His smile was hesitant at first, but grew with her presence.

"Well, it looks good," she said.

It had grown dark outside, and the tree lights made the office glow with the warmth of a home in winter. The day with Carlos had gone well, and she was feeling better than she had in weeks, both physically and emotionally. She sat across from Don and began to tell him about Carlos and Mrs. Luna, how they were in deposition with Reilly, and how they were with each other.

"He's such a cute kid," she said, "but you can feel the

sadness in him. I think Reilly could, too. That's probably scaring the shit out of him right about now." Bernie couldn't help but smile, realizing nothing she ever planned or researched could be as disarming as a little boy in an oversized chair talking about his mom and dad in heaven, pointing toward the ceiling, lifting his gaze higher.

Don nodded his head in agreement. "I'm looking forward to meeting them, but to tell you the truth, I already feel like I know them, especially Carlos."

"Did I ever tell you about Angelica Corona, the woman that the Lunas lived with before they died?"

"I'm not sure." He leaned closer, his attention keen on every word she said.

"I went to her house a few weeks ago; she's the one that had the box of letters and pictures we went through. Remember?"

"Of course."

"Well, at first, I thought she was some kind of gold digger looking for some way to get her hands on some of Carlos's money. I promised to pay her for the Lunas' bills that went unpaid, but that's only a couple of hundred bucks, no big deal. Anyway, today," Bernie paused and gazed around the room, searching for the words to articulate the feeling that had come over her earlier. "Today I was listening to her talk to Carlos. She was telling him about his mother, not in a sad mopey kind of way, but happy and very matter of fact. She told him that his mother, Lucero, was a star looking out for him, because Lucero means morning star. He kind of, I don't know, lit up at that. It was *something*. I guess it kind of lit me up, too, because I hit the day and Stuart Reilly with more energy and confidence than I've had in a long time." The flow of conversation spilling out of her was surprising, so natural and automatic, the expected awkward moment nonexistent.

"Wow. It sounds like things are going well for you, then. I mean, last time we saw each other was, well, probably not a good night for either one of us." His eyebrows lifted when he offered a brief smile and submissive nod of his head.

"No, and I want to apologize for that. For whatever good it might do, I'm sorry. I was out of line." The fingers on her right hand lifted from the table, a slight gesture, as if her hands had a distinct and separate will, eager to reach out for him. "A lot has happened since then, and uh . . ."

"No, Bernie, you don't need to explain. Let's leave that alone." He reached over and placed his hand over hers, squeezed gently. "Please. You're a lawyer, and part of being a good lawyer is digging into people's lives and peeling off the layers. It's not the worst thing I've been through."

"You didn't really lie, but I snooped. I could argue that those are all public documents, but you and I both know I was snooping into your private life. It was wrong." She could still feel his hand on hers, but she didn't know what to make of that. It was nothing more than any friend would do, almost gentlemanly, but she liked it all the same. She still liked his touch.

"It was wrong," he agreed. "But I'm over it, and you should be too. To tell you the truth, I never expected anyone to be interested enough to actually check me out. For the record, the Judgment is now entered; I'm officially divorced, and it's all a done deal. All of it."

Bernie didn't answer. The world had been spinning too fast for her lately, kicking up old secrets and lives like puffs of dust. Her restlessness and anger had slowly withered away to a small roar that allowed her to simply throw her hands up in surrender. She would never have all the answers, not now, anyway. Life was full of mysteries, and her past was overflowing with them. Pieces to the puzzle were there, but some were missing, lost forever, and nothing was going to change that. But she could change.

Long ago, Bernie had made a decision to work for the right thing, and to focus on one right thing at a time. At work, this week, it was the Lunas. At home, well, that was more complicated, but maybe it was time to throw her own life out there on the line. Noni was in the best place she could be. Bernie had a mother out there, even though she didn't really know her, and something told her that, if she wanted it, she could have a family too. For a moment, she had even considered that, maybe, she could have a man in her life, a relationship, but it didn't take long for Bernie to recognize that as foolishness and pushed that thought away. That was the fantasy of a winter night, sweet-smelling pine, and the magic of a six-year-old boy with no front teeth, his mother shining down on him from a bright star in the heavens.

"So," Bernie said, slowly pulling her hand away, changing the subject to the more comfortable and necessary realm of Don's pending deposition, "I have a mediation binder with everything perfectly organized, color-coded and labeled and ready to go; the great report you sent me is in there, too. I want to go over it with you line by line, but just when you got here, I couldn't seem to find it. I think Mrs. Gordon is messing with me, taking a turn with it."

"Who's Mrs. Gordon?" he asked, confused.

"She's our resident ghost. She hides files, occasionally

slams a door or two upstairs, drives poor Crystal crazy."

"That's right, you told me about her out at the cemetery." His voice softened, "Remember?"

"I do." She stood and headed for the door, happy to be moving, avoiding the crest of an emotional wave that seemed so close she could feel the spray and mist. "Even though I can recall every word in there, let me take one more look to see if I just missed it, because I really think you're Reilly's only hope to weaken this case. He has to minimize the damages; we've talked about that before, but . . ."

As she rummaged through the files stacked on Crystal's desk, double-checking everything, she noticed a brown paper package on the window seat. She recognized the handwriting, and for one brief moment, her breath halted. It wasn't heavy, just the size of a shoe box. She carried it to her office, holding it close to her breast, and before she even reached her desk, she saw the binder. It sat on the credenza, behind her chair. Was it possible that she looked everywhere but behind her, or was that damn spirit so conniving she found a way to make her search her secretary's desk after hours to find a package?

"Found it," she called, then turned to see Don standing back in the middle of the reception area, examining Crystal's decorating job. A broad timbre of light danced over him, the neighbor's new parking lights reflecting through the stained glass, refracted colors colliding with the subtle glow of flickering tree lights. It was as though the light hummed or buzzed around him.

"Your tree is beautiful," Don said.

Bernie moved beside him, hugging the binder and the package to her chest as they admired the decorations.

"Thanks, but I didn't have anything to do with it. Crystal and her husband did it all. It is nice though."

Don stood there in the light of the Noble Fir, quietly gazing at Bernie. "I've missed you," he said. "I enjoyed talking to you and I hope we can still be friends, and not just professionally."

Bernie swallowed hard. "I've missed you, too. It's been a weird time."

"What happened with your—God, I hope this doesn't cause a problem, bringing it up, but I want to know—what happened with your mother? Your birth mother."

"You know, it was a bit of chaos for a while. And I was right, Noni can't handle any of it, but, I think it's going to be okay. I guess you could say now that the initial drama is over I'm finally interested in what she has to say. I want to know her story, and my story too. In fact, it seems I got a package from her today, my mother, not Noni." She loosened her grip, showing him the box in her arms. Her eyes burned with a threat of tears and a lump rose in her throat, causing her voice to crack when she spoke. "God, where's that coming from?"

"Maybe you should open it now," Don said. "It might be something you need." With one hand he lightly touched her shoulder, guiding her to sit on the loveseat, a space for guests and visitors. "Unless you want to be alone for that, and I completely understand if you do."

"No; I'll open it with you here." She gently pulled the brown wrapping paper away, carefully tearing the taped ends, keeping the entire paper whole. Inside was a Christmas card, a colorful drawing of a horse-drawn sleigh carrying a man and woman down a snow-covered path on a moonlit night to their warm cabin glowing in the distance. The handwritten message was safely distant, simply telling her she hoped they could get together soon and wishing Bernie and her grandmother a very merry Christmas. The gift was, Julie wrote, something she'd treasured for many years, something Bernie might like to have. She ended the message by saying she hoped Bernie got everything she wished for this Christmas and always. Inside the box was an old stuffed baby doll with yellow hair and a pink gingham dress.

Bernie touched the nose of the doll, stroked it lightly, looked up to Don and smiled. "This is nice," she said. "I'm sure there is a story to go with this." She held the doll up to her face and took a deep breath. "Clean. She smells a bit like fresh linen."

"Maybe she kept it in the linen closet."

"Maybe." Bernie moved the box and paper to the floor then sniffed the doll again. "Or maybe she kept her in the laundry room with the dryer sheets."

"I doubt it."

"I didn't even think to get her anything. Of course, I didn't get anybody anything yet." She picked up her binder and her baby doll, then rose to her feet, ready to work some more. "When I have like a week or something, I'll tell you everything that happened, and I mean everything. But not now." Her voice trailed off and she shook her head slightly, "Not tonight."

Don moved closer to her. They stood inches apart, still and quiet. "At the risk of offending you or sounding foolish, would you like a hug? You look like you need a hug."

His eyes looked straight into hers, searching for any hint of rejection.

"Yes, I think I would," she answered. "That would

be nice."

He quietly wrapped his arms around and pulled her closer, his efforts stalled by an old rag doll and three-inch binder pressed between them.

"Perhaps I should put these down," she said.

Don took the bundle from her and set them down on the small sofa then took both of her hands into his own. Bernie didn't object or pull away. He lifted her right hand to his face and pressed her knuckles against his cheek, never shifting his gaze away from hers. When her index finger moved to stroke his face, he closed his eyes, a line of dark lashes fluttering. Still holding her hands, he lowered them to his sides and pressed his soft lips to hers. Two small kisses, one after the other, innocent and sweet. They released their hands and slowly moved apart, their eyes searching and unsure of what happened, but neither one spoke a word.

Under the glow of a shining star on top of the Noble Fir, their arms reached out for the other, first embracing and holding one another close, feeling the warmth of the other's body, the press of arms and hands on her back, caressing his shoulders, touching the back of her warm neck. Eventually, their mouths came together, lips parting to a perfect fit. He smelled like fresh air and tasted like a warm fire that Bernie wanted to fall into, happy to burn.

"Wow," she finally said, her voice low and deep. "That was some hug."

"I've wanted to kiss you since that rainy day," he said, "but . . ." He laughed and took her hand gently. "You aren't the easiest person to get close to, you know."

"Yes, I know." She laughed and moved away from him, embarrassed by her behavior, kissing in the office, like the stories of drunken Christmas parties at Bennett, Hart and Reilly. She reached for her doll and binder, desperate to escape the physical longing that seized her. "But, there's a reason," she explained, again clutching the doll and book to her chest. "We shouldn't have done that. If anything is going to happen between us, we should wait, not get into this until at least after the mediation." She inched away, her heart still pounding. "It's not professional."

"No, no, no. Bernie, if we try to pretend this," he reached over and touched her face gently, running his index finger along her lower lip, "didn't happen, then all through the deposition and mediation, you're going to be thinking of nothing but this moment right now. You can't unring that bell, you know."

She backed away and he followed her into the conference room where he stood close beside her, his hand only brushing against her. "You're right, you're right," she agreed, "but either way, this is a distraction and ..."

"I think the best thing, really, is to start from here and take it slowly." He took the doll away from her again, moving it and the binder to the table, then took her hand and held it in both of his. "Let's go home, Bernie. I'm ready for tomorrow. I know what the case involves, what the numbers are, what Reilly will ask, what you will ask, and what I will say. Let's just go sit in front of a fire, have a glass of wine, enjoy the evening together. Let's start over. Let's be the good friends we are, and see where that goes. Some of the best relationships start with friendship."

Bernie again felt the rising crest and shutter of a crashing wave, this time savoring the thrill of the ride. She could feel herself riding the wave, the sea and wind in her face, taking her breath away. She wanted it to go on forever. She wanted it more than he could ever know. She wanted it all: him, Julie, Noni, her dead mother and father, the riddle solved, to save the world one case at a time. She wanted that stream of light shining down from the stained-glass window to open wide and swallow her whole. But tonight, what she wanted most was to sit and drink some fine red wine with this man in front of a raging fire. She wanted to taste the fire.

Twenty-Two

The parking lot was nearly full, a sure sign of the holiday, family and friends dutifully filing in to share Christmas Eve with their aging parents and grandparents, fulfilling their obligation before Christmas Day. Bernie found a spot at the far end of the lot, near the statue of the Madonna, a young Jesus smiling in her lap, his chubby arms reaching out for someone to hold him. A lingering mist from a late afternoon rain glittered in the pool of blue light surrounding the holy mother, who seemed to shine brighter than usual on the night of her child's birthday celebration. Bernie flashed even the lifeless piece of stone a happy smile before heading in. It had been a good week, one of her best.

"Don't you look fancy," she said, bending down to kiss Noni's rouged and powdered cheek.

"Sister Anna fixed my hair." Noni lifted a quivering hand to touch the sides of her pinned up hair, her face. Her thin lips trembled to a weak smile.

"Well, you look beautiful. It's nice to see you up and dressed again." Ten days ago, she would have told her grandmother about the smudge of red lipstick on her teeth, but it now seemed somehow cruel, like telling a three-year-old girl playing dress up that her shoes didn't match her ball gown.

"What's that?" Noni pointed to the shopping bag Bernie carried.

"Oh, Santa asked me to make a little delivery for him." She winked and set the bag down near Noni's chair while she slipped off her raincoat. "No peeking, hear me?"

"Where have you been, Bernadette? I thought maybe you forgot where I lived." Noni reached over and pulled the edge of the shopping bag toward her, jutted her chin out and peered into the bag to see two bright gold boxes and silky red satin bows. "You shouldn't buy such an old woman presents. What could I need at my age?"

"Don't be silly. Now, do you want to open gifts now, or wait until after dinner?" She stood over her grandmother, hands on her hip, still pulsing with the energy of other last-minute shoppers panicking at Macy's. "I'm sure there will be Christmas carol singing later, so maybe we should have our party now, but it's up to you."

Bernie finally took her place in the rose covered chair, took her shoes off and tucked her feet up beside her, eager to share her good news with her grandmother, to spend some pleasant time with her for a change.

"I guess we should open them now, or you might have to stay out too late."

"Right, we'll open them now so that I won't be out past eight," she said, sending Noni an eyebrow raise. "It has nothing whatsoever to do with your dying curiosity to know what's in the box."

Noni nodded her head and gave a small chuckle. For the first time in weeks, Bernie felt like her old Noni was back, the one who made her furious with her endless advice, the one who made her breathe when life had seemed to smother her with unbearable loss, the one she loved more than anything.

Bernie reached into the bag and pulled out a small box and handed it to Noni, then patiently waited while she meticulously picked at the bow and tape to unwrap the package neatly, her quivering fingers working hard at the fine task until finally she dropped the paper to the floor and removed the small lid from the white box. "Oh, Bernadette," she sighed. "This is too lovely for me." She held up the pretty watch, then clutched it to her chest. "I love it. The numbers are nice and big, so I can see them."

"Yes, and all twelve of them are on there, just like you like. How do you like the band? It's tortoise shell and easy to snap off and on." She reached over and showed Noni how the bands pulled apart and snapped back together, no fiddling with a small buckle, or stretchy gold band that sometimes pinched the old woman's fragile skin.

"It's perfect. Just like you." She held her wrist up and admired her gift then lifted her arm for a quick hug. "What's in that other box?"

Bernie loved the childish eagerness of Noni on Christmas. "I guess you'll have to open it to find out," she said, handing the larger gift to Noni.

"I bet it's slippers. All the old ladies around here will be wearing their new slippers tomorrow." She picked at the gold bow, handed it to Bernie, then moved on to the taped ends again picking and pulling until she freed the box from its gold foil wrap. "I wouldn't want to be left out of the slipper parade."

"We'll see," Bernie said, tugging on her ankle, pulling her stocking feet close.

Inside the box was overflowing with gold, red, pink, green, blue, and silver foil-wrapped candies. Brach's candies to the brim. "Oh my," Noni said, "oh my goodness." She looked to her granddaughter and grinned. "Don't tell Lolly; she'll never leave me alone."

"Is that all there is?" Bernie asked. "Dig around in there."

Noni reached her hands down into the box and found the black velvet slippers. "They're beautiful," she said, lifting them out, letting pieces of candy spill all around her, in her lap, on the floor. "Oh boy, look what I've done."

Bernie laughed as she picked up the stray candies, taking time to unwrap a vanilla caramel for herself. "I hope you like them," she said, "the slippers, I mean. I know you like candy."

"Thank you, Bernadette. They're gorgeous, like you. Now, if you will open that top drawer, I believe there might be a little something for you."

Bernie knew it would be something from the gift shop; it always was. It didn't matter if it was yesterday's meatloaf wrapped up in a napkin. She felt like she had her Noni back, her sassy, grouchy love of a grandmother, and that was the best gift possible. Bernie opened the drawer and found the gift. Inside was a beautiful handkerchief, hand-embroidered with her initials.

"Mrs. Kennedy's granddaughter made it. She let us tell her what to put on there, so it would be special." She was proud of her gift, proud of her Bernie.

"Thank you, Noni. I love it, more than you know." She bent down and kissed her grandmother on the forehead and squeezed her frail hand. "Now we're both fancy," she said, folding the handkerchief into thirds and tucking it into the pocket of her blouse so that the embroidered initials stood out.

"So, tell me what you've been up to," Noni said.

"It might take a while," Bernie said. "I have had a pretty good couple of weeks." She settled back into her rose-covered chair and took a deep breath.

"First, I settled the Luna case—you know, the little boy whose parents were killed in the car accident."

"Oh yes, the little Mexican boy."

"Uh-huh, the one who was living with his grandmother in Mexico." She smiled at the reference to living with a grandmother, hoping Noni would feel her unspoken gratitude. "Well, Carlos will get 1.8 million dollars in a structured settlement and his grandmother, Señora Luna will get two hundred thousand." She clapped her hands together once and threw her head back. "Can you believe it? I still can't believe it. Policy limits, I got the policy without going to trial."

"Oh, Bernadette that's wonderful. How much do you get?"

"Well, just a percentage, but let's just say it's going to be a nice paycheck when the money comes in. Very nice. You know, I have a sneaking suspicion that our mediator comes from a family of migrant farmworkers. He was very sympathetic to Carlos and Mrs. Luna, said he hoped the American dream would still be a possibility for such a fine young man. Can you believe it?" Bernie gazed at the ceiling, her mind and heart still reeling from the mediation, the celebration, Don, even the look on Crystal's face when she handed her the biggest Christmas bonus she'd ever seen.

"Will they stay in Mexico with all that money?"

"I don't think so. Carlos is a citizen, but Mrs. Luna is

not. There's this woman, Angelica Corona, who has been very good to them. I didn't trust her at first, but she's kind of grown on me. I told her I would help her get guardianship if the grandmother approved. And, even though it's not legal, I think Mrs. Luna might just stick around longer than she's supposed to and maybe try to get a green card. She has money to hire a good immigration attorney." She lifted her shoulders, grinned mischievously. "What can it hurt to try? And, to tell you the truth, I think she wants Carlos to be here, even if she stays longer than she's supposed to. Seriously, who's going after a little old lady?"

"I always said you were the best lawyer. I'm proud of you, Bernadette, so proud." Her dark eyes, cloudy with old age, filled with the sting of tears. "You are too good for me."

"What do you mean, too good for you? I'm who I am because of you." She stretched one hand out and patted the old woman's forearm.

"That might be true, but there's so much you don't know." Noni turned her face away, avoiding her granddaughter's gaze. "Your real mother . . ."

"Noni, let's not talk about all that. I know who Julie Randall is, that she's my birth mother, but none of that matters. She didn't want me back then; you did."

Noni raised her hands to her face, her new watch hanging loosely on her frail wrist. "I think it's time, dear. I don't want to ruin your week, our Christmas, but I think it's time. This might be my last Christmas. I can't die with this weight on me." Her chin trembled violently as though she nibbled the air. "I have to tell you."

"Stop it, Noni. I don't like it when you do your I'm-dying-any-minute-now bit." Bernie dropped her feet to the floor, pressed her palms against her thighs. This was supposed to be a pleasant evening, no drama, no tension. Couldn't Noni for just once let things be, just enjoy the evening for what it was? Bernie let out a loud exasperated sigh, refusing to let anyone ruin her good mood.

"It's true, though. Every year, all of us here think about who was here last Christmas who isn't this year. It was a long list this year. It makes me think."

"Well think about something else, then." Bernie rose to her feet and gathered the loose bits of wrapping paper from the floor and shoved them into the bag. "It's Christmas, Noni. Don't spoil it. Please."

"Bernadette, sit down," Noni said, a command she had given hundreds of times in the past thirty-eight years. "I want to tell you something. Please, just let me do this now. It will be a gift to me."

Bernie sat down slowly, her jaw set and spine stiff as she leaned back in her chair of roses, prepared to listen to whatever Noni had to say. She sat quietly while Noni told her about the night Julie Randall came to the hospital, how Bernie had a little broken arm, how filthy they both were, how she knew Julie was lying.

So many of the pieces of the puzzle of Julie Randall's story began to fall into place, but there were still gaps and holes. Missing pieces. Noni knew some, but not all of Julie's story. Bernie did not want any more pieces of her life swept under the rug. She deserved to know the truth, and that meant getting both sides of the story, putting it all together.

"I thought I was doing a good thing," Noni whispered in her gravelly voice, rough with age. "Your mother, well, Patty, that mother, was going to leave Ron, your dad. She was always a bit flighty, you know, kind of a dreamer or something, wanted more than she had no matter how much there was. Well, she was going to run off with her boss, of all things. I didn't want her to go to hell. The church doesn't allow divorce, so I told her and Ron I had found a baby for them, a baby who was hurt and needed them to care for her, so they could be a real family. They had tried to have a baby for years, and nothing happened, so I knew Patty would want you. If she had a baby she never would be fooling around with that man; she would never want a divorce. Mothers don't leave their children."

Noni paused and sat quietly for a moment, her breathing heavy with guilt. "I told her I knew that a baby would save her marriage, that I would pay for everything. I didn't want her to commit such a sin that she would lose everything. Even God. Her soul. So, she stayed, and they had you to love, and I thought everything was good. I didn't think about my own sin. Until the other one, your other mother, showed up."

"It was a good thing that you did, Noni, not a sin. You just did what you thought was right, finding me a better home, giving me a better life." She wanted to say so much more. She wanted to scream. Instead, she sat and soothed her shaken, trembling grandmother, stroking the old woman's arm, her back, then her hand. "What's the harm in that? You're worrying about nothing."

"Well, I was not so fair to Miss Randall, I'm afraid. I made it so that she was, oh, how do I explain? It was so long ago, times were different. I didn't really give her any other option." She looked at Bernadette, searching for understanding, not wanting to say more than she had to about those days at the hospital, the pain in that young mother's face, the way she cried and carried on.

"Are you saying you forced her?" Bernie looked confused. "What do you mean, 'no option?"

"Well, I will let her decide what to tell you about that time. She wasn't in a good place back then. I know she wants to tell you what happened, so talk to her, let her tell you her own story, and please, tell her I'm sorry I hurt her." Noni paused to lift her hand to her mouth before going on. "Bernadette, I'm sorry I made your life so horrible, with everything that happened, but I only did what I thought was right." She shook her trembling head from side to side. "How could I know what would happen?"

"Noni, why didn't you tell me? All these years, I've wanted to understand what happened, where I came from." Bernie sat bewildered, unmoving as the weight of all this information sunk in. From the hallway, a child screamed and small footsteps could be heard slapping down the wooden floor. A mother called for her to slow down or she would hurt herself. Mothers and daughters. Families by birth or by design, there was a maternal mystery Bernie could not fully understand. "Noni, why would you keep all this a secret from me?"

"I didn't want you to go away from me," Noni finally answered. Her fingers fidgeted with the folds in her dress, picking and patting, smoothing and stroking, as though she was scraping to open another taped-up package. "I was scared," she whispered. "You were all I had left."

The two women sat silently, each of them lost in their own private turmoil; Noni desperate to know if she would lose the only love she had in her life, Bernie struggling to understand a history of lies and deception that had shaped the very heart of her. The very heart of her. Where did that really come from? Noni? Mom and Dad? Julie? Or was it her own making, her own life choices?

"So, what about Mother and Dad?" she asked, taking Noni by the forearm, compelling her to speak. "Do you know about that, too? I mean, you kept this from me. Do you know why Dad shot her?" Her grip on Noni's arm tightened, urging her to answer. Every beat of her heart pounded red hot through her, socking her in the guts, the throat, the head. All those stories under her bed. All those years of clipping bad news, wallowing in it.

Noni closed her eyes, shook her head from side to side, pained by the memory of the most tragic of their days. "Yes, I . . . I think maybe I know, but who really can know what happened that day but Ron and Patty?"

Bernie leaned forward, pressed her elbows into her thighs and buried her face in her hands, fighting back angry tears, feeling the scarlet heat rise to her face. "What happened?" she whispered through gritted teeth, her jaw fixed and tight. "Tell me. I can take it."

"Oh Bernie, your mother, she just wanted and wanted. She was seeing that man again, her old boss. She was going to go, said she was going to leave you with Ron, that you would be better off with him, so I finally told Ron about how I got you to make her stay the first time, but it was up to him this time. He didn't know about the first time, or that I arranged for you to be theirs. He just got so angry. Stormed out of the house, you probably remember that. I don't know what happened that morning, but I can only guess what Patty must have said or done. I loved her so much, but she could make you . . ." Noni again looked away, searching the closed door for some hidden wisdom and shook her head in bewilderment. "Still," she continued, turning back to meet Bernie's pale grey stare, "he had no right to kill her. No right to take her from us forever." Noni didn't cry, just sat waiting and trembling, finally ready to face her own fate.

"I don't know what to say, Noni. I don't know what I feel about all this, but I guess I should thank you for at least telling me now." A weight like a stone fell from Bernie's chest to her belly, making her legs feel like lead, heavy and immovable. If Noni were younger, she would get angry, tell her to go to hell, get lost, something, but it was too late for that. Noni was old.

Bernie sat quietly, her thoughts shifting to Judge Melton's closing words at the end of the Luna mediation, the large award already agreed upon. He'd sat at the conference table, Bernie and the Lunas on one side, all of them absolutely giddy; Reilly and his clients on the other, somberly getting through the final moments.

"Life is full of accidents," the retired judge had said. "Sometimes it's just a little thing like tripping over a curb, or cutting the wrong length of a board, or cutting a finger. Nothing too serious. Nothing more than a little carelessness. Nothing too difficult to fix. But sometimes, a little carelessness, even with the best of intentions, can cost a life, and that can never be fixed. All we can do is try to compensate for that loss in the best way possible, and in this case, a young child and an older woman can only be compensated monetarily. We cannot give them any more than that. I just hope that is enough to allow this young man and his grandmother to find their solace, their way to some kind of resolution of their loss, a chance at a future."

His words at the time had caused Bernie's spirit to soar. They now only caused her confusion. Money would not have made any difference when she lost her parents, but her grandmother had offered and given her that solace. Noni. She could not hate her. Not even now.

"There's so much we've been through just because I didn't know," Bernie said, talking to herself as much as to Noni. "All that therapy, all those nights. Wouldn't it have been easier to just tell me back then?"

"I'm sorry. I didn't ever want to tell you, figured that other woman got over all of it long ago, moved on with her own life, probably back with her abusive husband. So, I didn't tell you. Why should you know all that bad stuff from before? Then she showed up here in Fresno. I just about died right there when I saw her. It was in your car, Thanksgiving." Her tired eyes closed tight with the memory.

Bernie flashed back to the night of Noni's horrible attack of diarrhea, the weakness and illness. Noni was right, she didn't have many Christmases left. It was time for all of this to end.

Sister Anna knocked on the door before sticking her head in. "Good evening, ladies. Are you going to join us for our feast? It's all ready and waiting for you."

Bernie looked at Noni, so frail in her chair, then up to the ever-smiling nun, the nicest one at Nazareth, Noni's favorite. "Yes," she said, "we'll be right there."

After Sister Anna closed the door behind her, Bernie stood up and moved behind Noni. "I'll push you in," she said. "No need for you to crash into the Christmas tree."

"Thank you. Thank you." Noni's voice cracked as she

spoke, and she lifted her trembling left hand, her wrist adorned with her new watch, to wipe her murky eyes. "I love you Bernadette."

Sister Anna walked arm in arm with Mr. Wilson from down the hall, keeping pace with his short shuffling steps, patting his stubby hand. "Ah, there you are," she said. "Doesn't Isabelle look lovely tonight?" she asked Mr. Wilson, lifting her voice to a louder pitch for his failing ears.

He grinned at them, nodded sweetly. "Merry Christmas," he said.

"Will you be joining us tomorrow, too?" Sister Anna asked Bernie. "We're having a Barbershop quartet for entertainment. They're terrific."

"No, I'm afraid I'll have to miss that," Bernie said. She paused, placed her right hand firmly on Noni's shoulder, and gave a gentle squeeze. "I'm going to visit family up in the Bay Area, just across the Golden Gate."

"Oh," Sister Anna said, "I didn't know you had other family."

"Me neither," Bernie said, enjoying the confusion that washed across the nun's face.

Noni offered only a weak smile in agreement, her weak chin still trembling. Bernie felt lighter somehow, freed from the burdens of a life beyond her own. Though there was still more to learn, the echo of a lifetime of painful secrets and lies was silent at last. She pushed Noni down the corridor, happy to be there, happy to be going away.

This, Bernie thought, this must be joy.

Acknowledgments

I am grateful to many people for their constant support and encouragement to tell stories. First and foremost, I want to thank my dear friend Patti Ringo, for her own story that inspired the creation of Bernie Sheridan. Thank you to Mary Kate Monahan Zolin, and Maksim Zolin, who always make me believe in what is possible, and for giving us Darby Jay. Thank you to my brother, Robert Villanueva Nichols, a true friend. I want to thank all of my family, including my parents and brother, Dale, who left us too soon; my sisters Sylvia Scheitzach, Neena Dho, and Rose Hong Pham for the many stories that fueled our lives. Our dinner table was a patchwork of backgrounds and colors where refugees and wanderers were welcome, and for that I am especially grateful. And many thanks to the readers and friends who shared their time, energy and friendship to help this story evolve: Linnea Alexander, Amber Folland, Kristin FitzPatrick, Corrinne Clegg Hales, John Hales, Courtney Hughes, Donna McCloskey, Bill McEwen, Elizabeth Nunes, Amber Ulrich, Liza Wieland, Debbie Wray, and Steve Yarbrough. And thank you to Nelson Lowhim, Bobbie Ford, and the crew at Alternative Book Press who make it all happen.